A Tender Christmas

Bringing you the gift of love…

A Tender Christmas

THE UNLIKELY SANTA
by
Leigh Michaels

ALL SHE WANTS FOR CHRISTMAS
by
Liz Fielding

THE GIRL HE LEFT BEHIND
by
Emma Goldrick

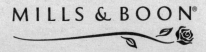

MILLS & BOON®

*MILLS & BOON and MILLS & BOON with the Rose Device
are registered trademarks of the publisher.
Harlequin Mills & Boon Limited,
Eton House, 18-24 Paradise Road, Richmond, Surrey, TW9 1SR*

A TENDER CHRISTMAS
© by Harlequin Enterprises II B.V., 2000

The Unlikely Santa, All She Wants for Christmas and *The Girl He Left
Behind* were first published in Great Britain by Harlequin Mills & Boon
Limited in separate, single volumes.

The Unlikely Santa © Leigh Michaels 1995
All She Wants for Christmas © Liz Fielding 1996
The Girl He Left Behind © Emma Goldrick 1990

ISBN 0 263 82422 5

05-1200

*Printed and bound in Spain
by Litografía Rosés S.A., Barcelona*

Leigh Michaels has always loved happy endings. Even when she was a child, if a book's conclusion didn't please her, she'd make up her own. And, though she always wanted to write fiction, she very sensibly planned to earn her living as a newspaper reporter. That career didn't work out, however, and she found herself writing for Mills & Boon® instead—in the kind of happy ending only a romance novelist could dream up!

Leigh likes to hear from readers; you can write to her at PO Box 935, Ottumwa, Iowa, 52501-0935 USA.

Look out for THE CORPORATE WIFE
by Leigh Michaels

in Tender Romance™, January 2001

THE UNLIKELY SANTA

by

LEIGH MICHAELS

CHAPTER ONE

BRANDI Ogilvie was not having a good day.

A shipment of Christmas supplies—twinkle lights, wrapping paper, and tree ornaments—which had been promised for delivery that morning had gotten lost somewhere between the warehouse and the store, and Brandi spent the better part of two hours on the telephone trying without success to track it down.

A sudden, virulent flu had taken out a half-dozen workers in the course of the morning and was threatening to decimate her staff before the week was out—hardly a cheerful thought for the first Monday in December. It was the crucial second week of the Christmas shopping season, and the Tyler-Royale store in Oak Park, Illinois, was a major department store, not a self-service discount outlet. As its manager, Brandi needed every person she could get on the sales floors.

And as if all that wasn't enough for one day, her secretary paged Brandi away from her lunch break before she'd eaten the first half of her hot pastrami sandwich. She sighed and picked up the other half to take back to her office, and as she was leaving the tearoom, two youngsters who were playing tag around the tables crashed into her. Mustard squirted from the sandwich over her new cream-colored silk blouse.

"Urchins," she said under her breath. "What are they doing in here anyway? And where are their parents?"

Brandi didn't expect an answer, and she was startled when a voice at her elbow murmured, "Right over there, drinking coffee and peacefully oblivious to their children's antics." Casey Amos, the department head of ladies' active wear, reached past Brandi to pick up a linen napkin from the nearest table.

Brandi took it and dabbed at the stain on the front of her blouse. "I'd like to ban kids from the tearoom altogether. That's why we put in the cafeteria downstairs, you know."

"You'd feel better if you sat down and ate something reasonable," Casey diagnosed.

"It's got nothing to do with where and what I eat. It's the season. Just between you and me, I hate Christmas, Casey."

"Now is that a proper attitude for the manager of a Tyler-Royale store? Don't you remember what Ross Clayton said at the sales conference just last week?" Casey struck a pose in imitation of the chain's chief executive officer and deepened her voice. "Always remember Christmas is the engine that drives retail sales. We'll do a third of our year's business between now and New Year's Day. And every single one of our customers is apt to walk through our doors in the next six weeks. Catch that customer and keep him or her happy!"

Brandi feigned a frown. "Does that mean you think our beloved leader would object if I spanked the brats?"

"Darling, I doubt you could catch them," Casey said frankly. "If you were eating properly and taking your vitamins, I'd put money on you, but..."

Brandi laughed. "All right, I'll order a salad next time. I suppose this serves me right for being in such a hurry— I shouldn't carry food around."

She could hardly go back to work drenched in mustard; her secretary would just have to be patient for another few minutes. Brandi stopped in Salon Elegance, the department that handled upscale women's clothing, and bought a duplicate of her blouse.

The clerk charged the sale to Brandi's Tyler-Royale credit card and offered to send the original blouse out for cleaning. "It may be too late already, Ms. Ogilvie," she said. "Mustard's a tough one. But we'll do our best."

Brandi pinned the white carnation that marked her as a manager to her shoulder, gathered up her receipt and wallet and made a mental note to compliment the woman's supervisor about her helpful attitude. Then she headed for the escalator and her office. She was feeling much better, now that she was properly dressed again.

Christmas was just a state of mind anyway—in less than four weeks the holiday season would be over. She'd survive the pressure this time just as she had for the past half-dozen years. It was simply part of the job. And someday, when she moved farther up in the corporate structure, she wouldn't have to deal with this sort of pressure around the holidays.

In Tyler-Royale's anchor store in downtown Chicago, the executive offices took up two whole floors, but in the rest of the chain—even the big suburban stores like this one—space was precious and managers made do with much smaller quarters. Brandi's office lay at the end of a narrow corridor on the top floor, cramped between the employees' lounge and a storeroom, and her secretary's desk occupied a tiny alcove just outside her door.

The secretary looked up with obvious relief at seeing her boss. No doubt, Brandi thought, that was because today the alcove seemed even smaller than usual—the single visitor's chair beside Dora's desk was occupied.

"Sorry I took so long, Dora," Brandi said briskly. "I had a little accident and had to change my blouse. Have I forgotten an appointment?" But she didn't remember scheduling a supplier or a sales rep today, and Dora usually let people like that sit in her office rather than subject them to the cramped alcove. So who was waiting for her?

The man rose with an easy, athletic grace Brandi couldn't help but admire. She was tall herself, but her nose was on a level with the knot in his tie—a black tie, over a white shirt, under a V-necked sweater in a bold black-and-white pattern. His eyes were almost black, as well, or was that just the effect of the dramatic clothing? And his hair was black; it looked silky and fine and soft.

Dora said, under her breath, "He's waiting for you, Ms. Ogilvie. He says he's your new Santa."

Brandi blinked and looked up at the man again. Mid-thirties, she estimated. There was not a strand of silver in his hair; his shoulders were broad and his stomach per-fectly flat, and his face—though far from unpleasant to look at—was too well chiseled to be called merry. His was hardly the sort of physique she normally sought for the job; this man looked more like a model—the rugged, out-door kind—than a stand-in for jolly old Saint Nicholas.

Furthermore, Brandi thought, he ought to have realized that much himself—unless he was suffering from some kind of delusion. Maybe he really thought he *was* Santa Claus?

"Did you call security, Dora?" she asked softly.

Despite her low tone, the man heard her. "No need for that, Miss Ogilvie."

His voice was low and warm and rich and reassuring; that much was exactly right for the part. But the rest of him…

Dora shook her head. "He didn't seem threatening, ex-actly, just determined."

Brandi didn't have any doubts about the determination.

She turned to face the man. "It's *Ms.* Ogilvie, please. And if you're looking for a job…"

His eyes dropped to her left hand, where a diamond cluster sparkled on her ring finger, then met hers again, without hesitation. "It's not a matter of looking, exactly, Ms. Ogilvie, I *am* your new Santa."

Brandi said dryly, "You'll pardon me for not recognizing you. Perhaps it's because you're out of uniform?"

His smile started in his eyes, she noted. It was quite a nice smile, slow and easy; it lit up his whole face and showed off perfect teeth and an unexpected dimple in his left cheek.

Dora cleared her throat. "Also, Ms. Ogilvie, there's a call for you from Mr. Clayton." She said the name with the same reverence most of Tyler-Royale's employees used when referring to the chief executive officer.

Brandi frowned a little. "And you've kept him waiting? Why didn't you tell me that right away?"

"He said not to disturb you, that he'd wait till it was convenient."

Brandi's frown deepened. That didn't bode well; Ross Clayton was a good and thoughtful employer, but it wasn't like him to be so very considerate of his man-ager's schedules. "I'll take it right now," Brandi murmured and turned back to her unlikely Santa. "Hiring isn't my department anyway. Perhaps you'd best speak to the personnel director—third door down the hall, on your right." Without pausing to see whether he obeyed, she closed her office door behind her and picked up the phone. "Ross, I'm sorry to keep you waiting."

"It's no problem. This is in the nature of a favor, so I didn't want to disturb your lunch."

"Don't let it worry you. You'd have been the least of the disturbances. What can I do for you?"

"I'm sending a man out to see you this afternoon."

Brandi closed her eyes. "Very tall?" she said warily. "With black hair and a grin so charming it almost makes you overlook the fact he's a maniac?"

"That sounds like Zack. He's showed up already, has he?"

Brandi rubbed the bridge of her nose. "Oh, he's here."

"He's generally on the ball. Good, you can put him to work right away. I know you can always use an extra Santa."

"With all due respect, Ross, I don't need another Santa. I have three perfectly good Santas hired already. Their work schedule is set up through Christmas Eve, and…"

"I hear the flu's getting really bad. What if you lose one?"

"That's why I've hired three. Ross, they're all honest-to-goodness grandpas, with real white beards and real white hair. They're even just about the same height so they can swap costumes. Tell me, where am I supposed to get a Santa suit for your Goliath? Besides, those kids are a tough audience. I can't just stick a couple of cotton balls on your friend's face and make him look believable!"

"I know you're a stickler, Brandi. But as a favor to me…"

Brandi wanted to groan. "Let me guess," she said crisply. "He's an old friend of yours who's fallen on hard times, and you're finding him a job?"

"He's got some problems just now," Ross agreed.

"That figures."

"It's only a seasonal job, Brandi. Just through Christmas."

"I don't need a Santa," Brandi muttered. "I need an assistant manager and another six clerks who can float to any department."

"What?"

"Never mind. Is this a direct order, Ross?"

"Brandi, you know I like to give my managers maximum authority. I try never to issue direct orders in matters that affect a single store."

"That means it is. All right, Ross—your Santa has a job." She put down the telephone and dropped her head into her hands for a few seconds. Then she punched the intercom. "Dora, is Santa still out there?"

"Yes." The secretary's voice was little more than a whisper. "He won't leave."

"I'm not surprised. Send him in."

Brandi sat at her desk and watched him as he crossed the narrow room and took the chair opposite her. He moved like an athlete, perfectly at ease with his body and in command of every muscle. She wondered if he was a dancer, too—there was something about the way he moved....

As if it mattered, Brandi reminded herself. She eyed his cable-stitched sweater and houndstooth-check trousers. He wore his clothes with an ease that said they weren't brand-new, as she'd half expected them to be. So Ross hadn't fitted his friend up at the downtown store before sending him out to Oak Park. And his clothes were expensive; Brandi had no trouble recognizing the quality of the whole outfit. Whatever hard times this man had fallen on were obviously recent ones.

She picked up a pen and doodled a square on the edge of her desk blotter. "Ross said your name's Zack?"

"That's right. And I'll happily let you call me that if you tell me your first name in return."

Brandi looked at him levelly, eyes narrowed. "Don't be impudent. I may have had to give you a job, but I don't have to make it easy for you."

He bowed his head. Brandi couldn't help but feel the submissive gesture was tinged with a good deal of irony. "Zack Forrest, at your service."

"That's better. Mr. Forrest, I'm sure you understand that Ross doesn't assign entry-level jobs in his stores. That's up to the managers. And right now I don't need a Santa. What I could use is floor help—clerks who float throughout a department and assist the customer to find what he or she wants. If you're interested, I can put you down in men's active wear this afternoon for training, and—"

He was shaking his head. "Ross sent me here to be a Santa."

"I just told you..." Brandi paused. "Look, I'm sure Ross meant well. But he doesn't know what's going on out here."

Oh, that was great, she told herself. The last thing she needed was for Ross Clayton's friend to go back and tell him that the manager of his Oak Park store said he had no idea what was going on!

"I want to be a Santa," Zack Forrest said. "In fact, I insist on it." If his voice hadn't been so deep, Brandi would have sworn he sounded like a stubborn three-year-old.

"Or what?" Brandi said in disbelief. "You'll report me to Ross? I don't know what kind of hold you have on him, but—"

"I wouldn't call it a *hold*, exactly," he said thoughtfully.

Brandi gave it up. "Why did he send you to me anyway?"

Zack shrugged. "He said this store has the busiest Santa's Workshop of any Tyler-Royale location."

"That's partly because I'm so careful who I hire to man

that department.'' Brandi paused and thought, I can't believe I'm explaining my hiring practices to him!

He treated her to another slow, unrestrained smile. ''I thought you said hiring wasn't your responsibility, Ms. Ogilvie.''

''You know, with that kind of attitude it's no wonder you're out of a job.'' Brandi stood up. ''You can report to the personnel manager and fill out the paperwork. Be sure to leave a phone number. Since it will take some time to find a Santa suit your size—''

Zack Forrest had risen, too, and Brandi let her gaze run from his face to his well-polished black wing tips and back, hoping the curt appraisal would take him down a notch. But he didn't even blink, just stood quietly and watched her face while she looked him over.

Brandi went on, ''We'll be in touch when we can put you to work. Don't expect a call for a few days, though, because I'm sure finding a suit to fit you will be—''

''No problem at all,'' Zack interrupted. ''I happen to have one in my car right now. I can go to work this afternoon.'' There was a glint in his eyes. ''If you like, that is.''

Brandi was taken aback. ''Fill out the paperwork first and we'll see,'' she said finally. ''I'll call the personnel director and tell him you're on the way.''

The corner of his mouth quirked as if with satisfaction, but he didn't say a word till he was at the door of her office. Then he paused and turned. ''You owe me one, though,'' he said gently.

Brandi had already picked up the telephone. She looked up from it, her mouth ajar. ''One what? Listen, buddy, if you think you're the one who's doing *me* a favor here—''

''Oh, no. I appreciate everything you've done for me.'' There was a faint note of irony underlying that rich, warm voice. "I just mean I've earned equal time to look you over as thoroughly as you've studied me, Ms. Ogilvie."

"I beg your pardon?"

"And I reserve the right to do so...someday." He sketched a salute and pulled the door closed behind him.

Brandi sank back into her chair. At this rate, it was going to be a very long time till Christmas.

Brandi couldn't settle to anything constructive that afternoon, because the face of her unlikely Santa kept popping up between her and whatever she was trying to do. Finally, she pushed all her paperwork into a desk drawer and went out to do her daily tour of the store.

Early in her training, Brandi had learned to pop into every department frequently but unexpectedly, just to be certain her staff was performing up to specifications. It had turned out to be a good habit; in her two years as manager of the Oak Park store, Brandi had avoided a lot of big trouble by catching problems while they were still small enough to handle. It was one of the reasons that her store consistently ranked near the top of the Tyler-Royale chain when it came to profitability.

Though if the CEO kept sending her employees she didn't need or want, her record was likely to be chipped away. What had gotten into Ross Clayton anyway? Zack Forrest had denied having any hold over him, but Brandi didn't believe it for a minute. It just puzzled her to think what it could be.

Mondays were always the least hectic day of the week in the retail trade, but already this was shaping up to be the busiest Christmas season Brandi had ever experienced, and despite the day the store was comfortably full of shoppers. Some were admiring the long double row of decorated trees that lined the atrium entrance, inviting the public to come in for a closer look. Others were already heavily loaded with bags and boxes in Tyler-Royale's trademark blue and silver. In the toy department, several women browsed, and nearby a line of children waited to reach the big chair that sat just in front of the elaborate facade of Santa's Workshop.

Wait a minute, Brandi thought. There wasn't supposed to be a Santa on duty this afternoon—not till evening, when children were out of school and families came to shop.

She paused at the railing that surrounded Santa's Workshop and helped to keep the line orderly in particularly busy times. This wasn't one of those times; at most, a dozen children were waiting to talk to the man in the red suit who sat comfortably in the throne-size chair with a child on each knee.

Brandi went to the nearest checkout station and called the personnel director. "Did you assign our new Santa to work this afternoon?" she asked bluntly.

The man sounded stupefied. "Of course not. I gave him the employee handbook and said we'd call him when we got the schedule straightened out, just like you told me to do."

"That's what I thought," Brandi muttered. She put the phone down. By the time she got back to Santa's Workshop, the two boys had gotten off Zack's lap and a little girl had climbed up.

Brandi leaned against the rail and watched for a moment. She had to admit that Zack Forrest made a better Santa than she'd expected. Despite some padding around the middle, he was still a bit on the lean side, and Brandi could tell from across the room that his beard was fake. But he'd brushed something into his eyebrows to turn them gray, and his suit was perfect—the heavy red velvet was trimmed in what looked like real white fur. And he hadn't settled for cheap black patent accessories, either—this Santa's belt and boots were top-grain black leather, polished to a gleam. So was the cover of the notebook that lay open on his right knee.

A notebook? Brandi thought in disbelief. Why on earth was he taking notes? And why was he even *here*, without orders? The sooner she dealt with this mutinous employee the better.

Brandi slipped through the gate and went to the head of the line. "I need to talk to you," she murmured.

Zack ignored her. All his attention was focused on the child in his lap. The little girl was about four, and she was chattering merrily in what could have been a foreign language as far as Brandi was concerned; she could make out little resemblance to standard English. But though Zack's brow was furrowed a little as if he, too, found it difficult to understand the child, he was writing down a word now and then as she talked.

"Did you hear me?" Brandi muttered.

Zack's gaze lifted to study the line. "Certainly. I'll see you after I've finished with the kids."

Brandi had to bite her tongue to keep from firing him on the spot—but how would that look to the dozen children, and their parents, who were waiting in line?

She waited impatiently, trying not to tap her toes, as he eased the little girl off his lap, then beckoned the next child up and began to chat. At this rate, she thought, he'd be all afternoon getting through the remaining dozen kids. Which was no doubt exactly what he had in mind—stalling till Brandi got tired of waiting.

She shut the gate so the line wouldn't get any longer and put out the sign, kept handy for all the employees' breaks, which announced that Santa had gone to feed his reindeer but would return soon. Then she went back to stand beside the big chair. There was an infant on Zack's lap now, and his mother was backing off to get a photograph.

But finally the line was gone. Brandi waited till the last child was well out of earshot, and then turned on Zack. "What are you doing here?" she demanded.

"I don't see how it could be any more obvious."

"You were told you'd be called when we had an assignment for you!"

"And just when was that likely to be, Ms. Ogilvie? I don't think it would take much effort for you to find an excuse not to call me at all, so when I saw there was no Santa scheduled to work this afternoon, I volunteered."

"Don't you understand the store has a liability, Mr. Forrest? You can't just walk into this job without training."

"What's to learn? Your personnel director gave me a list of all the rules, and they're easy enough to memorize. Let's see—don't promise any toy unless the parent gives you a signal, just say *We'll see* instead. Never comment on a request for a little brother or sister. Just pretend you didn't hear it. Don't wear strong cologne or after-shave. Don't give candy without the parents' permission. Make a tour of Toyland every day before going on duty, in order to be familiar with the merchandise. Help the child to climb up, but don't lift—we're less likely to have scared little ones that way..." He paused. "And fewer injured Santas, too, no doubt, if they're not straining their backs lifting tots."

"That suggestion may have come from the corporate legal department," Brandi said stiffly. "But I don't see what that has to do with—"

"It certainly sounds like it."

She raised her voice. "The point is—"

"The point is that I have the rest of the hundred rules down pat, too—so why shouldn't I be working? Why should the kids be cheated of their opportunity to talk to Santa, just because it happens to be Monday afternoon?"

Brandi folded her arms and put her chin up. "There seems to be a basic disagreement about who's in charge here, Mr.—"

"Careful," Zack warned, and waved as a child stopped hopefully by the closed gate.

"*Claus*," Brandi said through clenched teeth. "Perhaps we should have this discussion somewhere other than Toyland."

Zack snapped his fingers. "I think you've finally hit on a good point, Ms. Ogilvie."

It was midafternoon, and the cafeteria should be practically empty. "How about talking it out over coffee?" Brandi suggested.

The child at the gate looked disappointed when Zack stood up. "When will you be back, Santa?" she called. "How long does it take to feed your reindeer?"

"Just a few minutes," Zack said. "I'll be back soon."

"If I were you, I wouldn't make any promises," Brandi muttered.

The lunch rush was long over, and only a few patrons were in the cafeteria, having a soft drink and resting their feet while they checked over their lists and purchases.

Zack poured two cups of coffee and carried them to an out-of-the-way table while Brandi gathered up cream, sugar, and napkins and told the counter attendant to put the charge on her bill.

"I suppose Santa never carries money," she said as she set her awkward load down on the table.

"Of course I do. But you asked for this date, and judging by how sensitive you were when I got your title wrong, you're probably the sort to take offense if I insist on paying. I'd be happy to hold your chair, though, unless that would irritate you, too."

"Oh, sit down," she ordered.

But he held the chair for her anyway, before taking the seat across from her.

Brandi stirred sugar into her coffee and looked him over thoughtfully. "I feel as if I've walked into *Miracle on 34th Street*," she muttered.

Zack grinned.

The effect of his brilliant smile against the pure white beard and tanned face was stunning. He looked good in red, Brandi thought absently. The suit was a deep, rich ruby, and the color reflected nicely across his high cheekbones.

"If that's a polite way of asking if I think I'm the real Santa Claus, Brandi—no, I don't."

"Well, that's some relief. Wait a minute. How'd you know my name?"

Zack leaned forward confidingly. "Would you believe I used my X-ray vision to see through the file cabinets in the personnel director's office?"

"No."

"That's good. We've established two things. I don't think I'm either Superman or Santa Claus, and you admit I'm not deluded about it. Now we're getting somewhere."

"We're getting nowhere. I could fire you for this stunt, you know. You can't just go around putting yourself to work because you see a job you think needs doing."

"I don't expect to be paid for this afternoon. It's sort of like giving out free samples—I volunteered in order to show you how well I can do the job. And you must admit I'm good at it."

Brandi didn't want to admit anything of the sort, but she

could hardly deny it, either. "That's beside the point, don't you think?"

"Hardly." Zack leaned back in his chair. "Tell the truth. Would you have called me?"

"Not directly. It's not my job. But I'd have made sure the personnel manager kept you in mind."

"What a comfort." His voice oozed sarcasm. "I might have got to work by Christmas Eve!"

"You have to remember you're low man when it comes to seniority. Knowing Ross doesn't make a difference where that's concerned, and it's only fair that the three Santas I hired before you will be considered first."

"There. You see? That's why I felt it necessary to make my own hours."

"Look, Mr. Forrest, I can't have employees setting their own schedules without considering what's best for the store."

"I *am* considering what's best for the store. You've now got a dozen kids who are happier with Tyler-Royale than they'd have been if I wasn't on duty this afternoon. And you'd have a dozen more if you'd left me at work instead of dragging me down here to drink coffee. So if you'll excuse me, I'll get back to my job." He pushed his chair back and stood up.

"Just because you know the CEO doesn't mean you can make the rules," Brandi warned.

He looked at her, gray eyebrows lifted in what looked like long-suffering patience.

Brandi reconsidered. He'd been flagrantly in the wrong to put himself to work like that. Still, she had to admit she couldn't exactly fire him over it; she'd have a little trouble explaining to Ross Clayton what was so terrible about his friend volunteering an afternoon to play Santa in order to prove himself.

And Zack Forrest looked as if he knew very well what she was thinking. He was standing beside the table with an air of disdain, clearly waiting for her to admit defeat.

Brandi capitulated. ''You will not set your own hours anymore.''

Zack set a booted foot on his chair and leaned over her. ''How about if I promise to tell you before I go on duty?''

''That's not the same thing at all.''

He smiled a little. ''Well, I'm sure you'll work it all out. In the meantime, you know where to find me.'' He didn't pause till he reached the cafeteria door, and then only to politely hold it for a couple of elderly ladies.

There was no point in counting to ten in an effort to control her temper. Instead, Brandi counted the days till Christmas.

CHAPTER TWO

BY THE time Brandi left the store that night, it was almost closing time and the late-evening rush was beginning to die down. In the parking area of the enormous shopping mall, the cars were beginning to thin out. The air was cold and crisp; she knew she'd have been able to see the stars if it wasn't for the powerful banks of lights that held the winter darkness at bay. There would be no snow tonight.

A few miles away, in the big apartment complex where she lived, the windows of almost every unit glowed. In many of them, Christmas trees sparkled with light as tiny red and green and gold and white bulbs twinkled on and off. Almost every door displayed a wreath or a Santa or a Nativity scene.

And she could hear Christmas carols as she walked through the courtyard to her building. The sound of it made Brandi's head hurt. The music wasn't obnoxiously loud, but it was so darned distinctive, and so very inescapable. Christmas, she thought, had gotten out of hand.

Her own apartment, in contrast, was dim and quiet. She closed the door with a sigh of relief, turned on a couple of lamps, and put a classical CD on to play. Then she poured herself a glass of sherry and sat down on the couch to enjoy a little peace.

The room was something like a cocoon, cozy and comforting. The overstuffed furniture was covered in subdued colors and subtle patterns, nicely framed prints decorated the neutral-colored walls, and soft deep carpeting cushioned the floors. A room to be at ease in, it looked just as it did the other eleven months of the year—and that was one of the things Brandi liked best about it.

Here, there was no tree, no tinsel, no mistletoe. She didn't have to deal with the sights and smells of the holiday. She didn't have to listen to perpetual Christmas carols. In fact, when she was safely snuggled into her own living room, she could pretend it wasn't Christmas at all.

And considering the day she'd had, that was a blessing. She let her head rest against the soft back of the couch and closed her eyes. How on earth was she going to handle her new Santa?

In the two years she'd managed the Oak Park store, she'd never had an employee like him, that was sure. She'd never even *heard* of an employee who set his own hours in defiance of the store's schedule, who contradicted the boss, who acted as if he knew her job better than she did.

But then, she'd never hired a friend of the boss before, either. She'd like to call up Ross Clayton and ask what kind of blackmail material Zack had on him; it must be something extraordinary to account for the kind of special treatment the man seemed to expect. For the life of her, she couldn't think of anything that infamous.

She finished her sherry and wandered into the kitchen to dig through the freezer for something that would be easy to cook. There wasn't much variety left; she'd have to fit in time to stop at the supermarket in the next few days. Certainly she'd have to go before the weekend, when things would really get hectic again.

The phone rang. She made a face and thought about ignoring it, then sighed and picked it up anyway. There might be a security problem at the store.

Casey Amos said, "I saw you with Santa in the cafeteria this afternoon. What's going on, Brandi?"

"We were having a chat. Why?"

"You should hear what the grapevine's saying."

"Casey, I stopped being interested in store gossip a long time ago."

"All right, then, I won't tell you," Casey said cheerfully. "It's a good story, though. And I could see the sparks you were striking off each other."

"The only sparks you saw were pure irritation."

"Ah. Then it is true Ross made you hire him?"

Brandi kept her voice level. "I wonder who started that rumor."

"You just did—telling me you were irritated. If hiring him had been your idea, and he annoyed you so much, he'd have been out the door in two minutes flat."

Brandi wanted to bite her tongue off. Just yesterday she'd have had the sense to think it over before she spoke, and she'd have refused Casey's bait. Zack Forrest had struck once more. At this rate, by Christmas she wouldn't have a shred of judgment left.

"Instead," Casey went on, "he finished his shift and went home. In fact, since I was clocking out at the same time, he walked me to my car."

"Congratulations."

"He seems perfectly nice—but I didn't feel the same kind of sparks you were giving off this afternoon, so don't worry."

"Why do I put up with you, Casey?"

"Because I'm the best department head you've got, and when I get a store of my own next year you're going to cry over losing me."

"True. Still—"

"And because I'm so discreet. I won't pass along a word of what you've confided in me tonight."

"I wasn't aware I'd bared my soul," Brandi said acidly. "If that's why you called, I appreciate the thought, but—"

Casey's voice took on a more serious note. "No, actually I'm checking on the menu for the Christmas party. It's only two weeks off, you know, so I have to get an order to the caterer right away."

"Casey, you know I don't care what you serve at the Christmas party."

"We can do it for the same money as last year if we leave out the shrimp."

"Didn't you say the staff loved the shrimp last year?"

"Yes. Still, everything else has gone so high, and you did say we had to stick to the budget...."

"Have the shrimp. I'll make up the shortfall personally. Just don't tell anybody, all right?"

"And ruin your reputation as the biggest Scrooge in the chain? I wouldn't dream of it. Are you going to put your name in the gift-exchange drawing this year?"

"Of course not. Why do you think I insisted you make participation voluntary?"

"Still, you seem to be softening a little. Maybe it's Santa's influence. You seem inspired, somehow."

Brandi gritted her teeth. "The only thing my new Santa has inspired in me is fury."

"I wasn't referring to any person in particular," Casey murmured. "I was talking about the spirit of Christmas. But *you* assumed I meant your new Santa. How interesting that you thought of him right off!"

There were times when the cramped size of Brandi's office had its advantages; she'd found that meetings and conferences tended to move along very promptly when the participants found themselves sitting on bookcases and file cabinets.

Her usual Tuesday morning meeting with all the store's department heads was winding down, just a few minutes before the business day began, when Dora came into her office with a slip of paper and slid it across the desk without a word.

Brandi unfolded the note, still half-listening to the report from the head of the electronics department. "Mrs. Townsend of the Kansas City store wants you to call her," Dora had written in her cramped, neat hand.

That's odd, Brandi thought. If the matter had been crucial, Dora would have summoned her from the meeting. Since it wasn't, why hadn't the secretary just held the message till after the meeting broke up?

Then Brandi realized she'd overlooked the second part of the note. "And your Santa popped in just now to tell you he's going to work this morning," Dora had written.

Brandi sighed. Did everybody in the store now think of Zack Forrest as her very own private Santa?

She dismissed the department heads and followed them out to the alcove. "Dora, did Mrs. Townsend tell you what she wanted?"

"No. She just said to call her when it's convenient, that she'd be in the store all day." Dora warily eyed the slip of paper in Brandi's hand. "I didn't know what to do about your Santa."

"Neither does anyone else," Brandi admitted.

"I'm not even sure what he was talking about. I asked him why he didn't just punch the time clock like the rest of the employees instead of reporting to you, and he said you were expecting him. So I thought I should tell you right away."

I wish you hadn't, Brandi thought. If she didn't know Zack was down there in the big chair in front of Santa's Workshop, stirring up trouble, she could simply go about her business. Now that she knew, she'd have to do something about it—she couldn't simply pretend to be oblivious. No manager could let a brand-new employee go around creating his own schedule and making a fool of her. If that word got out, Brandi Ogilvie would be a laughingstock throughout the whole chain.

But she'd spent the night thinking about it, and she still couldn't quite imagine how she was going to stop Zack Forrest from doing precisely what he pleased.

She could refuse to pay him, of course, but she didn't think that would stand up long once he had another chat with Ross Clayton. After all, he was doing the work for which he'd been hired—and she didn't think the fact that he wasn't precisely up to Brandi's specifications would carry any more weight with Ross than it had yesterday when she'd tried to get out of hiring him in the first place.

Well, if she couldn't get rid of him, she'd better give him some regular hours. At least then she'd look as if she was still in control. ''Dora, will you find out when the next real Santa's due to come in?''

''Certainly.'' Dora looked a bit puzzled.

''Better yet, go over to the employees' lounge and make a copy of the schedule for the next week, and bring it into my office. Oh, and Dora—try not to let anybody see what you're doing.''

Dora looked even more confused. Brandi just smiled and went back to her office.

She dismissed Zack from her mind for the moment and settled back at her desk to call Whitney Townsend in Kansas City. She always enjoyed talking to Whitney; the woman might have anything in mind, from a personnel swap to a practical joke on the CEO. And since she was not only a senior manager but a vice president of the Tyler-Royale chain, she could get by with either—or almost anything in between.

Brandi's call was passed to Whitney's office with

machine-gun efficiency. "How are you?" Whitney demanded as soon as she picked up the phone. "I haven't heard from you in weeks."

"You know how things get this time of year."

"Exactly. That's why I expected a call before the Christmas season kicked into high gear. Don't you know you're supposed to phone your mentor once a month at least?" The smile in her voice took any sting out of the words.

"I've tried," Brandi said crisply. "But I didn't bother to leave a message last time I called, because you were in San Antonio sorting out the problems in the store there."

"Oh, that. Ross seems to be short a troubleshooter at the moment, so I got roped in to handle things."

"I assumed that's what happened. At any rate, I thought you probably had enough to deal with. The time before that you were vacationing in Hawaii when I called. Your secretary offered me the number, but I know better than to disturb you on a second honeymoon."

Whitney laughed. "Good thinking. No problems, then?"

Brandi thought about Zack Forrest, and sighed. She couldn't even begin to put that particular difficulty into words. "Nothing more than usual."

"Well, that's good. Nevertheless, I want to check for myself, so I'm coming up to see you at the end of the week. Hold Saturday evening open for me, all right?"

Brandi flipped the page in her desk calendar to write the appointment down. "You don't mean the night of the corporate Christmas party," she said slowly.

"That's exactly what I mean. And don't you dare miss it."

"Whitney, you know I hate those things."

"Yes, and I also know that every year you come up

with another spectacular reason for not coming. In fact, Ross suggested I not call you, because he wanted to see what you'd use to get out of it this time. You're running so late at sending your regrets that he figures it'll have to be a doozy of an excuse.''

''But of course you didn't obey his wishes.''

''Well, it wasn't quite a direct order,'' Whitney said reasonably. ''So I just ignored him.''

Brandi wished she'd dared to ignore Ross on the question of Zack Forrest. Someday, she thought dreamily, she'd be a corporate vice president and she could. Not that it made any difference right now. ''Can't we just have lunch instead, Whitney? We won't really be able to talk at the party, you know.''

Dora opened the door and quietly laid the Santa schedule on Brandi's desk.

Whitney said firmly, ''I'm flying up on Saturday afternoon and back on Sunday, so it's the party or nothing. I have a store to manage myself, you know.''

Brandi capitulated. ''Then I'll be at the party to see you. But I hope you don't insist on my having a good time otherwise.''

Whitney only laughed, and Brandi put down the phone and picked up the Santa schedule. Dora hadn't stopped with the week's calendar; she'd brought the whole month's, all the way through Christmas Eve.

Brandi had worked like fury on that schedule. It was the perfectly arranged product of two seasons' worth of observation of the store's mix of customers. Any time there was likely to be a large number of children in the store— late afternoons, evenings and weekends, mostly—there would be a Santa on duty. And the hours were perfectly divided between the three elderly, white-haired, bearded men Brandi had hired to play the part.

Now, in order to leave room for Zack Forrest, she was going to have to throw it all out and start over.

She wanted to growl. No, what she really wanted to do was go down to Toyland and give one irrepressible Santa a black eye. But that was guaranteed to make things worse.

She got out a frcsh schedule sheet and began to draw boxes.

Keeping things as fair as possible, while trying not to cheat any of the men she'd hired first, would be a challenge. In fact, just the idea of calling her handpicked Santas in and explaining the changes gave her heartburn. They weren't going to be happy at having their calendars rearranged for no reason, and she didn't blame them. But she could hardly come straight out and tell them they'd been displaced by an upstart who happened to know the boss.

Unless… Maybe there was another way.

She turned the original schedule this way and that, then smiled, reached for a red marker, and drew a series of neat lines. Then she tucked the page in the pocket of her suit jacket and left her office. "Dora, I'll be in Toyland talking to Santa."

"Good luck," Dora muttered. "I don't envy you the job."

The line outside Santa's Workshop was moving along faster this morning then it had yesterday; most of the children were very small, and the parents seemed more interested in photographs than in conversations. Brandi closed the gate, put the "Santa's Feeding His Reindeer" sign in place, and strolled to the head of the line to stand near the big chair.

Zack had seen her coming the moment she'd gotten off the escalator, Brandi was sure of that, though he didn't look up. In fact, an observer would swear Santa hadn't taken his attention from the child on his lap. But Brandi knew he was aware of her presence, because she could feel a sudden pulse of energy coming from him—as if he'd been waiting impatiently for her and was relieved that she'd finally appeared.

She stood beside the big chair, just inside his peripheral vision, and folded her arms, trying to look as if she could comfortably stay there forever. She knew better than to suggest Zack leave even a single child waiting, but perhaps if she just stood there silently, he'd get nervous and hurry things along.

A couple of minutes later he looked up at her with a quick smile and a quizzical quirk to his fake-gray eyebrows. ''Are you certain the reindeer need feeding *again*, Ms. Ogilvie?''

Brandi kept her voice level with an effort. ''I'm afraid they do, Santa.''

''And you came all the way down to help me. How thoughtful of you!''

The year-old child on Zack's lap gurgled, and her mother picked her up. ''Nice touch. I hope you both enjoy yourselves on your break.'' She winked at Brandi. ''Bet I can guess what you'd like for Christmas from this particular Santa.''

Brandi felt color rising in her face as she remembered what Casey had said about the sparks she'd seen passing between Brandi and Zack yesterday. The conclusion Casey had jumped to was an idiotic one, of course—and this young mother was being just as silly to think that the electricity she saw must have a romantic element to it.

But Brandi had to bite her lip hard to subdue the blush. She didn't look at Zack, but she could sense he was smiling, obviously enjoying her discomfort.

The next child had been listening to the exchange. He

marched up to Zack, folded his arms, and announced, "Santa's just for kids. My mom says so. Big people aren't supposed to ask you to bring them things."

Zack's eyebrows soared. "Why on earth shouldn't they? Big people have dreams, too." He looked up at Brandi appraisingly. "What *would* you like for Christmas, Ms. Ogilvie?"

"For New Year's Day to come three weeks early," Brandi said.

Zack choked, and it was almost half a minute before he recovered enough to take the child on his knee and get back to business. With her equilibrium restored, Brandi settled back to wait for him to deal with the rest of the line. At least, she thought, he wasn't likely to ask her any more leading questions in public!

He was better than she'd expected at the job, she had to admit. He'd done his homework, or else he was a phenomenal actor, for not a toy was mentioned that Zack didn't seem to recognize. And he didn't simply acknowledge the requests, either; he engaged each child in conversation about his wishes, and asked how he'd decided on that special item.

Brandi shifted impatiently from one foot to the other. "That's charming, Santa, but—"

Zack's eyes widened. "You mean you actually think I'm doing something right for a change?"

"Yes and no. I don't see the point of asking them why they've chosen a particular toy."

"I'm trying to make certain they really want it, and haven't simply been swayed by television ads or what their friends say."

A mother waiting in line nodded in approval. "Last year my son got everything on his list and didn't play with any of it. I was pretty annoyed, I'll tell you, when all those expensive toys turned out to be just a fad. I appreciate your taking time to make sure, Santa Claus.''

Zack shot Brandi a look that said, *See? Maybe I do know what I'm doing*.

She said, under her breath, ''I still think it's more likely you're trying to delay till I get tired of standing here.''

''You?'' he murmured. ''I'm beginning to think you're inexhaustible, Ms. Ogilvie.'' But eventually the kids were all satisfied, and Brandi and Zack were alone outside Santa's Workshop. Zack stood up, stretched, and tucked his leather-covered notebook into a capacious pocket. ''I must say it's nice to have a break. That chair isn't as comfortable as it looks. Coffee? It's my turn to buy, I believe.''

The same counter attendant was working in the cafeteria. ''Two days in a row?'' she murmured. ''This is getting to be a habit, Ms. Ogilvie.''

Oh, that's just great, Brandi thought. If Casey was right, the store's grapevine was already working overtime. By the end of the day, her two cups of coffee with Santa would probably have grown into a full-fledged affair. And if the tale escaped the Oak Park store and made the rounds of the chain, gossip would probably have her moving to the North Pole to live with him.

Zack stirred sugar into his coffee and looked thoughtfully across the table at her. ''So what do you really want for Christmas, Brandi?''

She decided to ignore the name; complaining, she suspected, would only encourage him. ''You're off duty now. Remember?''

He didn't seem to hear. ''Emeralds? They'd look good against that auburn hair and fair skin of yours.''

''I hardly think Santa's likely to bring me emeralds.''

''Well, that's true—at least this Santa. We hardly know each other, so it wouldn't be at all proper for me to give you jewelry.'' His gaze dropped to the cluster of diamonds on her left hand. ''To say nothing of the fact that Mr. Ogilvie would probably object. Tell me, *is* there a Mr. Ogilvie?''

This, Brandi thought, is getting out of hand. ''I can't think why you'd need to know.''

''Can't you? Well, never mind for now. Surely there's something you'd like for Christmas. Something simple, maybe, like peace on earth…'' Zack snapped his fingers. ''I know! How about a white Christmas?''

''That would be too late to do us any good,'' Brandi said crisply. ''On the other hand, a nice half-inch snowfall sometime this week would put every shopper in the holiday spirit and raise the season's sales by at least ten percent.''

Zack shook his head sadly.

''Only half an inch, though.'' Brandi sipped her coffee. ''Much more than that jams up traffic and people stay home.''

''You have a very unromantic view of the holiday.''

''So would you, I expect, if you'd been working Christmas retail for a decade.''

Zack looked startled. ''Ten years? You're not old enough.''

''Yes, I am. I started working part-time for Tyler-Royale when I was in high school, right in the middle of the Christmas season. But I didn't come down here to talk about me. I've got your work assignments for the rest of the month.''

Zack pulled out his notebook and flipped it open.

''That reminds me,'' Brandi said. ''Don't you think you ought to ditch the notebook?''

''Why?'' He didn't sound argumentative, just curious.

''Surely I shouldn't have to explain to you that Santa

remembers everything a child says and does. It's part of the mystique.''

Zack frowned. ''You mean you haven't ever heard of the old guy making a list and checking it twice? I take back what I said earlier, Brandi. You're not unromantic about Christmas, you're downright oblivious.''

Something about his tone annoyed Brandi; he didn't need to treat her like Scrooge, for heaven's sake. ''I must say I don't see what good it does to write down what a child wants. It's not like you're seriously going to hunt up these kids on Christmas Eve and deliver toys.'' She wrinkled her brow. ''Are you?''

''Of course not.''

''Right. How could you, when you haven't the foggiest idea who the child is or where he lives? That proves my point, you know. Writing all this stuff down takes up time and paper for nothing.'' She reached for his notebook, and knocked loose the white carnation pinned to the lapel of her forest green suit.

Zack slid the notebook out from under her hand and tucked it back in his pocket. ''On the contrary,'' he said soberly. ''Taking notes make the kids feel that I'm listening to them very seriously. They're reassured to know their requests are written down safely in Santa's book. So, while I thank you for your concern, I believe I'll keep on just as I've been doing.''

Brandi glared at him for an instant, then turned her attention to her carnation. It was useless to argue with him, she thought. She was obviously not going to convince him she was right, and the issue simply wasn't important enough to issue a direct order. That was why she'd asked a question in the first place, instead of just telling him to leave his notebook at home; Brandi had learned long ago to choose her battlefields more carefully than that.

Zack reached across the table. For an instant, his fingers almost encircled her wrist as he pulled her hand away from the carnation. Then he straightened the flower himself, setting the pin firmly into the wool of her lapel.

Brandi thought she could feel the warmth of his fingertips against her collarbone. The sensation was strictly imaginary, of course, she reminded herself, since not only the suit but a silky blouse lay between his hand and her bare skin. Still, the contact seemed to burn all the way to her bones.

"You said something about my work hours?" Zack reminded her.

Brandi pulled the Santa schedule out of her pocket and slid it across the table. "The blocks I've marked in red are yours."

Would he argue? she wondered. Or threaten? Would he get angry, or try to negotiate?

Zack studied the page, and then his gaze lifted to meet hers. At this distance, his eyes looked even darker than usual against the spun white floss of his beard. "You've marked all the times you hadn't already scheduled a Santa."

"Yes," Brandi admitted. "Since you seem to have adopted a good number of those hours anyway, I thought you might as well have every last one of them."

"It's generous of you, but—"

Brandi smiled. "Isn't it?" she said easily. "I *have* given you more time than any of the other Santas will work, so I hope you won't make an issue of it. They might feel left out."

"Considering the way these hours are spread around, I doubt they'll be jealous." Zack glanced at the paper again. "Two hours in the morning, one at closing time, a half hour through the supper break...this ought to keep me busy.''

''If you don't like the schedule, Zack...''

''Oh, I absolutely adore it. I can get all my Christmas shopping done while I'm between shifts.''

Brandi started to feel just a bit uneasy. The schedule she'd given him was nasty—the man wouldn't have an entire half day to call his own for the next month, but his work was so split up that all of his hours didn't add up to a full-time paycheck, either. Shouldn't he have at least tried to change her mind, to talk her into giving him some more reasonable hours? She studied him covertly. She couldn't detect a hint of strain in Zack's smile, and that worried her.

''Of course, I may have to pitch a tent in the parking lot to be sure I'm not late for any of my numerous curtain times,'' he said, ''but as long as you don't mind that little nuisance—''

Brandi relaxed a little. There was an edge to his voice, so slight that if she hadn't been listening intently, she'd have missed it. So he wasn't as sanguine as he'd pretended. Now he'd no doubt start to negotiate.

Well, that was all right with Brandi; she was perfectly willing to compromise. At least this time she'd be dealing from a position of strength, unlike the matter of his notebook. Brandi thought it made a nice change, everything considered.

''That's why I gave you your schedule for the whole month,'' she said agreeably. ''So you could plan ahead.''

''I'll do that. Now, since I'm supposed to be working at the moment, I'd better get back to it or you'll probably fire me for not showing up for my assigned times.''

He folded the schedule, tucked it into an inner pocket, and left the cafeteria without a backward glance.

Guilt washed over Brandi like a wave across the deck of a sailboat. The schedule she'd given him was worse than nasty, she admitted; it was unconscionable. She'd never before assigned an employee to that kind of random, scattered hours over such a long period of time, and she wouldn't stand for any of her department heads doing so, either. It wasn't fair to expect someone to be always on call and ready for work for a full month, without a single break.

Only store managers have to do that, she thought with a tinge of wry humor.

But why hadn't Zack made a fuss? Why hadn't he tried to get a change? Was he intending to go straight to Ross to complain?

She didn't think so. From what she'd seen of him so far, he wasn't the sort to hide his feelings or ask someone else to fight his battles. He hadn't hesitated to stand up for his convictions about the darned notebook so why would he have shrunk from arguing about his working hours?

Maybe he was simply further down on his luck than she'd thought. Maybe he really needed the work.

Brandi swallowed hard and tried to remember what the schedule had looked like. It wasn't too bad for the next couple of days, she thought. Not till the weekend did the scattered, fragmented hours really start. She'd see how it worked out for a day or two, and then...

Well, if she had to go to him and back down, it wouldn't be the first time Brandi Ogilvie had admitted to making a mistake.

She just didn't relish the thought of facing Zack with an apology.

CHAPTER THREE

BRANDI leaned on the fence that surrounded Santa's Workshop and watched admiringly as the white-haired man sitting in the big chair encouraged the child in his lap to tug on his long white beard. The child gave it a healthy yank, and Santa yelped in what Brandi thought was only slightly exaggerated discomfort.

The child's eyes widened. "Mommy, it's *real*," he said. "This must be the *real* Santa!"

Now that, Brandi thought, was more like it. Too bad Zack wasn't here to see a qualified professional at work.

Not that she was exactly anxious for him to show up. She hadn't seen Zack in nearly thirty-six hours, since he'd stalked out of the cafeteria yesterday morning. She suspected he was taking care to stay out of her way.

In fact, Brandi wouldn't have been a bit surprised if he hadn't shown up for work today at all, but instead had gone back to see his friend, Ross Clayton. She'd even wasted a little time considering what Ross might have to say about how she'd handled this entire affair, and she'd had to remind herself that her boss was generally a reasonable sort.

Still, she'd ended up sending Dora to the employees' lounge to check the time clock, and only when the secretary came back to report that Zack had indeed clocked in to work his assigned morning shift had Brandi really relaxed. Then she'd devoted herself to the paperwork that had been building up on her desk for the last week. She'd spent the whole morning and much of the afternoon in her office, and it was only as the early winter darkness was closing in that she finally pushed her papers aside and went to make her regular tour of the store.

She watched as Santa tipped his face down to look at a child over the top of his half glasses. The glasses were a perfect finishing touch, and the lenses were real—she'd made it a point to notice in the man's employment interview.

"Now that's a switch," a low, rich voice said beside her. "The admiring look on your face, I mean."

She wheeled around to face Zack. "What are you doing here?" She could have bitten off the tip of her tongue the second the words were out; why should it be any particular concern of hers if he wanted to hang around Santa's Workshop and observe?

The corner of Zack's mouth quirked, but there was little humor in the expression. "I'm just coming off duty, after a half hour in the chair while this guy had his dinner. Since it was your idea, I expected you'd at least remember."

Brandi had forgotten. Why hadn't she been smart enough to keep a copy of that ridiculous schedule she'd given him? Because it was so very ridiculous, she reminded herself, that she hadn't foreseen any possibility it would ever go into effect—that was why.

Zack must have just come from the small dressing room concealed within the shell of Santa's Workshop, for he was wearing street clothes. Brandi had gotten so used to seeing him in the red velvet suit and the white beard that she was startled by his gray trousers and matching cashmere sweater, and more so by his chiseled profile. He looked tired, and there was no hint of a dimple.

Brandi found herself wondering about that dimple. Had it been to the left of his mouth, or the right? She couldn't quite remember. Not that it mattered, of course; she didn't care if she ever saw it again. And it was no concern of hers whether Zack Forrest smiled or not.

''He's good,'' Zack said. He nodded toward the Santa.

Brandi was surprised that he'd volunteered so much. ''Of course he is. That's why I hired him.''

''Careful—you don't want the kids to hear that.''

She was annoyed with herself for the slip. ''Thanks for the reminder,'' she said sweetly. ''I'll be more careful now, so don't feel you have to stick around to keep me in check.''

Zack didn't seem to notice the saccharine tone. ''Where do you think I'd be going?''

''You surely don't expect me to believe you've actually pitched a tent in the parking lot. I assumed you were on your way home. If you've finished work—''

''But I haven't. I'm off for two hours, then I have another hour on duty just before the store closes.''

''But I thought, since you weren't in uniform…''

''I assumed you wouldn't like the idea of an extra Santa wandering around the store.''

''No, I wouldn't.''

''And since I have a tendency to get claustrophobic, I don't relish the thought of sitting in the dressing room. It's pretty tiny, you know. So that means changing my clothes every time I come off duty.''

Brandi bit her lip and debated how to confess that she really hadn't intended it to work out that way.

But before she could find the words, Zack added, ''I must admit my Christmas shopping is coming along well, though. I've been killing time by looking over the merchandise, and I've almost taken care of my whole list. What about you? Are you off duty now?''

''No—I'm just making my regular rounds. I try to walk through every department in the store at least twice a day.''

One of Zack's dark eyebrows lifted quizzically. "Is this your first trip, or have you been avoiding Toyland today?"

"I haven't been avoiding anything. It's a critical time of year, and I've been very busy in my office." Brandi didn't owe him any explanations, of course, but the question made her feel a little uneasy. *Was* that one of the reasons she'd kept herself so fully occupied all day?

"I'm glad you explained," Zack said earnestly. "You see, I thought it might have something to do with not wanting to run into me."

Brandi's uneasiness flared into full-fledged annoyance. Zack had no cause to indulge in that sort of speculation, and she'd better put a stop to it right away. But keep it light, she warned herself. "Why on earth wouldn't I want to see you?"

Zack started to smile. "You do, then? Well, that's reassuring. It makes my life worthwhile, to know that you've been looking forward to seeing me again after all."

Brandi winced. She'd walked right into that one.

Zack was merciless. "In fact, since we're both planning to stroll through the store right now, we can do it together. Won't that be fun? Which direction are you heading?"

Whichever way she indicated, he'd no doubt adapt his plans to trail along just to annoy her. Not that he wasn't already doing a good job of that—if there was a contest for irritating the boss, he could be named employee of the month.

"I'm not planning to stroll, exactly," she said. "I'm in a hurry, so—"

"Are you anxious to get done and go home after all?"

"Not particularly. I'll be here till closing time—I usually am this time of year. But I have other things to do. So, since I'd hate to rush you and keep you from looking around to your heart's content—"

Zack leaned against a pillar and folded his arms across his chest. "I suppose your Christmas shopping is all done?" he challenged.

"That's right."

"You don't even need to look for one little thing to finish out your list?" He whistled admiringly. "You know, I'd convinced myself that someone who's got such a case of glooms about the holiday would put off shopping till the last possible moment. But you are a wonder of efficiency, Brandi."

"Well, I'm glad the question entertained you, but—"

"I wonder how I could have been so wrong about you. Unless... Yes, I've got it. I'll bet you're giving everyone on your list Tyler-Royale gift certificates."

He was dead right, as a matter of fact, and that made Brandi nervous. How had he guessed that? "So what if I am? There's nothing wrong with gift certificates."

"I suppose not," Zack said. He didn't sound as if he believed it. "One easy stop at the customer service desk and you're done. Everybody gets what they want, Tyler-Royale rings up the sales, and you've even cut back on after-Christmas returns and exchanges. What a perfectly thoughtful solution for everybody!"

"You don't need to make it sound like a breach of good manners." Brandi stepped away from the fence. "It's been nice talking to you, Zack, but since we're not going the same direction..." She started walking down the broad aisle toward housewares.

Zack fell into step beside her. "Why *are* you so anti-Christmas? I'd really like to know. If you hate the pressure of retail sales at this time of year, there are other jobs, you know."

"I hope I won't always be at this level, so that I won't always have to deal with Christmas panic. But in the meantime, I live for my job the other eleven months of the year, and I've learned to simply endure Christmas. It equals out.''

"The job is what you live for?'' There was an incredulous note in his voice.

"What's so amazing? I have other interests, you know, but this season of the year there's no time for them. The job has to come first. Or don't you think any woman should be more interested in a mere job than in other things?'' Brandi's voice was tart.

"I wouldn't dare tell all women what to do. I just meant, if that's the case, there's obviously no Mr. Ogilvie after all.''

It wasn't a question, and yet, since it was pointless to evade such a direct statement, Brandi answered. "No, there isn't.''

"Has there ever been?''

She stopped beside a towering stack of small appliances—mixers, toasters, blenders. "I beg your pardon?''

"I just asked—''

"I know what you asked. My personal history is none of your affair.''

Zack shrugged. "All right. Whatever you say.'' He picked up a box. "Do you think my sister would like a vegetable steamer?''

"Since I don't know your sister, I haven't the foggiest.'' Brandi's voice was curt.

Zack didn't seem to take offense. "I've already bought her one, you see, but now that I think it over, it just doesn't seem right.'' His eyes lighted up. "Or maybe I'll just give it to you—you're the sort to appreciate a really practical gift. Well, I'll have plenty of time to think about it before

I decide. I've still got more than an hour to kill before I have to go back to work.''

That reminded Brandi of the damned schedule. The only thing she really remembered about it was that as the days went on the hours got worse. That meant this had been one of the milder days, even though the work shifts he'd described had sounded bad enough to send most employees into fits. She was going to have to back down, and the sooner she did so, the less painful it would be.

She took a deep breath. ''Look, Zack…if you want to simplify that schedule I gave you, it's fine with me. We don't really need a Santa during the dinner break, and it's a nuisance for you to sit around and wait in order to do half an hour's work.''

He didn't nod, or smile, or frown. He didn't do anything at all.

His lack of reaction puzzled Brandi. ''Or for the last hour we're open, either,'' she went on hurriedly. ''We don't need to offer a Santa then.''

Zack still gave no indication that he'd even heard her, but she knew he must have.

She tried to make a joke of it. ''All good little kids are home in bed by that time anyway. So if you'd like to call it a day right now—''

''You're cutting my hours?''

''I'm trying to give you a break!''

Zack shook his head slightly, as if he was disappointed in her. Or perhaps he simply couldn't believe his ears. ''Oh, no, Brandi. I wouldn't dream of asking for special treatment. You assigned me certain blocks of time to work, and I'm not complaining.''

Brandi blinked in astonishment. ''All right,'' she snapped. ''If that's the way you want it, go right ahead.''

Zack smiled, and his dimple flashed for just an instant.

"After all, you're not asking me for anything so out of the ordinary. I'm sure you'll be here every single hour that I am. Won't you?"

The dimple was in his left cheek. Brandi wanted to growl at herself for noticing.

She could feel the change of pace in the store as closing time approached. Even though she was still in her office, out of sight of the sales floors, she could almost hear the beeping of cash registers being cleared, of computers humming to a halt, of lights clicking off.

Brandi signed the last of a stack of letters and put them aside for Dora to mail in the morning. Then she took off her white carnation—a bit bedraggled now, after twelve hours pinned to her lapel—and dropped it into the wastebasket beside her desk.

The rest of the executive offices were dark, though in the employees' lounge next door several workers were putting on coats and boots for the journey home.

The store itself was never really dark; light was the best security measure. But the sales floors looked different with the banks of brilliant display lighting shut off. And the store sounded different, too. For one thing, the Christmas music, which was so cheerfully relentless all day, had at last died into blessed silence.

The escalators had already been shut off. Brandi walked down slowly, running a practiced eye over the entire floor. Outside Toyland, she spotted a red suit; Zack was leaning on the fence by Santa's Worship, talking to a group of kids. And what they were still doing in the store after closing time was anyone's guess. The kids were what had drawn her attention, she told herself. She certainly hadn't been looking for Zack.

A uniformed security guard called her name, and Brandi

met him in electronics, where he was checking the display cases to be sure they were locked. The Doberman by his side perked his ears and looked her over with interest. Brandi kept a respectful distance; the dog was securely leashed, but it would take only a nudge to his harness and a word from the guard to turn him into a vicious machine.

"The head of mall security warned me they had a strange-looking guy hanging around the parking lot earlier tonight," the guard said. "They're suggesting all employees leave by the main entrances. Santa said he'd walk you to your car."

"That's not necessary. Be sure you tell everybody."

He nodded. "I posted a sign on the employee exit."

Zack had shooed the kids toward the entrance, but he was still leaning on the fence, watching as Brandi approached. "Ready to go?" he said.

"You needn't bother, Zack."

"Don't flatter yourself. It's no bother at all, because I'm going that way myself."

"How gracious of you," Brandi murmured. "Still, you must want to change clothes before you go."

"Again? No, thanks. When I take off the suit this time, I'm getting straight into a hot shower."

Why that comment should make her face grow warm was beyond Brandi's understanding. It was a perfectly straightforward statement, nothing more. "Well, don't let me keep you from it."

"The only thing that's slowing me down is the fact that we're standing here talking," he pointed out.

That was true enough, so Brandi started for the entrance. But she murmured, "Can't you take a hint?"

"Of course I can. That wasn't exactly a hint you issued, that was a sledgehammer."

The metal-mesh gate was already closed, except for a

gap just wide enough for her to slip through. "I can get myself across the parking lot to my car, you know. We have these little episodes from time to time, and it never amounts to anything."

"But if you don't get to your car, and they find your body tomorrow…"

"You think the authorities will suspect you?"

"Of course they won't," he said promptly. "There must be dozens of people who'll fall under suspicion first. I just hate to think who Ross would replace you with."

"Thanks for keeping my ego cut down to size."

"You're quite welcome."

The grand concourse of the mall was quiet; the usual hurly-burly was reduced to the click of heels here and there and the quiet splash of the fountain. They crossed to the main door, and Zack held it open. Snowflakes swirled in on a blast of air, which sent chills up Brandi's spine.

Sealed in the artificial cocoon of the building all day, Brandi hadn't given a thought to the weather. "I didn't even know it was snowing. What a nuisance."

Zack bowed deeply. "My pleasure, madam. Half an inch of snow, delivered sometime this week, I believe you said?"

Brandi glared at him. "If you think you're getting credit for this because a couple of days ago I happened to say a little snow would help sales… Don't you have a coat?"

"I left it in my car."

"Not one of your brighter moves, I'd say."

"Oh, this suit's surprisingly warm. That's one of the things I've been meaning to talk to you about, by the way. Do you suppose we could turn down the heat around Santa's Workshop? Or the lights, at least? It's a little steamy."

Brandi shrugged. "Maybe if you weren't wearing so much fur…"

Zack brushed a few snowflakes off his white-fur lapel. "You mean this? It's fake. Kids might be allergic to the real stuff."

"I should have known."

"Besides, I'm not the only one who's uncomfortable with the temperatures up there."

"Oh? Have you polled the other Santas? I suppose next you'll try to organize them into a union and picket if you don't get what you want."

"Not a bad idea. I'll have to start making my list of demands. Where's your car?"

Brandi waved a hand toward the farthest row of the parking lot. "Sorry it's so far, but it was your idea to come out here."

"I'm not complaining."

But he must be cold, Brandi thought. Snow had already frosted his velvet cap, and a few flakes had caught in his eyelashes. She hadn't realized before how long and dark they were. She really ought to send him back to the mall, or directly to his car, instead of letting him walk on with her and get colder.

Right. She'd probably have just as much success at that as with anything else she'd tried to make him stop doing.

"I wasn't just talking about the Santas anyway," Zack went on. "The kids are uncomfortable, too. Most of them have their coats on, you know. In fact, a cooler temperature in the whole store might be more popular with shoppers."

"Why don't you start asking them? You can put that notebook to some good use for a change. Just write me a report in a couple of weeks and I'll take it under consideration."

But Zack didn't seem to hear.

Brandi followed his gaze. Twenty yards away, a woman and a small child were walking hand in hand toward a parked car. At least, the woman was walking; the child—perhaps six or seven years old—was hanging back, staring at Zack and saying two words over and over. "Santa Claus…Santa Claus!"

The woman frowned a little and shook her head. "Peggy, no. I told you we only came to look at the Christmas lights."

"But if I can just talk to Santa Claus—"

"What would you like to tell me?" Zack called.

"Zack," Brandi said under her breath. "Isn't this covered in the rules? The mother doesn't want you. And a Tyler-Royale Santa doesn't go marching up to kids. He waits to be approached."

"I'm not working for you at the moment, Brandi. Remember?"

Before she could protest, he was gone. His long stride ate up the distance despite the slick snow underfoot, and before Brandi could catch up he'd crouched down beside the child. "Are you going to come sit on Santa's lap tomorrow and tell me what you'd like for Christmas?"

"No," the child said. It was hardly more than a whisper.

"Why not?" Zack asked gently. "Surely you're not scared of me. I'm nothing to be scared of."

The woman said, "You can't give my daughter what she wants for Christmas, sir."

There was a note of pain in her voice—and a veneer of dignity—that made Brandi look more carefully at the pair. The child's winter coat was obviously not new and was much too big for her. The woman's was rather threadbare, and neither of them was wearing boots. But there was a pink ribbon carefully tied in the child's hair, and the mother's back was very straight.

Zack didn't move; he was still at the child's eye level as he glanced up at her mother. His voice was somber. "Maybe not," he said gently. "Some things are tough even for Santa." He slid a gentle arm around the child's shoulders. "But I'll certainly try. Why don't you tell me anyway, Peggy, just in case?"

The child sent a swift look up at her mother, then hid her face against his soft velvet sleeve. But her voice was clear. "I want you to bring a job for my mommy."

Brandi's heart squeezed painfully.

The woman looked down at her shoes. Brandi noticed that the toes were wet through. "I made the mistake of telling Peggy there won't be a Christmas at our house this year because I don't have a job. It's all she's thought of since. I'm sorry she's bothered you with it." The quiet dignity in her voice made Brandi ache even more.

Zack seemed to be utterly speechless.

He ought to have known better than that, Brandi thought. Now he'd gotten himself into a prize jam, with his big ideas about how easy it was to play Santa Claus. "That," she said under her breath, "is why we have rules."

Zack looked up at her innocently, as if he hadn't heard a word. "Brandi, didn't you say you needed floor clerks?"

"I may have. But—"

The woman interrupted. "Please. Don't trouble yourselves any further. Peggy, come along." She tugged the child gently toward the car.

Brandi scowled at Zack. Then she took one more good look at the woman and said, "Wait!" She reached into her handbag for a business card and a pen, and wrote across the top of the card, *Please do your best to find a position for…* "Ma'am? What's your name?"

The woman told her, with obvious reluctance. "Theresa Howard."

Brandi jotted the name on the card and handed it over. "Bring this to the third floor of Tyler-Royale tomorrow, and ask to see the personnel director."

The woman's eyes widened as she read the card. "Oh, Miss Ogilvie…"

For an instant, Brandi was afraid the woman was going to kiss her hand. "It will probably just be for the season," she said hastily. "But it will help."

Zack didn't say a word. They stood together in the snow until Theresa Howard and her daughter reached their car, and then started walking toward the far side of the parking lot again.

Brandi finally broke the silence. "There's no need to thank me for making you look good, Zack." She didn't look at him.

"I wasn't exactly planning to."

"Oh, you weren't?" Brandi stopped and faced him squarely, her hands on her hips. "How dare you put me in that position?"

"I didn't put you in any position. I just asked a question."

"You embarrassed me."

"Maybe I did. I'll admit I intended to. But I certainly didn't force you to hire her."

Brandi glared at him. "Well, at least you realize that much, so don't get any crazy ideas for the future. I do happen to need floor help, and Mrs. Howard looked like a good possibility. But that doesn't mean I'm going to start rescuing you if you make a habit of this."

"Of course you won't," Zack said.

Brandi thought he sounded just a little too agreeable,

and she shot a suspicious stare at him. He looked perfectly innocent.

"That kind of situation is why you need training," she pointed out. "Which is what I tried to tell you the first day, when you insisted this was such an easy job. The very idea of promising a child something without any idea of what she's going to ask—don't you even realize the damage you could do?"

"I didn't promise the child anything except that I'd try," Zack argued. "I certainly didn't tell her I could give her whatever she wanted."

Brandi thought it over and decided reluctantly that perhaps he was right—technically, at least. Still, he hadn't exactly used good sense.

He'd walked on, and she had to scramble a little in the snow to catch up. "You ought to know better than to plunge in like that and meddle, Zack. The mother clearly didn't want you to interfere."

Zack stopped walking and looked down at her. In the yellowish glare of the lights, his suit had an orange cast, and his eyes were darker than she'd ever seen them before.

"You know what I think?" His voice was light, almost careless—but there was an edge to it that made Brandi uneasy. "I suspect you're really not a person at all, *Ms.* Ogilvie. You're an alien. Or a machine. That's it—you're a robot. Unfeeling and inexhaustible. And I know just the way to prove it."

Before Brandi could do more than blink in surprise, he'd swooped on her. He seized her shoulders and pulled her against him so fast and so tightly that the air was forced out of her lungs with a whoosh. She tried to push away from him, and looked up into his face to protest. But even if she'd had the breath to speak, she wouldn't have been able to, for his mouth came down on hers in a forceful, demanding kiss.

Brandi stopped fighting. She intended to stay still for a few seconds, to allow him to think she'd capitulated, though she was really waiting for a chance to break free. If he relaxed his hold for just an instant... But his arms were like iron around her, and his mouth on hers was taut and fierce and searing.

And infinitely more exciting than anything she had ever experienced before. The beard he wore was soft as silk against her skin, and he tasted of coffee and citrus, and of something incredibly sweet....

Slowly, the anger seemed to drain out of him, and his kiss gentled and softened. At the same time, it became more terrifying—for as the element of force vanished, Brandi felt herself responding to his caress. Her lips softened to welcome him, and she pressed herself to him almost against her will.

Eventually he stopped kissing her, eased her head down on his shoulder, and laid his cheek against her hair. Brandi didn't want to admit that it was probably a good thing he hadn't let go of her; her knees were too weak to support her.

Still, after an episode like that, she could hardly stand there in the man's arms and not make an effort to assert herself. "I'll accept your apology now, Zack." Her voice shook, despite her best efforts.

"Will you?" He sounded a little odd, too, as if he couldn't quite get his breath. "Then of course I'll apologize. My way."

His hand cupped her chin, and turned her face very gently up to his. This kiss started out differently—soft and easy and tender—but it didn't stay that way, and by the time he'd finished, Brandi's heart was pounding at a threatening rate, and her breath was coming in sharp gasps.

Zack held her just a little way from him, to look down at her. Unable to face him, Brandi let her head droop.

"I must admit," he said huskily, "you sure don't kiss like a robot."

Slowly he released her, keeping a hand on her shoulder for a moment till she was able to steady herself. Brandi took a step toward her car and stumbled over something in the snow at her feet. She was too rattled even to think what it could be, till Zack bent to pick up the handbag she'd dropped. He brushed the snow off the leather and gave it back to her silently. Then he took her arm so she wouldn't trip again, and started toward her car.

The silence that surrounded them was complete, as if they were caught in a bubble, shut off from the outside world. There should have been traffic noises, and sirens, and voices. But Brandi could hear nothing save the beat of her heart and the whisper of their footsteps in the snow.

"What would you have done if I hadn't bailed you out?" she said.

For a few steps she thought Zack hadn't heard her. "Is that why you hired her?" he said. His voice sounded as if it came from a distance. "To bail me out?"

"Of course not. I told you, I need floor help." She didn't look at him. Instead she fumbled for her car keys.

Zack took them and unlocked the door. "Why do you want me to think you're heartless?"

Brandi slid into the driver's seat. She'd have closed the door, but Zack—absentmindedly, no doubt—was standing in the way. "I don't see that I have a lot to do with forming your opinions," she said. "And I must say it wasn't very nice of you to look so terribly astonished because I found her a job."

Suddenly Zack smiled, and the lights were back in his eyes, dancing wickedly. "I was only startled that you didn't crush her for calling you Miss instead of Ms."

"Go home," Brandi said tartly. "You're going to freeze to death."

"Yeah," Zack mused. "Good idea. I'm going to have a hot shower. Then I'm going to open a cold beer and put my feet up and think about everything I learned today." He leaned into the car and drew a fingertip down her cheek. "And I do mean *everything*."

CHAPTER FOUR

THE snow was falling harder by the time Brandi reached her apartment complex, and her car slid a little as she tried to maneuver it into a parking spot. At the rate the flakes were coming down, they'd have a lot more than a half inch on the ground by morning. So much for Zack claiming credit for giving Brandi her Christmas wish...

"I am not going to think about him," she muttered as she closed the door of her apartment behind her. She was off duty now; she'd simply forget about Tyler-Royale's problems till morning. And, after all, Zack was a store problem.

He certainly wasn't a *personal* one.

Brandi kicked off her wet shoes and flipped through the mail—three bills, a letter from a friend, and a catalog of exotic Christmas candies and nuts, which she dropped straight into the nearest wastebasket. Then she went along the hall to her bedroom to change clothes. As soon as she'd traded her suit for jeans and a sweater and put on her warmest wool socks, she could feel the tension of the day begin to drain out of her.

She took her hair down from the tight French braid and brushed it till it gleamed. Then she dropped her gold button earrings into her jewelry case and tugged the diamond cluster from the ring finger of her left hand.

"Is there a Mr. Ogilvie?" Zack Forrest had asked yesterday. Brandi could still hear the rich undercurrents of his voice echoing through her mind and making her feel warm and cold all at the same time.

It was a question Brandi hadn't expected. She'd been wearing this ring for two years now, and it had been a long time since anyone had actually questioned her about its meaning. Many people seemed to think it was a wedding ring, but that she didn't make a big thing of it because she preferred to keep her private life to herself. And as long as they didn't come straight out and ask, Brandi had never felt obliged to confide the truth.

She had never gone to any particular trouble to promote the illusion that she was married. The ring had been a reward to herself when she'd successfully completed her management training course and been assigned a store of her own, and it had never occurred to her that some people might think it resembled a wedding ring. Brandi didn't think it did; the center stone was much larger than the other gems, with a narrow band of diamonds below it and a sort of starburst above, and it had always looked to Brandi like the dinner ring it was.

But it was funny how suggestible people were. To some of them, any ring worn on the left hand must stand for a relationship. And when Brandi consistently came alone to company functions, never appeared anywhere with a date, and didn't invite anyone to her home—well, maybe it wasn't unreasonable for her employees to assume she was married, but her husband was some kind of hermit.

Brandi didn't mind. A woman's life was a whole lot less complicated when no one worried about her single status or tried to match her up with the right man. That was particularly true for a woman at management level, one who spent most of her waking hours involved with her career. It was dangerous for such a woman to date a man who worked for her—and where else was she likely to run into one, when she had so little time for pursuits outside her profession?

Not that Brandi had bothered to think that argument all the way through, because it held no importance for her. She had no interest in adding a man to her life. A relationship only complicated things; she'd learned that lesson long ago.

So why had she reacted so strongly to Zack Forrest tonight?

Just asking the question brought back tinges of the breathless, achy, almost dizzy feeling that had swept over her as he kissed her tonight in the parking lot. She told herself that her reaction was easily explained; the man had practically assaulted her, so it was no wonder she'd felt breathless and achy and dizzy.

But she couldn't quite explain why she'd eventually kissed him back. Why she'd clung to him. Why she hadn't given him the sock in the jaw that he deserved.

A tinge of loneliness, that was all, she decided. No matter how happy she was with her life—and most of the time she was quite satisfied—still, she was alone a great deal of the time. At the store she was surrounded by people, but apart from Casey Amos, Brandi had been careful not to make those people her friends. A manager had to keep a little distance from her employees in order to be effective.

And at home… Sometimes, she admitted, her own footsteps sounded loud in the quiet apartment, and sometimes it was a temptation to talk to herself just to hear a voice.

So perhaps it was no wonder that tonight, once Zack had stopped trying to prove his point, she'd gotten caught up in the moment. One thing she had to admit—the man certainly knew how to kiss.

But it wasn't going to happen again. Now that she was aware and on her guard—

The doorbell rang, and Brandi sighed and went to answer it. If it was Zack, she decided, she'd kick him in the kneecap and slam the door in his face.

But it wasn't Zack; her visitors were three pre-adolescent girls selling holiday garlands to raise money for their school club. "We took orders back in October," one of them explained, "but you weren't at home. Now we've got an extra garland, and we thought you might like to buy it. Since you don't seem to have any other Christmas decorations…"

Brandi said, "I don't have decorations because I don't want them, and I don't want a garland, either. Look, I admire your efforts, and I'll happily make a donation to your club, but the garland would be wasted on me. So give it to someone who'll get some good out of it, all right?" She wrote a check and closed the door with relief. At least that had been easily dealt with. If it had been Zack, on the other hand…

And just why had she jumped to the conclusion it might be Zack at her door? That made no sense at all. If the man had anything else to say, he'd surely have said it in the parking lot. Only an idiot would even dream that he might follow her home. By now he was enjoying his shower, or perhaps he'd progressed as far as the cold beer.

"And whatever he might be doing," Brandi said, "it certainly holds no fascination for me!"

It wasn't as if she wanted him around, that was sure.

The snowy streets slowed her down the next morning, and the regular monthly meeting of the store's employee association had already started when Brandi came in. Every chair and sofa in the second-floor furniture department was lined with employees. Many were ready for work when the store opened in an hour; others were in casual clothes because they were scheduled for the evening shift or had the day off. Brandi was still amazed, when she saw them all together, at how many people it took to run a store the size of Tyler-Royale.

Today's crowd was smaller than usual, however. The snow had continued through the night, and traffic was a mess. That, plus the longer-than-normal hours they'd all been putting in, had probably kept some of the off-duty employees from making the effort to attend so early in the morning. And the flu continued to be a worry; yesterday they'd had a dozen employees call in sick. Brandi wondered what the report would look like today.

She didn't realize she was looking for Zack till she found him, and then—when he met her gaze and smiled at her—she could have kicked herself. But in fact, it would have been hard to miss him; he was ready for work, and the red suit he wore, contrasted with the big, dark green wing chair he'd chosen, seemed to cry out for attention.

This morning his white Santa beard lay on his knee. Brandi wondered if he'd left it off because there would be no children here, or because it made his face itch. It was funny that she'd hardly noticed the beard last night, except for that sensation of silky smoothness as he kissed her....

And that, she told herself, is quite enough of that. She had far better things to think about than what had happened last night.

She didn't smile back at him. Zack made a show of pulling up his sleeve to check his watch, and he shook his head sorrowfully at her for being late.

Brandi scowled at him, leaned against a pillar at the side of the room, and tried to pretend Zack Forrest didn't exist. But it took effort to focus her attention on Casey Amos, who stood in the center of the room as she conducted the meeting, and a few minutes later Brandi found her gaze drifting toward Zack once more.

He caught her eye and pantomimed an invitation for her to come over.

Brandi suspected he intended to invite her to sit on the arm of his chair. Wouldn't that look cozy, she thought, and shook her head. Then she moved to the back of the room and leaned against a big armoire.

Casey said, "Those of you who want to take part in the employee gift exchange should put your names in the box in the lounge by next Monday."

One of the customer service representatives hurried in, looking a little frazzled. Zack waved her over and stood up, offering his chair.

"On Tuesday," Casey went on, "everyone who's put in a name will draw one out, and the exchange will be at the party on the following Sunday night."

Zack looked around the room, then lazily headed for Brandi's armoire.

Brandi's heartbeat speeded up just a little in anticipation of being close to him once more. Don't be silly, she told herself. What happened last night had been an aberration, born of mutual irritation and frustration, and it was over. She shouldn't be having any feelings about him at all.

Casey didn't appear to have her mind completely on what she was doing. Her gaze seemed to shift from Brandi to Zack, and then back to Brandi once more.

Her interest didn't necessarily mean anything, Brandi thought. That red suit was hard to ignore, and it must look to Casey as if the man was walking out of the meeting. Even with her eyes fixed on Casey, Brandi couldn't quite avoid seeing Zack at the edge of her peripheral vision, coming steadily closer. No wonder Casey was looking at him.

"Five-dollar limit, just like last year," Casey went on,

and glanced at the sheaf of notes in her hand. "The party will be downstairs in the atrium, with music by…"

Brandi tuned her out. The annual Christmas party was just one more nuisance in an already over-busy season, in her opinion. She wouldn't go at all except that it would hurt her employees' feelings if she didn't show up.

Zack appeared beside her. "Avoiding me?" he said softly.

He looked very comfortable, with his arms folded and his shoulder against the door of the armoire, right next to Brandi.

"I beg your pardon?"

"You heard me. You're avoiding me."

"Of course I'm not."

"Then why didn't you come over and sit down? I'm a gentleman. I'd have given you my chair. Or are you so firm a feminist that you wouldn't take it?"

"I'm only an honorary member of the employee association, so I try to stay in the background."

"Is that so? Don't you believe in clubs, either?"

"It's not a club, Zack. Since technically I don't work for the store itself but for the corporation that owns the chain, I'm really not eligible to belong to the employee association. But they invited me to join anyway."

He grinned. "I'll bet that made your day—being asked to join the play group."

Brandi tried to ignore him. It was difficult, he was close enough that the barest hint of his cologne—very light, very appealing—tickled her nose.

"Or did you think I might kiss you again?" Zack murmured. "Was that what scared you off? Let me assure you, I wouldn't."

"I should certainly hope not."

"Not in public, at any rate. In private, on the other hand, you could probably tempt me."

Brandi's jaw dropped and she turned to face him directly. "Touch me again," she warned, "and you'll be out on your ear—Ross Clayton's friend or not. Got that straight, Forrest?"

Zack didn't turn a hair. "I'll try to keep it in mind." He settled both shoulders against the armoire and looked out over the room. He was so close that Brandi could feel the heat of his body, but she knew if she moved, he'd understand perfectly well why she'd done so, and he'd be amused. And Brandi was just stubborn enough to refuse to give him the satisfaction.

She put her chin up, folded her arms in imitation of his pose, and turned her attention back to Casey Amos. Why in heaven's name wasn't the woman moving the meeting along? she wondered. They didn't have all day. Despite the snow, there'd be customers arriving in a few minutes. But there stood Casey staring at her....

Brandi swallowed hard and tried to imagine what that exchange had looked like from across the room. The only good news she could think of was that they were at the back of the room, so only Casey had been in a position to see much. At least, she hoped everyone else had kept their backs turned.

Casey cleared her throat and flipped to the next page of her notes. "We're going to need more volunteers than usual to help with the Wishing Tree. We've had six families register in the first week of the program, but then Pat Emerson got the flu and things have come to a screeching halt."

Brandi frowned. Pat was ill? That must have happened just yesterday, or surely she'd have heard it before now.

"What's the Wishing Tree?" Zack asked under his breath.

Brandi would have liked to ignore him, but that would no doubt be just about as effective as pretending an impacted wisdom tooth didn't hurt. "You've noticed the Christmas trees in the atrium?"

"They're a little hard to overlook. A dozen of them, each ten feet tall—"

"Most of them are just to set the mood for the store and show off special merchandise. But one is the Wishing Tree. Families who can't afford clothes and toys and special things for Christmas ask for what they'd like to have, and the wishes are hung on the tree. Then customers or employees pick out the person they'd like to shop for and buy the gifts."

Zack frowned. "You just let people walk in and hang their wishes on the tree? You've never struck me as such a trusting sort before, Brandi."

"Of course there are restrictions. In the first place, there aren't any names on the trees, just ages and sizes, and the customer service department takes charge of the gifts and delivers them to the right people. They also make sure the family is genuinely in need. People have to be registered with a charitable organization before they're eligible for the Wishing Tree. That's what Pat Emerson was doing before she got sick—coordinating all those details."

"Who's going to do it now?"

"I don't know." Brandi was racking her brain, without success. "Pat will be hard to replace. It takes a special kind of person to do that job—warm and insightful and empathetic, without being a pushover."

Zack shrugged. "Sounds like a management sort of problem to me."

"Management? If you're implying that I should take it over, Zack, let me assure you—"

"That you haven't the qualifications? I'm not surprised you'd say that. You might not actually be a robot, but—"

"What I haven't got is the time," Brandi pointed out.

Casey went on, "At least one person in every department should try to stay familiar with the needs listed on the tree in order to help shoppers. And if anyone can volunteer to fill in for Pat till she's back in shape, I'd love to stick around after the meeting and talk to you."

Zack raised a hand to draw Casey's attention.

"It takes a lot of time," Brandi warned. "Pat devoted herself to that project."

"Time I've got plenty of. Since I have to be here anyway, waiting around for my various shifts, I might as well be doing something constructive."

Brandi bit her tongue to keep from reminding him that she had offered to amend his working hours. "I should also warn you," she went on, "that Pat—"

Zack looked down at her, his eyes wide and looking even darker than usual, and interrupted. "Are you trying to stop me from doing a good deed, Ms. Ogilvie? It's bad enough that you're a Scrooge yourself, but to stand in someone else's way…"

Brandi gritted her teeth.

Zack raised his voice. "I'll volunteer."

Casey peered at him. "Hey, that's great. Stick around after the meeting—I'll get Pat's files, and Ms. Ogilvie will fill you in on the details." She turned to the next order of business.

Brandi looked straight ahead and waited.

A full minute went by before Zack said with deceptive gentleness, "What exactly did she mean, you'll fill me in on the details?"

''Pat was coordinating the program, but I'm in charge of the Wishing Tree. It's not just a store project, it's a corporate one—there are Wishing Trees through the whole chain.''

''I'm going to be working directly with you?''

The look on his face, Brandi thought, almost made up for the certain irritation of having to work with him for the next week or two, till Pat was back to full capacity. ''I tried to tell you before you committed yourself,'' she said sweetly. ''But of course it wouldn't have made a difference to you, would it? Since it's all in a good cause, I mean.''

The meeting was finally over just minutes before the store opened, and employees rushed off in all directions. Brandi waited till the confusion had eased before she tried to catch Casey. ''How long has Pat been ill?''

''Several days. Don't look at me like that, Brandi. I only heard it myself this morning, or I'd have told you. She had a couple of regular days off, and she thought she'd be over the flu in time to come back as scheduled.''

''That's going to create a major problem with the Wishing Tree.''

''Oh, I don't know. I imagine your Santa can handle anything he puts his mind to.'' Casey looked up at Zack and smiled. ''It's the hole in my department I'm not sure I can fill—Pat's my best saleswoman.'' She put a hand on Zack's sleeve. ''Let me give you just the highlights on the responsibilities. It's not difficult, really, once you get the hang of it, and I'm sure Brandi will—''

Just then, the clerk from Salon Elegance who had taken care of Brandi's mustard-stained blouse came up to her and held out a Tyler-Royale bag, and Brandi couldn't hear what Casey was saying about her. It was probably just as well; Brandi suspected she wouldn't have liked the program Casey was mapping out for her.

"Sorry, Ms. Ogilvie," the clerk said. "The cleaners did the best they could, but you can see they weren't very successful."

Brandi pulled the blouse out of the bag. It was perfectly pressed and neatly folded, but on the front was still an unmistakable blotchy yellow stain.

She thanked the clerk for trying, then crumpled the blouse into the bag and tucked it under her arm. But Casey had finished her instructions by that time, and Zack was fiddling with his long white beard, getting it anchored just right before he went over to Santa's Workshop.

"Was that a favorite blouse?" he asked. "It looks like it had a bath in mustard."

"It did, as a matter of fact," Brandi said. "And since you were the cause of its ruin, I'm tempted to take the price of it out of your pay. So if you're wise—"

"Me?" Zack sounded shocked. "How could I have caused that?"

"It happened the first time you showed up here, when my secretary paged me to come and talk to you, so technically you're responsible."

"Technically?" Zack started to smile. "Now why doesn't it surprise me at all that you'd think that way?"

The long white beard hid the dimple in his cheek, but Brandi knew precisely where it was. Suddenly she found herself wanting to slip a fingertip under the edge of the soft, fluffy whiskers and touch that tiny hidden spot. And then she wanted to tug the beard away so the dimple wasn't hidden anymore, so she could kiss it…kiss him… once more.

The desire was so strong, so sudden, and so irrational that she was having trouble breathing. What's happening to you, Brandi Ogilvie? she asked herself. You've lost your mind entirely, that's what!

"Don't you think you'd better get to work?" Her voice was a bit sharp.

"Yes, ma'am," Zack murmured. "Or I won't have enough of a paycheck for you to dock."

Brandi didn't watch him walk away. She didn't have to; she knew without even looking that he was in no apparent hurry. The public address system came to life with a crackle, followed by the opening note of "Jingle Bells." The mercilessly cheery sound was enough to push Brandi over the brink.

She squared her shoulders and turned to Casey. "By the way, would you kindly stop calling him *my* Santa?"

Casey's eyebrows soared. "Well, he does seem to be sticking rather close to you, don't you think?"

Brandi gave it up. Further protest would only call more attention to the situation than she wanted, and she'd already said more than her ordinary good sense would have allowed her to.

"I'd better get downstairs," Casey murmured. "Unless the snow keeps people away, I'm going to need six arms today."

"I might have a new employee for you."

"Joy," Casey said without enthusiasm. "Just what I need—someone to train."

"It'll make your time go faster," Brandi said with mock sympathy. "I'll tell the personnel director to send her down to you if she shows up."

"*If*? You mean you haven't actually hired her?"

"Not yet. It's a long story."

"I wish I had time to listen to it," Casey admitted. She started to walk away.

"Wait a minute," Brandi said. "Where'd you get that button?"

Casey fingered her lapel, where a small plastic-covered badge nestled discreetly against the white carnation that marked her as a department manager. "You mean this one?"

"Of course I mean that one."

Casey cupped a protective hand around the button so Brandi couldn't see it clearly. "Zack gave it to me this morning."

"I should have known Zack would be behind this. What's it about anyway?"

"You mean you haven't approved it? As cozy as the two of you have been—"

"Cozy?" Brandi's voice would have turned antifreeze to slush. "Give it here."

"Come on, Brandi, it's just a fun little gimmick."

"You know political buttons and protest ribbons and all those sorts of personal statements are forbidden in this store."

"This is hardly a political announcement, and you can't have my button. If you want one, go ask Zack—I'm sure he'll give you one. You just have to promise you'll do something nice for someone every day till Christmas, and he'll make you an official Santa's Friend, too. Look, I've really got to run—we wouldn't want to lose sales because the department's not open, would we?" She was gone—still wearing the button—before Brandi could object.

Brandi stalked across the second floor to Santa's Workshop. There were no children in line; nevertheless she firmly set the "Santa's Feeding His Reindeer" sign in place and closed the gate just in case someone came along before she'd finished with her errant Santa.

Zack had propped one elbow on the arm of the big chair

and stretched his long legs out as if he was admiring the high polish on the toes of his boots. As she approached, he rolled his eyes and stood up. ''Ms. Ogilvie,'' he said in a tone of long-suffering patience, ''at this rate, the reindeer are going to be too fat to fly.''

''Then we'll make venison sausage of them and you can ride the subway and the El on Christmas Eve,'' Brandi snapped.

Zack sighed. ''You know, I have this instinctive feeling you're unhappy with me. What is it now?''

''You mean there's more going on than just the buttons?''

''You're unhappy about the buttons?'' He sounded incredulous.

''Not the buttons themselves. It's a cute gag. But you can't just start that kind of gimmick without consulting me. There's a policy in the chain that no employee can wear political or religious jewelry or buttons—''

Zack's eyebrows almost disappeared under the white fur band of his velvet cap. ''So which category do you put Santa's Friends in?''

''It's the principle of the thing, Zack! If one kind of personal statement is allowed, where do you draw the line? What about black arm bands? Protest signs?''

''Has anyone ever told you you're a little intense, Brandi?'' He shook his head as if in confusion. ''And here I thought you were upset because I rearranged Toyland last night.''

Brandi was speechless. ''You did *what*?''

''Only a couple of the game displays. I got bored with shopping, you see, so I was just looking at the toys. Some of the shelves were too crowded, and it was hard to get one box out of the stack. I just moved them around so—''

''That's it,'' Brandi said. ''You're done. You're fired.''

Zack looked at her for a few seconds in silence. "Over a few buttons?"

"No. I'm terminating you because you're meddling in areas that are none of your concern. You were hired to be a Santa, not the manager of this store."

Zack pulled what looked like a television remote control out of the capacious pocket of his jacket.

"What's that?" Brandi asked.

"A cellular phone. You know, you can use it anywhere. It comes in very handy when Santa needs to consult the main data banks at the North Pole."

"Funny. What are you doing?"

"Well, I don't need to ask the elves whether you've been nice or naughty this year. I can draw my own conclusions. So I'm going to call Ross so you can tell him yourself why I don't seem to be working out." He punched a string of numbers and held the phone out to her.

"Dammit, Zack—"

The phone's buzz gave way to silence, and then to Ross Clayton's voice. It didn't surprise Brandi that there was a private number that rang directly into Ross Clayton's downtown office, bypassing switchboards and secretaries, but it startled her that Zack had it. Brandi had never been offered that kind of access; all her calls to the CEO took the standard route.

She glared at Zack, and then at the phone. He continued to silently hold it out to her, and eventually she took it. "Ross? It's Brandi Ogilvie."

"I'm glad you called. I've been wanting to talk to you."

"Have you?"

"Yes. Zack tells me he's thrilled with the cooperation he's getting from the whole store, especially you. From what I hear, things must be working out great."

Zack was looking at her with wide-eyed innocence, as if he could hear the entire conversation.

Ross went on, "Of course I could see that for myself when I was in the store last night."

"You were here?" Brandi's voice was little more than a gasp. "When? You didn't stop in the office."

"Oh, it was the middle of the evening. You'd probably been at home for hours."

Last evening, she thought. Before closing time. Before that kiss in the parking lot.

"Kelly and I brought the kids over to visit Santa. Not Zack, of course—they'd have been onto him in a second—so we waited till the next one came on duty. But afterward he was telling me how much he's enjoying himself."

"I'll bet he told you all this while he was rearranging the displays in Toyland," Brandi said dryly, and waited for the reaction. Surely Ross wouldn't condone this take-over, no matter how good a friend Zack seemed to be.

"As a matter of fact, yes—that was what he was doing. It looked pretty good when he was done. The department manager seemed to like the new look, too."

Brandi's head was swimming.

"And the Santa's Friend buttons are cute. Which reminds me, I haven't done my good deed for the day yet. So what's on your mind? Surely you're not canceling out of the party now."

"The Christmas party? No," Brandi said weakly. "I'll be there."

"Good. I know Whitney's looking forward to seeing you. In fact, I think you're the main reason she's coming this year. What can I do for you, Brandi?"

"I was just..." She hesitated. "I called to tell you Zack's the most...innovative employee I've had in some time."

Ross laughed heartily. "Now that doesn't surprise me. Take good care of him, and keep in touch, all right? I'll see you Saturday night."

"Sure." She didn't meet Zack's eyes as she handed the phone back to him.

He punched the cutoff button and dropped the phone into his pocket without a comment.

Brandi gathered her dignity. "I may have acted a little too hastily."

Zack looked astounded. "*You*, Ms. Ogilvie?"

"Don't rub it in, Forrest."

"So that means I still have a job?"

"If I were you, I wouldn't take on any long-term debts," Brandi snapped. "But for the moment—yes, you still have a job." She stalked toward the gate and set the sign aside.

"Oh, Brandi," Zack called.

She didn't turn around. "What is it now?"

"Did I hear you say you're going to the Claytons' Christmas party Saturday night?"

"Yes. Why?"

"So am I," Zack said easily. "How would you like to go with me?"

CHAPTER FIVE

BRANDI considered picking up the "Santa's Feeding His Reindeer" sign and hitting Zack over the head with it. She settled for saying, as evenly as she could manage, "No, thank you."

"Parties like that are a lot more fun when you have a date," he pointed out.

"I happen to already *have* a date," she snapped. Her arrangement with Whitney Townsend might not be quite the kind of date Zack was thinking of, but in Brandi's opinion it was just as important—and more enjoyable, too.

Zack didn't answer. That made Brandi nervous, and finally, unable to control her curiosity, she turned around to face him. He was looking at her with what appeared to be amazement.

Brandi was annoyed. "You don't need to look astonished about it."

"I'm not astonished. I'm merely overwhelmed by disappointment." He didn't sound particularly discouraged, though. He went on blithely, "Well, that'll teach me to ask earlier. About this Wishing Tree business…"

"What about it?"

"I'll be off duty most of the afternoon. Shall we have lunch and you can tell me all about it?"

"I expect to be very busy this afternoon." If the tone of her voice didn't freeze him out, she thought, nothing would.

It didn't. "How about later, then? I'll do my dinnertime stint and we can spend the evening on the Wishing Tree."

"I hardly think it will take all evening."

Zack grinned. "Oh, in that case," he said, "we can use the rest of the time to get to know each other. Won't that be fun?"

Brandi finished analyzing November's sales figures and signed the final report for Dora to fax to the main offices downtown in the morning. It was well past six, and Dora would have gone home by now.

Or perhaps she wouldn't wait for morning and her secretary—almost every department in the store was running slightly ahead of her projections, and that was the kind of news Brandi always liked to share.

She was surprised at the time. It seemed she'd been occupied with the sales reports for no more than an hour, but the whole afternoon had sped by while she worked. And there hadn't been a word from Zack. Maybe he'd had to be on duty at Santa's Workshop later than he expected. Or maybe he'd decided they didn't need this little heart-to-heart chat after all. Wishful thinking, she chided herself.

Brandi was startled to find Dora still at her desk, which was covered with the advertising layouts that would run in the next few weeks. Brandi checked her watch again to be sure she hadn't misread the time. "What are you still doing here, Dora?"

"You told me not to interrupt you this afternoon," Dora said comfortably.

"For heaven's sake, I didn't mean you couldn't go home when you were finished with your work!"

"But I'm not finished. Besides, your Santa—"

Brandi frowned a little.

Very smoothly, Dora went on, "I mean, Mr. Forrest was in. I told him I had orders not to disturb you, and he waited for a while."

"And then he just went away? You amaze me."

"He said he'd be in Toyland where he could do something constructive while he waited."

"I suppose that means he's rearranging the whole department."

"He didn't say what he intended to do. At any rate, I was afraid if I left he'd sneak back up here and barge in on you, so I stayed. The advertising slicks needed sorting anyway."

"Thanks, Dora. I don't deserve such loyalty." Brandi handed over the sales report. "Would you fax this downtown? And then just leave the rest of the advertising—tomorrow's soon enough to finish it."

She took the escalator down to the second floor. The store wasn't crowded; the snowstorm was over, but the aftereffects were still keeping many people at home, just as she'd predicted. Till the streets were completely cleared, Christmas shopping would suffer. At least the season was still only halfway along; this kind of storm just a few days before the holiday could cripple the store's bottom line.

Her favorite Santa, the one with the half glasses, was holding court by the Workshop, and Brandi paused for a moment to admire him in action. It wasn't that Zack was out of place in that chair, exactly; he did just fine—far better, she had to admit, than she'd originally hoped for. But she'd prided herself for years on perfect Santas like this one. He looked so at ease, so natural, so comfortable in the big chair....

Except he wasn't sitting in the regular Santa chair, but in a dark green wing one—the chair Zack had been occupying this morning up in the furniture department during the employee meeting, and then had given up to the woman who'd come in late. Brandi didn't want to think about how he'd managed to talk the department manager into letting him requisition it. Or maybe he'd just moved it over to Toyland without anyone's approval....

Santa looked up from the child in his lap and called, "Thanks, Ms. Ogilvie! It was very thoughtful of you to change the chairs. I really appreciate a comfortable seat— you know, those packs of toys are heavy, and I have to take care of my back." He turned his attention once more to the child.

Brandi didn't bother to tell him she'd had nothing to do with the chair. She just waved and went on into Toyland.

She almost tripped over Zack; he was siting cross-legged in the middle of an aisle with a couple of youngsters, and they'd spread the pieces of a train layout all over the floor. The kids were assembling the wooden track while Zack took the engines and cars out of the box.

Brandi leaned against a case full of fashion dolls. "Zack, what are you doing?"

He looked up. "Demonstrating the flexibility and creativity of this particular model of train kit."

"It looks to me as if you're playing."

"Well, yes," Zack admitted.

"I thought so."

"That's part of what makes this a very special toy, you understand. It not only captures the imagination of children and releases their creative side, it intrigues adults, as well."

Brandi ignored the nods of the man and woman—obviously the children's parents—who were standing nearby. "You're sure you're not just talking about *some* adults?"

"If you're implying I'm a case of arrested development—"

"Well, I don't see a lot of men your age sitting on the floor playing with wooden trains. Is this the height of your ambition, Zack?"

"Of course not." The track was assembled; Zack set the train down on it and leaned back against the nearest display case while the kids took over. "I hope someday I'll be sitting on the floor playing with trains with my own kids."

Suddenly Brandi could almost see that picture. A towering Christmas tree loaded with lights, a pile of packages, a train spread out on the floor, a couple of pajama-clad youngsters—and Zack.

Brandi shook her head in amazement. The man was hypnotic; she didn't even like Christmas, but he could still evoke in her mind an image straight out of Norman Rockwell. She could almost smell the turkey cooking.

She was annoyed with herself, and so her tone was sharp. "I thought you said you wanted to take care of the Wishing Tree business tonight."

"You'll have to pardon me for keeping you waiting." He didn't sound in the least sorry. "Of course, the dragon on your office doorstep left me kicking my heels for half an hour without even telling you I was there—but I'm sure you can explain to me how that's different."

"Dora's not a dragon. She just knew I was very busy this afternoon."

"Right." Zack stood up. "I'll be with you in a minute. Let me check with the department manager first."

"Why?"

"To make sure he can do without me. It's not terribly busy just now, but he's short a couple of clerks tonight—the flu got them. In the meantime, why don't you go get your coat?"

"What for?"

"Because I'm taking you out for a sandwich or something."

Brandi started to protest, but she realized abruptly that

she was hungry. Still, there was something uncomfortable about going out with him. "Let's just go to the tearoom."

Zack shook his head. "Now that you've broken your self-imposed isolation, everyone in the store probably wants to talk to you."

"And you want me all to yourself?" Brandi's voice was saccharine. "How charming!"

Zack's eyebrows lifted slightly. "It's not that. I just don't care to risk you being paged. You might spray mustard all over me this time, and I'm particularly fond of this sweater."

Brandi could understand that sentiment; today he was wearing hunter green cashmere.

Before she could open her mouth to argue, however, he'd vanished toward the cash register, and by the time he returned she'd thought better of her insistence on the tearoom. It was handy, yes—but the last thing she needed was for another dozen employees to see them together and draw their own conclusions. Besides, though Tyler-Royale food was good, during this season she seldom had time to go anywhere else, and she knew the menus of both the tearoom and the cafeteria by heart. So she went meekly back to her office to get her coat and boots, and met Zack by the employee exit.

The parking lot had been plowed, and the snow that remained underfoot was polished smooth by traffic. But in areas where the snow lay as nature had intended, the crystals caught the lights and sparkled as if a generous hand had scattered diamonds across the soft-sculptured drifts.

"My car or yours?" she asked outside the employee exit.

"Mine's no doubt closer." He showed her to a dark sedan not far from the store.

The car was covered with snow, so Brandi couldn't tell

much about it. But she looked thoughtfully at the distinctive trademark embossed into the leather seats, and listened to the soft purr of the engine coming to life. "You know, Zack, when Ross asked me to hire you, he said you'd been having some tough times lately."

"Oh, I have." His voice was emphatic. "Yes. Very tough."

"Obviously he didn't mean financially."

"What makes you think that?"

"I'm not an idiot, Zack. That Santa suit of yours is velvet, and the boots are top-grain leather—"

"Rented," Zack said succinctly.

"You're carrying a cellular phone. That's not an inexpensive toy."

He shrugged. "I'd have to buy my way out of the service contract, and that would cost as much as using it the rest of the year. I'm very careful not to exceed the amount of time my contract allows, though, so I don't have to pay extra."

"I'll bet you are. And you're driving a very nice car."

"It's the darnedest thing, but I can't afford to sell it."

"Oh, really?"

"I'm serious. You know how tough it is to get the full price out of a new car. Once you drive it off the lot, it drops ten percent in value just like that." He snapped his fingers. "So I might as well keep it for a little while."

"Till it's repossessed?" Brandi said dryly.

"If it comes to that. After all, if I sold it I couldn't clear enough to buy something else, and then how would I get around?"

"You could always use the reindeer. What are you really, Zack? A corporate spy?"

"Brandi, don't you think if Ross wanted to plant a spy in your store he could have hidden me better than this?"

"I wasn't thinking of Ross."

Zack grinned. "Now that's a unique point of view. Would it make you happier if I started wearing a trench coat and dark glasses and slinking around behind displays?"

"So you're admitting it?"

"I'm not admitting anything."

"Well, if you're just a Santa, I'm—" She stopped. A half-formed suspicion stirred to life in the back of her mind, but she couldn't quite put her finger on it. Until she could think it all out, there wasn't much point in pursuing the matter. And in the meantime she was still thoroughly stuck with the man.

"As long as we're speaking of Ross," Zack went on, "are you sure you won't reconsider and go to the party with me Saturday?"

"I thought this was a corporate party," Brandi pointed out. "Last year nobody below assistant manager status was invited."

"I know. Sounds deadly dull, doesn't it—all those assistant managers drinking champagne and buttering people up?"

"So the Claytons are planning to enliven the party by including you?"

"Well, not just me, I'm sure," Zack said modestly. "A few friends here and there. You haven't answered my question, you know."

"I don't believe in breaking a date because another one comes along."

"Even if it's a better one?"

"Now that's a matter of opinion, isn't it?"

She expected he'd take offense, but he didn't seem to. "Italian food all right?"

"It's fine with me."

A couple of miles from the mall, Zack parked the car beside a restaurant and came around to open Brandi's door. "You know," he said, "I've been thinking."

"That sounds dangerous," Brandi said under her breath.

"Well, it was quiet all day. Not many kids, so I had a lot of time on my hands, even while I was occupying Santa's chair."

"Speaking of Santa's chair, Zack—"

"I know, if there's any wear on it you'll take it out of my paycheck."

"That wasn't what I meant."

"It wasn't?"

"No. I haven't sat in Santa's chair, so how would I know it's uncomfortable?"

"Didn't I tell you it was?"

"Well, maybe you did, but you've told me so many things I never know when to take you seriously. I just wish you wouldn't go off on these tangents without checking with me first. You've already got Casey starting to question policy."

"Maybe that's a good thing, if she's going to be managing a store of her own next year."

"I don't want to get into an argument with you about details, all right? The point is, I can't have every stock boy and salesclerk setting their own rules, but with you as a stunning example, I'm apt to have mutiny in the ranks by Christmas."

"Is that all that's bothering you?"

"*All*? Don't you think that's enough?"

"Well, maybe you've got a point," he conceded. "In that case—"

The hostess greeted Zack by name and showed them to a table with a checked cloth and enormous red napkins. The menus were huge, too, and seemed to list every conceivable combination of pasta and sauce. Brandi glanced at hers and put it aside. "You were saying?"

Zack looked at her over the top of his menu. "I knew you were decisive, Brandi, but really—"

"The only thing I've decided is that I'm not going to read the whole menu. Since you obviously come here often, you can choose."

"And that way you can concentrate on me," Zack mused. "What a perfectly charming—"

Brandi interrupted. "Just make it something that doesn't take hours to cook. Now I believe you were going to agree to some terms concerning your job?"

Zack held up a hand as if he was taking an oath. "I'll check out anything important with you before I do it."

Brandi supposed she'd have to be satisfied with that, inadequate as it was. What was his definition of important anyway? "All right. Now we can talk about the Wishing Tree."

"Just a minute. I want to tell you about my idea first."

Brandi looked at him a little doubtfully. "Zack—"

"You said not two minutes ago that you wanted me to consult you before I did anything else," Zack reminded her.

That does it, Brandi thought. I'm caught in my own trap. "What now?"

"Have you considered keeping the store open extremely late one night a week till Christmas, so parents can leave the kids at home and come to do their Santa shopping in peace?"

Brandi frowned. "Can't they just get a sitter during normal hours?"

"Not as easily as they can once the kids are in bed. Besides, the kids are apt to know where they've gone, and there are boxes and bags to hide when they get back. If it's the dead of night and the little ones are asleep, it's much easier to sneak the packages in and keep the Santa myth intact.''

"How do you know so much about kids?" Brandi challenged. "If you don't have any of your own yet—''

"Oh, there are a dozen or so who have adopted me as their favorite honorary uncle." He ordered manicotti for both of them and a bottle of red wine, and leaned across the table to drape Brandi's napkin solicitously across her lap.

"And that's why you thought being a Santa would fill in an awkward spot in your life?"

"I suppose that's what brought it to mind. What do you think? Shall we organize Parents' Night Out?"

"Aren't you going to have enough to do with your job and the Wishing Tree?"

"What's to do? A little advertising, a few signs in Toyland…''

"A few employees who are disgruntled at having to work even crazier hours."

"I don't think that will be a problem. I've talked to several, and most of them think it's a good idea."

"And I suppose you've already mentioned it to Ross, too."

"Well, yes. I didn't think it would hurt."

Brandi sighed. So much for checking things out before he acted! "Go ahead, then—ask the manager of Toyland and see what he thinks. But you're only authorized to proceed if he wants to, and if you can get the mall management to agree to let us break the rule about normal business hours. Understand that, Zack?"

"Absolutely," he said airily. "And while we're on the subject, what about a special night for senior citizens to shop? I bet they'd like not being knocked over by the regular shoppers. We could organize buses to go around and pick them up—''

''One thing at a time, Forrest. What are you doing anyway? Maneuvering for a job in public relations?''

''Now that's a thought.''

''Well, take my advice and don't settle for a single store. With all your ideas, you could keep the whole chain hopping.''

''Thank you.''

''I didn't intend it as a compliment.''

The waiter brought their wine. Zack tasted it and nodded, and the waiter filled their glasses and silently went away.

Brandi swirled her wine and sipped. ''Take those crazy buttons, for instance…''

''What about them?''

''Where did you get the things anyway?''

''The notions department made up a thousand for me. They did a good job, didn't they?'' He reached in his pocket. ''I've got an extra if you'd like it.''

''No, thanks.''

He tipped his head to one side and studied her.

''You don't think I'm capable of doing a good deed a day, do you?'' Brandi challenged.

''I'd sure like to watch you try.''

''Well, that's got nothing to do with it. There's a corporate policy that forbids wearing that kind of thing, and until it's lifted, I feel I have to abide by it—even if I end up blinking at violations by every member of my staff.''

''Ross has a button.''

''I know. He told me. That's different, because Ross makes the rules.''

''The idea seems to be working anyway. I just started handing the buttons out yesterday, and I think the store feels more cordial already. Everybody likes being Santa's friend, you see. I think that good feeling could transfer into the Wishing Tree program, too." He leaned forward confidingly. "We could end up with the biggest Wishing Tree program in the chain."

"It's not a competition, Zack."

"Pity. So tell me what I've let myself in for."

"Mostly a whole lot of paperwork and detail. The family comes in to talk to you. You check with the agencies to be sure they're really needy."

Zack frowned. "I can't imagine someone applying for charity if they don't need it."

"Then you'd be surprised."

"But their pride—"

"Exactly. The people who need help the worst are the ones who are too proud to ask for it."

"Like Theresa Howard," Zack said.

Brandi nodded and made a mental note to check with Casey Amos and the personnel director tomorrow about whether the woman had come in. "On the other hand, there are some who are out to get anything that's available. Pat used to spot-check some of the families whose stories sounded a little fishy—she'd go drive by the address and be sure the pieces all fit together."

"And did they?"

"Not always. But don't go on a crusade. The majority are legitimate. It's basically pretty simple. The family makes a list of their needs, and you'll fill out a star for each person and put it on the tree, with age and clothing sizes and likes and dislikes, so the person who chooses that star to shop for has some ideas. Then as the wishes are filled, the customer service department will let you know, and you'll pack things up and deliver them."

Zack shrugged. "You're right. It sounds pretty easy."

"I said *simple*, not *easy*. There are always snags. Gifts don't come in at a nice, steady pace, and sometimes one member of a family is passed over altogether. There's a fund provided by the store, so you can go shopping to fill in all the gaps."

Zack didn't look enthusiastic at the prospect.

The longer Brandi thought about it, though, the happier she was that he'd taken over the Wishing Tree. If he gave the project the attention it needed, he wouldn't have time to annoy her. "Just think," she consoled him, "all that time you've spent wandering around the store looking at the merchandise won't be wasted after all. I'm sure *somebody* would like that steamer you bought for your sister."

The manicotti was perfectly cooked but literally too hot to eat, so they dawdled over dinner, and it was midevening before they got back to the mall. "Are you going into the store or home?" Zack asked.

Brandi yawned. "Home, I think. After a couple of glasses of wine I probably wouldn't get much done in the office anyway."

Zack eyed her in mock disappointment. "I'm shocked at you, Ms. Ogilvie. *I* have to go back to work. And you were late this morning, too. Maybe I should report you to Ross."

"Go ahead. You'll no doubt find him at home."

Zack parked his car next to hers. "Meaning that he doesn't work sixteen-hour days? That's a good question, you know. If the CEO doesn't have to, why do you?"

"Because he's the CEO, and I'm not. He's already at the top and I'm still climbing. Sit still, Zack—don't bother to come around and help me out."

Her protest came too late, though; he was already out of the car. She'd parked in the farthest corner again, and the lights were dimmer here. Zack seemed to loom over her as he had last night—right before he'd kissed her. He was awfully close. Brandi wondered if he was thinking of doing it again, and told herself that the odd little ripple in her nerves was anxiety.

"Thanks for dinner," she said quickly, as she slipped her key into the door lock. "I still think you should have let me pay for it, though, since it was store business."

"That's okay. You can take me out for lobster someday, and I promise not to protest." But he smiled as he said it.

She couldn't close her door because he was standing in the way, almost leaning over her as if he was inspecting the equipment—or her. "And you said *my* car's nice," he murmured.

Brandi almost laughed in relief. "If you think I'm going to get into that argument, you're crazy." She turned the key in the ignition. The only sound was an ominous clicking from somewhere in the engine. "What the—" She tried again.

"Your battery's dead, so you might as well give it up." Zack put a fingertip on the switch that controlled the headlights and gently pushed; the switch clicked off.

Brandi groaned. "The sun was just coming up when I got to work this morning, and I must have left the lights on. What an idiotic thing to do!"

"No, it's not. But why don't you use the setting that automatically turns the headlights off?"

"Because I don't trust it to work," she admitted.

Zack didn't laugh; she gave him credit for that. But even in the dim glow of the parking-lot lights, she could see the gleam of humor in his eyes.

"All right," she said irritably, "so I'm a fool, too."

"I didn't say that, Brandi."

"Well, you don't have to stick around. Though I would

appreciate it if you'd pull out your magic little telephone and call a wrecker for me."

Zack shook his head. "I would, but—"

"I know, you've used up all your free time."

"It wouldn't do any good to jump-start the engine unless you plan to drive around for an hour or two to recharge the battery. Otherwise, it'll be dead again by morning."

"Oh. I hadn't thought of that."

"Besides, do you really want to sit here in the cold and wait? The wrecker guys are probably hours behind on their calls, with the snow. You'd be better off to leave it till tomorrow."

Brandi had to admit he was right. "In that case, Santa's Friend, how about doing your good deed for the day?"

"And take you home? I'd love to, but I'm supposed to go on duty in fifteen minutes, and I'm afraid if I don't turn up for my last half hour of work the boss will fire me."

"Zack—" She waved a hand at the thinly populated parking lot. "Skip it. Nobody's there anyway."

"Certainly. But may I have that in writing?" Brandi stuck her tongue out at him. Zack grinned and helped her into his car again. "Did you lock your car?" he asked.

"You think someone's going to hot-wire that vehicle and drive it off if I didn't? Of course I did, Zack—I've lived in this city all my life. I always lock doors."

"And turn off headlights?" But the smile that tugged at the corner of his mouth made it a teasing comment, not a tormenting one, and Brandi was surprised to find herself feeling almost warm because of it. Warm, and a little confused. What was happening to her anyway?

She gave him directions to her apartment complex, and when they arrived she unfastened her seat belt and let him help her out of the car. "Would you like a cup of coffee,

Zack? Nothing fancy—I haven't been to the supermarket in days—but…''

It was the least she could do. He'd bailed her out of a jam after all. It was only friendly to offer him a hot drink. He'd probably turn her down anyway; he'd be anxious to get home, too.

Zack smiled and said, ''I'd like that.''

Brandi swallowed hard. It wasn't fair, she thought. All the man had done was smile, and the odd, breathless ache she'd felt this morning—when she'd been assaulted by that sudden, idiotic urge to kiss the dimple in his cheek—swept over her once more.

She found herself wondering what he'd have done if she actually acted on that kooky impulse. Not that she had any intention of finding out, she assured herself. A cup of coffee, a little polite conversation, and he'd be out the door.

Just outside her apartment was a visitor, obviously waiting for the bell to be answered. As they approached, the girl swung around to face them, and Brandi recognized her as one of the three who had been selling garlands the night before. Her arms were full of evergreens.

''Oh, you're finally home,'' she said with obvious relief. ''I've got your garland, you see.''

Brandi frowned. ''I thought I told you to give it to someone who wanted it.''

''But I can't. My mother got really annoyed with me, and said I couldn't sell things to people and then not deliver them. So here.'' She thrust the sharp-scented greenery into Brandi's arms and hurried away.

''Well, isn't that a switch,'' Brandi muttered. ''All I tried to do was make a donation, and now I'm stuck with this thing.'' The bundle was huge and prickly; she shifted it gingerly and tried to reach her key. ''And I do mean *stuck*. Do you want a garland?''

"No, but I'll hold it for you." Zack rescued her from the evergreens. "Can't you use it?"

"I don't decorate for Christmas."

"Not at all? Don't you celebrate it, either?"

"Of course I celebrate, in my own style. I'll collapse and rest up from the rush and get recharged for the next one—the after-Christmas sales and returns."

Zack frowned. "That doesn't sound like much of a celebration. Don't you have a family?"

"Not really. My mother died when I was eighteen."

"That's a tough time to lose a parent."

She nodded curtly and went on. "My dad's in California. They divorced when I was little, and he's got a second family."

"So you don't feel you fit in?" Zack's tone was gentle.

His conclusion was true, but Brandi didn't feel like admitting it. The last thing she needed was well-meaning sympathy. "It's got nothing to do with that. I can't go dashing off halfway across the country in the midst of my busiest season for the sake of carving up a turkey."

"So you stay home and have a bologna sandwich by yourself."

"Something like that." She wasn't about to get drawn into a discussion of her habits. "Just dump the garland anywhere."

"What are you going to do with it?"

"I'll put it out with the garbage if I can't find anyone who wants it. Maybe some of your Wishing Tree people would like to have it. Coffee or hot chocolate? I think I have some of that powdered mix."

"Coffee's fine." He was still standing in the center of her living room, the garland in his arms, looking around. "It's a shame, you know. You've got a perfect place for a tree, right by the balcony doors so the neighbors can enjoy it, too.''

He had to raise his voice, since Brandi had gone on to the kitchen. She put the kettle on and called back, ''That's it, you see. On the rare occasions I'm in the mood to look at a Christmas tree, I just step onto the balcony and enjoy everyone else's. No fuss, no muss, no dropped needles...''

Zack didn't answer, and Brandi busied herself finding a tray—since she didn't entertain often, she had to look for it—and setting it up. ''I don't have any fresh cream,'' she warned.

''I don't use it, remember? You know what you need to get you into the Christmas spirit? A couple of kids.''

Brandi choked. ''Oh, no. Never.'' She stepped around the corner and almost dropped the tray. Most of the garland was now draped neatly over the mantel; Zack was arranging the last few feet. And the gas log in the fireplace was burning brightly. ''Make yourself at home,'' she said dryly.

''Thanks. Why no kids?''

''They're altogether too much responsibility.''

Zack tipped his head to one side. ''Were you a difficult kid?''

Brandi was puzzled at the question. ''No more than most, I suppose. But it's a different world these days. People who aren't willing to be at home with their kids shouldn't have them in the first place.''

''And you aren't willing?''

''Not particularly. I could hardly quit—I have enough to do making a living for myself as it is, without taking on a couple of people who'd need college educations one day. Besides, I told you I love my job.''

''To say nothing of your ambitions for the future.''

''That's right. Zack, the garland's kind of cute, but—''

He hadn't paused as they talked, and the last bit of greenery seemed to nestle down around the mantel as if it belonged there. "Doesn't that give the whole place a festive air?" He came to take the tray out of her hands and set it on the wicker trunk in front of the couch. "I didn't mean permanent kids anyway."

"You mean I could be sort of an adopted aunt to someone else's? I don't know any kids all that well. Besides, I don't seem to have the knack for getting along with them, and it's dead sure I don't have the time to learn it, even if I wanted to."

Zack didn't answer. He sat quietly, cradling his coffee cup in one hand, staring at the fire.

Brandi wondered what he was thinking, and the suspicion she'd felt earlier in the evening stirred to life again. But this time, as if her subconscious mind had spent the intervening time chewing on the problem, it was not just a half-formed hunch but much more.

She'd asked if he was a spy, and without pausing to consider, Zack had made a joke about Ross. Was it her imagination, or had there been something almost Freudian about how fast that answer had come? Did it mean he was working not for some rival of Tyler-Royale's, but for Ross Clayton himself?

He'd even had that very private telephone number, she reminded herself.

Brandi stirred sugar into her coffee and leaned back in her corner of the couch. "Ross has always had a trouble-shooter he can call on," she said almost dreamily. "Someone who can go into any of the stores and diagnose and fix problems."

Zack's eyebrows rose. "What brought that up, Brandi?"

She didn't answer the question. "A few years back it was Whitney Townsend, but now she's settled in Kansas

City. At the moment there doesn't seem to be a trouble-shooter, because when San Antonio got into some minor difficulty a few weeks ago, Whitney went down to sort it out.''

"I don't quite—"

"Or maybe there is a troubleshooter—but for some reason Ross doesn't want anyone to know just now who's doing the job. So he sent Whitney to take care of the small problem, and held the real troubleshooter in reserve for the big one.''

Zack shrugged as if he was willing to humor her by playing along. "Secrecy could be an advantage for Ross at times, I'm sure.''

"Exactly.'' Her fingers were trembling. "And that's what made me start to wonder tonight about what you're really doing here. You're certainly not an ordinary Santa, Zack, so what are you? Are you Ross's troubleshooter? And if that *is* what's going on—then why are you here? What's wrong with my store? And why didn't I realize there was a problem before the head office did?''

CHAPTER SIX

THEN Brandi held her breath. Was her suspicion the truth? Was the trouble Ross had spoken of that first day not Zack's personal problem at all, but something wrong with the store?

And if it was, would Zack admit it?

The suspicion had been building in her mind all evening, and so quietly that Brandi had been unable to put her finger on it. Her misgivings had started when he'd showed her to his car—or maybe long before that, when she'd first noticed the quality of his Santa suit—and had finally burst forth in full flower.

The trouble was, even though the theory was her own, Brandi couldn't quite make herself believe she'd hit on the right answer. She couldn't imagine how she could be oblivious to a problem large enough to cause that kind of response; even now, she couldn't begin to think of anything going on in the store that would upset anyone in the head office.

But there was something strange going on—and she could find no other combination of circumstances that made sense. Zack's explanation of why he was still using his cellular phone despite a financial downturn might hold water—but the easy dismissal of his expensive car didn't.

"You may have to run that one past me again." Zack sounded as if she'd hit him solidly right in the diaphragm.

As if he was startled, Brandi thought. But was he surprised at the accusation because it was false, or because he'd been discovered?

He went on, "Ross wouldn't go behind your back like that, would he?"

"He has before," Brandi said. "Not with me, exactly. I mean other managers, in other circumstances. Whitney Townsend's told me some tales about investigating a store without telling the manager."

"How could you be unaware of a problem so bad that Ross would go into overdrive about it?"

Brandi's eyelids were stinging. She shut her eyes to try to keep the tears from showing. She was a professional woman, and she didn't cry about business matters; what had come over her anyway? "I don't know," she mumbled. "I don't know."

The silence was oppressive.

Zack hadn't really answered her question, she realized, and she found herself wishing that she hadn't said anything at all. If it was true, she wasn't helping the situation by blubbering about it like a baby. And if it wasn't true, she'd simply made a fool of herself.

Zack slid closer. She could feel the warmth of his body next to her even before he slipped a hand under her chin and raised her face to his. "Brandi, look at me."

She had to make a great effort to open her eyes.

Zack's voice was husky. "Nothing like that is going on. The troubles I'm dealing with are my own."

Her unshed tears made his face look blurry, but despite that fact, Brandi thought he had never looked better. "You're telling the truth, Zack?" she whispered.

"I swear it. From everything I can see, the store is doing beautifully, and you..." He paused, and said something under his breath that Brandi didn't quite catch. Then he bent his head to very deliberately kiss a tear from her eyelashes. "And you are beautiful, too," he whispered, and his mouth claimed hers.

Already emotionally off balance because of her fears, Brandi reacted to his kiss almost as she would have if she'd stepped off a cliff. She was dizzy, and her stomach had an all-gone feeling as if she'd looked down and found nothing but air beneath her feet. Her breath came in painful gasps, and she clutched at Zack.

He eased her back against the couch, but that didn't seem to help, for each kiss increased her dizziness. The only thing she could depend on was the strength of Zack's arms holding her, cradling her, keeping her safe. He was the one remaining solid object in a world gone suddenly topsy-turvy, and so she pressed against him and kissed him back, until suddenly she didn't care if she fell all the way to the center of the earth, so long as he was with her. Her ears were ringing already—had she fallen so far?—but she hardly noticed.

Zack pulled back a little. Brandi murmured a protest and tried to draw him down into her arms once more, but he resisted.

Brandi frowned a bit. Her senses came flooding back, and she realized the telephone was ringing. How had she gotten so frazzled that she hadn't even heard it? And what did Zack think of her preoccupation—for obviously *he* hadn't been so carried away that he'd missed it.

She was still a little light-headed, and she had to clutch at the door frame to steady herself as she went into the kitchen to answer the phone.

She recognized the voice; it belonged to one of the security guards at the store, and he sounded tense. "Ms. Ogilvie? There's been a little trouble down here. It's over now, but I thought I should call you anyway."

Brandi shook off her giddy feeling. "What happened?" Midway through the guard's explanation, she cut him off. "I'll be there as soon as I can."

Zack was standing in the center of the carpet when she came back into the living room. Had he heard the conversation, Brandi wondered, or was he on his feet because he intended to leave just as soon as possible?

While she wasn't naive enough to think Zack hadn't enjoyed that kiss, the whole situation *was* a little awkward. She'd kissed the man as if she was starving—as if she expected never to have another chance to be held and caressed. She wondered if he thought she'd thrown herself at him; she couldn't blame him if he did.

Her voice was a little tense. "I hate to ask for another favor, Zack, but can you take me back to the store?"

He reached for the coat he'd draped across the back of a chair. "Trouble?"

"Remember the weird guy the security guard warned us about?"

"You mean the one who was hanging around the parking lot last night?"

Brandi was momentarily distracted. Had it really only been last night that Zack had walked her to her car—and kissed her? She pushed the memory to the back of her mind. "Tonight he tried to hold up the clerk at the perfume counter just inside the main door from the mall. She reached for the panic button instead of the cash, and he gave her a shove and ran." She slid her arms into the coat he was holding for her. "I should have been there."

Zack gave her shoulders a sympathetic squeeze. "And just what do you think you'd have been able to do about it?"

"That's beside the point. It's my store, and my job." She flipped her hair over her coat collar, and the gleaming auburn mass hit him squarely in the face. "Sorry. I didn't mean to swat you with my hair."

Zack shook his head a little, as if the blow—light as it was—had stunned him. "A robbery—right in the mall?"

Brandi nodded. "Crazy, isn't it? He'd have to run a hundred yards down the mall to get outside."

"Or else cut across the store to the parking-lot exits."

"Yes—but either way, he might run into any number of security people before he got out of the building and away."

"Did they get him?"

"I guess not," Brandi said reluctantly. "By the time the clerk could stop screaming and tell anyone what had happened, the guy was long gone."

"Then maybe he wasn't so crazy after all."

Brandi settled into the passenger seat and nibbled at her thumbnail. "Fortunately the clerk wasn't badly hurt—just shook up and maybe bruised a bit. You know, I've always felt we were safe from that sort of thing, just because there are seventy stores and hundreds of people around all the time, and it would be so difficult for a robber to get away."

"Maybe this kook isn't smart enough to think about things like that."

Brandi shivered. "If you're trying to make me feel better, Zack, you're not getting the job done. I'd rather think a would-be robber would be smart enough to think through the consequences, because if he isn't, anything might happen." She lapsed into silence, which lasted till they arrived at the mall.

Closing time had passed, so Zack ignored the no-parking signs and pulled up in the fire lane beside the mall entrance nearest the Tyler-Royale store. Just a few yards away were three police cars, lights flashing.

"Zack," Brandi said slowly as they crossed the side-walk to the mall entrance. "About what I said earlier—

I'm sorry I accused you of being involved in some kind of plot.''

Zack silently held the door for her.

Brandi went on. ''I must have sounded absolutely paranoid. When something threatens this store, or even appears to...well, I go a little crazy, I'm afraid.''

''Brandi—''

The tone of his voice scared her; he sounded almost somber. Brandi hoped he didn't intend to discuss the kiss they'd shared, and how it fit into the pattern of her behavior. She couldn't look straight at him. ''This isn't the time or the place for a chat, Zack. So can we just forget it happened? Please?'' She didn't wait for an answer.

Inside the Tyler-Royale store, a knot of people was gathered around the perfume and cosmetics counter nearest the atrium entrance. The still-shaken employee was sitting on a tall stool, twisting a handkerchief in her fingers and talking to two policemen. She didn't even see Brandi.

The security guard came hurrying up. ''I'm sorry if I woke you, Ms. Ogilvie, but I thought—''

''You didn't, John. I'm glad you called.''

''Oh? You sure sounded funny, like you'd just dozed off.'' The man glanced from her to Zack, who was standing just a step behind her, and suddenly a tinge of red appeared in his face.

Obviously, Brandi thought, he'd gotten the wrong idea. There was no point in trying to correct his impression, though; any kind of protest would sound fishy. She said crisply, ''Where's the Doberman?''

''In his kennel. I thought with all the cops around, we didn't need the confusion of a dog just now.''

''You're sure you won't need him?''

The guard nodded. ''The guy's long gone. Lots of people saw him go, but they didn't realize what was happening in time to stop him.''

"Of course." Brandi turned to Zack. "This is obviously going to take a while. You don't need to wait around.''

"How would you get home if I left?"

"Someone will give me a ride. Or I'll take a cab.''

The perfume clerk heard her and turned around. She looked pale and shaken, and when Brandi patted her shoulder, she burst into tears.

Brandi put both arms around the woman. "It's all right," she whispered. "You did just fine.''

"But Ms. Ogilvie," the woman wailed, "the policeman says I should just have given the robber the money!''

Brandi shot a look of acute dislike at the nearest cop. No doubt he was right; no amount of money was worth the risk of a life. But now was hardly the time to suggest to a shaken woman that she'd done precisely the wrong thing. "Well, it's done now," Brandi said soothingly. "And you did the very best you could. When you're finished with the interviews, we'll make sure you get home, and you can take as much time off as you need.''

The policeman said gruffly, "I'm finished. She should probably be checked out at a hospital, though." After the employee had gone, leaning on a co-worker's arm, he turned back to Brandi and folded his arms across his chest. "Worried about the money, are you? Well, he didn't get any, so I guess in your view she handled it exactly right.''

"Of course she didn't," Brandi snapped. "But did you really think you'd make her sleep better tonight by pointing out she could have gotten killed because of the way she handled it?''

Zack moved a little closer. "Brandi…''

Brandi bit her lip. She didn't look at Zack, but at the policeman. "I'm sorry. Look, if you want to come back and teach all my employees the proper response, I'd be glad to have you. But scaring her a little more tonight isn't going to help anything.''

She thought she saw, from the corner of her eye, a smile tugging at Zack's lips.

The police looked for another half hour to be certain the would-be robber hadn't left any fingerprints or dropped any belongings, but finally they finished up, and Brandi was free to go. The store was quiet by then. She could hear the soft click of the Doberman's toenails against the hard-surfaced floors as the guard made his regular rounds. Brandi yawned as she said good-night, and wondered how long it would take for a cab to show up.

But Zack hadn't gone after all. He was sitting quietly on a carpeted display cube at the far side of the atrium, and when Brandi came toward him he stood up and slid a hand under her elbow.

The warm support was welcome, but Brandi wasn't in the mood to talk. Zack seemed content with the silence, as well. It wasn't until they were almost back at her apartment complex that he said, ''You're a thoroughly confusing creature, Brandi.''

She was puzzled. ''I don't know what you mean.''

Zack didn't answer. Instead he said, ''You'll be all right alone?''

It didn't sound like a question, but a statement. Obviously, Brandi thought, whether she'd invited him or not, he didn't intend to come in. Well, that was all right with her; it was late, and she was drained.

Still, she couldn't help but wonder what his reasons were. Was he simply tired himself? It would be no wonder; he'd had a long day, too. Was he being sensitive to her exhaustion? Or was he still wary of what had happened between them earlier this evening?

"I'll be fine," she said. "After all, I'm not the one who got held up."

He parked the car and helped her out. "You don't depend on anybody but yourself, do you, Brandi?"

She shrugged. "Who else am I supposed to depend on?"

He didn't answer that, and he didn't make any other move to touch her. He leaned against the passenger door and watched till she was safely inside the building.

Despite the central heating in her apartment, Brandi felt cold. That was the aftermath of shock, no doubt, from the evening's events. Tyler-Royale had its share of shoplifters. The main office had discovered an embezzler once, and now and then a store was burglarized. But so far as Brandi knew, this was the first time any of the stores had actually been robbed during business hours.

It was no wonder she was still feeling stunned. But was the robbery the only reason she was upset? Was she still suffering the aftereffects of that kiss, as well? Things had come very close to getting out of control. What would have happened if the security guard hadn't interrupted?

Nothing, she told herself. She certainly knew better than to allow it.

She warmed her hands over the fireplace. She'd been in such a hurry to get to the store that neither of them had remembered to turn the gas log off. Fortunately Zack had put the fire screen in place, so there had been no danger.

The sharp scent of evergreen seemed to float from the garland atop the mantel and fill the room. Zack had done a good job of arranging it; nevertheless the greenery was a little bare. Brandi knew exactly what would make it look right—some twinkling lights twisted through the branches and a scattering of small, bright-colored ornaments. Then the barest dusting of spray snow on the end of the needles, with some glitter for emphasis, and the garland would be perfect.

Not that she would do any of those things. There wasn't any point to it when she was scarcely ever home.

Zack had said this evening that she needed a couple of kids to get her into the Christmas spirit. Well, she didn't know about getting into the spirit—it seemed to her that having a couple of little people around for the holidays was likely to do nothing but increase her level of exhaustion.

The mental image she'd created in Toyland this evening, as she watched Zack playing with the kids and the train, sprang unbidden to her mind once more. In fact, if she closed her eyes halfway she could almost *see* that scene. A decorated tree stood beside the patio doors where he'd said it should go, and the train went round and round the track as two children in fuzzy sleepers knelt to watch. She couldn't see their faces, but they weren't very old.

Once, she had assumed she'd have children one day. It wasn't something she'd thought a great deal about; she'd never been around children much, and she had no great longing for them. But kids were part of the package of life—when the time was right, there would be a man and a marriage, and ultimately, a family.

And up to a point, things had followed the pattern. There had been a man; there had very nearly been a marriage. Thank heaven, she thought, that it hadn't come to that, for Jason didn't really want a wife, he wanted a caretaker.

Zack had observed tonight that she depended only on herself. Brandi could have told him, if she'd wanted to, how she'd learned that lesson not once but over and over. First from her father, who'd seldom shown interest in her after the divorce. Then her mother had died, and—unfair though it was to blame her for that—Brandi had felt abandoned once more. And, finally and most cruelly, there was Jason, who said he admired her independence, but meant only that he appreciated the freedom it offered him to be untroubled and irresponsible.

But she hadn't told Zack any of that, and she wouldn't. Sharing so much with someone she barely knew would be asking for another kind of hurt, and Brandi had learned the hard way not to allow herself that kind of weakness. She didn't need anyone to confide in anyway. She was used to depending only on herself. That she knew how to do.

The apartment was so quiet she could hear her own heartbeat. So quiet that she was tempted to talk to herself just to hear a voice.

Maybe she should get a cat to keep her company. Talking to an animal was nothing like talking to herself. Nobody would think she was crazy if she talked to a pet.

And having a cat around would certainly be less troublesome than dealing with a man. Particularly, she thought, with her sense of humor restored, a man like Zack Forrest!

Brandi was running late. Saturdays were always busy at the store, and this afternoon she'd had to deal with a series of unhappy customers who wanted to talk to the manager. Then the personnel manager had come in to complain that Zack was sending half his Wishing Tree clients upstairs to apply for jobs. And after that, she'd stopped to visit the perfume clerk to see how she was getting along after the robbery attempt.

As a result, Brandi was still feeling a little frazzled when she turned her car over to the valet in front of Ross Clayton's lakeshore mansion, and her palms were just a little damp as she started up the long walk to the immense carved front door.

Under the circumstances, she'd rather be almost any-where than here tonight. If it wasn't for Whitney Townsend's order to attend, she'd probably have found a last-minute excuse.

Brandi had never been particularly fond of business events that masqueraded as parties. It seemed such a waste of time to get dressed up to go out with the same people one saw regularly through the course of the job. If people were going to talk about their work anyway, she thought, why not just put them in a boardroom and let them get on with it? And if they weren't going to talk business, why were they bothering to get together in the first place? The only thing all these people had in common was Tyler-Royale.

No—*most* of these people had only the stores in com-mon, she corrected herself. There was Zack, of course, and whatever other friends the Claytons had decided to include tonight to liven things up. Though even Zack had ties to the store...

Suspicion flickered once more at the back of her mind, and resolutely Brandi extinguished it. He had reassured her that her store was in no danger, and she had no reason to disbelieve him.

She might not even see Zack tonight anyway. She'd be busy with Whitney Townsend. Besides, there were so many Tyler-Royale executives that it was quite possible to circulate all evening and still not see every single one of them.

Every leaded-glass window in the Claytons' Tudor Revival mansion was aglow. Standing guard at each side of the walk were huge evergreens, crusted with snow and golden lights, which were reflected from the snow-covered grass.

Before Brandi reached the house, another car pulled up;

she recognized the manager of the San Francisco store and paused on the sidewalk to let him and his wife catch up. She'd done part of her training in the San Francisco store, but she hadn't seen much of the couple since.

The night was cold and still; her breath hung in a cloud, and the manager's wife scolded her for waiting outside.

Brandi smiled and kissed her cheek. "I'm used to this kind of weather. And I wanted to say hello before we got into the crush inside." It was true; the fact that she didn't particularly want to walk into the party alone had little to do with it.

Why should she be feeling sensitive about that anyway? Certainly the crowd wasn't going to pause and hush to admire her new black velvet dress. All the Tyler-Royale people were used to Brandi appearing by herself; they'd hardly even notice.

But Zack would. And even though she'd told the truth about having a date, if he saw her coming in alone, he'd have good reason to wonder.

Not that he'd be looking, she reminded herself. So it was silly to go to any extra effort for his sake.

Just inside the massive carved oak front door, Ross Clayton and his wife were greeting their guests. Brandi hung back to let the San Francisco couple go ahead of her, but within a minute Ross took Brandi's hand and murmured, "Now who wins the honors for getting you to show up here tonight, I wonder?"

Brandi let her eyes widen just a little. "What on earth do you mean? Ross, you know I'd never miss a Tyler-Royale event unless I had overwhelming reason."

Ross chuckled. "I know. It's just our bad luck that you always seem to have overwhelming reason. Why not this time, that's what I'd like to know. Which reminds me, you've been awfully quiet all the way around for the past couple of days. How are things in Oak Park?''

Brandi shrugged. ''Hectic, but what else is new? Have you ever considered moving the company Christmas parties to July? It would be a whole lot easier to fit them into everyone's schedules.''

''You mean you'd actually like to fit them into yours? You amaze me.''

Brandi bit her lip.

He smiled a little. ''It's not a bad idea, actually. I'll consider it. You know, Brandi, that's one of your strengths. You always have a different way of looking at things.''

''Thanks,'' Brandi said crisply. ''At least I think that was a compliment.''

Ross laughed. ''Is Zack still working out so well?''

Brandi's eyes came to rest on the velvet lapel of Ross Clayton's tuxedo, where one of Zack's buttons proclaimed that he was Santa's Friend. ''Depends. Do you want reassurance, or the truth?''

''Ouch. Maybe we should talk—''

Ross's wife interrupted. ''Don't you think that's enough business, darling? You did promise me you'd lay off tonight and let everyone have a good time.'' She offered her cheek to Brandi. ''We're using the guest room at the top of the stairs for the ladies' coats. The maid will take yours up if you'd like.''

The San Francisco couple had already handed over their coats and moved off into the throng, and the guests who had followed Brandi in showed every sign of monopolizing Ross for the next ten minutes at least.

''Thanks,'' Brandi said, ''but I'll go and comb my hair, too.'' That way, when she came back down, it wouldn't be like walking into the party alone. It was silly, she knew—all her life she'd been walking into parties by herself, so why should it bother her tonight?

She slowly climbed the massive staircase. From one of the lower steps, she had a good view of the big formal living room, and she paused to look over the crowd. She told herself she was trying to spot Whitney, but she was terribly aware that there was no sign of Zack, either. That should be no surprise, she decided; there were more guests here tonight than Brandi had seen at any other Tyler-Royale party she'd ever attended.

There were several women in the guest room, chatting as they fussed with their makeup, and the air was heavy with cologne and hair spray. Brandi laid her coat on the bed, ran a quick comb through her auburn curls, and left. It was better to take the chance of being considered rude then to risk a full-fledged sneezing fit by sticking around for another minute.

But even such a short stay in the overfragrant room had made her eyes water, and Brandi paused in a little alcove in the hallway, leaning against the paneling and trying to blot the moisture away with the edge of a lace-trimmed handkerchief.

Party noises drifted up the open stairs. From the room she'd just left came a woman's voice and an answering laugh. And from down the hall came a peal of childish giggles.

The Claytons' kids, she thought. No doubt their parents thought they were safety tucked away for the night. Brandi took a step toward the sound and then stopped; it was none of her business after all. Probably the children were with a sitter or a nanny anyway. She didn't know much about kids, but surely these were too young to be left on their own with their parents so busy.

A door opened, sending light streaming into the dimly

lit hallway, and a small girl, perhaps three years old, appeared. She was holding the hem of her pink flannel nightgown up with both hands, and her chubby knees pumped as she ran down the hallway toward Brandi.

A man followed. The dim lights and the moisture in Brandi's eyes prevented her from seeing him clearly, but he looked incredibly tall compared to the child, and one of his steps corresponded to half a dozen of hers. Before the little girl had covered more than a couple of yards, he'd caught up with her, bent, and tossed her over one shoulder.

The child squealed happily.

"Shush, Kathleen," the man said, "or we'll have your mother up here and nobody will have any more fun."

His voice was rich and warm, and—despite the warning—loaded with good humor. At least, Brandi thought, this little scene explained why Ross had thought Zack would make a good Santa Claus.

She stepped out of the shadowed alcove. "Hello, Zack. Having a bit of trouble?"

"You might say," he answered. "The little varmint gave my bow tie a good yank and then ran."

Brandi took a good look at him. His dark trousers looked just a little rumpled, he wore no jacket over his stiffly pleated formal white shirt, and the ends of his tie dangled loose. She thought he looked wonderful.

The child giggled and grabbed for the tie again. "I got you, Uncle Zack! Didn't I?"

Uncle Zack? He'd mentioned a sister. Was it possible she was Ross Clayton's wife? And how did that all fit together?

"And now I've got you, nuisance." Zack shifted the child to a more comfortable position.

"Uncle Zack?" Brandi asked. "I didn't know you were related."

"I'm not—it's purely an honorary title." He studied Brandi's face. "Is something wrong?"

"No. Why?"

"You look as if you've been crying."

"Oh." She shook her head and tucked her handkerchief into her tiny black evening bag. "It's just all the scents in the cloakroom. I have to be careful at the store, as well. Too much perfume in the air and I'm a mess."

"That's good. I thought it might be something serious."

The child squirmed to get down, and effortlessly Zack rotated the little body into a firmer hold so she couldn't escape.

"You're obviously no amateur at this sort of thing," Brandi said. "Though I must say you don't look like a baby-sitter."

"Oh, after you turned me down for the party I figured I might as well be useful. These affairs are so deadly dull. Come and join us if you like."

His words were casual, but the way he looked at Brandi was anything but. Ever so slowly, his gaze roved over her, from the loose cloud of auburn curls, over the sleek black velvet of her dress to her high-heeled pumps, and back to her face again.

Brandi felt herself growing warm, and she had to force herself to stand still. He had warned her the day they met, she remembered, that sometime he'd give her a good looking-over. She supposed this was it.

"We were halfway through a game when Kathleen attacked me," Zack went on, "so I'd better finish or I'll have a mutiny from her big brother. Coming?"

Brandi hesitated. "I don't think so. I don't know anything about kids."

He smiled a little. "How do you think people learn?"

"Anyway," Brandi remembered with relief, "some-one's waiting for me."

Zack's gaze skimmed her body once more. "Yes," he mused. "And getting impatient, no doubt. I can understand why they would be."

His voice was very slightly husky, and its effect on Brandi was like silk rubbing softly against her skin, creating an electrical charge that fluttered her pulse and did funny things to her breathing.

She retreated toward the stairs, trying her best to look dignified. She wasn't sure she succeeded.

CHAPTER SEVEN

BRANDI reached the bottom of the stairs before she realized she hadn't even been looking for Whitney. Instead, she'd been basking in the memory of Zack with the little girl in his arms.

The child had been charming. And Zack hadn't exactly been hard on the eyes, either, Brandi had to admit. Despite his slightly rumpled appearance—or perhaps because of it—he had a personal magnetism that she'd bet few of the other men at this party did. Zack looked better in half a tuxedo than most men did in the whole thing, and there was something heartwarming about a guy who ignored his dress-up clothes in order to play with a couple of kids—

Brandi shook her head in rueful disbelief. What was happening to her, for heaven's sake? She was suddenly discovering a romantic streak she'd never dreamed she possessed! What was it about kids anyway? It wasn't that she had anything against them—in fact, she'd hardly been around any kids since her own childhood days—but she'd never been one to coo over babies or be charmed by tiny tots. So why should she suddenly find Zack's Father Goose act appealing?

She tried to focus her attention on the swirl of guests. Surely by now Whitney would be here, and once busy with her friend, Brandi would forget all about Zack.

The party had grown even larger in the few minutes Brandi had been upstairs. More guests were streaming in, and she had trouble making her way through the entrance hall and into the living room. Standing near the enormous, glittering Christmas tree in a bay window was a group of executives; they waved her over, but Brandi smiled and shook her head, and went on looking for Whitney.

The massive doors between the main rooms had been thrown open, and waiters were circulating with trays of drinks and hors d'oeuvres. Brandi took a glass of champagne and wandered toward the dining room.

But her progress was slow; several times she was interrupted by people who exclaimed over how well she looked and how long it had been since they'd seen her. They made such a big deal of it that Brandi began to feel guilty. Just how long *had* it been since she'd attended one of these parties anyway?

She'd just spotted Whitney, at the far side of the dining room, when the manager of the Minneapolis store buttonholed her to ask how she was planning to handle the new bookkeeping system that the head office was putting into place. It took twenty minutes to dislodge him, and by then the cocktail hour was over and people were starting to drift out of the room.

Brandi was just looking around for her friend again when Whitney appeared beside her, tall and sleek in pure white silk and a neckline that outdid every other woman in the room.

"*There* you are," Whitney announced with relief. "I was beginning to think you'd stood me up after all."

"I wouldn't dare," Brandi admitted, and gave her a hug. "You look wonderful!"

The man beside Whitney gave a little snort. Whitney turned to him with a stunning smile. "You've already made it clear what you think of the neckline, Max, so no further editorial comment is necessary. You remember Max, don't you, Brandi?"

"Of course." Brandi extended a hand to Whitney's husband.

Whitney glanced around the room. "I suppose we'd better move toward the pool—that's where dinner is being served." She eyed Brandi. "It's very polite of you not to wrinkle your nose. When I first heard about it, I couldn't help telling Ross he had to be kidding."

"Well…it is a beautiful pool. But—"

"Not anymore. His newest innovation is a portable dance floor that sort of hangs over the water. Can you imagine?" But Whitney seemed only half-interested; her gaze was moving steadily across the room. "Drat the man, where *is* he? I saw him just a minute ago."

"You mean Ross? He was in the front hall when I came down from the cloakroom, but that was at least half an hour ago."

"Why would I want Ross?"

Brandi's heart gave an odd little leap. "Then who are you searching for?"

Whitney said sweetly, "Don't look at me like that, darling. I'm not matchmaking."

"Of course you're not. You've got far better sense than that." But Brandi's breath was doing odd little things, nevertheless.

"Not that I wouldn't, if I thought it might do some good," Whitney admitted. "But in this case I'm completely innocent. The new manager of the Seattle store is here, and it's his first corporate party, so I thought it would be nice to make him feel at home."

It wasn't Zack, then. And come to think of it, why should Brandi have jumped to the conclusion that he was the one Whitney meant? Zack could hardly be the only unattached male in a crowd like this. Who was to say Whitney even knew him? In fact, Brandi was sure she'd mentioned Whitney's name the other night, and Zack hadn't reacted at all.

None of which explained the twinge of disappointment she felt—which of course was an utterly ridiculous reaction. "It's sweet of you to look out for him."

"So's he," Whitney murmured. "Sweet, I mean. Not that I'd expect you to notice that on your own. We may as well go on. He'll catch up with us sooner or later, as the seating's all arranged."

The pool occupied a much newer wing of the house. The high-arched ceiling and glass walls allowed the space to act as a conservatory, as well, and huge green plants softened the sharp angles and hard surfaces. Tonight, since the snow-covered lawns outside were lit as brightly as the interior, the glass almost vanished and the pool wing seemed to be an island of tropical warmth floating freely in a sea of winter.

Tables for four were set up all around the perimeter of the room, and a band's equipment was ready in a corner. It took a close eye to recognize the pool in the center of the room, covered as it was by a hardwood dance floor, elevated a step above the surrounding area.

"It looks pretty solid," Brandi said.

"Well, that's one thing in its favor," Whitney murmured. "If it hadn't, I wouldn't have set foot on it."

A dark-clad arm slid around Whitney's waist, and she gave a little crow of surprise as Zack kissed her cheek.

Brandi was startled. Zack in half a tux had been impressive enough, but the complete picture was stunning. She'd known from the first time she met him that he looked wonderful in black, but she hadn't dreamed of this magnificence. He certainly didn't look as if he'd been roughhousing with a couple of children within the last hour.

He wasn't paying any attention to Brandi, but looked instead at Whitney as if she was the focus of all his dreams. "Lovely dress, dear," he said. "Of course, I'm surprised Max let you out of the house displaying that neckline."

"Watch what you say, Zack," Max warned. "Or you'll have a whole lot of guys laughing up their sleeves at you when your wife turns up wearing a dress like that."

There was a strange all-gone feeling in the pit of Brandi's stomach. A wife? But he'd asked her to come to this party with him!

Of course, no one had ever told her Zack *wasn't* married. And there was certainly no reason she should be feeling let down over it, Brandi told herself crossly.

"And I will happily help her choose it, too," Whitney said. "Though I'll no doubt be hobbling 'round the store with my walker by the time you get married."

The surge of relief that sang through Brandi's veins made her feel weak—and then angry. What was happening to her anyway?

"I'll take my chances," Zack murmured. "Our table is right at poolside." He smiled at Brandi and took her hand, holding it between his two. "Isn't that delightful?"

Our table? But hadn't Whitney said just a minute ago that the seating was prearranged? "Hold it," Brandi said. "*He's* the new manager in Seattle?"

Zack looked horrified. "Who told you that?"

"Of course he's not," Whitney said. "And he's not joining us for dinner, either. As a matter of fact, I'm not even going to introduce him to you. Look, Zack, just be a good boy and go away, will you?"

"You don't have to introduce us," Brandi said. "We've already met." The way he was looking at her made the room feel a little too warm all of a sudden. He was still holding her hand, too, but Brandi noticed that fact only when he raised her fingers to his lips.

Whitney looked exasperated. "How?"

Zack said, "I make it a point to get acquainted with every pretty woman at a party." He drew Brandi toward the table and pulled out her chair.

"I know you do." Whitney's voice was dry. "And that's exactly why I wasn't planning to introduce you— I'm not about to give you my seal of approval. Brandi isn't simply a pretty woman at a party. She's worth three of you, Forrest. So go away, will you?"

Zack gave no indication that he'd even heard the order.

Brandi decided it was nice to know that it wasn't just her he ignored in order to do as he pleased. It was some relief to find that Zack could be as immovable as the Rock of Gibraltar where others were concerned, too.

He seated Brandi with a flourish and moved around the table to hold Whitney's chair, as well. Whitney glared at him; he simply pointed at the tiny name cards that adorned each place. She read them, and finally sighed and sat down. "Is there nothing you won't descend to, Zack?" she asked. "I thought rearranging place cards was too low even for you, but…"

He looked innocent. "I never touched them."

"Then you bribed somebody who did," Whitney muttered. "It's the same thing."

"Oh, you really wouldn't have liked the Seattle person. He's too agreeable—he'd have bored you stiff before you'd eaten your appetizer."

"Well, there's certainly no danger of that with you, is there?" Whitney said sweetly. "How did you two meet anyway?"

"Zack's the newest Santa at my store," Brandi said.

"*Zack*?" Whitney sounded horrified.

"Didn't Ross tell you?" Zack asked.

"Don't tell me it was his idea," Whitney said firmly.

Brandi murmured, "It certainly wasn't mine."

Max leaned forward. "We haven't had a chance to talk to Ross. We just got in a half hour before the party."

A uniformed waiter brought their appetizers, huge, succulent shrimp marinated in a vinaigrette dressing.

After the waiter was gone, Zack added thoughtfully, "Ross probably didn't mention it because he felt bad for me. This is just to tide me over some troubled times, you understand."

"No doubt you'll get back on your feet eventually," Whitney said.

"Oh, I'm sure of it."

"I can't wait to see this," Whitney said.

"What? Getting back on my feet, or playing Santa? You can catch the late performance tonight, if you like—I'm scheduled to work the last hour the store's open." Zack glanced at his watch. "You'll help me keep an eye on the time, won't you, Brandi?"

"That's a crazy schedule," Whitney said.

"I'm not complaining."

"You'd better not be," Brandi said softly, "because you chose it yourself."

"You were very firm about the idea of my setting my own hours."

"I also told you I was willing to negotiate that schedule, Zack."

He smiled. "Does that mean you'd rather I stayed here tonight instead of going back to the store? That's wonderful, Brandi, because it was going to make a terrible dent in the party for both of us if I had to leave."

Whitney looked as if the shrimp she'd just bitten into tasted sour, but she didn't say anything.

Brandi studied her with puzzlement. She'd known Whitney Townsend for several years, ever since Brandi had started her management training course under Whitney's supervision, but she'd never seen the woman at a loss for words before.

"It's a fascinating job," Zack went on airily. "I'm getting quite attached to it. There's no predicting it, you see. One minute I'm getting smeared with chocolate-covered kisses, and the next I'm defending the whole idea of Santa Claus to a kid who's really too old to be sitting on anyone's knee. Yesterday I not only rescued a lost child, but I stanched a bloody nose after two kids got in an argument about whose turn it was. I felt immensely valuable."

Brandi frowned. "I didn't see a report on that."

"What? The bloody nose? It was no big deal. They stopped the fight themselves as soon as they remembered Santa was watching."

"Anytime a customer needs medical attention, I should be notified, Zack."

"The situation didn't require medical attention so much as comfort. It was a very minor bloody nose."

"Still—"

"You know, Brandi, it wouldn't hurt if you'd learn to delegate some authority."

Zack's tone was mild, but the reprimand stung a bit anyway. Brandi was annoyed not only at the remark but at her reaction to it—why should she be feeling sensitive over his criticism? It was her store, and her responsibility, and he had no business criticizing her.

And he ought to have notified her; the policy handbook he'd been given stated very clearly that any time a customer needed medical attention, no matter how minor the situation appeared, the matter was to be brought to management's attention. Minor ailments could become big ones, and the store could end up being held responsible, especially if there was no proof of what had actually been done for the customer.

Didn't Zack understand that rules weren't simply made for the fun of it, but for good reason? Just a couple of days ago he'd agreed to consult her on important matters—but already he was taking things into his own hands again.

"Too bad it's such seasonal work," Whitney was saying. "You could make a career of it."

"That's a thought. Maybe I could play St. Valentine next, and then a leprechaun. And I'm sure there's an opening for the Easter Bunny. The costume might be a little uncomfortable, though—all that heavy fur."

The band had begun to play by the time they finished their appetizers, and Max leaned across to Brandi and asked her to dance. There was nothing Brandi wanted less right then, but good manners forbade her to refuse.

The music was slow and easy, and she could look over Max's shoulder and see the two at the table deep in conversation. "I wonder what they're talking about," she said finally.

"Probably not the Easter Bunny. Beyond that, I haven't a clue."

Ross Clayton appeared beside them. "May I cut in, Max?"

Brandi waited till Max was out of hearing, and said, "What kind of hold has Zack Forrest got on you, Ross?"

"You mean like blackmail material?" Ross was obviously amused. "Why? What's he been telling you?"

"Nothing much. That's part of the problem." Brandi stopped herself just in time; it wasn't exactly prudent to complain to the boss about a difficulty she ought to be able to solve herself. "How well do you know this guy, Ross?"

"Pretty well. Don't worry—he's a bit of a free spirit, but perfectly harmless."

Brandi looked up at him through narrowed eyes. "I'm charmed to hear it," she murmured, and wondered what her personnel director would have said about that. Sending the Wishing Tree clients upstairs for job interviews was another thing she'd have to bring up the next time she got a chance to talk to Mr. Free Spirit in private; he apparently thought he was running an employment agency. "He seems to be enjoying the Wishing Tree, at any rate."

"I think he'd like to be more involved," Ross went on.

"Oh, don't worry about that." Brandi's voice dripped irony. "He does just fine at minding other people's business."

Zack tapped Ross's shoulder. "Something tells me I'm being discussed," he murmured. "Ross, did Brandi tell you the manager of Toyland wants me to replace him when he retires after Christmas? No? I didn't think she would." He slid an arm around Brandi just as the music changed to a soft, slow, romantic beat, and drew her close.

"I didn't tell him because I didn't know it." Brandi missed a step, and Zack's arm tightened a little more.

She was feeling a little light-headed, but she wasn't sure if it was because of the intimate way he was holding her or the announcement he'd made. The idea of having Zack around on a more or less permanent basis was enough to make any store manager lose her grip, that was sure.

She lifted her chin. It was uncomfortable to look straight at him when he was holding her so close. "The only thing he's said to me is that you're running him off his feet with special orders for oddball toys."

"I know. He's extremely proud of me. The increased volume alone—"

"Oh, really? I thought he sounded plenty worried. It'll

be wonderful if everything comes in, of course—but what if it doesn't, Zack? We're going to have a lot of unhappy parents and infuriated kids.''

"So that means we shouldn't try? I didn't make promises, you know.''

Brandi shook her head. "Sometimes it doesn't matter how carefully you say it, customers still think you've promised. Maybe I'll just put you in charge of complaints, and then you'll have to deal with the mess you've made.''

"Do you always assume it's going to be a mess, Brandi?'' His voice was easy, almost casual.

The question startled her a bit. "Of course not. The store would never get anywhere if I had that attitude. We'd never try anything new.''

"So your hesitation only applies to me?''

"You must admit you're a bit more challenging than the average employee, Zack.''

He didn't smile as she'd expected he would. A moment later, he said, "Can we leave business for another day and just enjoy the party?''

Brandi shrugged. "I'm enjoying myself as it is.'' She was a bit surprised to find that she was telling the exact truth, and also a little concerned that Zack might think she meant it was his presence that pleased her so much. "I mean—''

"Are you happy, Brandi?''

Happy? That was an odd question. "If you mean does the blood sing joyfully in my veins every single minute of my life, no. But I'm content. I like my job—''

"Is that all you want? All you need? Are you satisfied to be just content?''

"I have goals, of course,'' she said a bit stiffly. "But you said you didn't want to talk about business. What do you mean anyway? Not many people are all that wildly happy, you know. Simply being content isn't a bad thing at all.''

"It's not enough for me. I want the world—all the wild swings and the breathless joy and the overwhelming ecstasy there is to be had.''

Brandi shook her head. "Sounds uncomfortable.''

"At least it's never boring.''

"Just because something's consistent doesn't make it boring, Zack.''

He was silent, as if he was thinking that over.

Brandi decided the conversation had gotten a bit too serious. Why was it that talking about happiness could be so depressing anyway? "By the way, what did you do to the man from Seattle?''

He smiled. "Nothing much. I simply introduced him to the sultry lady clothing buyer from Atlanta.''

"Was that before or after you switched the place cards?''

"I'm wounded, Brandi. I didn't do that—he did.''

"At your suggestion?''

"Well, I did tell him where everyone was sitting,'' Zack admitted. "Don't take it personally, though—she really is very attractive, and he hadn't caught so much as a glimpse of you at that point.''

"I'm surprised, if she's such a stunner, that you didn't reserve her for yourself,'' Brandi said sweetly.

Zack slanted a look down at her and smiled, and Brandi's heart seemed to turn over. She couldn't look away, and for an instant, her body felt numb and completely out of her control. She stumbled, and Zack drew her closer still. She could feel his breath stirring the hair at her temple, and the warmth of his hand seemed to melt the black velvet at her waist. She wanted to stretch up on her toes and kiss that delightful dimple in his cheek, and then close her eyes and let her head droop against his shoulder and forget the party in order to lose herself completely in him.

She had to use the last bit of common sense she possessed to tear her gaze from his face and turn her head away. She realized gratefully that the waiter had returned to their table with their entrées.

Zack had seen, too. "Mighty inconvenient timing," he murmured as he guided her to the edge of the floor.

Brandi pretended not to hear, but her pulse was thumping madly. What had he been thinking just then? she wondered. And if they hadn't been in the middle of a crowded room, what might he have done?

As they sat down once more, Whitney studied them with an impartial, level gaze. It wasn't an unfriendly look, just an appraising one. Still, it made Brandi a bit nervous, and she tried to laugh as she said, "You usually look at things that way when you're considering damage control."

Whitney didn't answer. Instead she said, "I hear you had some excitement at the store the other night."

"You mean our robber?" Brandi tried a bit of her prime rib; it was so tender that the weight of the knife was almost enough to cut it. "I suppose next we'll have to start combat training for all employees."

"It's got to be a fluke," Whitney said.

"Would you want to take a chance?"

Zack said, "How's the employee doing?"

"Incredibly well, from what I can see." Brandi put her fork down. "I went to visit her this afternoon, and she insisted she'll be back to work tomorrow."

"So soon?"

"Don't look at me that way, Zack. I suggested she take a few extra days off, but she thinks the longer she stays away the more difficult it will be to come back, and it's hard to argue with that logic.''

"Especially when you're short of help," Zack murmured.

"Exactly." It was the perfect opening to mention his habit of sending prospective employees up to personnel. "And as long as we're on the subject of employees, Zack..."

"Yes?"

Brandi thought better of it. That kind of discussion was far better held in private, and it seemed she'd lost any desire to delve into business tonight. "Never mind. We can talk about it later."

Zack smiled, and the talk moved on to other things. As soon as they'd finished dinner, he drew her back onto the dance floor. The band was playing a series of slow, soft, dreamy numbers, and Brandi had no idea what time it was when Zack shifted his hold on her in order to check his wristwatch.

"You don't have to do your last shift," she murmured.

Zack's voice was soft and lazy. "You *are* having a good time, aren't you? The store's been closed for hours. It's almost midnight."

"Really?" She was vaguely surprised that it didn't bother her much. "Are you afraid I'll turn into a pumpkin when the clock strikes twelve?"

"Do you usually?" He didn't wait for an answer. "The kids were planning to drive their baby-sitter nuts by trying to stay awake all night, and I told them I'd peek in at the stroke of midnight to find out how the slumber party's going. Want to come?"

She didn't even hesitate. "All right."

The room he'd come from much earlier that evening was quiet and shadowed now, the only light falling from a night-light on a desk in the corner. It was obviously a boy's room; he was curled up in the top bunk, under a coverlet decorated with cowboys. In the bottom bunk, surrounded by a couple of dozen dolls and stuffed toys, was the little girl Brandi had seen earlier. Her rosy cheeks were flushed, and her cheek was pillowed on the fat tummy of a furry panda bear. She'd kicked off her frilly quilt.

Zack tucked it back around her. "Baby-sitter one, kids zero," he murmured. "I didn't think they'd make it to midnight."

Brandi studied the softness in his face. "You're very attached to them, aren't you?"

"They're very special kids." He gave a last pat to the cowboy quilt and drew Brandi back into the hallway. In the quiet little nook at the top of the stairs he stopped and turned her to face him.

Almost automatically, Brandi put her hands on his chest—to keep a little distance between them, she thought. Or, perhaps, so she could feel his warmth and the strong beat of his heart through her palms.

Even in the dim light, the diamond cluster on her left hand sparkled. Zack caught her hand and turned it to watch the stones at play. Then he said quietly, "Allow me," and slid the ring from her finger. Brandi started to protest, but she hadn't finished forming the words when he slid it into place on her right hand instead. "That's much better," he murmured, and kissed the bare spot at the base of her engagement finger.

Brandi had never realized that was such a sensual spot. She gasped a little, and Zack let go of her hands and drew her into his arms.

In the space of an instant, Brandi considered all the reasons she shouldn't let him do this. Then she dismissed them. She relaxed into his embrace and raised her hands to cup his face and draw him down to her.

This was very different from the other times he'd kissed her. This time he seemed almost hungry, as if only she could satisfy the needs he felt, and the sensation rocked Brandi to her bones.

She didn't know how long he kissed her, only that it seemed forever and still wasn't long enough. When Zack raised his head, his voice was almost hoarse. "I need to talk to you. But this isn't the time or the place."

She couldn't speak; her throat had closed up. She shook her head, meaning to agree that this was hardly the best choice for a heart-to-heart discussion, but before she could do more, they heard footsteps coming up the stairs, and they moved apart just in time.

"There you are, Zack," said a jovial voice. Brandi didn't recognize the man; he must be one of the Claytons' friends, not a Tyler-Royale executive. "How are you enjoying the toy business? I wanted to ask you—"

Zack made an impatient gesture, as if to cut him short. Brandi knew exactly what he was feeling; she would have little patience right now with another discussion of bookkeeping systems. What she needed was a few minutes by herself to clear her head. "Excuse me," she murmured.

"I'll wait for you downstairs," Zack said, and Brandi slipped away for a moment to the cloakroom.

Whitney was seated at the dressing table, tipping her lashes with mascara. She looked at Brandi in the mirror, and her eyes narrowed slightly.

As if, Brandi thought guiltily, she can see the kisses still burning on my lips.

Whitney replenished her mascara wand and leaned closer to the mirror. "I should probably bite my tongue

off rather than say this,'' she murmured, ''but watch out
for Zack.''

Brandi didn't look at her; she dug through her bag in
search of a lipstick. ''Why? Don't you like him?''

''Of course I like him. Everyone likes him; he's perfectly charming, just as most love-'em-and-leave-'em guys
are. But you never know what's he's up to. This whole
Santa episode makes no sense whatever.''

Brandi carefully outlined her lips. As casually as she
could, as if it didn't matter, she said, ''I thought maybe
he was really working for Ross as the new troubleshooter
or something.''

Whitney gave a genteel little snort. ''I doubt you'd ever
catch Zack doing anything that responsible.'' She snapped
the catch of her handbag. ''Watch out, Brandi.'' She left
the room without waiting for an answer.

For a couple of minutes, Brandi was alone in the cloakroom, but then it began to fill once more. The laughter and
heavy mix of perfumes made her head start to ache, and
she went back out to the hallway.

Zack had already gone down to the party; the shadowed
little nook at the top of the stairs was empty. Brandi paused
for a second at the top of the steps, trying to regain her
mental balance, when she heard a voice from the room
across the hall from the cloakroom.

It was Whitney's voice, low and urgent, with a hard
edge that made the hairs at the nape of Brandi's neck rise.

''What's going on, Ross?'' Whitney said. ''Zack
wouldn't tell me the reasons, but I've mentored Brandi for
years, and I have a right to know. Why have you planted
Zack in that store?''

CHAPTER EIGHT

BRANDI'S hand closed on the newel post with a grip so tight it should have hurt, but she was too stunned to notice.

Just two nights ago she'd asked Zack if he'd been sent to investigate her store, and he'd denied it. He'd said straight out that the problems he was dealing with had nothing to do with the store, or with her. His troubles were his own, he'd said; the store was performing beautifully....

At least, that was what he'd seemed to say. And then he'd kissed her so intensely and thoroughly that Brandi had stopped thinking about her suspicions. She wondered now if that was why he'd kissed her—because it was the simplest way to distract her from an inconvenient line of thought. It had been a very effective move, if so.

But Zack had been lying. Or perhaps he had told the literal truth, but phrased his words so carefully that she'd missed the underlying reality. It didn't make any difference, really, which it was—the intent had been to deceive.

Or was it possible instead that Whitney was simply wrong?

Brandi seized on that explanation with relief. It was easier to dismiss Whitney's intuition and business experience than to believe Zack had lied to her. Whitney's judgment was at fault, that was the problem. For some reason Brandi didn't understand, Whitney had taken a dislike to Zack, and she was willing to believe the worst of him.

Now it all made sense.

Brandi had actually taken the first step on her way downstairs when Ross said quietly, ''I have my reasons,

Whitney. And I'm not able to discuss them with you at this point.''

The words hit Brandi with the force of a pile driver. Then Whitney's suspicions, and her own, were the truth.

Zack had lied.

Before she could recover her balance, Brandi heard the creak of a hinge as the bedroom door started to open. Ross and Whitney were coming out.

Brandi couldn't risk meeting them just now. She was in no shape to confront her boss and ask for an explanation—not on a matter of this much importance. And she was not up to seeing concern and perhaps pity in her friend's eyes, either.

But she couldn't just run downstairs. She couldn't brave meeting Zack at this moment; she didn't have enough self-control for that. She would need a chance to sort out her thoughts before she did anything at all.

Without making a conscious decision, Brandi fled back to the cloakroom and extracted her coat from the pile on the bed. She waited a couple of minutes, giving Ross and Whitney a chance to return to the party, and then tried to make herself invisible as she slipped down the stairs. If she could just get outside before anyone noticed...

But luck wasn't with her. She was almost at the front door when Ross called, ''Brandi! You're leaving already?''

She turned, keeping her head down and drawing her shoulders up till the high collar of her coat hid a good part of her face. ''It's been a lovely party,'' she said, ''but I'm sure you'll forgive me for ducking out. I've got another long day tomorrow.'' Her voice was huskier than she'd have liked, but she hoped he wouldn't notice. He didn't argue, and she nodded a goodbye and went outside.

The temperature seemed to have dropped like a rock

during the hours she'd been inside—or perhaps it was just that shock and fear had made her more sensitive to the cold. As Brandi stood on the curb and waited for the valet to bring her car, she tried not to look over her shoulder. With any luck at all, Zack would still be waiting for her in the party rooms, unaware that she was running away.

Which was, she freely admitted, exactly what she was doing.

I need to talk to you, he'd said. Brandi wondered what he'd been planning to tell her. Would he confess? And if so, what sort of explanation would he have for why he had lied to her before?

Maybe tomorrow she could listen to him. Right now, she'd probably start screaming.

She could see her breath, but by the time the valet returned with her car, Brandi had stopped feeling the cold. No amount of chill in the air could match the frigid brittleness deep inside her.

Even the long drive across the city with the car's heater running full blast didn't warm her up. Once inside her apartment, she lit the gas fire with shaking fingers, and huddled in front of it.

Just a couple of hours ago she had been happier than she had been in years, so happy that all sense of time had vanished in the enjoyment of Zack's company, of the warm security of his arms around her, of the delicious sense that the world was a saner place when she was with him.

But he had lied to her, and now all the freedom, the enjoyment, the hope that she had thought he represented were gone.

Only once before in her life had she felt this confused, this upset, this frozen. Once before she had given her trust, and she had been betrayed.

But that time, she had believed that she had known the man she trusted. As it turned out, she'd been wrong, and the disillusionment she'd suffered had kept her from making the same mistake for years afterward. In fact, she'd thought the memory of her pain would keep her from repeating that particular error forever.

But it hadn't. In fact, this mistake was worse, if anything. She had never allowed herself to believe that she knew Zack at all—but still she had allowed herself to trust in him, to believe that he was different, special. The kind of man she could truly care about.

Brandi sat beside the fire, listening to the soft hiss and crackle of the flame, smelling the sharp pine fragrance of the garland Zack had so carefully fitted over the mantel two nights ago, and staring at the diamond-cluster ring that he had moved from her left hand to her right. It had been such a romantic gesture—such a touching, world-shaking signal that he was serious about her.

Oh, he was serious all right, she reflected. Serious about deceiving her.

She tugged the ring loose and put it back on the hand where it belonged. The hand where it would stay.

Brandi was in the store early the next day, though she had to admit that her almost-sleepless night had left her with less than her usual concentration.

She normally enjoyed Sunday mornings. The quiet hour before the employees started to come in was a perfect opportunity to walk through every department, undistracted by customer problems or employee concerns. On her normal walk-throughs, she was watching her people as much as the store itself. On Sundays she could concentrate on the merchandise, keeping a sharp eye out for displays that looked tired, mannequins that sagged, stacks that had been pushed out of line. It was tiny details like these that made Tyler-Royale stand out among other department stores, and Brandi was determined her store was going to be the cream of the crop.

But today it took effort to focus on the job. The store was too quiet, and her mind kept slipping back to the party the night before. Surprisingly, though, it wasn't only the abrupt end of the evening that seemed imprinted on her mind, but the earlier fun. Even the night before, with the pain still fresh and raw, whenever she had managed to close her eyes it hadn't been the shock at the top of the stairs she remembered, but the hypnotic rhythm of dancing with Zack....

And that kind of thinking, she told herself, was going to get her precisely nowhere.

She pulled her mind back to the task at hand. They were halfway through the Christmas season, and the biggest shopping days of the year were still to come. Did the store have enough stock in the areas that were selling best? Was there an excess of certain merchandise? If so, perhaps it should be marked down to speed its sale, or perhaps offered to other stores in the chain where the demand might be heavier.

The computer in her office would give her the numbers, of course, but Brandi had long ago learned to put more faith in her instinct than in statistics.

She paid particular attention to Toyland, since it was the busiest single department at this time of year. The stock was starting to drop, she noted, but so far there seemed no shortages anywhere. Extra supplies of toys and games were no longer stacked clear to the ceiling, but the regular shelves were still full and inviting.

She wondered which displays Zack was responsible for rearranging. He'd said something about games, hadn't he?

There was a pile of board games laid out in an eye-catching pattern at the end of an aisle.

Not that it mattered, she told herself, and went on to electronics and housewares before she could dwell on the subject of Zack.

Before Brandi was quite finished with her tour, employees were coming in. The lights came up, the Christmas carols began to play, and soon the great doors opened and the first wave of customers poured in. Sundays during the Christmas season were always busy, but this was a particularly hectic day. Shopping urges that had been pent up by the week's snowstorm seemed to have been released in a frenzy.

Every department seemed to be overrun, and Brandi found herself pitching in on the floor, greeting customers in the atrium entrance, directing them to the merchandise they wanted, even ringing up sales for a while in the ladies' active-wear department, when Casey Amos and her new trainee—the woman Zack had discovered in the parking lot the night of the snowstorm—got behind.

Theresa Howard was apologetic. "I'm sorry I'm so slow, Ms. Ogilvie," she said. "Sometimes I think I'm all thumbs and I'll never learn this job."

Brandi smiled. "Casey and I have trained a lot of people," she reassured the woman. "You're doing just fine."

Finally the pressure let up. She showed Theresa Howard how to greet three customers at a time and still make each of them feel valuable, and then retreated to the executive floor, where the paperwork she'd intended to do before the store opened still waited.

But as she passed the customer service department, just down the hall from her office, Brandi saw that the two representatives were being run off their feet settling problems and wrapping packages. There was not only a line waiting for help, but a woman who wanted to apply for Wishing Tree assistance. Brandi took her off to a corner and went to work.

Where was Zack when she needed him? she thought irritably. There wasn't time to check the schedule to see if he was due to come in today—but she rather thought he was. She seemed to remember that the kooky schedule she'd arranged hadn't given him a single day off. Though, since she *had* told him last night that the schedule was more flexible than it implied, perhaps he'd decided to go back to setting his own hours.

Or maybe he didn't intend to come in to work at all. Maybe Whitney's question to Ross had tipped a balance somehow, and now that the secret was at least partially out, there was no further point in having Zack play his role.

Brandi wondered for the thousandth time what had happened last night after she'd left the party, and how long Zack had waited for her.

The client said hesitantly, "Excuse me?" and Brandi pulled herself away from the fascination of imagining the look on Zack's face when he realized she wasn't coming back.

"I really appreciate this, you know," the client said. "It's—well, it's the only way we'd have a Christmas, through the generosity of other people." Her voice was thick with emotion.

Brandi smiled sympathetically, but she didn't answer; she knew how close the woman was to tears. Instead she said gently, "What about you? Now that we've got the kids' lists made, what would you like?"

The woman shook her head. "Oh—nothing. The best gift for me will be if people care a little about my kids."

Brandi looked down at the form she had just finished

filling out, and her eyes began to prickle uncontrollably. It was such a simple list—warm jeans and boots for a couple of little boys, and a snowsuit and a baby doll for a three-year old. "You'll get everything on your list," she said firmly.

A sudden tingle in the back of her neck warned her that Zack was somewhere around. She sneaked a look through her lashes and spotted him near the door of the employees' lounge. He was leaning against the wall and watching her.

Brandi found herself feeling hot and cold all over, and all at the same time. She tried not to look at him again, but it was impossible to keep her gaze from straying in his direction.

No Santa suit today. He was still dressed for the street, in a black leather jacket and jeans. His garb was the most casual she'd seen him wear, and it made him look tougher somehow—as if he no longer needed to project a sophisticated veneer.

The client thanked her, gave Brandi's hand a fierce squeeze, and left.

Brandi stacked the papers she'd filled out in a folder, fussing till she had them lined up just right. She didn't see Zack leave the lounge area and come toward her. She didn't have to; she could feel his closeness as easily as if she'd suddenly sprouted radar antennae.

He didn't take the chair across from her where the client had sat, but leaned against the table beside her instead, his hip almost brushing her arm. "Now who's making rash promises?" he said.

She tried to keep things casual. "It wasn't rash. I'll take care of it myself. You needn't even put those stars on the tree."

"Shopping and everything? You amaze me, Brandi."

She could feel his warmth, but there was no place to

move. Her chair was already against the wall, and the dominating position he'd assumed not only blocked her from slipping past him but made her feel tiny and helpless.

Though Brandi wasn't about to admit that; no one was going to bully her simply by sitting on the edge of a table and looking down his nose. "The manager of the supermarket down at the other end of the mall offered to fix food baskets for our Wishing Tree people," she said. "You might want to go talk to him about it."

Zack nodded. He didn't speak, and he didn't move.

"I suppose you'd like to look over the application?" Brandi held out the folder. "I hope I did it to your standards."

Zack didn't reach for the paperwork. He folded his arms across his chest instead and looked down at her. She followed his gaze; he was looking at the diamond cluster on her left hand, and there was a shuttered wariness in his eyes that she'd never seen before.

She put the folder down. "Don't look at me like that, please. You know, I wouldn't have objected if you'd wanted to take over that job—it is your department after all."

"You were obviously almost finished." His voice had a rough edge. "Besides, I didn't want to take the chance that you'd scream and run if I approached you too suddenly."

"What?" Brandi was honestly at a loss.

"You didn't seem to want to talk to me last night," he reminded her.

"Well, I certainly wouldn't scream and run here."

"Oh, that's right." There was an edge of irony in his tone. "We're in the store now, and all the rules are different."

She watched him warily. He sounded angry—no, it was

more than that. There was a tinge of bitterness in his voice, and that made Brandi furious. Did he honestly expect that he could lie to her and get away with it forever?

She was aware that the crush at the customer service counter had abated, leaving the clerks free to observe. She should probably take him back to her office and close the door and have it out.

Before she could suggest it, though, Zack said softly, ''Why did you run away last night?''

She couldn't deny it, for it was true, she had run. But she wasn't going to let him put her on the defensive. ''I don't owe you any explanations, Zack.''

''What the hell does that mean? Of course you owe me an explanation! How do you think I felt when I discovered you'd slipped out without even telling me?''

''Guilty, maybe?'' Brandi guessed.

There was a flicker in his eyes, as if the jab had struck deep into his soul. His voice grew softer, but it was no less resolute. ''I told you I needed to talk to you, and you promptly vanished. Were you afraid to hear what I had to say, so you ran?''

''Maybe I just wasn't ready to listen to another round of lies just then.''

''Lies?'' The softness had vanished. ''Dammit, Brandi—''

''Oh, come off it, Zack! The innocent act might still be convincing if I hadn't heard Ross telling Whitney last night that he planted you in my store.''

''He said *what*?'' Zack sounded astonished.

''She asked him why he'd put you in this store,'' Brandi said impatiently, ''and he said he wasn't at liberty to tell her. Now correct me if I'm wrong, Zack, but a few days ago I asked you the same question, and you denied it— right?''

He shook his head a little, more in confusion than denial. "You asked me if I was Ross's troubleshooter, and I said no, I'm not. Which is the absolute truth."

"Oh, I beg your pardon! Perhaps I got the details a little askew, but—"

"I'm not here because of Ross, Brandi."

"Oh, really?" Her voice dripped sarcasm. "I suppose I imagined him telling me to hire you?"

"I mean, he suggested this particular store. But playing Santa was my idea."

"Well, maybe you should tell me what this is all about!" She didn't realize how shrill she sounded until she noticed both of the customer service representatives watching her intently, mouths ajar.

"I tried last night," Zack said. "You wouldn't listen."

Maybe he had intended to tell her, she thought wearily. She'd have to give him the benefit of the doubt on that question. "Well, I'm all ears now."

Zack glanced over his shoulder at the customer service representatives. "You and a lot of other people," he said dryly. "Perhaps we could go into your office?"

They were in Dora's alcove when the manager of Toyland came bursting out of the elevator. "Ms. Ogilvie!" he called. "There you are! I've been trying to find you."

Brandi paused. "What is it?"

"Not now," Zack said through gritted teeth. "Can't you, just once, let the store go to hell?"

She glared at him. "When I've got an undercover agent standing right here? Of course not!"

"And Zack," the department manager said with relief. "Man, am I glad to see you." He seized Zack's arm with both hands.

"If you're short a clerk, I'm sorry," Zack began. "But—"

The manager shook his head. "It's a whole lot worse than that. This afternoon's Santa came in to work all right, but he's in the dressing room now—as sick as anyone I've ever seen."

"The flu?" Brandi asked.

"Sure looks like it. He's far too sick to do his job— he'd expose every kid in the store to this bug. But there's a line from here to the moon waiting to talk to Santa. Zack, you'll help me out, won't you? I've got to have a Santa!"

Zack didn't answer.

Brandi looked up at him. His gaze was dark and steady and watchful, as if he was asking a silent question.

But there could be only one answer; the needs of the store came first. "I'll have to ask you to pitch in," she said levelly. "We'll talk later, Zack."

"You can bet on that." There was a steel thread underlying his voice.

Brandi put her chin up. "Believe me, I'm as eager as you are to get this sorted out. But in the meantime, look on the positive side. You'll have all afternoon to get your story straight!"

Brandi made it a point to be highly visible for the rest of the business day. Zack was not going to be able to accuse her of hiding away in her office. Besides, though she wouldn't have admitted it to him, she couldn't have settled down to her regular work if her life had depended on it.

Her mind was going a million miles a minute, trying to anticipate his explanation—but she couldn't think of any that made sense.

If he *wasn't* in the store because of Ross…but Ross had said quite plainly…

Give it up, Brandi, she told herself finally. She'd simply

have to wait till she heard his side of it and make her judgment then.

She got caught up in a crowd on the escalator and her white carnation was smashed. She was in the employees' lounge, digging through the refrigerator for a replacement, when a couple of clerks came in to put their names into the jar for the Christmas gift exchange. "You're going to be in it this year, aren't you, Ms. Ogilvie?" one of them asked. "It's just good fun."

Brandi shook her head, but after the clerks were gone she pinned her flower in place and thought of what the Wishing Tree client had said—about how the best gift would be knowing that people cared.

Maybe she should take part, she thought. It was such a simple little thing. And it was Christmas after all—the time for caring.

Before she had a chance to argue herself out of it, she'd written her name on one of the little cards Casey Amos had left beside the jar and dropped it in.

She walked through Toyland several times during the afternoon, watching the line inching past Santa's Workshop, and happened to be there for the big stir of the day, when a couple brought in their infant quadruplets, dressed in identical red velvet suits, for their first visit with Santa.

"Makes quite a picture, doesn't it?" a bystander asked Brandi, chuckling at the sight. "Santa's got his hands full, holding all four of 'em at once."

She nodded and leaned against the fence to watch. The babies were three months old, their mother told her, and for a moment Brandi lost herself in sheer enjoyment not only of their antics but the way Zack handled them. The babies wriggled, made faces, and yanked at his beard; Zack watched them with a tenderness in his face that tugged at Brandi's heart.

Then he looked up and caught her eye, and the tenderness faded, to be replaced with something that looked more like a challenge—and Brandi stepped away from the fence and almost tripped over her own feet in her eagerness to be away.

Last night he had held her and kissed her, and he had seemed to say that he had serious feelings about her. For why would a man move a ring from her left hand, unless he intended to make room for a more important one?

But today...today he had looked at her almost with scorn.

Closing time approached, and the crowds began to thin. Brandi waited beside the perfume counter nearest the main entrance till a customer turned away with a bag full of fragrances.

The clerk was back at work as she had promised. Brandi thought she looked a little shaky, as if she wasn't quite over her shock. That would be no surprise, she thought, and wondered if she should have refused permission to let the woman come back just yet.

But the clerk greeted her with a wide smile. "It's good to be back," she said. "I wondered if I'd have the jitters all day, but it hasn't been bad at all. Of course, it's been busy, and that helps."

The clerk turned away to help a customer, a long-haired young woman wearing faded jeans and a canvas vest, its pockets stuffed with odds and ends. "I'd like an ounce of Sensually Meghan," she said, and pulled a credit card out of her back pocket.

Brandi's eyebrows went up just a fraction of an inch. The woman didn't look like the Sensually Meghan type— that particular scent cost three hundred dollars an ounce these days. It was just another example demonstrating that customers couldn't be judged by appearance. She made a mental note to mention the incident at the next full staff meeting as encouragement to her employees not to jump to conclusions based on a customer's clothes.

The clerk was processing the charge when the customer asked, "How long does it usually take after closing for all the people to clear out of the mall?"

Brandi's sixth sense started to quiver. "On Sundays, not long," she said. "Why?"

The woman smiled at her. "It is an odd question, isn't it? We work for an advertising agency." She gestured toward the main entrance, where two men with video cameras waited. "We'll be shooting footage for ads for the mall."

Brandi relaxed. Really, she thought, since the robbery attempt, I'm starting to get paranoid.

"We don't want our equipment to get in the way," the young woman went on, "but frankly, we're not wild about working Sunday nights, either, so if we time it just perfectly we can shoot and get out and not annoy anyone."

"I think I'd get started setting up," Brandi advised. "If you're off to the side of the main doors, no one will trample you."

"Hey, thanks." The customer stuck her expensive perfume carelessly into a pocket and headed for the entrance.

"You just never know, do you?" the clerk said.

The public address system crackled to life and announced that the store was now closed, and the clerk began to clear the cash register. Brandi dug out her keys and went to shut the big metal gates that barricaded the Tyler-Royale store from the rest of the mall.

She stopped the gate just short of full closure to allow procrastinating shoppers an exit, and watched the camera crew setting up their tripods and lights just outside the store.

But her mind wasn't on them, but on the coming confrontation with Zack.

Thinking of him seemed to have the power to conjure him up, for just a couple of minutes after the closing announcement she saw him coming down the now-stationary escalator. He was still wearing his Santa suit.

"I'd have waited for you to change," she said as he came up to her.

"Then I will. I saw you hovering down here as if you were ready to run, and I thought perhaps—"

He broke off as a scream sliced through the air.

Brandi looked around frantically. The only thing she was certain of was that the sound hadn't originated anywhere inside Tyler-Royale. Sound echoed oddly in the huge open mall, however, and the scream could have come from a hundred places.

Just outside the gate, a member of the camera crew said, "What the—"

Another scream sounded, and a man erupted from the cookie and snack shop next door to Tyler-Royale and started down the length of the mall at a dead run. Under his arm was what looked like a brown paper bag.

The perfume clerk gasped, "That's the guy who tried to rob me!"

Zack shot one look at the clerk, pushed Brandi out of his way, and took off after the robber.

Propelled by the push, Brandi collided with the metal gate and grabbed the rods to keep herself upright. She was shrieking something; she thought it was his name.

Time seemed to stretch out in slow motion as she clung to the gate and watched the chase. Ever so slowly, stride by stride, Zack gained on the man with the bag, till with one final lunge he slammed a shoulder into the robber's back, and the two of them went down together onto the hard tile floor.

As they rolled, Brandi saw the flash of metal in the robber's hand. Was he holding a knife? A gun?

In her terror for Zack, she screamed again. It was a useless warning for him, but a blinding revelation for her.

As the two man grappled for the weapon, Brandi knew, with the terrible clarity that sometimes comes with shock, that it didn't matter to her what Zack had done, or who he was, or why he was in her store. Or even whether he had lied to her after all.

That was all unimportant, less than nothing beside the fact that somehow, while she wasn't even looking—much less protecting herself—Zack Forrest had crept into her heart.

Last night she had been hurt by the discovery that she had let herself trust him despite her lack of knowledge of what he really was. Now that discovery paled beside the blinding realization that this was not only a man she could care about if the circumstances worked out just right, but the one and only man she loved.

CHAPTER NINE

THE struggle in the mall could only have lasted for a minute or two, but to Brandi it seemed to go on for years. Where were the mall security guards? she wanted to scream. What good did it do to have people on the staff if they weren't there when they were needed?

Finally, the guards converged on the pair in the hall. Two of them sat on the robber; another helped Zack stand up. Logic told Brandi he wasn't hurt after all, for the first thing he did was to dust off his red velvet suit.

Nevertheless, she was still shaking minutes later when the camera crew came triumphantly down the corridor. She hadn't even noticed they were gone, and she paid little attention to the video cassette the young woman in the canvas vest was waving over her head.

"What a piece of action!" she was saying. "We'll be on the news on every station in greater Chicago. Santa Claus busts a robber, and we've got it on tape!" She grinned at Brandi. "What can you tell me about your Santa—besides that he's in great shape under the velvet suit?"

Brandi noticed with almost clinical detachment that each of her fingertips was quivering to a different rhythm. "Not much," she said. "His name's Zack Forrest, and he's a temporary employee, just for the season. That's all I really can—"

"Zack Forrest?"

Something about the woman's tone made Brandi's eyes narrow in suspicion. "That's what I said, yes."

"You mean the toycoon?"

"What did you call him?"

"*Toycoon*. It's the nickname Wall Street gave him last spring when he bought Intellitoys. You know, the educational-toy maker."

The little oxygen still in Brandi's lungs rushed out with a whoosh. *How's the toy business*? one of their fellow guests had asked Zack last night. Brandi had thought the guest meant the Santa job.... Zack owned a toy company?

"We were shooting an ad for one of their new products last week," the young woman went on, "and I did my research. I wonder what he's up to? Why's he playing Santa anyway?"

From the corner of her eye, Brandi glimpsed a red suit, and she turned around to get a better look.

Zack's hair was ruffled, and his fake beard hung askew. He'd lost his velvet cap in the fracas, and he sounded as if he was still a little breathless. "I'm just doing my volunteer stint for the children," he said, and smiled at the woman who held the videotape.

Brandi was torn between the desire to fling her arms around him and kiss the dimple in his cheek in gratitude that he was safe, or slap him across the face as hard as she could for taking a foolish risk.

"Perhaps I'm being immodest to ask," Zack went on, "but am I the star of that videotape you're waving around?"

The young woman grinned. "Yeah. You can watch yourself on TV tonight—I bet every station in the city will want this. Maybe even the networks."

"Ah," Zack said knowingly. "Doing a little moonlighting, are you?"

"Anything wrong with that?" A defensive note crept into the woman's voice. "There's no clause in my contract with the advertising agency that forbids me to make a little money on the side.''

"Of course there's nothing wrong with a little enlightened capitalism," Zack soothed. "Though, as long as the tape's for sale…" He reached for his wallet. "How much do you think they'll pay? And how many stations are there?"

The woman told him, and then looked at him incredulously while Zack counted a series of bills into her hand.

"There," he said. "And a little extra for good measure. You've turned a profit, and this way you don't even have to mess around making copies for all the stations." The videotape vanished into a capacious pocket of the red velvet suit, and Zack looked around with a smile. "I think you might want to reschedule your regular business, though. It looks as if the mall will be tied up for a while tonight."

In the meantime, Brandi saw, the police had arrived in force. She watched while they cordoned off the snack shop and the videotape crew packed up their equipment and left.

Only then did she speak, still without looking at Zack. "What are you planning to do with the videotape?"

"Haven't decided. But it was obviously a once-in-a-lifetime opportunity, so I thought I'd better grab it while I could."

"You could always show it at parties. I'm sure it would be a hit."

"Now that's a thought," Zack said agreeably. "People who don't know that's the most incompetent robber in the Western hemisphere would think I looked like a hero."

Brandi nodded. Her voice was perfectly calm. "That was a sizable amount of money you just handed over for someone who implied a few days ago that he couldn't quite keep up with the payments on his car."

Zack had the grace to look ashamed of himself.

Brandi didn't wait for an answer. She looked straight at him, and fury hardened her voice. "Dammit, Zack, why didn't you tell me who you are? Or what you do? Why the big secret?"

His tone was even and perfectly calm. "Because I didn't want to advertise the fact that Intellitoys is in big trouble."

She shook her head more in confusion than disagreement. It seemed such an inadequate reason.

A burly policeman came up to them. "Uh…Santa. We'll need a statement from you, sir."

For a moment Zack ignored him; he was watching Brandi. Finally he sighed and said, "I'll be back as soon as I can, Brandi."

"I'll be in my office."

It was more than an hour before he tapped perfunctorily on the door and came in. He'd taken the time to change clothes, she saw, and he was once more wearing the jeans and leather jacket he'd had on when they'd started this conversation earlier in the afternoon.

It felt to Brandi as if that had been a very long time ago. Back then, she'd known only that he had the power to hurt her. But she hadn't understood how deep that power ran, or how devastating the hurt could be. She hadn't yet realized that she loved him, and she hadn't begun to conceive of the deception he'd practiced.

Now she felt as if he'd torn her heart from her chest without bothering with anesthesia.

She'd been trying to concentrate on a supplier's catalog with little success. She put it down when Zack came in, but she didn't say a word.

Neither did Zack; he pulled a chair around and straddled it, his arms crossed on the back. Brandi wasn't surprised that he felt as if he needed a shield.

For a full minute it seemed as if they might sit that way forever. Silent as the confrontation was, however, the air between them seemed to sizzle.

When Zack finally spoke, it was almost as if he was picking up in the middle of a conversation. ''Intellitoys' advance orders for the Christmas season were reasonable,'' he said quietly. ''Not good, but acceptable. But as the holiday got closer, we started getting cancellations from stores because merchandise they already had on hand wasn't selling. And soon a fair performance was turning into a disaster. We could absorb a single season of low sales, even a Christmas season, but there was a larger problem—nobody seemed to know why the sales were down. And unless a company knows why it's not selling merchandise, next year is apt to be nothing but worse.''

Brandi fidgeted with a paper clip. She couldn't argue with that logic as far as it went. She just didn't understand what it was supposed to have to do with her.

''It was apparent to anyone with eyes that the marketing firm we were using didn't have a clue,'' Zack went on. ''They kept saying it was just a cyclical drop that would correct itself with time, but we haven't got that kind of time to play with. The company could be dead and buried by the time they'd admit they might be wrong.''

Brandi knew the helpless feeling he must have suffered—knowing action was required, but not knowing which direction to move.

''So I fired them,'' Zack said. ''It was an impulsive decision, I admit, but it left me no worse off than I was before.''

Brandi didn't intend to rescue him, but she couldn't help but agree with that philosophy. ''Bad information is worse than having none at all.''

Zack smiled approvingly, as if she were a particularly

bright student. "Very true. But firing the marketers didn't solve the problem, either—we still had to somehow find out what was going wrong. Why did kids suddenly not seem to want our products, and why had parents lost interest, as well?"

"So you decided to become a Santa?" Brandi shifted restlessly in her chair. "Pardon me for questioning your judgment, Zack, but there's more than one marketing firm in the world. Couldn't you just hire another one and use focus groups? Get a bunch of kids and parents into a room and ask them what they like? Putting on a red suit and a beard is just about the silliest—"

"Oh, is it really? Focus groups are no more honest than statistics, you know—it's not at all hard to skew the results, even with the best of intentions. I figured I'd ask the real authorities—the kids themselves, and the parents. And how better to get their honest feelings than to sit in Santa's chair?"

"It's not what you'd call a scientific sample."

"Scientific samples take time, which I haven't got. Right now, I don't need analysis, I need a gut reaction of what's wrong. Which, I might add, I started getting the first day I was out there."

"With a notebook," Brandi reflected.

"You'd better believe I was taking notes. I didn't want to forget a single comment because that's a good way to be led astray, too. It's easy to remember only what you want to."

"And you think you've got the answers?"

"No—but I know which direction we need to go." There was confidence in his voice.

Brandi sighed. There wasn't much point in arguing with him; Zack was convinced he'd taken the right course. In any case, it didn't matter, because his reasons for starting this masquerade weren't really important. "So why didn't you tell me what you were up to?" she asked softly.

He shook his head as if in disbelief of her innocence. "The stock-market wizards would have been on me like the sharks they are. With the first drop of blood, those guys go into a feeding frenzy. That in turn would have very nasty effects on my stockholders' confidence level."

"No doubt, but—"

"What would you think if the president of the biggest manufacturer of light bulbs in this country showed up at the corner drugstore demonstrating them, and asking people why they suddenly seemed to prefer other brands to his?"

Brandi shook her head. "No. You're telling me why you didn't want it known, and I understand all the reasons. But that's not what I asked, Zack. Why didn't you tell *me*?"

He seemed to be staring at his feet. "It was important that I be just an ordinary Santa," he said. "A working stiff with no stake in the answers I got. People are amazingly adaptable at telling a survey taker what they think he wants to hear. If I stood out in any way, it would affect what I was trying to accomplish."

As if this unlikely Santa hadn't stood out from the beginning, Brandi thought wryly. "And just what did you think I was apt to do? Call a press conference and announce your little project?"

"I didn't know you, Brandi," he said softly. "How could I possible have had the answer to that question?"

And what about later, she wanted to ask. What about after he'd had a chance to get to know her?

But too many of the possible answers to that question scared her. She didn't think she could stand to sit there, loving him as she did, and listen as he told her that he still didn't trust her to keep his secrets—at least, not enough to volunteer them without being forced.

And so she didn't ask.

"It was safer if you didn't know," Zack went on. "No one could get information out of you if you didn't know it in the first place."

The gentle note in his voice made her want to hit him; the desire was even stronger than it had been a couple of hours ago, right after that crazy stunt he'd pulled.

"Ross thought it was better if nobody knew. That way there couldn't be a slipup."

Brandi swallowed hard. "So Ross didn't trust me, either?"

"It's not that, Brandi. Honestly, it's not. But Ross is a major stockholder in Intellitoys, and if it got out that he was worried about the company…"

There was no need to finish that sentence. Once Wall Street got hold of that information, there would be nothing left of Intellitoys but splinters.

"Or, for that matter," Zack went on, "if the other toy companies that Tyler-Royale deals with discovered that Ross was favoring my business over theirs by using his stores as a laboratory, they'd be unhappy."

That was an understatement. Brandi knew from long experience what suppliers could be like if they thought someone else was getting an unfair break. She shivered.

"I see you understand the problem," Zack said. "Even Tyler-Royale's board of directors might well have had a collective fit. Maybe Ross was wrong to keep you out of the loop, Brandi—"

"*Maybe*? Didn't it occur to either of you that if I knew, it might keep me from saying something I shouldn't?"

"Yes. But you must admit, right or not, Ross had good reason for asking me to stay under wraps."

Brandi thought it over, and finally nodded. She still thought Ross and Zack had been wrong, but she didn't have to agree in order to understand.

But somehow, she thought, she was never going to feel quite the same about Ross Clayton again. And as for Zack…well, she'd have to think about that one for a good long time.

"So that's why Ross wouldn't tell Whitney what was going on," she mused.

"If he thought you didn't need to know," Zack said reasonably, "why would he be willing to tell Whitney?"

She couldn't argue with the logic of that, either, but it made her furious that she couldn't find a flaw in his reasoning.

Zack's voice was soft. "I wanted to tell you, Brandi, when you asked me about the troubleshooter and whether the store was in trouble. But it wasn't altogether up to me. You understand, don't you, that it was Ross's secret as much as mine? I couldn't spill it without warning him."

And that, Brandi thought wearily, told her exactly where she ranked, didn't it? Well down toward the bottom of his list.

Suddenly the office felt stuffy, as if they'd used up all the oxygen, and she felt an almost overpowering need to get out of the store and into the fresh cold air.

"Goodness knows I understand putting business first," Brandi said crisply. "In fact, it's nice to know that you have enough sense to do that—at least when it's *your* business that's concerned." She knew she sounded a bit catty, and she didn't care. "I think we've covered everything, don't you?" She stood up and came around the corner of the desk. It was the most obvious dismissal she could imagine.

Zack put a hand out toward her.

She took a half step back, well out of his reach. "Or is there something else you'd like to tell me, Zack?"

For a moment, his eyes looked cloudy, as if he was staring into the distance at something she couldn't see. Then his dark gaze focused once more on her face. "No."

"Then I suppose the only thing left is to agree on an explanation of why you're suddenly not playing Santa anymore."

Zack didn't move. "Why?"

"To avoid any uncomfortable questions, of course. Would you rather I say you've had a job offer you couldn't turn down, or that illness in the family called you away? Either way, I could imply you've gone out of state. Or maybe that's not far enough. How about out of the country?"

"I'm not planning to quit now, Brandi."

"You certainly can't keep on."

"Why not? I'm not finished. I told you I've got direction now, but not answers. Ross agreed with me that you'd have to know, but there's no need to bring anyone else into it."

"Wouldn't you be better off finishing your research somewhere else?"

Zack looked up at her for a long moment. His eyes had narrowed, and they looked darker than she'd ever seen them before. "You really want me to leave, don't you? Why, Brandi? Is it because I'm some kind of threat to your peace of mind?"

"A threat? To me? That's a joke." To her own ears, Brandi's voice lacked conviction. "But if you insist, stay. Goodness knows, I don't want to take chances with my career by making Ross mad at me."

Zack didn't seem to hear her. "You haven't answered

my question yet about why you didn't stick around and listen to me last night.''

She shrugged. ''The delay doesn't seem to have made much difference. Or isn't this what you were planning to tell me?''

He hesitated, and then said quietly, ''Not exactly.''

He no doubt meant he'd had an edited version in mind till he'd been caught out and had to tell the whole story. Well, that didn't surprise her. ''If you'll excuse me, Zack, I still have work to do.'' She sat down behind her desk again and picked up the catalog she'd been holding when he came in. She couldn't even remember what she'd been looking at.

He stood and slid the chair into position across from her. ''Then I'll see you tomorrow.''

Only if I don't see you first, Brandi thought.

If she'd had more energy, Brandi would have pulled the pine garland down from the mantel, shredded it needle by needle, and flung it like confetti over the rail of her apartment balcony to mulch the garden below.

If the fireplace had been real instead of merely a gas log, she'd have stuffed the garland in and set a match to it, and sent the whole thing up in one explosive puff of resin.

But perhaps it was just as well that she didn't; demolishing the garland might have been cathartic, but Brandi knew the memories it represented would not be so easily destroyed. As long as she lived, she would remember the night Zack had so carefully draped the greenery—and then kissed her, to cover up...not an outright lie, perhaps, but certainly a half truth.

Part of the trouble was that she truly understood the position he'd been in. He'd given his word in a matter of business, and an honorable man didn't go back on that. She understood that Zack had been caught in a situation where he couldn't—technically—do anything at all. He couldn't tell her the truth without first warning Ross, but he couldn't tell her anything else without lying, at least by implication.

The same thing had happened to her on occasion, and she'd handled it the same way. So how could she blame him for doing what he'd had to do?

But her heart still told her that if he had cared about her...

Stop tormenting yourself this way, she told herself. Loving wasn't always reciprocal—hadn't she learned even that much from Jason?

She'd cared desperately about him, that was sure. After it was over and the pain had receded, she'd realized that perhaps her desperation had been even stronger than her caring. She'd lost her mother not long before, and she'd needed someone to make her feel valuable, connected to the world. Jason had been quite happy to fulfil that role—as long as it was convenient, and as long as Brandi had required nothing more serious of him.

But Zack was different, and she'd known it at some level all along—even while she'd thought that the experience with Jason would keep her safe. Even when she'd thought Zack was just another careless, happy-go-lucky young man out for a good time with little thought for the future, somewhere deep inside her heart she'd recognized how different he was.

Jason would never have challenged her decisions, her orders, as Zack had; it would have been too much trouble. Jason had never fussed about the hours she worked, for it gave him time to tinker with his novel; Zack had seemed worried about her. Jason had often told her how proud he was of her independence; he would never have cared for her as tenderly as Zack had—taking her home, walking her to her car, making sure she wasn't alone at the party.

Jason had been a cardboard figurine. Only after he was gone from her life did Brandi realize how little she had known him, and how much of the man she thought she'd loved had been constructed from her own imaginative longings.

But Zack...Zack was a living, breathing, three-dimensional man. Sometimes difficult, often opinionated, always challenging.

But always lovable. That would never change.

On Tuesday, her secretary came into Brandi's office with a computer printout and a worried expression. "You know how we open a charge account automatically for every new employee?" she began.

Brandi nodded impatiently. "What about it, Dora?"

"We've got a new hire who's charged almost up to the limit."

Brandi put out a hand for the printout. "One of Zack's finds from the Wishing Tree project, no doubt?"

"No. It's Zack himself."

What a way to hide out, Brandi thought. For a man who said he wanted no special treatment—nothing that would distinguish him from the ordinary employee—Zack was hardly fading into the wallpaper. Of course, Zack could create a storm in a teacup and probably never realize it. He was so supremely confident of himself that he thought everyone else was just as self-assured.

But she wasn't going to get caught up in thinking about his attributes today, she reminded herself.

She ran an eye down the list. Most of the charges were on the small side, but there were a lot of them. No wonder

Dora's attention had been drawn to this; what was the man thinking of?

Brandi sighed. "I'll talk to him. In the meantime, I don't think you need to worry about it."

Dora looked doubtful, but she didn't argue. Brandi went back to work, but the printout on the corner of her desk seemed to be looking at her, and finally she couldn't stand it for another minute. She'd managed to avoid him since Sunday, but she would have to seek him out now.

It was the dinner hour, so he was apt to be down in Santa's Workshop, filling in during the break. She picked up the printout and took the escalator to the second floor.

The crowd was small tonight; in fact, just one man in a trench coat and a couple of small children were inside the fence that surrounded Santa's Workshop. The man was chatting with Zack while the kids climbed all over him.

She set the "Santa's Feeding His Reindeer" sign in place and closed the gate. Zack looked up as if her presence was magnetic, and Brandi felt her heartbeat flutter a little under his steady gaze.

The man in the trench coat turned, and only then did Brandi realize it was Ross Clayton. "Hi, Brandi. Is it time for Zack's dinner?"

"No. I just needed to talk to him a minute."

Ross grinned. "I'll get my angels out of the way, then. I'll give you a call this week, Brandi. There are a couple of things we need to talk about."

She nodded. No doubt Zack had told him how upset she was. Well, that was all right; she still had a few things to say to Ross about this whole affair, and the sooner the air was cleared, the better.

Zack slid the little girl off his knee and stood up. The child took two steps toward Brandi. "I remember you," she announced. "You were at the party."

Brandi nodded. "You have a very good memory, Kathleen."

The child nodded without self-consciousness. "Uncle Zack said maybe we could see you again and help put up your Christmas tree. Then he said he didn't think so after all. Why not?"

Brandi shot a glance at him. What had he been planning anyway?

Before Brandi could answer, Kathleen's brother, with the arrogance of a couple of extra years, announced, "Because it's too late, dummy. Everybody's got their Christmas trees up by now."

"Don't call your sister a dummy," Ross said.

"Even if she is?"

Ross gave Brandi a crooked grin. "See all the fun you're missing by not having kids?"

It was a teasing comment, of course, but Brandi watched them till they were out of sight. She felt lonely, as if she'd thrown away something she hadn't even looked at yet—and only now realized that it was too late to change her mind.

Uncle Zack said maybe we could see you again and help put up your Christmas tree…

Brandi closed her eyes and remembered her brief vision of a track set up under a decorated tree, with a couple of children watching blissfully as a train went round and round, and Zack—

Stop it, she told herself. Just stop it.

"I thought Ross didn't want them to see you in costume," she said.

"Oh, they overheard some talk about my new job, so he thought it would be better for them to see me in the role than use their imaginations."

"They seemed to take it well."

"Maybe it's the fact that I've been trying toys out on them for months, so it seems an appropriate job for me to have."

"I see." She stuck her hands in her pockets; her fingertips brushed the folded computer printout and reminded her of why she'd come downstairs. "I need to warn you that you've just about exhausted your credit limit. If you need an increase, I'm afraid you'll have to convince the credit manager that you have resources beyond what we're paying you." There was a faintly ironic note in her voice.

Zack ignored it. "That's all right. I didn't feel I should profit financially from this little experience, so I've been buying some extras for the Wishing Tree. I'll just turn over my paycheck to pay the bills, and we'll be square."

Brandi nodded. "All right." The public address system crackled to life, and Dora asked her to come to the office. Great timing, Brandi thought; she couldn't have planned it better if she'd tried. "I'll see you later, then."

She hadn't quite met his eyes the whole time she'd been standing there, and she didn't intend to. It would be not only too painful, but too revealing. But as she turned to leave, he said her name, and the note of longing in his voice sabotaged all her intentions.

"I've missed you," Zack said huskily.

Brandi couldn't deny the ring of truth in his voice. And she could see desire in his eyes. He wanted to kiss her, and every cell in her body knew it and was recalling precisely how it had felt to be in his arms, to be held and caressed and kissed till nothing mattered but him....

"I thought maybe we had something special," Zack said.

Brandi swallowed hard. "Not without some trust."

He nodded. "I was wrong not to tell you."

"You certainly were."

"I'm sorry."

Every nerve was tingling. Was he really saying what she thought he might be—what she hoped he was telling her—that these few days of separation had made him realize, as she had, that he cared? *I thought maybe we had something special*, he'd said. Was it possible there was a second chance after all?

The last remaining fragment of common sense reminded her that this wasn't exactly a private spot for a conversation, much less anything more. Zack certainly couldn't kiss her right outside Santa's Workshop, in full view of every kid and parent in Toyland. Could he?

She couldn't help it; the urge to sway toward him was an irresistible one.

At the gate, a child cried, "But there's Santa! He's not gone after all!" and sanity returned with a snap.

"Later," Zack said.

Brandi nodded and hurried away. He hadn't even touched her, but her skin was tingling as if electrical jolts were running through her. Later, she thought dreamily, when the store was closed and the kids were gone, they could explore what he'd meant. What they meant to each other.

In the alcove outside Brandi's office, Dora looked relieved to see her. "I was starting to fret that you hadn't heard the page," she said. "Mrs. Townsend's on the telephone for you. She said she'd hold as long as it took, but—"

Brandi had forgotten all about Dora's summons. Feeling guilty, she hurried into her office and grabbed the phone. "Whitney? I'm sorry I took so long."

"Don't fret about it. I'd have waited forever."

There was a tense, almost harsh edge to Whitney's voice that scared Brandi. "What's going on?"

"I found out what Zack's up to."

Brandi relaxed. She turned her chair around, propped her heels on the corner of her desk, and considered how much to tell Whitney. She wouldn't volunteer that Intellitoys was in trouble, of course—but how much did Whitney already know?

Thank heaven Zack had told her everything, she thought. If he hadn't, she might have said the wrong thing just now and destroyed his plans—and maybe even his business.

"A little extra market research," Brandi said airily. "Finding out what kids want for Christmas. I know all about it."

"Oh, that much was obvious." Whitney's voice dripped impatience. "Good heavens, before he bought the company he was asking all the kids he ran into for their opinion of Intellitoys, so of course a stint as Santa would be right up his alley. But there's more, Brandi."

She means the drop in sales, Brandi told herself. But she couldn't quite make herself believe it. There was a black hole of dread in the pit of her stomach.

"I asked Ross last weekend why he'd planted Zack in your store," Whitney said, "and he wouldn't tell me."

Brandi didn't mean to admit to anything at all, but before she could stop herself she said, "I know." Her voice was little more than a croak.

"What did you say? Anyway, he wouldn't tell me right then. He was keeping his mouth shut because he knew I'd do exactly what I'm doing right now—I'd call you up and warn you. But now that he's made up his mind…"

Brandi's palms were damp. "*Warn* me? About what?" She could hardly force the words past the lump in her throat. Then there was something wrong! What disaster was about to descend on her?

Surely, she thought, she ought to *know*. Simply admitting that she didn't have the vaguest idea what was going on was tantamount to confessing that she wasn't fit to manage a store!

"Ross is going to offer you the job as his troubleshooter."

For a moment, Brandi thought she couldn't possibly have heard correctly. That wasn't a disaster; that was a promotion beyond even her craziest dreams.

She said, "I never in my life considered that."

"Well, think it over before you jump," Whitney said dryly. "Don't let yourself be awestruck into taking it. It's not all that great a job, aside from the fact that it puts you straight on the fast track to the head office."

Brandi shook her head a little. "Is that what you're warning me about—that the job has its disadvantages?"

"Not entirely." Whitney sighed. "In fact, that's not it at all, and this isn't going to be easy. Ross knows you're a good manager, but the next step up is a big one, and he wasn't so sure you were ready for it. So he sent Zack out there to do a little undercover work to see whether you had the right qualities to move up to the next level. Watch out for Zack, Brandi. He's there to spy on you."

CHAPTER TEN

BRANDI'S brain felt frozen. *Is there anything else you'd like to tell me*, she'd asked him. And Zack had said no, there wasn't.

Of course not, Brandi thought. He wouldn't *like* to tell her that his main reason for being in her store was to spy on her. Accidentally, she'd phrased the question so he could answer it with total truthfulness and still not be honest. He must have loved that!

"I'm terribly sorry to do this to you," Whitney said. "It's a rough blow, but perhaps it's better that you know it now. I could tell just from seeing you with Zack that you'd gone head over heels where he's concerned—"

"Head over heels? Don't be silly." Brandi's voice was a little shrill.

"Listen, kid, don't try to fool me. I know you too well. I just wish I'd found this out earlier."

"That makes two of us," Brandi admitted wearily. There was an instant of sympathetic silence, and Brandi, fearful of what Whitney might say next, hastily changed the subject. "There's something I don't understand about all this. How could I possibly be Ross's troubleshooter? I could hardly go under cover because everybody in the chain knows me."

"They know your name, but your habit of avoiding corporate parties works to your advantage. Not all that many people would recognize you on sight. Besides, troubleshooters don't stay anonymous for long, Brandi. About fifteen minutes after the job's offered, the grapevine starts spreading the word. You think everyone in the whole chain didn't know me?''

''I always thought—''

''And don't overestimate the amount of secret work that's to be done. Most of the time it's pretty straightforward. It's not an easy job, though—it wears people out and burns them up, and it doesn't take long for travel to lose its glamor. I held that job for almost three years, and I think my record stands to this day. But if that's what you want…''

Brandi considered the warning in Whitney's voice. But there really was only one answer she could give when the question was asked; this promotion was what she had worked for and dreamed of. It was another important step up the ladder to ultimate success. She had earned it, and she deserved to enjoy it. It was impossible to consider turning down such a plum.

''It's what I've always wanted,'' Brandi said quietly.

''Then you have my very best wishes, my friend. But at least think it over before you jump.''

Brandi thanked her and put down the telephone. She should be feeling wildly elated, she told herself. All her hard work had finally landed her on the fast track to the top of the corporation. Someday she might even sit in the office that was Ross Clayton's now, as the head of the whole chain.

When the shock wore off, she told herself, she'd be happy about her promotion. But just now, her head was spinning with fury and disappointment and sadness.

By the time Brandi came out of her office, Dora had gone; the lights were still on in the alcove, but the computer was hooded and her desk was neat. Down on the second floor, the Santa with the half glasses had returned from his dinner and taken his place in the big green wing chair outside the Workshop. Beneath his white whiskers, his face still looked a little pale from his bout with the flu, and Brandi wondered if she should send him home despite the doctor's release that said he was fit to return to work.

He greeted her with a smile, however, and a hearty Santa chuckle. "If you're looking for your young man, Ms. Ogilvie, he's back in the dressing room."

Your young man. The words fed the flames of Brandi's irritation. Did everyone in the store think that she was helplessly in love with Zack Forrest? Even Zack? Had he, perhaps, fed that rumor on purpose? Maybe it was even part of his effort to predict how she'd handle the stress of the new job!

She might not be able to wipe him out of her heart as easily as she'd like, but she could certainly put a stop to this nonsense. She could make it clear to everyone that they were not, and were never likely to be, a couple.

Brandi stalked around behind Santa's Workshop to the dressing-room entrance and, without pausing to think, yanked the door open.

Zack was standing with his back to her, tucking in the tail of his long-sleeved shirt. He half turned and grinned at her. "Hi, there. Is it my imagination, or are you a little impatient to get out of the store tonight?"

"I need to talk to you."

His eyebrows rose a little at her tone. "Give me a minute to put my shoes on," he said. "I'd invite you in, but as you can see, there's hardly room for both of us."

He was right. Santa's Workshop was a masterpiece of illusion. The interior was much smaller than the structure looked from the outside, and a closet and dressing table took up the majority of the dressing room's space. The ceiling was scarcely high enough to clear Zack's head.

Next Christmas, Brandi thought, they really ought to

make it larger. But of course, next Christmas it wouldn't be her concern.

"Something wrong?" Zack inquired.

He actually sounded as if he didn't have a suspicion, and Brandi's exasperation rose another notch. She leaned against the door frame and folded her arms across her chest. "You know, Zack," she said, trying to keep her voice light, "I can't make up my mind whether to thank you for my promotion or throw you bodily out of my store for lying to me."

His eyes narrowed, but he didn't say anything.

"Of course it wouldn't be prudent to fire you now, would it?" Brandi mused. "So I guess I'll settle for thanking you for the recommendation you obviously gave me."

"I didn't have anything to do with your promotion, Brandi."

She hardly heard the denial because of the accompanying admission—that there was to be a promotion, and Zack quite obviously knew it. If he hadn't, he'd have said something else altogether. "Nothing at all?"

Zack shook his head. "It was Ross's decision. I didn't make any recommendation."

Brandi's voice was deceptively gentle. "You know, Zack, if you'd tell me the moon was shining, I'd go and check it out before I'd believe you."

He flushed a little, as if he felt ashamed.

"You've lied to me at every turn, and even when you've told the truth, it turned out to be a lie, too. You're a master of careful phrasing, aren't you? How dare you sit there in my office and say *there's nothing else I'd like to tell you*!"

"Brandi—"

She considered, for an instant, that it wasn't wise to say all this, that it would be better to keep her feelings inside and never let him see. But hurt and fury and disappointment welled up in her like an oil gusher, and once the surface calm had cracked, there was no stopping the flow.

"I suppose you believe the end justifies the means, Zack? Well, no matter how thrilled I am with my promotion, I think the way you conducted yourself is a disgrace. I can't ask you never to set foot in this store again, but I can promise that any further conversation between us will be limited to business. And I thank heaven it's only ten more days till Christmas, so you can get out of that ridiculous Santa suit and go back to playing with toys yourself. Have I made myself perfectly clear?"

"Oh, yes." Zack's voice had a hard edge to it. "And considering the circumstances, I can't imagine wanting to talk to you about anything. Will a handwritten resignation letter do, or shall I go over to electronics and type one?"

"Unless you're planning to give it to Ross, don't bother," Brandi snapped. "You've certainly never answered to me, and I wouldn't want you to pretend to start now!"

She turned on her heel and stalked off across Toyland.

At least that was all over, she told herself when she reached the safety of her office. It was finished. She didn't have to be concerned about Zack anymore, and she could relax and enjoy the challenge of her new promotion.

As soon as her head stopped aching.

The week edged by, and Brandi didn't hear from Ross. There wasn't even a phone call, much less an offer of a promotion.

After a couple of days of silence, she considered the possibility that Whitney's information might have been wrong. But she soon dismissed the idea. Zack had known about the promotion offer, too. It was real—or at least it had been at the time.

Of course, it was quite possible that after her explosion Zack had reconsidered his recommendation. He might well have gone back to Ross to report that Brandi Ogilvie was an uncontrollable maniac, unfit even for the position she already had, and completely unsuitable for anything higher.

Brandi thought that over and decided she didn't care. If the price of telling Zack exactly what she thought of him turned out to be the sacrifice of a job, then she was willing to accept the loss. At least she'd been honest. She could live without the job, and there would be another promotion someday—one she didn't owe to Zack Forrest.

In the meantime, she split her days between the store and the Wishing Tree. Someone had to take over, since Zack had walked away and Pat Emerson's flu was proving to be worse than the average case.

Actually, however, Zack hadn't quite walked away. He'd left a telephone message for her the day after he left the store, asking her to let him know if he was still needed to finish up the Wishing Tree. Brandi had asked Dora to call and tell him no.

She was surprised to find that she really enjoyed working on the Wishing Tree. Sorting through the requests, matching up the gifts that customers brought in, and making sure that every person on the tree was remembered was a detailed and time-consuming task, but it absorbed her attention in a way nothing else seemed to. Sometimes it hurt, though; every time Brandi looked at an application that displayed Zack's signature approving it, she felt as if she'd been stabbed anew.

To escape the paperwork, she started shopping for the family she'd adopted—the one she'd signed up on that Sunday afternoon when she'd first challenged Zack for the truth. Warm clothes for the children were easy enough, but shopping for the mother was difficult—what did one buy a woman whose only request had been for her children? And toys gave her a problem, too. She wasn't sure what to buy for boys.

More than once she found herself wishing that Zack was still around to ask. When that happened, she gritted her teeth and plunged back into work again.

She was in ladies' active wear one afternoon, looking at a casual slacks-and-sweater set and wondering if she could guess the size the woman wore, when Theresa Howard finished with another customer and came up to Brandi.

"That's a nice combination," Theresa said.

Brandi held up the sweater. "Do I hear a little hesitation in your voice?"

"Oh, no. But is it for you? I think the blues would show off your gorgeous hair better than pink would. May I show you?"

Brandi laughed. "Very tactful," she complimented. "You're obviously taking to this job. Actually, this is a gift."

Theresa relaxed. "Oh, in that case…" She was ringing up the sale when she added, "If you need help delivering all the Wishing Tree stuff, I'd be happy to volunteer. I'm still trying to get on my feet financially, so I can't donate much money, but I'd like to give something back, and I thought perhaps if I helped with deliveries…"

"I *will* need help, thank you." Brandi picked up the neatly bagged sweater and slacks. "I believe I mentioned right at the outset that this was probably just a seasonal job, Theresa?"

"Yes, ma'am. And I understand that, I really—"

Brandi interrupted. "I've been talking with Miss Amos

about your performance, and we've agreed that you can consider this position permanent.''

Theresa's eyes filled with tears. ''Oh, Ms. Ogilvie…''

''Unless, of course, you leave it to move up,'' Brandi added hastily, before she could start crying herself. ''And don't thank me, because you've earned it.''

Besides, she thought as she walked away, tucking the bag under her arm, if there was anyone who deserved Theresa Howard's thanks, it was Zack.

That reminded her of the snowy night in the parking lot and the first time Zack had kissed her, and she had to bite her lip hard to drown out the pain in her heart.

When she returned to her office, Ross Clayton rose from the chair beside Dora's desk. ''Finishing up your shopping?'' he asked cheerfully.

Brandi stared at him in surprise. It had been days since Whitney had told her of the promotion, since her confrontation with Zack. What was Ross doing here now? ''This is the last of it,'' she admitted, and ushered him into her office. She put the bag on the corner of her desk, so she wouldn't forget to wrap it to match the rest of the toys and clothes she'd bought for her Wishing Tree family, and sat down.

''I'm sorry it's taken me so long to get back to you,'' Ross said. He pulled up a chair across from her. ''I've been out of town, sorting out some trouble in the Phoenix store. That's a good deal of what I wanted to chat with you about. I need someone to do that job for me.''

Brandi's head was swimming. Did this mean the job offer was still good? But after the way she'd yelled at Zack…

Ross said, ''You've talked to Whitney, no doubt?'' Brandi nodded, and he smiled. ''I knew I could count on her to pass the word along. What about it, Brandi? Are you interested in being my troubleshooter?''

Brandi looked down at her hands. Of course I'm interested, she thought. This was what she'd worked for since the very first week she'd been a salesclerk, when she'd set her sights on a much higher goal. She was going to have a career, not a job that simply let her get by....

''I think you're ideally qualified,'' Ross went on, ''because you're not only experienced at the store level, but you're bright and you're a creative problem solver. But I won't sugarcoat this offer—it wouldn't be fair. This isn't an easy or a popular job.''

''I've always liked challenges, and I've never worried about being popular.'' But Brandi's voice sounded odd to her own ears, as if it belonged to someone else.

Ross leaned back in his chair as if confident that he had his answer. ''The thing that convinced me, you know, was when you sniffed Zack out. There was no reason to think his being here had anything to do with you—but you knew it. That's exactly the kind of sixth sense I'm looking for.''

Brandi didn't think it was necessary to tell him that that hadn't been her managerial instincts at work, but an awareness of an entirely different sort. *My nose for trouble*, she told herself, aware that wasn't quite true, either.

''I can't legally ask you whether you plan to stay single,'' Ross went on, ''but I must warn you that this kind of job is terribly hard on families and friendships.''

Brandi closed her eyes, and once more let an image wash over her, of two small children and a train and a Christmas tree...and Zack. The scene was faded now, as if it was a photograph that had been left out in the sun, but it still had the power to move her.

''You can plan to be on the road up to six weeks at a time,'' Ross said, ''and away from home about fifty weeks of the year. If you want to try it, I would like to have a commitment from you for two years in this job. After that, we'll talk about what you want to do next. Maybe move through the district managers' positions, getting to know the whole chain.''

She took a deep breath and wondered why she wasn't happier. Certainly he was not making the job sound like a plum, but that was no surprise; Ross wasn't the kind to hide the disadvantages of whatever he offered. Brandi had known about the difficulties of the job anyway, so why was she reacting now as if they were insuperable? Why did she have this nagging feeling, now that the plum lay within her reach, that she really didn't want it after all?

She was being stupid, she told herself. Zack would never be a part of her life. The children she had once visualized so clearly were nothing more than a wispy dream. She was free as a cloud, responsible only to herself. And *for* herself. Certainly for the sake of her future, it would be wise to take the promotion. And yet…

Her gaze fell on the blue-and-silver paisley bag that lay on the corner of her desk. She wanted to take the necessary time to wrap that package as beautifully as she could. She wanted to be there to watch as it was opened, and perhaps to get to know that woman better.

She wanted to watch Theresa Howard grow in confidence, move up in the department, maybe eventually take it over after Casey Amos left.

She couldn't do those things if she took the job Ross offered, for she would not be able to stay in one place long enough to nurture a friendship. Not as the troubleshooter. And probably not afterward, either, if she had to move around the country in order to continue up the corporate ladder.

Perhaps she wasn't as free as she'd believed. Perhaps

her treasured independence had truly been self-imposed isolation instead.

A year or two ago, she wouldn't have given a second thought to leaving everything and everyone behind for a new challenge. Now, without even realizing it, she had grown roots here.

"If you'd like a chance to think it over before giving me an answer…" Ross began.

Brandi shook her head, almost automatically. "No. I can answer you now." She wet her lips and said, "Thanks, Ross, but I'm happy where I am."

He was obviously startled. "Perhaps I shouldn't have hit you with this in the midst of the busiest season. Take a while to think, Brandi. After Christmas is over and things settle down a bit, you may change your mind."

"It won't make a difference," she warned.

He studied her thoughtfully for a moment, and then his eyes began to sparkle. "I see. My wife and Whitney both said there was something cooking between you and Zack—"

Brandi said steadily, "This has nothing to do with Zack. It's just what's best for me."

Ross gave her a knowing grin.

Obviously he didn't understand, Brandi thought. But then, she hadn't expected him to.

The employee party was always held on the last Sunday before Christmas, starting just after the store closed. There had been a an air or excitement all afternoon; Brandi caught the drifts of enthusiasm as she walked through the store shortly before closing time. She even caught herself humming a snatch of "Jingle Bells" once.

She wasn't precisely happy, of course. She thought it would probably be a long time before the ache in her heart receded enough to be ignored, and she didn't even dream of a day when she might altogether forget the twin agonies of loving Zack and discovering his lies.

But there were increasing stretches of time when she was content, for she was certain the decision to stay at the store was the right one.

She'd done as Ross asked; she'd spent many hours thinking about the job he'd offered. Sometimes, in the darkest hours of the night, she'd found herself thinking that perhaps she *should* take it. In the troubleshooter's post she could get away from almost everything and make a fresh start.

But that was the problem, Brandi concluded. The things she *could* leave behind, she didn't particularly want to. And the memory of Zack—the one thing she'd have liked to forget—would accompany her no matter where she went or what she did.

By the time she got downstairs to the party, the store was officially closed, the caterers had set up the long buffet tables in the atrium, and stacks of brightly wrapped packages of all sizes were appearing under the largest of the Christmas trees.

Brandi slid the package she'd brought into the nearest stack as discreetly as she could. As she turned away from the tree, she ran headlong into Casey Amos, who hunched protectively over the packages she carried. Her eyes widened when she saw Brandi.

Brandi shook a playful finger at her. ''You look guilty,'' she chided. ''I'll bet you took an extralong coffee break this afternoon to wrap those, didn't you? Shame.''

Casey swallowed hard. ''You want some shrimp?'' she said weakly. ''Let me get rid of these and I'll join you.''

The caterer's table was a masterpiece, loaded with simple food beautifully arranged to tempt the palate. Brandi picked up a plate and pulled a giant boiled shrimp off a lettuce-wrapped stand.

From the corner of her eye, she caught a glimpse of a red velvet suit, and her heart seemed to do a somersault. Don't be silly, she thought. In the first place, Zack couldn't possibly be attending the employees' party, because he wasn't an employee anymore. In the second place, he certainly wouldn't be wearing a Santa suit.

Very deliberately, she turned around to prove to herself that the suspicion was only a figment of her imagination, and discovered that she'd been half-right. The Santa she'd seen was the one with the half glasses, who hadn't bothered to change clothes after his shift.

Zack wasn't wearing red velvet.

He was standing at the entrance. His black-and-white patterned sweater seemed to Brandi's eyes to swirl like an optical illusion, and she thought for a moment that she was going to faint.

She had convinced herself that she was better, that the agony was receding, that someday soon she would forget him. Now she knew how foolish she had been. She had been hiding from the pain, but seeing him again brought it all bubbling up like an acid bath. And she had to admit that she would never be all right, that she would never forget, and that she missed him more than she had thought it possible to long for another human being.

She had thought she loved Jason, and time had salved the wound. But this was different. This was forever.

Beside her, Casey Amos heaved a long sigh, as if she'd made up her mind about something desperate. "I'd better confess."

"What?" Brandi said tersely. "That you invited Zack?"

"Is he here?" Casey looked over her shoulder, only

half-interested. "No, it's not that. I hope you won't hate me, but I put your name in the gift exchange drawing."

"Is that all?"

"I thought it was too bad for you not to be included. But it hit me when I saw you putting a package into the pile a minute ago that you'll be the only employee to get two gifts tonight."

A couple of weeks ago Brandi would have been a bit annoyed at being dragged into something she had no interest in. As it was, she thought the mix-up was mildly funny; she'd probably be teased for a day or two and then the event would be forgotten. "Don't worry about it, Casey. I just hope you got something nice for the person whose name I'm supposed to have drawn in return." Her gaze drifted toward Zack once more; he'd moved toward the Christmas tree.

Across the serving table, Theresa Howard turned pale and dropped a shrimp. "I put your name in, too," she whispered. "Casey said something about your being left out, and I thought…"

The humor of the situation—and the rightness of the decision she'd made—struck Brandi sharply, and she started to laugh uncontrollably. "What a party," she managed to say finally. "I wouldn't have missed this for the world!"

Even if Zack *was* there, for he stayed at the fringes of the crowd. Brandi had started to relax, thinking that he was as intent on avoiding her as she was on staying out of his way, when they abruptly came face-to-face at the portable bar.

"How's business?" Brandi asked, trying to keep her voice light. She squeezed the twist of lime into her club soda and wiped her fingertips on a napkin.

"Busy. We're reorganizing produce lines, repackaging

some toys in smaller units…nothing earthshaking in itself, but I hope it will have an impact well before next Christmas season.''

''I'm sure it will.'' She didn't look directly at him. ''I'm happy you found what was wrong.''

For a moment, she thought he wasn't going to answer. Then he said softly, ''And I'm happy you're getting the job you want.''

Before Brandi could tell him any differently, he'd walked away. Not that it mattered, she thought. But the ache in the pit of her stomach—the nagging pain that had been her constant companion since the day she'd found out he'd spied on her—intensified.

The gift exchange proceeded with more than usual hilarity; Brandi's three packages got exactly the reaction she'd expected. Then a fourth was delivered, and she laughingly demanded, ''All right. I know about Casey and Theresa, but who else has been setting me up?'' Too late, she looked across the circle at Zack. He, too, had thought she was a Scrooge who needed a dose of Christmas spirit.…

Dora sheepishly raised a hand, and also the manager of Toyland, who said, ''I thought it would be sad if you weren't included on your last Christmas—'' He caught himself too late and clapped a hand over his mouth.

Brandi sighed. Obviously Whitney had been right about the corporate grapevine. Too bad the gossips hadn't picked up on the latest installment. ''No, I'm not terminally ill,'' she said over the speculative whispers. ''And no matter what rumor says, I'm not leaving to take another job, either.'' She looked down at the stack of gifts in her lap. They were small things, even silly things, but the thought that had gone into them meant a great deal to her. ''I'm happy here—with my friends." It was mostly true, she told herself. She was as happy as she could be just now.

The party ended early, since they were going into the final and most wearing week of the season. Zack left among the first group, walking out with Theresa Howard. Brandi tried not to notice. She stayed till the caterers had cleaned up the last scrap of turkey, and then she locked the employee exit behind her and went home.

Another ordeal survived, she told herself. It would get easier with time, though she could no longer fool herself that the pain would end entirely someday.

She made a hollow in the garland on the mantel so she could set up one of her gifts there—a ceramic statuette of a winking Santa—and she was just setting him in place when the doorbell rang. Through the peephole, she recognized Zack, and with resignation she opened the door.

"I'm glad you didn't pretend not to be home," he said. "I'd have looked pretty silly climbing up the drainpipe and over the balcony rail."

Brandi didn't invite him in, but leaned against the jamb with the door open only a few inches. "I can't see why that would be necessary. If you left something at the party, you can get it at the store tomorrow. I'm not going back tonight."

Zack shook his head. "That's not why I'm here. Didn't Ross come through with the job offer?"

"Why not ask him? I suppose you're worried because you recommended me and I didn't live up to expectations."

Zack looked exasperated. "Look, must we have this conversation with my foot in the door?"

"I didn't invite you here."

"Brandi, I don't blame you for being angry with me. And I'm not justifying what I did. But I'd like to have a chance to explain it—so you'll know I didn't do it for fun, or without thinking it through.''

Brandi shrugged and moved back from the door. ''I suppose I have nothing to lose by listening.''

She purposely didn't offer him a cup of coffee, and she didn't sit down. Zack didn't seem to notice; he moved around her living room with the nervous energy of a caged panther, stopping for a moment to look at the ceramic Santa on the mantel. Brandi had forgotten that, or she'd have left him standing in the hall.

''Ross and I have been friends since college days,'' Zack began. ''In fact, we met in the dean's office—both of us were close to being thrown out of school because of a little too much high-spirited fun. Ever since then, we've pitched in to help each other when trouble's brewing, so of course when I started getting bad news about my Christmas sales, I called Ross.''

Brandi decided to hurry things along. ''And he thought it would be a good idea to kill two birds with one stone by sending you to spy on me.''

Zack winced. ''He didn't, Brandi. All he asked of me was an opinion about how well you'd be suited to the job he was thinking of offering you.''

''That's what I called it,'' Brandi said softly. ''Spying.''

''No. He was just asking for another point of view— it's the kind of thing I've done myself a thousand times, with Ross and with others. He knew you were good, you see—that was never in doubt. But he questioned whether you were flexible enough for the fast changes and the constant shifts that a troubleshooter faces every day. All he wanted was an opinion. The decision would be his, no matter what I thought.''

She shrugged. That must be what he meant when he

said he hadn't actually made a recommendation. It ended up being the same thing.

"It seemed a very small favor," Zack said softly, "compared to the one he was doing for me, so I agreed. I didn't realize then—how could I, Brandi?—that it wasn't just Ross's employee I'd be looking at." Zack was looking very steadily at her. "I had no idea that I was going to meet a very special woman here."

Brandi swallowed hard. *A very special woman.* It wasn't all she wanted; in fact, it wasn't really very much at all, but she would treasure those words forever. It was half a minute—an achingly long silence—before she regained her balance enough to say coolly, "That's touching, Zack. But once that possibility occurred to you, didn't you think about backing out of your promise and telling me what was going on?"

"Yes—but don't forget that by the time I realized I needed to tell you the truth, I was in pretty deep. I warned Ross the night of the party that I was going to tell you the whole thing—my reasons for masquerading as Santa, the troubleshooter job…"

Brandi's body went absolutely still. He had intended to confess the whole lot?

"And I tried," Zack went on softly, "but you ran away rather than listen to me. The next day, when you found out about Intellitoys, you didn't even try to understand that there might have been a reason for not telling you right away. You didn't ask questions. You just attacked."

I was hurt, she wanted to say. I was aching with love for you, and you didn't even seem to care that I might have liked to know what was going on! "I suppose that's why you didn't make a recommendation to Ross, because I'd conducted myself so badly. Why didn't you just tell him I'd be a terrible troubleshooter?"

She thought for a moment he wasn't going to answer. Then he said quietly, "Because I thought you'd make a damned good one."

A very special woman... She felt as if he'd snatched away the fragment of joy that comment had held for her; obviously he'd meant it professionally, not personally, after all. She ought to have known that from the beginning.

"Even after that I wanted to confess it all," Zack said, "and at least be square with you, whatever else happened. But don't you see, Brandi? If I told you what Ross was considering, and you changed your behavior in the least— as you'd be bound to do, it's only human—he would never have offered you the job. I was caught in my own trap."

She nodded a little.

"So I told Ross I couldn't make a recommendation, that I was too personally interested in you to have a valid opinion."

"And he believed that?" Brandi's voice was dry. Then she remembered what Ross had said about his wife's suspicions, and Whitney's. Maybe Ross *had* believed it.

"Any reason he shouldn't?" Zack sounded a little annoyed. "Just because you can't stand having me around—"

Brandi's heart seemed to give a sudden jolt and stop beating altogether. "What did you say?"

"Look, you've made it obvious how you feel, Brandi. Your career comes first, and I respect that. I don't have much choice about it, do I?" He zipped his leather jacket. "All right, I've said what I came to say. At least you know I didn't lie to you for the sheer enjoyment of it, so I won't bother you anymore."

As he brushed past her, Brandi's hand grasped his sleeve. The contact seemed to burn her fingers, and Zack stopped as if he'd run into an electrical field.

Brandi stared up at him, willing him to stay, knowing that if he left she would always regret letting him go. Her fingers tightened.

Slowly his hand closed over hers and tugged it loose. But instead of letting her go, he cradled her fingers on his, and ever so slowly raised her hand to his face.

She let her fingers curve around his jaw, savoring the warmth of him and the faintest prickle of his beard. If she could never touch him again, she thought, she would treasure this moment, this memory. She smiled just a little, and her eyes misted, and so she couldn't see clearly what emotion was in his face as he pulled her tightly against him.

He kissed her as if he couldn't deny himself, and his hunger woke a passion in her that was deeper than anything Brandi had ever felt before. This is where I belong, she thought, and burrowed against him as if she was trying to make herself a part of his body.

Eventually he stopped kissing her and simply cradled her close, his cheek against her hair. "Dammit, Brandi," he said unsteadily, "you're not my kind of woman."

Slowly, sanity dawned. Brandi tried to pull away from him, embarrassed at her own uninhibited behavior.

But Zack wouldn't let her go. "I've always made it a point to steer clear of high-powered career types."

"Love 'em and leave 'em," she said coolly, remembering what Whitney had said.

"No," Zack corrected. "Have fun, but don't get serious. And I planned to do the same with you. But it just didn't work, you see." A note of bitter humor crept into his voice. "I came here tonight to confess—so I might as well tell it all, right? I didn't realize right away why you affected me so. I thought for days that I was always on edge around you because I didn't like you at all."

"Gee, thanks." The crack in Brandi's voice robbed the comment of irony.

"The night you asked me if I was Ross's trouble-shooter... You were so vulnerable, so helpless, so open, and I began to think that you might be what I'd been looking for all these years. It was almost a heretical thought—that my idea of the perfect woman had been so far from the reality. But then at the party, I saw you with the kids—and I couldn't help but think that you wanted that, too. I guess it was wishful thinking, wasn't it?"

Brandi's throat was tight with pain and unshed tears.

"I was going to propose to you that night," Zack said softly. "And then—if you accepted me—I planned to throw myself at your feet and tell you the truth."

She'd asked him what he was going to tell her that night, and he'd dodged the question instead of answering—and so she'd assumed he'd intended to share only a version of the truth. How could she have been so blind?

"But you wouldn't stick around to listen. The only thing I could think was that you knew what I wanted to say— and you didn't want to have to turn me down, so it was easier to run away than to hear me out."

Brandi put her hand to her temple, where a vein throbbed.

"I knew then I'd read you wrong after all, that your career was more important than I could ever be. And I loved you so much I wanted you to have what you wanted—even if it wasn't me." He kissed her hair gently, and set her aside. "It isn't too late, I'm sure. I'll talk to Ross—"

Brandi had to clear her throat twice before she could say, "He offered me the job. I turned it down, Zack."

He stood as if turned to stone. "What?"

"Why do you think I blew up at you like that? I didn't

do it on purpose, exactly, but I thought if I exploded at you, you'd tell Ross I shouldn't get the job.''

''You *wanted* that to happen?''

''I didn't reason it out ahead of time. But yes, I think I did.''

''Why don't you want the job?'' He sounded as if he'd been hit a solid blow just beneath the ribs.

Brandi didn't look at him. She picked out a spot on the front of his jacket instead and stared at it. ''A long time ago, I thought I was in love,'' she said slowly. ''He was a charming man, but he liked things easy—so when he found a woman who had family money, he dumped me. And I decided never to let anyone get that close to me again. Especially not the happy-go-lucky sort who didn't worry about where the next car payment was coming from—''

''And who'd take a temporary job as Santa Claus to make ends meet? I think I begin to see.''

She nodded. ''I wasn't looking for a man at all, but even if I had been, you were so obviously not what I wanted that it never occurred to me to be wary of you. But before I realized what had happened, you'd crept into my heart—and made me want to feel again, and to give, and to be close to people....''

Zack drew her tightly against him once more. He kissed her temple, and the pain went away. But there was still a knot in her stomach. ''I love you. But I don't know, Zack,'' she said on a rising note of panic. ''I'm scared. Kids are so important to you. What if I can't be a good mother? I'm not exactly promising parent material!''

He smiled down at her. ''If you weren't,'' he said softly, ''it would never occur to you to ask the question. We'll wait till you're ready, that's all. And if you're never ready, I can live with that—as long as I have you.''

Slowly, the knot eased. "You scare me to death sometimes," she confessed, "but I've never been as alive as when I'm with you."

"Can you forgive me for not being completely truthful with you?"

Brandi nodded. "Now I can. Now that I understand why."

He kissed her again; it was as much a promise as a caress. "If you still want the job, Brandi, we'll make it work somehow."

She considered the question, and shook her head. "My career is important to me, Zack. But it's not all-important anymore."

Zack's hands slid slowly down her back, drawing her even closer against him. "And what *is* all-important?"

Brandi looked up into his eyes, and the last whisper of doubt disappeared. This was right, and real, and forever. "You are," she confessed. "And you always will be—my unlikely Santa."

Born and raised in Berkshire, **Liz Fielding** started writing at the age of twelve when she won a hymn-writing competition at her convent school. After a gap of more years than she is prepared to admit to, during which she worked as a secretary in Africa and the Middle East, got married and had two children, she was finally able to realise her ambition and turn to full-time writing in 1992.

She now lives with her husband, John, in West Wales, surrounded by mystical countryside and romantic, crumbling castles, content to leave the travelling to her grown-up children and keeping in touch with the rest of the world via the Internet.

Look out for HER IDEAL HUSBAND
by Liz Fielding

in Tender Romance™, January 2001

ALL SHE WANTS FOR CHRISTMAS

by

LIZ FIELDING

CHAPTER ONE

'Is THAT Ursa Major?' Maddy quickly pointed to the familiar constellation as Rupert made a move to seize her hand. But he wasn't to be diverted by the diamond-spattered velvet darkness of the Caribbean sky.

'Who cares?' he demanded, and Maddy gave a startled cry as he grabbed her waist and pulled her roughly into his arms. 'You know what I want.' And with a crazy little laugh he began to plaster her face with kisses.

'Rupert,' she gasped, turning her head from side to side in an attempt to avoid his questing mouth, 'don't—'

But he wasn't taking no for an answer. 'You must know how I feel. You've set me on fire, Maddy!' he declared. 'I must have you. . .I will have you.' She was trapped, the hard stone balustrade protecting her from the sharp drop to the sea digging into her back, Rupert blocking the way to the house with his body. 'I will have you,' he repeated. 'No matter what it takes.'

'No!' she protested, desperately trying to push him away. They were supposed to be friends. Just friends. And because of that she had fallen for the oldest line in the book. "Come and look at the stars. . ." How on earth could she have been so stupid? 'You know you don't mean this, Rupert,' she declared. but he wasn't listening and Maddy suddenly had the most awful premonition that he did mean every word.

'I know you think I'm a fool, but I've never been

5

more serious in my life. . .' he proclaimed. 'I'll show you. . .' He fumbled in his pocket and produced a heavy, ornate ring set with rubies and diamonds and held it under her nose. 'This was my grandmother's engagement ring. That's how serious I am.' He was triumphant. 'Nothing will keep me from you. . .'

He was still speaking but Maddy no longer heard him, only the shocking echo that boomed in her head. . . 'This was my grandmother's engagement ring'. . .'my grandmother's ring. . .'

The stars began to spin, the terrace dissolve, but as Maddy swayed towards him Rupert misunderstood. He captured her hand and pushed the heavy ring onto her finger. 'I know I'm not much of a catch. . .not clever like you, but marry me and I'll make you Lady Hartnoll one day—'

The light spilling from the open doorway caught the stones and they flashed fire—hateful red fire. She tugged at the ring, hating the sight of it on her finger. 'You're right, Rupert.' Her voice seemed to come from far away, brittle and light as spun sugar. 'You're not in the least bit clever or you'd know better than to offer rubies to a redhead. You'll have to do better than your grandmother's precious bauble—'

'I'll get you another ring,' he said, a little desperately. 'Anything you like. . .' But his words didn't register as she twisted the ring back and forth, desperate now to be rid of it, to get away, but her knuckle, broken once when she was a child and awkward ever since, refused to give up its treasure. 'You can have everything I've got, Maddy,' he insisted.

'And what's that?' Was that her laughing? Surely not. She hadn't laughed before. . . 'A second-hand ring and a second-hand title? It's not very original of you,

Rupert; it's all been done before, you see...' All she wanted was to lash out, hurt the man who had brought her nightmare to life... 'For heaven's sake, you don't even have any *real* money...' For a moment there was silence. Blissful silence.

But Rupert's shocked voice broke the peace. 'My God, it's true! Charlie Duncan warned me that underneath you were as hard as nails, but I didn't believe him...'

'Well, you should have,' she declared as with one final twist the ring suddenly came flying from her finger to clip his cheek, the heavy, clawed setting breaking the skin before hitting the stone floor of the terrace and rolling away into the darkness.

Rupert touched his face where the ring had struck him, staring in disbelief at the smear of blood on his fingers. Then with an anguished cry he dived to the ground and began a frantic searching for his family heirloom. This final touch of farce was too much for Maddy and a bubble of near-hysterical laughter caught her unawares. She clapped her hand over her mouth and spun quickly away, determined to make the safety of her bedroom before she gave vent to her feelings, whatever they might turn out to be. But as she turned she blundered into a figure standing in the purple shadow of the bougainvillea that tumbled about the French windows that opened from the drawing room.

The man caught her and held her as she stumbled, his strong hands grasping her waist to steady her, and Maddy found herself looking up into a pair of fiery green eyes that for a moment regarded her with an unreadable expression that seemed to play havoc with her senses and eat into her very soul.

He was tall—he had to be if she was forced to look

up at him—with the kind of dark, weather-beaten good looks that made women weep, and for a moment she remained transfixed, mesmerised, with Rupert, the terrace, the scented Mustique night all forgotten.

'You can put her down now, Griff, darling.' A cool, feminine voice brought her sharply back to earth and she turned, hardly believing her ears.

'Zoe, I didn't know you were coming to Mustique. When did you arrive? Have you rented somewhere? Stay with us. . .we've loads of room.'

Zoe glanced over her shoulder at Rupert who was by now frantically quartering the terrace in his search for the precious ring, but she made no comment. 'No, darling,' she said. 'I'm on my way to Palm Island and since the *Dragon* was on her way down there to pick up a charter I've hitched a lift. I know it's rather late to call, but we're leaving at first light and I wanted to speak to your father.'

Griff? Zoe had had a number of what she referred to as "little flings" since her divorce ten years earlier. But this man was very different from her godmother's usual sleek, well-groomed, well-heeled companions. In his mid-thirties, casually dressed in a pair of lightweight trousers and an open-necked shirt, he was clearly much younger than her godmother, and Maddy, still held by those strong, vital hands, felt herself grow hot. 'You captain the *Dragon*?' she exclaimed quickly, pulling herself free. 'I saw her anchored off Barbados. She's very beautiful.'

'Of course he doesn't,' Zoe said, a little impatiently. 'The yacht has a full complement of crew.' So—he was just along for the ride. 'You can join us if you like.'

'No,' Maddy said, unnerved at the thought of being confined in a yacht, no matter how luxurious, with Zoe and her young lover. Then, aware that she had been a little abrupt, she added, 'It's very kind of you, but I can't leave Dad all by himself.'

'You're quite sure?' Zoe asked. Maddy found herself staring once more up into the green eyes of her godmother's companion.

'Positive,' she said too quickly. 'Did you say your name was Griff?' she queried, the chill in her voice an attempt to disguise her sudden confusion—an intensity of feelings that she didn't fully comprehend but didn't like one bit.

'*I* didn't say anything.' His voice had a low and gravelly sound that seemed to unravel her nerve-ends. And the slightest stress on 'I' suggested that *she* had said something. Far too much. She felt the heat rise to her skin under his discomfiting gaze.

'Just Griff?' she demanded pertly, in an attempt to put him in his place. Even as she said it she realised how ridiculous that was. This man wasn't "just" anything and his "place" would be wherever he chose.

'Hugo Griffin,' he replied formally, with the smallest of smiles. 'But Griff will do.' He extended his hand. Maddy did not want to take it, but he waited. She ran her tongue nervously over her lips and offered him her fingers, but he grasped her hand fully, holding it, swallowing it up in his own strong hand, holding it for far longer than politeness dictated. It was as if a current of electricity were being fed into her body, lighting her up. It was frightening, exciting, appalling because he was in some subtle way taunting her. She jerked her hand free and turned quickly to her godmother.

'Have you seen Father?'

'He's on the telephone.'

'Still? I don't know why he bothered to come on holiday. Come and have a drink.'

'Don't you think you'd better stay out here and help your friend find his. . .er. . .bauble?' Maddy flushed scarlet as Griff, one brow raised the merest fraction, caught her eye. She glared at him, then glanced back at Rupert, who was now crawling about under the seating in the summer house.

'I'm sure he'll manage,' she said abruptly, and, brushing quickly past Griff, she went inside.

'I've been blown to bits driving in that wretched Moke, Maddy,' Zoe said. 'Will you point me in the direction of a mirror?'

Zoe was the most elegant woman that Maddy had ever met and she looked as if she had stepped straight from some exclusive hair salon, but Maddy didn't argue. 'You can use my room. Up the stairs and—'

'Show me the way, darling,' Zoe said, and the edge to her voice suggested that the desire for a mirror was simply an excuse to singe Maddy's ears over the scene she had just witnessed on the terrace.

Maddy turned to Griff and waved vaguely in the direction of the drinks cabinet. 'Please, help yourself. . .' she said, and flushed once more as he regarded her with an expression that made her feel as if she had said something. . .suggestive.

'Darling, this is *gorgeous*,' Zoe said, sitting on the edge of a lace-hung four-poster bed. 'The whole house is a delight.'

'We were lucky to get a Christmas cancellation. Why don't you stay here and spend the holiday with us?'

'Christmas?' She pulled a face. 'I've never much cared for tinsel in the Tropics. . . Besides, Griff and I have something special planned. We weren't going to stop in Mustique at all, but I wanted to speak to your father and when his office told me he was here on holiday...' She paused. 'What do you think of Griff?' she asked, so carelessly that Maddy's heart sank. She thought that Griff was likely to break her godmother's heart. She had never seen her so lit up, excited...

'Something special?' she repeated, with a sudden dreadful premonition. 'Zoe—'

'Don't ask. I know everyone will try to talk me out of it, so it's going to be a secret until afterwards...' She briskly changed the subject. 'Besides, it's you who has some explaining to do. How on earth could you be so unfeeling to that poor boy? He's obviously head over heels in love with you.'

'Nonsense. He's a clown.' A stupid, sweet, foolish clown. She had told him that she couldn't be anything but his friend but he had refused to believe her, and tonight he had blundered unknowingly into a hurt that she had buried so deep that she thought she had forgotten it.

'Well, you certainly made him look like one tonight. Money's spoiled you, my girl.' Zoe took a brush from her bag and began to tidy her hair with little fidgety movements that betrayed her anger. 'You're a very beautiful young woman. But handsome is as handsome does. Just because you've been hurt once it doesn't excuse unkindness.'

'No...'

Zoe's face softened. 'Oh, my dear girl, I wish I could tell you, show you what you're missing—' She stopped as she saw Maddy's face. 'Run along down and keep Griff company, darling. I can find my own way down.'

Keeping Griff company was the last thing she wanted

to do, but there was something. . . 'I think I'd better go and make sure Rupert's found his. . .er. . .'

'Bauble?'

'Help yourself to anything you want,' Maddy muttered, and fled, determined, somehow, to make her peace with Rupert.

'What did you think of Zoe's new. . .friend?' Michael Osborne enquired of his daughter over breakfast the following morning.

Hugo Griffin was the last person that Maddy wanted to think about, but her father was waiting. 'I hardly spoke to him.' But she had been aware of his eyes on her all the while her father had been talking to him. 'He seems very fond of Zoe,' she replied noncommittally.

'Is he genuine, do you think? She was asking me about selling stocks. A lot of stocks. I've a very nasty feeling that he's at the back of it.'

'Surely not!' She began furiously buttering toast. 'I mean, surely she gave you a reason for wanting to sell? Didn't you ask her?'

'It's really none of my business, Maddy. But she sidestepped all my efforts to discover what was going on with such determination that I'm seriously concerned.' He shrugged. 'I just hate to see a friend, a woman at a vulnerable age, taken advantage of by some unscrupulous. . .' He shrugged again. 'Well, I don't have to draw a picture.'

Maddy's appetite had suddenly deserted her as she remembered their brief conversation the night before, that feeling that Zoe was on the verge of something rash. 'Poor Zoe.'

Michael Osborne pulled a wry face. 'If Zoe was poor

there wouldn't be a problem. I want you to try and find out what's going on.'

'How can I?' The last thing she wanted was to get involved in Zoe's romantic entanglement with Griff. 'And she wouldn't thank you for interfering,' she added quickly. 'Surely you can use your business contacts in Barbados to check up on him?'

'And if he finds out? Tells Zoe?' He shook his head. 'I'll make some discreet enquiries when I get back to London.'

'But that won't be until after Christmas,' she pointed out. Her father pulled a face. 'Oh, I see. Your telephone call last night means you have to go home.'

'I'm sorry, sweetheart, but I've got to get back before the weekend.' He held up his hand to stall her protest. 'Don't you see? It gives me the perfect excuse to ask Zoe to have you to stay with her on Palm. After all, I can't leave you here alone over the holiday. Such a pity that Rupert had to rush off. . .' He grinned wickedly as two bright spots stained her cheeks.

'For heaven's sake, Dad, I'm twenty-three years old, I have my own flat in the centre of London and I run my own business. I'm perfectly capable of looking after myself.'

'Of course you are. More than capable. But surely appearing to be a helpless little brat isn't too much to ask if it means protecting Zoe from some good-looking confidence trickster? I thought that you, more than anyone, would want to save a friend from that.'

'I've never flown in a seaplane before,' Maddy said in a brittle attempt to appear friendly. But she couldn't meet his eyes; instead she looked beyond Griff's sharply defined features to the small craft moored against the jetty as he lifted her luggage from the Moke.

Her father had spoken to Zoe and arranged a direct flight to Palm by seaplane. That at least had been something to look forward to. Until she'd seen who the pilot was. He tossed her bag into the tiny hold and indicated the passenger seat with a curt nod of his head. 'Unless you climb aboard instead of standing about chattering,' he informed her, 'you won't be flying on this one.'

Maddy felt her mouth nearly drop open. *Chattering!* She had merely tried to ease the almost palpable tension between them, but clearly he was furious that she was being foisted on Zoe.

Reluctantly she turned to face the man. His sea-green eyes were regarding her intently and she had the uncomfortable feeling that he was capable of peeling back the layers of her mind to discover what she was thinking. Could he possibly suspect the real reason for her visit?

She regarded him coolly from beneath long dark lashes. He was tall, with the brawny, well-tanned physique of a man who spent most of his time out of doors; his shorts, faded T-shirt and bare feet pushed into leather-thonged sandals were in stark contrast to the expensive if casual cut of the clothes he had worn when he'd come to the house—a stark contrast to the immaculate white uniforms worn by most charter pilots. He wouldn't last long with Dragonair unless he made more of an effort, she thought. Or had he other plans? There were plenty of rich widows and divorcees in the Caribbean. Women like Zoe. . .alone and vulnerable to the flattery of a good-looking man.

'Well?' he demanded, raising one sharply defined

brow. 'If you've seen quite enough. . .?' Maddy felt a blush steal over her cheekbones. He'd thought she was ogling him for heaven's sake! The sheer nerve. Flustered, she turned to the aircraft, which bobbed gently on its floats against the jetty, and indicated the fierce red dragon painted on its tail.

'Don't Dragonair pilots normally wear a uniform?' she demanded imperiously in an effort to cover her confusion.

'Normally,' he conceded. 'But who said this was a normal charter?'

'You're just doing this as a favour for Zoe on your day off? Won't your employer object?' she queried.

The expression in his eyes was unreadable against the dancing reflection of the sea, but the low, warning timbre of his voice sent a little shiver of goose-flesh rippling up her spine. 'Are you coming?'

Maddy gave an imperceptible shrug and lifted her chin just a touch. 'I don't seem to have much choice. Zoe is expecting me.' If she had hoped to prod him a little with this, she signally failed.

'She didn't have much choice either, the way I heard it. After all, you mustn't be deprived of your holiday.'

'I thought you were in a hurry,' Maddy snapped crossly. Then, as she made a move to board the seaplane, it rose and fell slightly against the dock on the swell of the tide, and she hesitated.

'Afraid of getting your feet wet?' he asked.

She threw him her most withering glance, but he didn't wither. On the contrary he put two hands about her waist, lifted her from the jetty and swung her across the gap, holding her for just long enough over the space where the ocean sucked against the jetty to let her know that he was seriously considering whether to dump her in it. A little gasp escaped her lips at such brazen intimidation and, apparently satisfied that he had made his point, his mouth twisted momentarily into a tormenting little smile. Then he placed her very gently on the seat of the plane. 'I. . .I. . .' But Maddy was finally lost for words. It was going to be hard work denting this man's composure.

Griff raised a dark brow with speaking insolence at her inability to say precisely what was on her mind. 'Yes?' he prompted.

Burningly conscious of the pressure of his fingers through the fine silk of her biscuit-coloured camisole, the invasion of the broad pads of his thumbs beneath the flare of her ribs, she was horrified to discover that she was blushing for the second time in less than five minutes. Her immune system was normally alert to all the danger signals, but this man had somehow slipped under her defences while she'd been reeling from her scene with Rupert and she was very much afraid that he knew it. She had to disabuse him of the fact, and quickly.

'One hand would have done,' she said. It was meant as a rebuke but her voice was oddly breathy and it came out all wrong.

The lines that bracketed his mouth deepened and he very nearly smiled. 'Valuable cargo must be treated with care,' he replied.

'Valuable cargo?'

'Zoe told me that you are an heiress to a considerable fortune.'

Maddy felt a little chill invade her soul. 'Is that all she had to say?'

'She's been going on all week about how charming you are. It's odd, because she's usually so discerning. . .'

'Thank you,' she said, as crushingly as she knew how.

But he wasn't crushed either. 'Anytime, Miss Osborne,' he replied with grave formality. But at least he had removed his hands and she could breathe again.

'Now, would it be too much trouble for you to move over? You're sitting in my seat. Unless, of course,' he added, with a wry twist of his mouth, 'you would prefer to fly yourself to Palm Island?'

'I. . .' She snapped her mouth shut and scrambled across the tiny cockpit into the passenger seat. She had been about to tell him that she was perfectly capable of doing just that, and wipe that mocking smile right off his face, but she had no wish to encourage further conversation.

Besides, it wasn't strictly true. Maddy had recently obtained her pilot's licence but she'd never flown a seaplane, although the controls looked familiar enough. If the pilot had been anyone else she might even have dared to ask if she could take the controls for a while, but she wasn't about to ask 'Griff will do' for any favours. Which was probably just as well, because she was pretty sure that he wasn't in the mood to grant her any.

Nevertheless, she watched him with the fascination of the newly addicted, following every movement as he ran through his pre-flight checks, wound up the engine and then called the control tower on his radio for permission to take off.

The crackling voice on the radio gave him a heading and height and he threw her a glance to check that she had fastened her seat belt before casting off and closing the cockpit door. The snap of the lock made her jump. It had an almost ominous finality about it, as if the two of them were cast adrift from the rest of the world.

'Ready?' Griff asked.

'Yes,' she said quickly. 'Yes, of course.' She gave herself a firm mental shake and looked out of the window, determined not to say another word until they reached Palm.

Griff taxied out into the deserted bay, waiting a moment for clearance. Then he opened the throttle and, unable to help herself, she turned to watch, holding her breath as the plane surged forward under his steady hand and skimmed over the clear turquoise water for dizzy, breathless moments. Muscles flexed on strong, tanned forearms as he pulled back on the control column, their strength defined by the fine line of hairs, once presumably as dark as the untamed mop that decorated his well-shaped head but now turned to dark gold from constant exposure to the sun.

For a moment her back was pressed hard against the seat and then quite suddenly they were airborne, free, and Maddy gave a little sigh of pure pleasure that drew a brief, enquiring glance from the pilot, but she didn't notice. Maddy was staring down at the ocean, at the unfamiliar view of a string of islands that disappeared into the hazy distance, each with its own protective circle of reef.

The plane banked steeply, giving a breathtaking view of the exquisite colours of the bay beneath them, every shade of turquoise, then jade and bright emerald-green until beyond the white ruffle that betrayed the hidden reef the water turned to deepest sapphire. As they gained height a yacht, brilliant white against the sparkling blue depths of the ocean, shrank to the size of a child's plaything and Maddy had a brief glimpse of the wreck of the *Antilles* which years before had run onto the reef between Mustique and a nearby island and broken its back. Then there was nothing but a cloudless blue sky.

Maddy watched intently as Griff made the small adjustments for straight and level flight, envying the sure, confident touch of his long, sun-darkened fingers on the controls, recognising a man in his element. As if sensing that he was being watched, he turned, and for a moment their eyes, the tawny and the green, clashed

'Don't do that,' he said abruptly.

'Do what?' And she knew instantly that even thinking the question had been a mistake. Asking it out loud had been madness.

'Flirt when you don't mean it. Flash out signals like a firefly on heat. I realise there is a type of woman who can't resist the challenge but—'

'I beg your pardon?' Maddy gasped.

'I said—'

'No,' she said quickly, with a tiny gesture of dismissal. 'Forget that. I heard what you said; there's no need to repeat it.' And she snapped her head round to stare straight ahead at the achingly blue sky, painfully aware that once more she had flushed hatefully beneath her delicate tan, but this time she refused to let it go. 'You're quite wrong, you know. I wasn't trying to flirt with you.' Damn. Why on earth had she said that? Far better to have ignored it. Palm wasn't far. Much better to keep her silence. 'I was just interested in the controls.' No! No! She hadn't meant to say that! It was as if her tongue had a life of its own.

'The controls?' Griff gave a short laugh. 'Of course you were, Miss Osborne.' Before she knew what was happening he had grasped her dismissive hand and laid it over his on the control column, holding it captive, small and white between his own strong, workmanlike ones. 'Like this?' he asked, his decisive mouth far too close for comfort.

'No!' Maddy was desperate to pull free from the exhilarating touch of his hands but her brain was ignoring the urgent signals for help.

'Will you show me how you do that?' he mocked, his voice slipping easily into a fluttering, breathy impersonation of her own, so good that if she hadn't been thrown totally off balance by the swiftness of his attack, by the unexpected surge of warmth as the palm of her hand was pressed against his dark knuckles, she might just have found it funny. 'Oh, Griff, aren't you strong...' His voice wavered in a perfect imitation of the kind of woman she had heard a dozen times during the past couple of weeks, the kind of woman who hung around the muscular young men who worked around the hotel and on the beaches. The kind of woman he preyed upon? If so, why wasn't he encouraging her instead of mocking her? Could it really be true that he was ready to fleece Zoe? If that was the case Griff wouldn't want Maddy telling her godmother that he had made a pass at her, would he?

He made no move to hold her as she snatched her hand away, seething with indignation. 'Maybe half the women in Mustique have thrown themselves at you, Mr "Griff will do", she told him with considerable force, 'but, I can assure you, you are perfectly safe from me.'

'I'd be perfectly safe from you if you stripped naked and danced the limbo. I don't like heartless girls who tease.' His green eyes, hard as the heart of an emerald, flickered carelessly over her, apparently unmoved by her outburst. 'And, judging by the performance I witnessed yesterday, you're obviously a past master. Or should I say mistress?'

'Mistress?' Maddy, who prided herself on her ability to take most things in her stride, felt a flutter of confusion ripple the smooth surface of her life. Disturbed, unsettled by the man's insolent manner, she lashed back, 'Hardly that. It was doubtless his desperation to get into my bed that drove Rupert into offering marriage,' she responded vigorously, without pausing to consider the wisdom of such a statement.

'There's no need to explain; the picture came over loud and clear.' His voice was barbed. 'If you can drive a man that far you must have a rare gift for the game.'

'It's not a game,' she said stiffly, fervently wishing that she had kept to her plan to ignore him. But it was impossible to ignore him in the tiny confines of the aircraft. He reached across the small space between them to graze her mouth with the edge of his thumb and she gave a shuddering little gasp.

'Your lips drip ice, Miss Madeleine Osborne, but your eyes are on fire. A dangerous combination.' He tucked his thumb beneath her chin and forced it up so that she was looking straight up into those insolent green eyes. 'One day you'll meet someone who won't take no for an answer.'

'You?' She had intended cold mockery, derision. The word came out as a breathy little gasp, an invitation.

'Would you like to find out?' He didn't wait for her answer but reached for the dark glasses perched on the ledge above the instrument panel and slipped them on.

And, following his example, she slipped on her own sunglasses and pushed them firmly up her arrow-straight nose, signalling that as far as she was concerned the conversation was at an end. It should never have started. She wasn't so easy to provoke under the normal course of events, but this man had rattled her from the

first moment she'd set eyes on him. Tease indeed! As if
Rupert Hartnoll's proposal had been welcome... On
the contrary she had been less than happy when he had
arrived unexpectedly in Mustique a few days after them,
especially since he had so easily persuaded her father
to let him stay at the villa they had rented. But then
Michael Osborne was impatient to become a grandfather and, presented with a perfectly eligible suitor, he
had been a more than willing accomplice.

Maddy glanced at Griff from behind the relative
safety of the darkened lenses. She wasn't in the least
surprised that he appealed to women like Zoe with too
much money and nothing to keep them occupied. He
had the kind of body any woman would find irresistible
and, if not precisely handsome, his strongly moulded
face and the well-defined curve of his mouth suggested
a sensuality...

Confused at the turn her thoughts were taking,
Maddy tightened her lips. Handsome is as handsome
does, she reminded herself very firmly, then threw an
exasperated glance at the cockpit ceiling. Oh, Zoe, she
thought, why couldn't you take up knitting and grow
old gracefully?

Griff reached up for the radio, speaking to traffic
control to inform them that he was approaching
Paradise Island.

'See you in a couple of weeks, Griff. Have a good
holiday,' the voice crackled back before signing off. He
hooked the radio back up. Maddy frowned, surprised
that he hadn't immediately contacted the next control
area. But she had learned to fly in the busy airspace
near London. Out here everything was more—well,
relaxed.

'You're going on holiday?' she demanded. The words

were out before she could recall them. She had assumed that he would be working, that she would at least have some time alone with Zoe to find out what was going on. But if he was going to be there all the time. . . He was staring at her. 'The air traffic controller said. . .' she began, then coloured. 'It doesn't matter.'

'A couple of weeks' fishing, if you've no objection,' he said abruptly. He didn't elaborate and she left it. It didn't matter to her what he planned to do, and since she knew Zoe loathed fishing they would at least have some time alone to talk.

She glanced out of the cockpit. They had dropped height considerably, she noticed with surprise as they approached a small island. From the air it seemed deserted. Not a sign of life, no craft to mar the perfection of a narrow horseshoe inlet that ran up to a small, sheltered beach fringed with palms and tumbled rocks. There was no dwelling to spoil the perfect natural mop of lush greenery that decorated the hilltop centre although she knew that could be deceptive. Few islands were totally uninhabited and the windward side might be choc-a-bloc with holiday-makers. But somehow she didn't think so.

'Is that Paradise Island?'

'Like to have a closer look?' It wasn't a polite invitation and she turned at the sudden tenseness in his voice. Then the engine gave a little splutter and the propeller ceased to spin. Maddy watched, fascinated, as Griff switched off the engine, pushed in the throttle, turned off the fuel—classic textbook procedure prior to an emergency landing. . . 'Shoes, glasses, false teeth,' he snapped urgently. 'Open your door. Now!'

Her eyes saw what was happening but her brain wasn't taking any calls. 'I haven't got false. . .' Then the sudden realisation that the engine had cut out, that the crackling chatter from the radio had abruptly ceased and that the only sound was the air rushing past the fuselage broke through the disbelief and she reacted. She kicked off her shoes, flung off her glasses, flipped the doorlock before burying her head in her lap.

CHAPTER TWO

MADDY, her head buried in her lap, waited for the impact and prayed. As they hit the water, there was a jolt that rattled her teeth and threw her against the restraints and she kept her hands tight about her head as they bounced across the smooth water of the inlet, biting down hard to stop a scream escaping. She was so tense that she didn't realise the plane had finally come to a halt until there was a touch on her shoulder. 'You can come out now, Miss Osborne.'

She lifted her head a little, hardly able to believe that they were riding on the glassy smooth water of the inlet. She knew enough to understand the skill it had taken to glide the little seaplane to a safe landing and she cleared her throat to tell him so. But when she tried to speak nothing came out. She cleared her throat again. 'Well, any landing you can walk away from. . .' she said, somewhat flippantly, only to be surprised by the unexpected shake in her voice.

'In this case, swim away from.' They had come to a standstill in the middle of the bay. 'Or rather, paddle away from.' He glanced at her. 'At least you didn't have hysterics, for which small mercy I suppose I should be grateful.'

'I never have hysterics,' she said, but what had started as a rebuke degenerated into a nervous giggle that sounded stupidly loud in the utter silence of the inlet. 'Would now be a good time to start?' she asked.

'Why don't you save it until we reach dry land?' he suggested. 'Then you can really let yourself go.'

Griff opened the cockpit door on his side and climbed down onto the float, rocking the machine precariously. Maddy finally succumbed to a little scream and, terrified that the plane would tip over and sink, rapidly followed suit, slipping precariously as her legs buckled beneath her, unexpectedly all rubber. She clung for a moment to one of the wing struts, clenching her teeth to stop them chattering as, somewhat belatedly, she began to shake with the shocking realisation of just how close to catastrophe they had come.

Griff, however, was sitting astride the other float apparently quite unconcerned. Perhaps emergency landings were a regular occurrence for him and he took them in his stride. He turned and, seeing her clinging to the strut for dear life, raised a sardonic brow. 'What's the matter?'

'N-nothing.' It was suddenly quite ridiculously important not to appear a shivering wimp. 'I. . .I'm just not dressed for a swim, that's all.'

He turned and looked at her, a slight frown creasing his forehead. Then he shrugged. 'Strip off if you don't want your clothes to get wet,' he invited somewhat astringently. 'It won't bother me.'

She glared at him. 'I remember. You're impervious. Well, thanks all the same,' she replied with resolution, 'but I'm sure I'll manage. And I'm not about to do a limbo dance, either.' His eyebrows rose a touch and too late she remembered that, as her father had suggested, she was supposed to be the epitome of helplessness. 'Just in case you were wondering,' she added, and turned quickly away to stare down into water so clear that she could see the ripples of sand on the bottom.

But that gave no indication of the likely depth—it could just as easily have been five feet or fifteen. And the beach was a couple of hundred yards away. Rather more than a paddle.

She lowered herself into the sea. As she'd suspected, it was too deep to stand. For a moment she hung onto the float, then she pushed off and headed towards the island, the desire for solid land, to feel the soft white sand of the beach beneath her feet suddenly quite overwhelmingly strong as her crisp, incisive crawl drove her through the water.

'Where are you going, Miss Osborne?' Griff's voice carried clearly across the surface of the sea and, surprised, she stopped and turned, treading water. Where on earth did he think she was going? He was still sitting astride the float, his strong, tanned thighs lapped by the wavelets.

'Sightseeing,' she snapped, and spluttered as the seawater lapped into her mouth. 'Where do you think?'

'Haven't you forgotten something?'

Her only thought had been to get ashore. Despite the appearance of total isolation, there *had* to be someone about who could help them. 'What?' she demanded.

He pointed above his head. 'We can't leave this out here. When I said paddle, I meant paddle.' He demonstrated by dipping his hand in the water and using it like an oar to propel the aircraft forward.

'But. . .' He was right, of course. The plane couldn't be left untethered in the middle of the bay. Even a gentle breeze could blow it out onto the reef, or onto the rocks that tumbled around the little bay, although right at that moment she was in no mood to care.

'But you're so *strong*, Griff,' she pointed out with just

a touch of malice. 'You don't need little me to help you.'

His grin was heart-lurchingly unexpected. 'In this instance, Miss Osborne, strength has nothing to do with it. If I paddle on my own, I'll just go round in circles.' And he drew a small, insolent circle in the air with his hand. 'And since Paradise Island is uninhabited for most of the year our best hope of early rescue is if I can get the radio working.'

'Most of the year? What about now?' she asked hopefully. She found the thought of leaving him to paddle around in circles a tempting one.

'You're out of luck, I'm afraid. The owner doesn't have too much time for sunbathing.'

'And you would know?'

'Yes, I do.' She regarded him through narrowed eyes. He might, of course, be bluffing. She was quite certain that he was capable of bending the truth to his own ends. But what ends? And his warning that they could not look for help from the island only confirmed her own impression from the air. The radio did seem to be their most likely hope of immediate rescue. And immediate rescue was very important. She hadn't the slightest wish to be stranded on a desert island with this particular man for a moment longer than she could help. If that meant helping him paddle his damned plane, then so be it.

She swam back to the plane and hauled herself onto the float she had so recently abandoned, but this time she had sea-water streaming from her hair and clothes.

'Pity about that,' Griff said, a little smugly, she thought as she wrung out her hair. 'You should have taken my suggestion. Wet clothes are so. . .uncomfortable.' She was painfully aware that her silk camisole was clinging revealingly to her bare skin, that he could not fail to notice that she was not wearing a bra. He was enjoying her discomfiture; his sympathy, in fact, was pure mockery.

'They'll soon dry,' she snapped, although neither the top nor her fine linen calf-length shorts were likely to recover from their unscheduled drenching. 'Shall we get on?' she demanded, only too aware of his amusement and afraid that she had blushed once again. The afternoon sun drying the sea-water on her face made it difficult to tell.

Griff obligingly opened the float locker and, producing a couple of oars, tossed one across to her. She caught it, regarded it doubtfully, then following Griff's example she dipped it into the water and began to paddle. It took a few minutes to get the hang of it, and she was painfully aware that Griff was watching her floundering attempts at oarsmanship with amusement.

Maddy had to work twice as hard as he did to keep the plane going in a straight line, but she refused to beg him to take it more slowly. By the time they neared the beach the muscles in her arms, her back and legs felt as if they were on fire. As she lay weakly along the float, however, Griff jumped down into waist-deep water.

'We can push from here,' he said, then clicked his tongue against his teeth. 'Come along, Miss Osborne, there's no time to relax; we're not finished yet,' he said briskly, as out of breath as if he had just been for a gentle stroll along the beach.

Relax? But she didn't even have the strength to scowl. Instead she slid from the float and, ignoring her screaming muscles as best she could, helped him to ground the plane on the safety of the beach, then she simply fell back against the sand and closed her eyes.

The sand was soft and blissfully warm, and she could have lain there for the rest of the afternoon, but Griff had other ideas.

'No time for sunbathing,' he advised. 'You'd better make a start collecting something to make a fire.'

'You're joking.' She didn't move. 'It's got to be eighty degrees.'

'I wasn't planning to sit by it and keep warm.'

'A signal fire?' Still she hadn't moved, but she opened her eyes, lifting her hand to shade them from the sun to look at her tormentor. He was standing ankle-deep in sand, muscular arms akimbo, regarding her recumbent body with irritation. Maddy, riled at this, said, 'How quaint. But wouldn't it be simpler to radio for help?'

'I don't expect you to understand, Miss Osborne, but the aircraft suffered a complete electrical failure. That's why we're in this predicament.'

'Can't you fix it?'

'I will certainly give it a try,' he conceded, 'but I'm a pilot, not an electrical engineer.' He shrugged. 'Of course, if you feel you are more qualified than me to check it out, I'd be quite happy to trade places.'

'I put a plug on a hairdryer,' she offered. 'Once.' Not quite the truth, but she had very little insight into the workings of a radio.

'Then I'll leave you to start building a fire.'

Maddy eased herself into a sitting position, stifling a groan as every muscle protested. She had thought she was fit, but clearly her daily swim hadn't prepared her for the kind of punishment her body had just endured. 'Surely you carry flares?' she asked. 'Isn't it mandatory?'

He regarded her thoughtfully. 'Probably. I'll organise some next time I'm in dock.'

'I should have thought Dragonair would have insisted on it.'

'Dragonair?' He glanced up at the plane then offered a regretful smile. 'I'm afraid this old crate doesn't belong to Dragonair. I bought it from them a couple of months ago.'

'And they didn't bother to remove their logo? A little careless of them.'

'An oversight.'

'And in the meantime you're trading on their good name...' He regarded her with a wry smile, but Maddy wasn't interested in his shady trading practices. She had thought of something far more disturbing. 'That means...they won't be looking for you when you're overdue.'

'There's no reason why they should,' he agreed, apparently without concern. 'But I'm sure Zoe will raise the alarm, eventually. Meantime...'

'Firewood.' She glanced around. It was suddenly very important to start a fire. The small beach was thickly rimmed with palms that occasionally dropped storm-damaged fronds. It shouldn't be too much hard work to gather a few. 'Where do you want it?'

'Far enough away from the plane not to set light to it, wouldn't you say?' He grinned. 'Better keep that as a final resort.'

Maddy hauled herself to her feet and staggered up the beach. She had been flying in a pensioned-off crate flown by some ne'er-do-well pilot that her godmother had taken a fancy to. She threw him a sideways glance as he climbed into the cockpit. No. That wasn't fair. He was a first-class pilot. It was down to him that she was still in one piece.

And when she didn't arrive at the appointed hour

Zoe would certainly raise the alarm. In fact, she thought with a sudden brightening of spirits, it was possible that a signal fire might bring help more quickly than Griff's attempts to repair the radio. This encouraging thought gave her all the incentive she needed and she moved more eagerly to gather palm fronds.

She was standing, hands on hips, admiring her handiwork when Griff joined her.

'Was that all you could manage?' He gave the structure a prod with his foot and her neat wigwam effect collapsed in an untidy heap. 'Well, it's a start, I suppose. You'll just have to put your back into it tomorrow.'

'A start. . .?' she spluttered.

But he didn't give her a chance to tell him just how hard she'd been working. 'You can leave it for now. No one is going to be looking for us before morning and we've more urgent things to consider.'

'What could possibly be more urgent than a signal fire?'

His green eyes seemed to dance in the light reflected off the sea. 'Fresh water, food. And then there is the small matter of where we are going to spend the night,' he said. And he smiled.

'Spend the night?' she repeated dully. And suddenly the importance of what he'd said about the fire sank in. She would have to put her back into it tomorrow. Tomorrow!

In a sudden panic, she looked around and to her dismay saw from the angle of the sun that it was already well into the afternoon. Calm. She must keep calm. Easier said than done.

'Didn't you manage to fix the electrics?' she demanded. Then, realising that she sounded just a touch hysterical, she added as airily as she could manage with a throat that the very mention of fresh water had rendered a desert, 'Perhaps we'd better light the fire now.'

'That pathetic heap won't last long enough to attract attention,' he said dismissively.

'I'll fetch some more fuel,' Maddy said, and without waiting for his answer took a step towards the palms. He captured her wrist, halting her abruptly and preventing her from moving away. She tried to shake him off, be about her business. 'Let me go,' she demanded. 'I've got to—'

'Miss Osborne, right now it's more important that we prepare ourselves for the night.'

'I disagree,' she said.

'When I'm forming a committee I'll let you know. In the meantime, just do as you're told.' She tried to pull free, but made no impression on the firm grasp about her wrist and furiously opened her mouth to protest, but he wasn't interested. 'So, unless you can fish. . . ?'

'Fish? Of course I can't fish.'

'Well, since the island doesn't boast a local branch of Fortnum's one of us has to provide supper.' He glanced towards the tangled heap of palm fronds, a wicked glint lighting his eye. 'You could, of course, try sending a smoke signal. . .'

'Very funny.'

He shrugged. 'It's important, I find, to keep a sense of humour under even the most difficult circumstances.'

She glowered at him. 'Ha, ha.'

'That's the spirit. And tomorrow I'll teach you how to survive in the wild. If we're here long enough you might eventually catch something other than a cold—'

'Long enough!' she exclaimed.

He shrugged. 'I don't suppose it will be more than a

day or two, Miss Osborne,' he said, and his mouth twisted into a dangerous little smile. 'You'll be home in time to unwrap the gifts heaped beneath your Christmas tree.'

'All I want for Christmas is a quiet holiday in the sun,' Maddy declared.

'Maybe.' He looked unconvinced. 'But we'll have to pass the time somehow.'

'In your dreams,' she snapped. His jaw tightened and this time when she wrenched on her wrist he did not detain her.

'There's a pool up there; I suggest you fetch some water.' Griff pointed to what might have been an overgrown path leading from the beach and held out a bucket that he had brought from the plane. In it were her sandals and a machete. In his other hand he carried a small fishing spear. 'A fair division of labour, don't you think? And, traditionally, fetching water is women's work.'

She ignored the bucket. 'You Tarzan, me Jane?'

He took her hand and placed the bucket handle in it. 'In your dreams, darling,' he murmured, with a grin that infuriated her far more than his words.

'Nightmare, more like,' she retaliated.

'How pleasant that we agree about something. And if you're back before me, light a fire,' he tossed over his shoulder as he turned away, apparently certain of her obedience.

'I haven't got a match,' she snapped. 'And, before you dare ask, I was never a boy scout!'

He turned then. His slow, appraising glance began at her feet and rose by way of a pair of long, willowy legs dusted with powdered white sand, the crumpled ruin of her shorts draped over well-rounded hips, a neat waist and the all too obvious curve of firm breasts unhampered by a bra under the damply revealing silk of her camisole. Then he met her eyes. 'Miss Osborne,' he said finally, 'I promise you that I would never, in a million years, mistake you for a boy scout.' He grinned as she gasped at his impudence, but, unabashed, he tossed her a lighter. 'Don't lose it,' he warned, 'or you'll be eating raw fish.'

'You've got to catch it first,' Maddy reminded him, before turning abruptly towards the dense green thicket at the edge of the beach. By the time she had reached it and stopped to put on her shoes, Griff had disappeared. For a crazy moment relief and panic in almost equal measure overwhelmed her, but panic was the marginally stronger feeling and she came close to chasing after him. begging him not to leave her alone.

Oh, wouldn't he like that? she thought, deriding her own weakness. What ironical little twist of fate had stranded her on an uninhabited island with the most insolent, vexing man she had ever had the misfortune to meet? A vivid recollection of the way he had picked her up so effortlessly and swung her into the aircraft intruded uncomfortably. Vexing, perhaps, but dangerous too. She hadn't forgotten the unexpected jolt as his hands had grasped her waist, that long raking look that had burned into her soul.

Maddy felt a sharp stab of guilt. She had angrily denied his accusation of flirting and yet she had found it hard to keep her eyes off him, and her reaction to his touch had hardly been discouraging. . .

'Oh, come along, Maddy,' she said firmly to herself. 'Zoe will be raising the alarm at this very moment.' And with that thought to comfort her she grasped the machete and with a savage swipe attacked the overgrown path. The eldritch screech of some unseen, unknown creature, caught up and echoed through the forest by a host of unearthly voices, almost undid her.

For a moment she stood rooted to the spot, heart pounding, her tongue like a lump of wood in her mouth, incapable of raising a cry for help. Then she saw the innocent agent of her terror flapping noisily high above her in the trees—a bird of some kind, brilliant blue, and then another and another. She began to laugh. Too many shocks for one day, that was all. That was all.

She sank onto her knees on the sand. She was laughing, but there were tears rolling down her cheeks. She knew she was near hysteria and tried to fight it, dragging in air in a desperate fight for breath, but it was running away with her, unstoppable, until, without any warning, she was wrenched to her feet.

'Stop that!'

She tried to speak, to explain that she was trying to stop, wanted to stop, but she couldn't. Instead she continued to laugh uncontrollably, her tear-filled eyes rippling over Griff's angry image until his face swam before her. He shook her but that just seemed to make things worse, then unexpectedly he released her shoulder and slapped her.

Abruptly she stopped, her hand flying to her cheek, her head all too painfully clear in the sudden silence— clear enough to want to strike him back. But as her tawny eyes sparked a storm warning a long, shuddering sob shook her entire body and, with an impatient exclamation, Griff caught her in his arms, holding her against the broad strength of his chest while she shivered and fought him. 'Stop that,' he demanded harshly, then, a fraction more gently, 'Stop it, now.' Just as quickly as it had seized her, the hysteria left her and she stopped fighting, slumping against him, her cheek pressing against his warm shoulder, her head filled with the slow, comforting thump of his heartbeat. 'It will be all right,' he murmured. 'Trust me.'

Maddy raised long, damp lashes to look up into his face and for just a moment was certain the expression that darkened his eyes was concern. For a lingering moment she clung to that, needing to be held, comforted, then she gave a little gasp.

'I wouldn't trust you half as far as I could throw you,' she said, pulling abruptly away from the dangerous comfort of his broad chest, wiping away the shaming tears with the heel of her hand.

'I'll put your rudeness down to delayed reaction,' he said with a clipped, dismissive edge to his voice, and he released his hold on her and stepped back, leaving her swaying slightly on still unsteady legs. 'Just this once.'

That tone was all Maddy needed to stiffen her backbone, restore her to her senses. 'Were you waiting for me to thank you for such prompt intervention?' She raised her fingers tellingly to her cheek, stretching her jaw in a somewhat exaggerated fashion.

'No. But you have my assurance that you are entirely welcome, Miss Osborne.'

Her tawny gold eyes flashed angrily. ' "Miss Osborne," ' she mimicked. 'Such formality seems a little out of place in these surroundings. Particularly since I just gave you the opportunity to do what you've clearly been itching to do ever since you set eyes on me.'

She knew even as she said the words that she was being very stupid—stupid in a way that was quite unlike her—but the moment she had set eyes on this man she had recognised some primeval attraction between them.

He was regarding her now with a look that made her curl her toes as she fought the desire to lash out.

He reached out and captured a bright, wayward tendril of hair, wrapping it around his fingers and holding it up to the light. 'Red hair and a temper to match. A dangerous combination, Maddy Rufus,' he said, with that drawly, teasing voice that got right under her skin. She flushed, furiously, unaccountably angry with Zoe. Had she amused her young lover with the tale of how Maddy, furious at the bestowal of Rufus as a nickname because of her copper-red hair, had defiantly painted every strand of it scarlet? She whipped herself with the thought.

'I think, after all, that I prefer Miss Osborne,' she said coldly.

'You're quite sure about that?' He raised darkly defined brows in sardonic mockery.

She swallowed, hard. It was time to take back some measure of control. 'Quite sure, Mr Griffin.'

He pulled his fingers from her hair, leaving a soft ringlet where they had been. But the moment of danger was over. 'I told you, everyone calls me Griff.'

Maddy, almost herself again, arched one darkly winged brow. 'Of course. "Griff will do",' she said, not bothering to hide the edge of sarcasm. Then she gave a little shrug. 'Nothing wrong with it as far as it goes. Such a pity the same can't be said of the manners.'

Griff's mouth straightened in a mirthless smile. 'Let's be honest. . .Miss Osborne. . .you have a few failings in that direction yourself.' Before she could respond he handed her the bucket. 'Now, do you think we could resume this conversation some other time? It isn't going to stay light for much longer.'

*

For a while she took considerable satisfaction in imagining that each branch, each overhanging leathery leaf that she slashed in two with the machete bore the arrogant, overbearing, infuriating features of 'Griff will do'. The nerve of the man, to suggest that she was bad-mannered when he... But then she burst upon a scene so enchanting, so magical that it would have warmed the most cynical tour operator's heart and she instantly forgot her anger.

A shimmering cascade of water dominated the clearing, falling dizzyingly from some unseen source, tumbling and spilling out in tiny diversions to spray over moss-laden rocks and tropical ferns in a lacy mist before plunging into a large dark pool. Delicately patterned wild orchids trailed carelessly over the surrounding glade, epiphytes sprouted from the branches of trees that might have been there for a thousand years. A fairy scene from the Garden of Eden.

But if she had been Eve, Maddy thought with an unexpected giggle, and Griff had been Adam the human race would have had a bumpy start. *Oh, really?* Startled by this unexpected sideswipe from her subconscious, she found herself remembering all too vividly the feel of his arms about her. 'Really!' she said, out loud, as if this put the matter beyond doubt.

But the light was going under the eerie green canopy of the forest and she didn't have time to worry about her body's unexpected response to a man her head disliked quite intensely—or time to linger by the pool, strip off her clothes and wash away the salt and sweat that clung to her skin. Instead she scooped up a bucket of water and poured it over herself, gasping at the unexpected chill, then relishing the slow trickle of water through her hair, over her shoulders and down her body.

Tomorrow she would bathe here, she promised herself, dipping her hand into the pool, raising it to her lips to slake her thirst with the wonderfully clear water, before filling her bucket in much the same way as women have been doing since the beginning of history and making her dripping way back to the beach.

There was no sign of Griff, but Maddy had no need to be driven to build a cooking fire; she was hungrier than she had been since the beginning of her holiday. It didn't occur to her to doubt that he would succeed in the task he had set himself. Griff would succeed at anything he set his mind to. And just what has he set his mind to regarding you? her subconscious prompted. 'Nothing. He doesn't even like me,' she said, but couldn't help remembering that moment when he had looked at her, held her protectively... 'I'm immune,' she protested, shivering just a little. 'And besides, there's Zoe.' And, having cleared up that point, she set about making a fire.

When Griff returned with his catch she was coughing from the smoke that had blown in her face as the wind had eddied across the beach, waving her hand frantically to clear the air. He had stripped to the waist, his shoulders and chest were dewed with sea-water and his dark hair was slicked back. His shorts were still dry. Had he swum naked? She quickly dropped her eyes to the fire, glad that her cheeks were already pink from the heat, but if she had expected praise for her efforts she was doomed to disappointment.

'You were right about not being a boy scout,' was his only comment as, bare, sand-encrusted feet planted firmly apart, he stood over her and tossed a fish down beside her—for all the world, she thought furiously, like some caveman hunter bringing home the fruit of his labours. It was a grouper—a brown-mottled, bewhiskered fish, ugly as sin, but excellent to eat. This one was small for the breed. They could, Maddy knew, grow to positively monster proportions in the underwater caves where they lurked, but this one would make a good meal for the two of them. Griff had gutted and cleaned it, clearly assuming that she would take over the woman's role and do the rest. She looked at it uncertainly. It wasn't that she couldn't cook. She poached a fine salmon when the occasion demanded, but cooking a grouper on an open fire without utensils had somehow been overlooked on her cordon bleu course.

Ignoring the fish, she scrambled to her feet and followed Griff in the direction of the plane. 'I'd like my bag,' she said stiffly, and waited for him to get it for her. 'I need a change of clothes.'

'Help yourself,' he said carelessly, taking the mooring rope and walking up the beach to the nearest palm, leaving her to pull her own heavy bag from the hold.

Maddy was achingly tired but she wasn't about to give this obnoxious creature the pleasure, the satisfaction of seeing that she was as near the end of her tether as she had ever been. She caught the handle and pulled furiously. The bag swung free rather more easily than she'd anticipated and she staggered back and sat abruptly on her backside with it in her lap. For a moment—one miserable, split-second moment as she sat on the wet sand—she wished that she really were one of those helpless, pathetic women who just cried when things got beyond them—the kind of woman whom men rushed to comfort at the drop of a hat, the kind of woman whom she was certain Griff would pick up, wrap in his strong arms and hug better. But she wasn't. She was a hard-working businesswoman who plastered her own cuts, and she reminded herself very firmly that she preferred it that way.

She scrambled quickly to her feet and searched for her sunglasses where she had thrown them on the floor of the aircraft. They weren't there and she climbed into the cockpit, finally spotting them poking out of the map pocket where Griff must have put them for safety. As she pulled them out an envelope came out with them, falling to the floor and spilling its contents—a cheque and a note.

She didn't mean to look but Zoe's familiar signature was unmistakable. And the sum made her gasp.

CHAPTER THREE

'DID you find what you were looking for?'

His voice, just below the cockpit window, made her jump and guiltily she pushed the cheque and note back into the envelope, stuffing them deep into the map pocket. 'Yes, thank you.' Forcing a smile to her lips, she turned and glanced down at him. 'Just my handbag.' She held it up.

'Your lipstick could certainly do with a retouch,' he agreed, but he held out his hands. 'Come on, I'll give you a hand down.' Surprised by this unlooked-for gallantry, she put her hands on his shoulders and allowed him to swing her to the ground. He held onto her waist for a moment longer than absolutely necessary. 'And if you want anything from the cockpit just ask me in future.'

Because she might see something she shouldn't? Too late for that, Mr Griffin, she thought. 'I'm not entirely helpless,' she said stiffly, trying to ignore the the perilous nearness of his body. She didn't normally find it so hard. But then Hugo Griffin ignored every 'keep off' sign that she had erected with such care over the years. . .

'Whether you are helpless or not remains to be seen, but you won't be much use to me if you break your ankle, will you, Maddy Rufus?'

'I've no intention of breaking anything,' she snapped, but although his words were apparently callous, she knew he was right. It didn't make it any easier to take.

He released her and returned to his task of tethering the plane and she found herself letting out a long, slow sigh of relief as she knelt and opened her bag to search for a T-shirt.

But Griff hadn't quite finished. 'I do realise that you wouldn't dream of sitting down to dinner without changing first,' he said, giving the rope a final tug. 'But since, for once in your life, you're going to have to cook it it might be advisable—'

'I wasn't actually planning on wearing an evening dress. . .' she began, then saw amusement flicker momentarily in his eyes as they swept her damp, bedraggled figure before lighting on the elegant black gown that lay on top of her bag. 'At least, not this one. A little too formal for the beach.' She flicked it to one side. 'Now this. . .' She held out a simple slip of a dress, cut on the bias from heavy cream silk.

His eyes snapped. 'I don't like you in that.'

Maddy stared at the dress. It was a favourite; she had been wearing it when Rupert had flung himself at her. . . Suddenly she didn't much care for it herself. 'No?' She dropped it and rose to her feet. 'I suppose it'll have to be the black, then.'

'I look forward to it. In the meantime your fire appears to have died down sufficiently to bake the fish.'

Her fire indeed! She laid no claim to it. 'And just how do you propose I do that?' she demanded. 'Or do you have a secret supply of aluminium foil?'

'No, but there's plenty of the local equivalent.'

'The local equivalent?' She propped her fists on her hips. 'I really can't wait to hear this.'

'Banana leaves.' He began to walk away, then stopped and turned back. 'Just watch out for the spiders.'

Maddy's scalp prickled. 'Couldn't you—?' she began, then saw his slow smile.

'You're not scared, are you, Maddy? Only, you did say you weren't entirely helpless. . .'

'No, of course I'm not scared,' she said, too quickly, but in the face of his cool appraisal she clung stubbornly to her pride. 'I'm not in the least bit frightened of spiders.'

'No?'

Maddy disdained to answer but threw him a look that should have fried him on the spot. Disappointingly he appeared not to notice. In fact he walked away without so much as a scorch-mark.

It wasn't far to the spot where she had seen a banana tree and, knowing it would be fatal to stop and think, she immediately hacked off several of the thick, leathery leaves, leaping back as they crashed to the floor. Then she grabbed them by the tip and almost ran back to the beach, stumbling over roots as she went, her skin almost crawling as she flung the leaves from her and stepped quickly back, half expecting a host of hairy beasts to leap out and devour her. Nothing happened. Of course nothing happened. He had wound her up and she had performed, as obliging as a well-oiled clockwork toy.

'All right. . .Maddy?' Griff said lightly as he joined her, hardly bothering to hide his amusement.

'Just fine. . .Griff.'

'Now, while dinner bakes I suggest you give a little thought to where you're going to build your shelter.' Startled, she looked up. 'You're more than welcome to share mine, of course,' he offered with mocking courtesy. 'But something tells me that you wouldn't be very keen on the idea.'

'Then you're more perceptive than I thought,' she replied, with considerably more poise than she was feeling, glad that the heat from the fire covered her blushes. 'I'd rather sleep on the beach.'

He smiled. At least, she thought that minute contraction of the lines fanning out from shaded eyes might just be his idea of a smile. 'Well, there's plenty of it to choose from. Help yourself,' he said provokingly.

Damn! She'd done it again—put his back up when he might have helped her. But she was not about to beg him to do anything for her if that was what he was hoping. Or was it worse than that? Was he taking advantage of the situation to make a little money from a wealthy young woman who was at the mercy of the elements? The thought was not a very pleasant one and, despite her father's suspicions, if she hadn't seen Zoe's cheque she was certain that it would never have crossed her mind. But now as she tried to push the idea away it seemed to take hold and grow. Well, there was only one way to find out.

She looked up at him, trying to ignore the strong line of his jaw, the blazing green eyes that promised so much. . .hypnotising her, enticing her into dangerous waters. 'How much would you want to build me a shelter?' she said abruptly.

'How much?' He said it lightly enough, yet his eyes had clouded and a muscle tightened at the corner of his mouth. 'It's odd but for a moment I almost believed you when you said you weren't entirely helpless.' He shook his head. 'There's no room service in paradise, Maddy. If you want a shelter you're going to have to build one yourself. I'm not for sale.'

Stunned, she remained motionless as he strode swiftly away from her. She should have been angry, but she

wasn't. Her heart was singing at his swift rejection of
her offer of money. Then she came down to earth with
a bump. With Zoe's cheque tucked away in his plane,
he wasn't likely to risk everything for what she might
offer.

'Damn! That wasn't very clever.' She glanced at the
fire, but there was nothing left to do. 'Better change for
dinner, Maddy, and put your thinking-cap on.'

At the far end of the beach the rocks formed a small
enclosure, wide open to the sky but offering enough
privacy to strip off and wipe herself down with the still
damp flannel from her sponge bag before applying a
generous helping of body lotion to her thirsty skin and
brushing out her long copper hair. She applied insect
repellent to the most sensitive areas and then dressed
in a pair of thin cotton trousers and a long-sleeved T-
shirt.

'You smell good enough to eat,' Griff remarked when
she rejoined him. Maddy raised her eyebrows to cover
her confusion at this unlooked-for compliment. 'I'm
sure the bugs will be grateful for the invitation to
dinner.'

'I'm wearing an insect repellent,' she replied, irritated
with herself for falling into his trap.

'Really?' He regarded her thoughtfully. 'If I was an
insect, I don't think I'd be repelled.'

'If you were an insect, I'd swat you,' she retaliated. It
was his turn to raise a sardonic brow and it occurred to
Maddy that if he were an insect, he would be a very
large one and swatting him would not be so simple. 'Do
you think the fish will be ready yet?' she asked quickly.

'No,' he said, and she had the uncomfortable feeling
that he knew precisely the reason for her abrupt change
of subject. What was it about him that set the hairs on

her skin up like the fur of a cat rubbed the wrong way so that she constantly lashed out at him? His arrogant manner infuriated her, it was true, and she had concrete evidence that his interest in Zoe involved money in some way. They were reasons enough to dislike him, distrust him even, but that wasn't what bothered her. Her reaction to him was on a deeper, more unsettling level altogether. He had the kind of power that did something impossible to her insides whenever he was close. And, like iron filings near a magnet, she could find no way to escape.

As if to give the lie to this thought she moved away from him and threw herself down on the sand. But still her eyes were drawn irresistibly to him. The sinking sun lit his profile against the darkening rocks, glowing against the warm skin of his shoulders and chest. She shivered. There was something almost savage about him, as if this untouched wilderness was his perfect environment. And yet in the cockpit of his plane was Zoe's cheque. Civilisation with a vengeance.

A while later he tossed a couple of coconuts onto the sand beside her. 'I've no rum to make a punch, but it will help the fish down.'

'I prefer my coconut milk straight.'

'Just as well, under the circumstances.'

'But it's a bit rough on you,' she said with mock concern. 'You were going on holiday, weren't you?'

'Was I?'

'The traffic controller hoped you had a good time when you signed off.' He frowned and her heart gave an odd little lurch. Had she heard something she shouldn't? 'Were you going somewhere nice?' she asked, hoping she sounded a great deal more casual about it than she felt. Or had he been going somewhere with a numbered bank account where he stashed his ill-gotten gains? Was that why he had been so put out at having to come and fetch her?

He shrugged and stretched out on the sand beside her, propping himself on one elbow. 'Just a couple of weeks' fishing. Here will do as well as anywhere.'

'You'll understand if I don't share your enthusiasm. I have absolutely no desire to spend two weeks here,' she said. His eyes danced over her face and she received the distant impression that she had said something to amuse him. But he didn't say anything. 'There isn't much in the way of home comforts or entertainment,' she reminded him.

'No, but I have you.'

'Me?' The word was startled from her.

'You are an endless source of entertainment, Maddy Rufus,' he said softly.

'I'm glad I prove useful for something.'

'Oh, you're going to be useful,' he assured her. 'Tomorrow you'll get your first fishing lesson. As for home comforts. . .' He waved a careless hand, taking in the scene around them. 'Perhaps you've been pampered long enough. It's time you had a taste of the *real* world.' Had she imagined the emphasis on 'real'? She certainly hadn't imagined the challenge in his voice, but she refused to apologise for her choice of holiday.

It was her first in the three hard years since she had started her own business. Spot a gap in the market and supply the need, was her father's philosophy, and never forget that people will always pay for the best. And after listening to his endless complaints about the poor quality of clerical staff available she had taken him at his word. But it had been hard work establishing her business and making it one of the most successful staff agencies in London. 'It looks,' she said somewhat pointedly, 'as if I'm going to have a taste whether I like it or not. At least until morning.'

'Well, don't worry. Paradise Island might be a little short on champagne but it has everything necessary for survival—good, clean water, fish to eat and fruit growing wild if you know where to look for it.'

'And coconuts,' she said, with just a touch of irony. 'Pity about the hot shower, a bed, and a well-stocked refrigerator.'

His eyes met hers. 'You don't need a refrigerator, there's a shower at the pool and if you want to sleep in comfort you could always weave yourself a hammock from wild vines.'

'Thanks, but I don't plan on stopping that long. The beach will do for tonight.'

'I do hope, for your sake, that the wind doesn't blow up.'

She picked up a handful of sand and let it trickle through her fingers. A windy night would be uncomfortable but she wasn't about to admit it. 'You've obviously been here before.' He didn't answer. 'When you've brought the owner here? Tell me about him. What's his name?' A thought suddenly struck her. 'Surely he has some kind of house here? Maybe even a radio?'

'Did you see any sign of a house?'

'Since I had my head in my lap I didn't see much at all.' She shrugged. If there had been a house, a radio, he would have used it. 'Do you think Zoe might have raised the alarm by now?'

'Maybe.' He sounded doubtful. 'The trouble is, I didn't tell her precisely when to expect us. Just some time before dark.' He paused. 'Or, if I had something to drop off at one of the other islands, maybe tomorrow morning.'

Maddy stared at him, not wanting to believe it but knowing only too well that in the laid-back, easygoing atmosphere of the Caribbean it was all too possibly the truth.

'Tomorrow morning?' she said, very softly, scarcely trusting herself to say the words out loud.

'In fact I don't suppose she'll actually begin to worry until the evening. My schedule was a little hazy when I spoke to her this morning.'

For the first time since they had made their unscheduled and somewhat precipitate landing, Maddy felt like screaming—just opening her mouth and screaming. But she didn't. It was far more important to find out just what he meant by 'hazy'. 'Did you say *tomorrow* evening?' she asked, with what she considered to be admirable self-control.

'That's not a problem, is it?' he drawled, with a stunning lack of concern.

'Problem?' She stared at him in total disbelief. 'Why on earth should that be a problem?' She didn't wait for him to answer but leapt to her feet and walked quickly down to the edge of the water. The sea swirled around her feet, sucking away the sand a little at a time, undermining her. Griff was doing that too—pulling away the certainties on which she had built her life, one by one: the certainty that she was firmly in control, the certainty that she knew exactly what she wanted, the certainty that she could never again feel anything. . .

'Time for dinner.' Griff's voice at her elbow a while later made her jump. He had piled a neat helping of the grouper's white flesh onto a piece of banana leaf and now offered it to her with mocking deference. The effect was somewhat sabotaged by his appearance. His shorts were oil-stained from his battle with the engine; he was wearing a fresh T-shirt, it was true, but the sleeves had been hacked from it without much consideration as to the aesthetics of the matter and his thick dark mop of hair looked as if it had been combed with his fingers.

'I'm not hungry,' she said, turning away, but he caught her chin and turned her back to face him so that the salty scent of the fish caught at the back of her throat.

'Of course you are. It won't hurt you to manage without cutlery and napkins for once.'

'I've eaten with my fingers before,' she said stiffly, lifting her chin away from his fingers.

'Really?' He sounded disbelieving. 'Don't worry, I won't tell. And the sea makes a pretty convenient finger-bowl.'

She gave him a cool glance, then shrugged and took the makeshift plate. 'Thank you,' she said, unbending slightly.

'You're very welcome.'

Maddy gave him a sharp look, but despite her suspicion that he was mocking her he appeared perfectly sincere. She settled back onto the sand and began to pull the fish to pieces with her fingers. Griff stretched out beside her and followed suit. She tried to ignore him, but short of turning her back to him that was impossible. And he would still be there. Probably until tomorrow evening. Better to try for some kind of truce.

'The last time I had grouper it was an enormous beast coated in rose mayonnaise, decorated with cucumber scales and with stuffed olives for eyes,' Maddy said, making an effort at neutral conversation but realising immediately that he would certainly take her words as a criticism of his efforts. She waited for Griff to make some disaparaging remark. He said nothing and somehow that was worse. Maddy felt her hackles rise. 'At a reception at the High Commission,' she added, forgetting her attempt at a truce in an effort to provoke him to some response.

Her father had business interests in the Caribbean and they had stayed in Barbados for a couple of days. Maddy, eager to get to Mustique had found it all rather irritating at the time, but the contrast between that event—the beautiful gowns of the women, the attentive, well-groomed young men eager to dance attendance on her every whim—and her present situation couldn't have been more spectacular.

'How did it taste?' he asked.

'Taste?' she asked absently.

'The fish?'

'Oh, the fish.' She considered the remains of her food. 'Not as good as this,' she admitted with some surprise.

'I don't suppose you'd worked as hard for it.'

She stiffened at the implied criticism. 'I certainly hadn't been in a plane wreck and hacked down half a jungle, if that's what you mean.'

'What else could I mean?' There was a teasing lilt to his voice and it was difficult to ignore the inviting way his eyes crinkled at the corners but Maddy did her best. 'You've the makings of a fine alfresco cook,' he said.

She had no wish to be thought a fine cook of any kind. 'I didn't do anything.'

'I've known women who could burn water,' he assured her.

'Really?' What women? How many? She slapped the errant thoughts away. 'Ah, well, there's a bit of a knack to water. I'm sure they had other talents that more than made up for it.'

He grinned. 'You may be right,' he said, and stood up, unfolding himself from the sand with the power and grace of a large cat. 'I think I'd better get the coconuts.'

Maddy bent to dip her hands into the sea to wash the fish from her fingers. The light was dying from a sky deepening rapidly from rose to purple. The swiftness of the Caribbean night never failed to startle or excite her. Already stars were appearing—glittering spots that would cluster and thicken in the intense darkness, so different from the pallid London sky that she was used to.

She turned as she heard Griff's feet on the sand behind her. He hefted a huge nut still encased in the thick green outer husk and with one swipe of the machete neatly sliced the top off. He handed it to her with a mock bow. 'I'm afraid you'll have to manage without a straw.' She pulled a face, then while he repeated the action with the second nut she tipped hers to her lips. Some of the milk made her mouth, most of it went down her chin.

'Next time I'll fly a scheduled airline,' she spluttered, attempting to capture the drips in her palm. 'They carry such simple necessities as straws.'

'But they're so predictable, so boring.' He took the nut from her and hacked a chunk of husk away to make it easier to drink from.

'You mean they fly to a schedule and don't strand you on a desert island?' she said.

'Not without the statutory eight gramophone records to keep you entertained for the duration. And a packet of straws for the coconuts. Shall I sing to you?'

'That depends. How good are you?'

'I'm certainly the best baritone on this island.'

'You're the only baritone. . .' He grinned. 'Why don't you sing "Show me the way to go home"?' she suggested.

'London? In December? No, thanks.' He lay back on the sand, staring up at the stars, his hands linked behind his head. 'Most people dream of living like this, in paradise. For the moment it's all yours. Why don't you relax and enjoy it while you can?'

'Relax? I've never worked so hard in my life.'

'But that's part of the pleasure. And this is the reward.' Above them the stars had clustered thickly, seeming almost close enough to touch against the velvet darkness of the night. She followed his example and lay back against the sand. 'Money can't buy this.'

'Easy for you to say. I'll bet whoever owns this island would tell a different tale.'

'You really shouldn't judge other people by your own standards.'

'At least I have some. . .' A shooting star streaked across the sky but before she could say anything Griff had seized her hand.

'Don't waste your wish, Maddy,' he warned. 'You'll be rescued soon enough.'

'I've nothing else to wish for.'

'Nothing?' Griff demanded, rolling over and propping himself upon his elbow. For a moment he stared down at her, a small crease furrowing his brow. 'I think that's the saddest thing I've ever heard.'

'Nonsense,' she said a little defensively. 'What's sad about it? I've everything that I could ever want.'

'Everything?' His frown deepened. 'You're a healthy young woman. Have you no desire for a family of your own?'

'How typical,' she declared, sitting up abruptly, and, pulling her hand free, she hugged her knees. The question was too personal, too intimate; it touched a raw and empty place within her. 'How typical of a man to believe that all any woman wants from life is a chance to wash his socks.'

'I doubt you'll ever have to wash anyone's socks,' he said with just a touch of sarcasm.

'The socks were metaphorical,' she said crushingly. 'It's the attitude—' She broke off, rather afraid that the small sound that had escaped his lips might have been stifled laughter. 'Besides, I have to find the right man first.'

'One with metaphorical feet, presumably.' He turned away and began to pick up small shells and toss them into the sea. 'What was the matter with the guy you turned down the other night?'

'You wouldn't understand,' she said.

'You could try me. We've nothing else to talk about.'

'We could talk about you for a change. What brought you to the Caribbean, for instance?'

'A job. The chance to do what I love most.'

'Flying? Don't you miss home?'

He turned to her. 'This is my home.'

'But you're English.'

'I've nothing to go back to Britain for. My father died in a mining accident when I was seven, my mother worked herself to death to give me an education—' He stopped abruptly. 'You're not getting off that lightly. You've a wish to make.'

She felt she had touched something, come close to what drove Hugo Griffin. But his face was shuttered and barred. 'There is something,' she admitted. 'I wish I had a cup of tea.'

He threw back his head and laughed. 'Make it a pot, I'd enjoy a cup, as well.'

'It's my wish,' she said primly, then stretched back on the sand and closed her eyes. 'If you want a cup of tea, you must wish for one yourself.'

'You'd enjoy it more if you shared,' he advised her, making her feel rather small. 'Besides, I've already made my wish.' This unexpected admission startled her into opening her eyes. He had rolled onto his stomach and was looking down at her, staring most particularly at her mouth, and her lips began to throb in time with her heartbeat.

'What?'

'If I tell you what it is, it won't come true. But I promise you I didn't waste it on a cup of tea.' His voice was velvet-rich and, to Maddy's ears, heavy with meaning. For a dangerous moment she was certain that he intended to kiss her and for a dangerous moment she wanted him to do just that.

'You mustn't wish for money,' she said quickly, with just a touch of panic in her voice. 'It has to be something totally impossible. A dream. . .'

'I know the rules and I'm very much afraid I've complied with every one.'

'An impossible dream?'

'"If ever any beauty I did see / Which I desir'd and got, t'was but a dreame of—"' He stopped abruptly, but Maddy didn't notice. She had seen something out of the corner of her eye and leapt to her feet, showering him with sand, oblivious to his furious exclamation.

'The fire,' she said. 'We've got to light the fire.' Without thinking she grabbed his hand. 'There! Look, a light. . .'

'It's very faint.'

Barely there at all. A tiny light that came and went with the motion of sea. It was probably miles away. 'But it might be a yacht!'

'It might just be a fisherman in a dinghy. Whatever it is, it's a long way away, Maddy,' he warned.

'But if we can see them they must be able to see us.'

'Only if they're looking.' Still he hadn't moved and time was passing.

'We have to try!' she insisted, groping in her pockets. 'Where's the lighter?'

'You used it to light the fire.' He was right but she didn't have it now. Had she dropped it? Her heart was beating too fast. Too fast to think clearly. Why wasn't he doing anything? 'Did you leave it in your shorts?' Had she? She threw a panic-stricken glance out to sea. Was the light still there? She searched frantically for a moment and then saw it once more. Further away?

Ignoring Griff's sharp exclamation, the jab of pain as her foot snagged against a shell half-buried in the sand, she turned and pounded along the beach to the pale smudge where her shorts were draped over a rock to dry.

For a moment her fumbling fingers missed the cheap little plastic throw-away tube that might save them and she was certain that the only means of signalling her presence on the island was lost somewhere in the sand. Then her fingers closed about the lighter and relief surged headily through her veins.

'Found it?' She hadn't heard Griff come up behind her and she jumped, quite literally, and for a moment the lighter wobbled precariously. His hand closed about her fingers, steadying them. 'Give it to me.'

He gathered the sprawled heap of palm fronds, scattered where he had kicked at the heap she had so neatly arranged, and Maddy fumed at the delay as he gathered a few pieces, broke them up to make kindling. Then she heard the snap of the lighter. There was a spark, but no flame.

'Come on,' Maddy urged.

'The lighter's wet,' he said, trying again.

'Let me try,' Maddy demanded impatiently. 'I did it before.'

He looked up, staring out to sea for a moment before handing over the lighter. She clicked it and it immediately burst into a bright flame but her shaking fingers couldn't make the kindling catch.

'Leave it, Maddy.' Griff's voice was gentle. Too gentle. He touched her shoulder. 'Whatever was out there has gone.' She refused to give up. 'The light has gone,' he repeated, then sank down onto his heels beside her and caught her hand, taking the lighter from her. Then he put his arm about her and pulled her to her feet, leaving the dark sea to confirm what he'd said.

She stared beyond him, scouring the surface of the water, determined that he should be wrong. But only starlight silvered the tips of the gentle waves.

'Oh.' The word was a little gasp as she realised just how much her hopes had leapt at the possibility of rescue. 'I'll organise everything better tomorrow. If only the lighter hadn't been wet...' She frowned. 'It worked when I lit the cooking fire.'

'These throw-away jobs can be temperamental.'

'I suppose so. And it doesn't matter,' she said, lifting her chin a little to hide her disappointment. 'We'll be missed sooner or. . .' The gentle hiccup of a sob broke through her brave words and somehow, before she knew what had happened, she was enfolded in a pair of strong arms and held against Griff's shoulder, his fingers tangling in her hair as he attempted to comfort her. And, heaven knew, she wanted to be held and comforted.

'Not quite as hardbitten as you thought?' he murmured, but she shook her head. He didn't understand. She was very far from being hardbitten, and right now the desperate see-sawing of her emotions had left her quite beaten. 'You're tired, Maddy. Come on. You should try and get some sleep.'

'Sleep?' The impossibility of sleeping under such circumstances appeared to have escaped him. But she didn't argue, allowing herself to be half led, half carried up the beach to the little lean-to hut he had built.

She was oddly reluctant to let go of him. It was dark and the little noises of the Caribbean night reached out from the forest, the ardent call of a bullfrog overlaying the stridulations of a million tiny creatures that from the fortified, nature-defying terrace of the Mustique beach house would have sounded charming. Here everything was so much closer, and as he set her down on the sand she clutched at him. 'Don't leave me.'

'I'm not going anywhere,' he said a little wryly as he detached her hands from his shoulders. 'Go on now. Go to sleep.'

She slid beneath the dark thatch of the makeshift hut and curled up into a defensive little ball like a miserable child. He had laid something—a towel, perhaps—over the sand. To her weary limbs it felt as soft as a feather bed. For a moment she lay there, conscious of tears welling in her eyes as she wondered whether her father was safely home. He would phone Zoe, expecting to speak to her. What would Zoe tell him? Then her brief descent into self-pity filled her with disgust and she rubbed angrily at her wet cheeks. She never cried. Griff was right—she should try and get some sleep. Everything would seem better in the morning.

Maddy eased off her trousers and rolled them up to make a pillow and then stretched out. Tomorrow they would be rescued and all this would just seem like a dream, she decided as she was caught out by an unexpected yawn. A very bad dream. Then she closed her eyes.

Maddy woke to a brilliant light shining in her eyes. And she blinked, trying to think where she was and why the bed was so hard. Then as she half turned to ease herself one thing became startlingly apparent. She was not alone.

CHAPTER FOUR

PARADISE. She was in paradise and Griff's smoothly muscled arm was about her waist, holding her fast against the warm, comforting frame of his body. She had asked him not to leave her and he had taken her at her word.

And shining in at her was the moon, huge and white, lighting a white path across the inlet as it sank slowly into the sea. For a moment Maddy watched entranced, the curve of her back nestled against his chest, her long legs tangled with his, which were longer still and shockingly hair-roughened.

For a moment she lay there, surprised by the rush of warmth, the unexpected pleasure of lying tucked within the protective curve of his body. Then his hand moved gently over her stomach to cradle the soft swell of her breast and Maddy froze. He had assumed her mute acceptance of his presence meant something else. In a moment of weakness last night she had wanted comfort, needed comfort But not that kind. She erupted from his grasp, leaping up without a thought as to the consequences.

'What on earth. . .?' He swore volubly as palm fronds showered down on him, the lean-to disintegrating about his ears. 'What the hell are you playing at?' he demanded, leaping to his feet and turning on her.

'Nothing. I have no desire to play.'

'And you think I have. Don't flatter yourself, woman,' he retorted, flinging off a palm leaf that clung stubbornly to his back. 'You were the one who begged me to stay with you; I was just—'

'Just what? Helping yourself?'

'If I had any intentions of helping myself, do you think you'd be talking about it right now? I *don't* help myself—'

'Oh, really? Well, I suggest you remind your roving hands,' she threw at him. 'They're not quite so restrained.'

For a moment he stared at her. 'My roving hands?' He said the words slowly, deliberately and took a step towards her. Maddy took a nervous step back. 'Where did they rove, Maddy?' She took another step back from eyes blazing darkly in the moonlight.

'I. . . I don't want to talk about it,' she snapped.

'Oh, but I insist. I want to know what fantasy has been conjured up by that overheated imagination of yours.'

'No fantasy,' she declared hotly, and this time as she stepped back she felt the sand wet beneath her feet.

'You don't imagine I was going to. . .take advantage of you, do you?' Maddy was beginning to regret her somewhat precipitate reaction. No doubt Griff had simply taken what had seemed to him the obvious and sensible decision to sleep alongside her, and if she didn't object to taking it further—well, she was certain that, despite his protestations, he would be more than happy to oblige. Or maybe he thought that she would willingly accept the situation in return for his protection. He seemed to have a pretty low opinion of her generally. . . 'Well?' he demanded. He was in front of her now, stripped to the waist, his powerful shoulders and broad chest far too close.

'You were half-asleep,' she said placatingly, retreating again into the water. 'It doesn't matter. Leave it. Just. . .oh, just go away,' she said helplessly, putting out a hand to fend him off.

'I'm going nowhere, and neither are you, Maddy Osborne. And I think it's about time you learned a few manners.'

The water was well up around her calves now. 'There's nothing wrong with my manners. You're the one who should learn to—' He didn't wait to discover what she thought he should learn. Instead he plunged forward and grabbed her arms and she let out a startled little scream.

He grinned. She saw the white gleam of his teeth and wondered how anyone quite so objectionable had managed to keep them for so long. 'Come on,' he taunted. 'You can do better than that. Or are you waiting for me to give you something to really scream about?'

'You already have,' she replied, perhaps unwisely, because he stepped a little closer and without warning shifted his grip to her waist.

'Oh, no, Maddy Rufus. You really can't expect to get off that lightly. I'm not one of your pet playboys to he twisted around your little finger then humiliated for your amusement.'

'I didn't—' But as he jerked her body close to his there was no time to explain. 'What are you going to do?' she gasped.

'I wonder what it would really take to make you scream as if you meant it,' he drawled, with a voice like velvet being shredded very slowly. 'Just a kiss, perhaps?' Maddy stood very still, steeling herself for the ordeal, her mind flashing a warning to her treacherous body that even now, as the cooling sea swirled around her thighs, was beginning to pound with her overactive heartbeat.

'No—' But her protest was cut off as his lips brushed hers as delicately as if he had touched them with the curved petals of a hibiscus. It sent a tiny tremor winging through her body like a thousand panicking butterflies. His hands were no longer hard upon her waist. They still held her, but lightly, drawing her traitorously willing body closer until her thighs were pressed against his legs. She was wearing only a pair of the most delicate silk pants, a T-shirt that clung revealingly to betray the eager thrust of her breasts, but she made no move to pull away. 'Griff. . .' she pleaded, but had no idea what it was she wanted.

'No scream that time, Maddy Rufus,' he said, his breath as soft as down against her cheek. 'I'll have to try harder.'

The muscles in her stomach contracted as she sensed a more demanding edge to his voice. 'No!' This time her protest was more urgent as she came to her senses and began to struggle. This wasn't her. She didn't. . . But as she flung a fist at his shoulder he bent and caught her behind the knees, swinging her up into his arms. 'Let me go! You can't. . .you mustn't. . .' For a long moment he looked down at her, his dark eyes challenging her to prove that she meant what she said. Too long. She suddenly realised that she had ceased to struggle and was lying back in his arms, no longer sure of anything. 'Let me go!'

His mouth curved into the most sensuous of smiles. 'Now?' he asked, very softly, and without waiting for her reply he did as she asked.

It was as if she fell in slow motion, hitting the sea with a splash that sent streams of phosphorescent water rising high above her in a bright arc. It almost seemed to Maddy that she could count every drop as it fell back to the sea before everything went momentarily black then white as she was submerged in the maelstrom of water churned up by her struggle to right herself.

After a moment she found her feet and burst from the surface, waist-deep, gasping with shock blazing with indignation, and this time there was no mistake about the scream. Uncontainable fury, all the repressed emotion of a terrible day, sheer outrage at the cavalier way she was being treated by this arrogant monster of a man rent the air and found a sympathetic echo in a flock of startled birds who flapped and shrieked at being disturbed so early from their roost.

Griff was standing, arms akimbo head thrown back, laughing with undisguised delight at the mayhem he had caused. 'Now, that scream,' he said, shaking his head, 'was very convincing. I suggest you remember it for future use.' Then he flipped the button on his shorts and Maddy backed rapidly away.

'What—what are you doing?' she spluttered.

'I'm going for a swim. You can join me if you like.'

She blushed fiercely as the pre-dawn light glistened on the hard planes of his magnificent naked body as he turned away and tossed his shorts onto the beach. 'Not if you were the last man on earth,' she retorted indignantly.

He grinned at her. 'Better hope you're rescued soon, then.'

'I'll make certain of it!'

But despite her angry words she couldn't stop herself from turning back to watch him as he powered away across the water in a fast overarm crawl. The pre-dawn light was enough for her to have determined that his glistening body was all one colour, confirming her suspicion that he was a stranger to a swimsuit. And, alone in paradise, who needed one?

Except that right now he wasn't alone.

He really was the most infuriating man she had ever met. She raised her fingers to her lips and discovered that despite everything she was smiling. Infuriating he might be, but it could not be denied that he was a great deal more invigorating than the likes of poor Rupert Hartnoll. She caught herself. And a great deal more dangerous. If she wasn't careful she would still be standing there when he returned to the beach. That thought alone was enough to make her move. Fast.

Maddy rescued her trousers from the wreckage of Griff's hut, shook out the sand and folded them neatly. She did the same for the towel. It was blue—a very large and expensively thick American plush towel. The kind that Zoe loved. She dropped it quickly and stepped back. Then she turned and ran.

Her bag was in the hold of the aircraft and she wasted no time in sorting out some fresh clothes for what would undoubtedly be another difficult day. She pulled out a tiny white bikini, then hurriedly replaced it with a more decorous one-piece bathing suit in her favourite dark mossy-green. It would be madness to be unnecessarily provocative.

She added a baggy white T-shirt, picked up her sponge bag and towel and as the sky turned pink with the rising sun, headed up the path to the pool for the bathe she had promised herself.

It was strange climbing up the empty path with only the chattering of birds and insects to disturb the silence. She might have been the first person in the world. Even as the thought entered her head she turned nervously. There was no sign of Griff, but she wasn't alone and the thought that he wouldn't swim forever spurred her on.

The pool was, if possible, even more beautiful in the early-morning light. A delicate mist was drifting off the water and curling over the lush vegetation, wrapping itself around the trailing orchids and morning glory vines already beginning to unravel their vivid blue flowers to the first early rays of the sun.

Maddy made her way to the side of the pool where the flying spray had been diverted to miss the pool and fly off onto a flat slab of rock, providing a natural shower—the work of the absent owner presumably. But whoever had done it she was grateful. She stripped off and stepped beneath it, gasping at the sudden chill on her warm skin. But after a few moments she quickly became used to the temperature and turned to a nearby rock to reach for her shampoo. As she did so, a particularly piercing wolf-whistle rent the air.

Furiously, Maddy grabbed for her towel. Holding it in front of her and sweeping her streaming hair from her face, she turned to confront her tormentor and tell him exactly what she thought of him. But Griff wasn't to be seen. She frowned. Griff was no voyeur, she thought edgily. He was far more likely to have stripped off and joined her under the shower. And this thought made the fine hairs on the back of her neck rise and her skin prickle nervously. Because if Griff wasn't whistling at her, then who was?

'Griff?' Maddy called uncertainly.

'Griff?' The word was echoed mockingly back at her, perfectly catching the hesitant inflection of her voice.

'Griff! Stop it! she said abruptly, and took a step forward. 'It's not funny.'

'What isn't funny?' Griff asked as he appeared on the path below her. Sea-water glistened on hard shoulders and the sculpted muscles of a chest scattered with dark hairs that curled lazily down his taut belly and disappeared beneath the towel tied carelessly about his loins. She jerked her eyes away, certain that he was wearing nothing else.

'*You* aren't,' she snapped, clutching her own towel tightly before her, glad of the dim light to cover her blushes. Anyone would think that she had never seen a man before—and in the briefest of swimsuits that were far more revealing than his towel. But not, she was forced to admit, a man like this. She shook herself angrily. A beautiful body meant nothing if the spirit was corrupt—she knew that. No one better.

Griff raked his fingers through the tousled, sun-kissed warmth of his dark brown hair turned momentarily black by the deep shadows. 'You've lost me, lady,' he said. 'But if you've finished with the shower. . .?'

'No, I haven't as well you know.' She made a grab for the shampoo bottle but it slipped through her wet fingers and fell with a splash into the pool. Unable to reach for it without exposing her naked rear for his amused inspection, she watched helplessly as, driven by the spray from the falls, it bobbed out of reach. 'Could you pass that to me?' she asked stiffly, aware, despite his perfectly straight face that he was deriving considerable amusement from her predicament.

'I could,' he said, but made no move to help.

'Please,' she added, a little belatedly.

'You're learning, Maddy Rufus,' he said, with an insolent little smile that sent shivers dancing along her spine, before reaching out to fish the plastic bottle from the water. But he didn't immediately surrender it. Instead he opened it and poured a little into the palm of his hand. 'Smells expensive.'

'It's just ordinary shampoo.' She held out her hand.

'Turn around; I'll wash your hair for you.'

'No,' she said, spotting the quizzical glint in his eyes too late. She took a deep breath. 'I can manage. If you will just pass me the bottle.'

'It's no bother at all,' he assured her, moving easily towards her, and she backed nervously under the shower. 'And while I'm doing it you can tell me what didn't make you laugh.' In Griff's distracting presence, she had forgotten about the wolf-whistle, but he didn't give her an opportunity to remonstrate with him; instead he put a hand on her shoulder and turned her round to face the water before whipping the towel away. 'You don't want it to get wet, do you?' he asked with all seriousness as she made a frantic grab in an attempt to keep it, and he tossed it out of reach so that she was left with no means to cover herself, apart from her arms.

She employed them swiftly and strategically and keeping her back turned firmly towards him, spat fiercely, 'Go away!'

He took no notice and she fumed, trapped and helpless, as he stroked the shampoo down the length of her hair. 'Your hair is a beautiful colour, Maddy,' he said. 'Like a skein of copper silk Have you ever been to New England in the fall?' he asked conversationally, apparently unaffected by the fact that the hairs on his chest were brushing against her shoulderblades, raising goose-flesh in a way that the chilly water had failed to do.

Maddy tried to speak but found that she had to clear her throat and concentrate very hard before she could answer. 'No,' she said, a little hoarsely.

'The trees have just this tint. Are you cold?' he asked with every appearance of concern. She was shaking, but not with the cold, and she was convinced that he knew that it was the touch of his fingers working slowly over her scalp, the pads of his thumbs pressed lightly against her temples, that was sending the shivery sensation to every nerve-ending. But she didn't have to make a complete fool of herself and admit it.

'Yes,' she said, crossing her fingers hard. 'The water's freezing.'

'You'll get used to it. And cold showers are good for the soul.'

'Have you rinsed out all the soap?'

'Not quite.' And he seemed in no hurry to end her torment, no matter what the cause. Instead, he lifted her hair through his hands, offering it to the spray. 'Quite beautiful.'

'I thought perhaps you didn't like redheads,' she said, not wishing to hear his smooth compliments.

'Really? Just because I haven't joined the army of admirers willing to fall in homage at your feet? Are you conceited as well as unkind?'

'Unkind?' She half turned, then, remembering, quickly turned back to the shower. 'If you're referring to that idiotic scene with Rupert, I apologised to him.'

'I would have thought that took a bit of doing.' As Maddy jerked angrily away from him she found herself hauled back by her hair, which had somehow become entangled in his fingers. 'The colour is immaterial,' he continued, apparently oblivious to her outburst. 'I just like hair to be long and shiny.' A long, raucous wolf-whistle echoed that sentiment and Maddy swung her head round to stare at Griff.

'It wasn't you!' she exclaimed.

'What?'

'The wolf-whistle.'

'Was that why you were all steamed up?' he asked.

'I thought you were playing a rather nasty joke,' she said indignantly. 'Trying to frighten me.'

'Not my style, lady.' He turned and looked up into the trees and then gave a lazy whistle. A small brown parrot, with pale blue head-feathers and a bold flash of yellow and orange on his wing, flapped down from the canopy and alighted on a nearby rock. The bird put his head on one side and peered at her with bright, beady eyes. 'Maddy,' Griff said, 'meet Jack. Jack, say, How d'you do?'

'How d'you do?' the parrot obediently repeated.

Maddy gave an uncertain little laugh. 'He's tame.'

'No. He was once, but he must have escaped from a passing yacht, or a nearby island. He's a St Vincent, so someone local probably owned him. He comes when he's whistled; he enjoys human company.'

'He's lovely. But he must be lonely, or does he have a mate?'

'No, he's quite alone. Freedom always has a price. And he's no lonelier than he was fastened to someone else's perch.'

'The perch has certain advantages.'

'An endless supply of sunflower seeds? A life of ease? Well, you should know. You live in a gilded cage. Jack and I have other ideas.' She was going to protest, tell him indignantly that he didn't know what he was talking about, but he had already turned away to retrieve her towel. He wrapped it around her, tucking it in firmly at the back, and as his knuckles grazed her shoulderblades her tongue seemed to have momentarily turned to wood.

She turned and looked up at him and for a moment he met her gaze head-on, his eyes, ocean-deep, daring her to challenge him and take the consequences, and for a moment she confronted him, taking on the razor-edged scorn. She'd done it countless times. She had no trouble facing down men who thought a woman in business was an easy target, men who refused to accept that she had no desire to indulge in a little meaningless sex.

But Griff made her feel vulnerable, uncertain and she faltered under that sharp, unwavering focus and finally dropped her eyes.

'Can you spare a little of your ordinary shampoo?' he asked, apparently careless of the fact that her heart was beating like a power-hammer. She wanted to tell him to go to hell in a handcart, but he was already reaching for the towel that snaked about his hips.

'Help yourself,' she said, snatching up her clothes. And she fled.

Back on the beach she quickly donned her swimsuit and applied sun block to every exposed inch, before covering herself with a baggy white T-shirt that came almost to her knees. Then, firmly ignoring her stomach's demand for breakfast, she began the earnest task of building the largest signal fire she could manage. It had suddenly become very important that she get back to civilisation.

Griff reappeared after a while, carrying what looked impossibly like a pineapple. But she studiously ignored him, intently ferrying back and forth across the beach to add to her pile of debris. When she was satisfied she collected the machete and began to hack some of the green fronds from a palm that overhung the beach.

'What are you doing?' Griff interrupted the shredding of a coconut with a clasp-knife to enquire.

'I'll need some green stuff to make smoke.'

'Oh, serious stuff,' he said with a grin.

'You could help.'

'I could. Except, of course, that I'm not in your desperate hurry to return to civilisation.' She refused his invitation to spar. 'Well, you'd better come and have some breakfast or you'll faint before assistance arrives.' Maddy was already beginning to feel a bit light-headed and didn't argue. 'And you should be wearing a hat.'

'The maid at the villa fell in love with mine so I gave it to her. I was going to buy a new one on Palm.'

'That's a pity. If you get sunstroke, who'll build the fire and fetch the water?'

'It's possible that you might have to do it all by yourself.'

He laughed, deep lines biting into his cheeks—the white flash of teeth, the sheer unexpectedness of it leaving her completely unguarded. 'Here, try this.'

He had cut a coconut in half to provide them each with a bowl and into it he had piled the shredded flesh of the nut and some pineapple, moistening the mixture with the coconut milk.

'This is delicious,' she said, scooping it up with her fingers. 'You have the makings of a fine al fresco cook.' She met his glance without flinching and felt quite proud of herself. 'Is it fish for lunch?' she continued, pushing her luck.

'Unless you can think of anything more original.'

'I don't have time to think. I have a bonfire to light.

Has the lighter dried out, or am I reduced to rubbing two sticks together?'

'Don't tempt me!' He glanced at the sea. 'Hadn't you better wait for a boat or something to signal to?'

'Like last night?' she demanded, with a warning flash from her eyes. 'I plan to keep the fire going all day if necessary. That way I won't miss anything.'

'Then you'll be kippered by tonight,' he said with a careless shrug as he tossed her the lighter and turned to walk away.

'You could stay and give me a hand,' she pointed out. 'Unless you've something more important to do?'

'I'm on holiday, remember. Besides, I can't bear to watch a woman work.'

'Then don't stick around or you're likely to faint dead away from the shock.' She nodded in the direction of the plane. 'You could always have another go at the radio.'

'Indeed I could.' And he smiled as if something had greatly amused him. It did something impossible to his face, deepening the lines carved into his cheeks, straightening the sensuous curve of his mouth, and it made his pirate's eyes sparkle like the ocean in the early-morning sun. It was an almost irresistible combination. Maddy turned abruptly away before she succumbed and returned his smile, but as she bent to light her signal blaze she discovered that it required two hands to keep the lighter steady.

Drat the man, she thought crossly as the dry kindling began to burn and she settled back on her heels. If he really disliked her so much, why wouldn't he help with her attempts to signal for rescue instead of wasting his time messing about with a radio that he had already admitted he couldn't fix? Surely he had no more wish to be stuck with her company than she wished to be inflicted with his?

She twisted her head to glance back over her shoulder. Griff was sitting in the cockpit, the radio receiver in his hand and for a moment her heart leapt in dizzy expectation that he had managed to bring it to life. Then as he saw her looking he idly waved a screwdriver in her direction.

She turned sharply away and gave the fire a poke with a large stick. Sparks flew upwards as a sudden draught from the sea whipped it into life, and within minutes a satisfactory column of smoke was rising from the slower-burning sappy leaves. Maddy, well pleased with her efforts, sat back to scan the horizon. But for an area where the sea was a way of life for the local people as well as a haven for holiday-makers it was oddly empty. She had hardly expected to attract the attention of one of the liners that carried the tourists from island to island. But there was not one yacht, not one tiny fishing boat.

'You've made a pretty good job of that,' Griff said, a few minutes later, coming to rest on his haunches alongside her, his knee perilously close to hers.

'It's just a pity there's no one to see it.'

He gave her a sideways glance. 'Did you expect a major search to be under way for you by now? Fleets of boats searching for wreckage? Aircraft scouring the sea? Newsmen pouring in from the four corners of the earth to cover the story?'

Maddy was temporarily lost for words. 'Why on earth would the Press would be interested?'

'It will surely cause a ripple of excitement if it becomes known that the daughter of one of Britain's most wealthy entrepreneurs is missing?'

'Perhaps,' she conceded, a little uneasily. 'But because of your lackadaisical attitude to schedules apparently even Zoe hasn't yet woken up to the fact that I'm more than half a day overdue.'

'But she will,' he replied evenly. 'Eventually.' If he noticed her furious scowl he didn't let it show. 'Meanwhile,' he continued, 'since you aren't hurt and you aren't about to starve, why don't you just relax and discover the simple pleasures of life? It's surprising what fun you can have without resorting to the bottomless credit card.'

'Enjoy myself! How can I?' She jabbed furiously at the sand with her stick. Griff reached across and took it from her, his long fingers brushing against the back of her hand, to send a tiny quiver of excitement through her. She glanced sideways from under lowered lashes at Griff's powerful figure. Was that the problem? Was that why she was so scratchy and bad-tempered? She was with a man who on the surface appeared the perfect companion for a desert-island idyll, to whom she reacted in a way she had long thought impossible. But he wasn't perfect—far from it. She looked up at him. 'Zoe will be concerned about you as well,' she said, hoping to shame him.

'Zoe isn't expecting me.'

'No?' Had he made some excuse to drop her at the dock and run now he'd got his money? Was there someone else waiting for him? 'Someone will surely be worrying?'

'A girl on every island?' he offered, as if he could read her mind and she blushed a deeper pink than the heat from the fire could quite account for.

'Except this one,' she snapped back.

'Except this one,' he agreed, unconcerned by her

hostility. 'I prefer my women warm-hearted and generous.'

'With long, shiny hair.'

'Nice,' he agreed, 'but not essential.' But the warm heart and generosity were? she thought. Particularly the generosity. 'Here, I've brought you a hat.' He removed an elderly panama from his head and placed it on hers pulling it down over her eyes. 'Now shall we try that fishing lesson?'

'No, thanks,' she said with a bright smile. 'I'll look after the fire. It wouldn't do to let it out.'

'We'll fish here. You can keep an eye on your fire.' He picked up a rod he had brought from the plane, took her hand and she was on her feet before she could object.

'But I've never even held a fishing rod,' she objected.

'It's not difficult.. I'll show you how.' He led her out into the inlet until the water was lapping around their thighs. Then he made a cast, sending the line flying out towards a tumble of rocks. 'There's a small cave under the water just there where the fish hide.'

'How do you know?'

He turned and looked down at her. 'Trust me. Now take the rod.' He placed it in her hands, standing behind her, holding her shoulders. 'Wind it just a little so the spinner tempts the fish,' he instructed her. 'Like this.' He reached around her and, placing his hands over hers began to reel in the line, very gently.

Maddy laughed and turned to look up at him. 'Could I really catch something?'

'I think it's entirely possible that you already have, Maddy Rufus,' he said, rather brusquely, then the line jerked, would have pulled the rod from her hands if Griff had not been holding it too, and for a few breathless seconds the pair of them wrestled with whatever was on the end of the line, until, without warning, the line went slack and they staggered back together.

'It got away,' she said, laughing a little, breathless too. 'Can we try again?' But this time when she turned to look up at him he stepped back.

'Later.'

'But—'

'Isn't that a boat?'

She turned to scour the horizon and, sure enough, a small, brightly painted dinghy with an outboard engine was moving quite swiftly past the inlet, a little way beyond the reef.

'Well, don't just stand there,' she erupted. 'Do something!'

She raced up the beach to the fire and began fanning it furiously and the flames crackled into life. She threw on a few sappy leaves to produce more smoke then looked up to where Griff was standing near the waters edge. 'Well?' she demanded. 'Did he notice us?'

'He waved back,' Griff said.

'What do you mean, waved back?'

'You said to do something,' he said carelessly, 'so I waved. He waved back.'

'Then he's seen us,' she said with relief. 'Where is he?' She strained to look, but the boat had disappeared.

'He didn't stop.'

'What?' She took a step nearer the edge of the water. 'What do you mean, he didn't stop?'

'I imagine he thought we were camping.'

'Why didn't you shout?' She glared at him furiously, her breast heaving with indignation. 'Damn you, Griff! Why didn't you do something? You just stood there and. . .and. . .waved as if this was a Sunday afternoon picnic.'

'Maddy—' he began, but she wasn't interested in his excuses. She swung wildly at his chest, pounding at him with her fists, tears of frustration glistening in her eyes.

'I don't believe you want to be rescued.' He caught her wrists but she struggled to free herself, determined to continue her battering. 'This is some big game to you, isn't it? A bit of a joke. Make Maddy Rufus suffer because she was nasty to poor Rupert—'

'Stop it,' he said, and gave her a little shake.

'Well, let me tell you about Rupert—'

He clasped his hand over her mouth. 'I don't want to hear about Rupert, or the rest of your unfortunate lovers. . .'

Driven to impotent fury, she began to kick out at him. Her bare toes made little impression on his shins, but with an exclamation of irritation he shifted his grip on her wrist in order to hold her away from him, and immediately her fist flew upwards, her knuckles catching his lip a sharp, glancing blow.

'Well, big man?' she demanded as he released her mouth with an oath. 'Are you going to hit me back?' Then she gave a little gasp as she realised that she had made a serious mistake.

Maddy wanted to tell him—tell him that she hadn't meant it. Her lips parted to plead with him, but no words came forth; her toffee-coloured eyes only widened like those of a startled gazelle. She wanted to run, escape the ominous darkening of his eyes. But she couldn't. Even if there had been somewhere to run to, she was held fast, riveted, not just by the hand that still grasped her wrist but by the retribution that blazed from Griff's eyes—retribution which, she understood, the slightest movement would bring down upon her head.

For a full second nothing happened, and, letting out the breath she was holding, very slowly, very quietly, she thought she might—just—get away with it. Then as she began to relax he caught her waist and hauled her up into his arms and his mouth came down hard upon hers.

CHAPTER FIVE

MADDY couldn't resist, couldn't fight. Her feet were inches from the ground and she knew with a deep, instinctive knowing that to struggle against his fast hold, his implacable thighs, the hard and dangerous plane of his hips would be utter madness. For a moment she remained determinedly still in his arms while his mouth ground down on her lips, his insistent tongue storming the negligent portcullis of her teeth to take total possession of her mouth.

Her mind tried desperately to shut him out, but the firm stroke of his tongue seemed, in a moment, to steal away her will, sapping her resistance to his determined, blissful assault upon her senses as he explored the secret, sensitive places of her mouth with the skill of a master. A warmth was gradually stealing through her body, making her conscious as never before of the yearning tension of her breasts as they peaked against the smooth cloth of her swimsuit, longing for the rougher touch of the hair that darkened the glistening, sun-drenched skin of his chest. A trembling heat surged through her abdomen, flooded her thighs with a delicious ache that urged her to press closer to him as her body rejected the intellectual games her mind was playing.

It had recognised the sexual tension that had ignited between them the second their eyes had met and now her arms wound themselves about his neck and her body invited him in. For a long, blissful moment she felt the warm, muscle-packed flesh of his shoulders quiver beneath the spread of her fingers, his hair-roughened thighs against her own, smooth skin, the more urgent thrust of his desire as he held her close. Then, as suddenly as it had begun, it was over. With an almost painful rejection, he thrust her away from him, his hands still hard about her waist as she swayed uncertainly, her legs turned to butter that was melting under the heat of his kiss.

For a moment they stood locked together in shocked silence, while Maddy's heart thumped painfully beneath her ribs. Griff's expression was adamantine, impenetrable. 'It would have been a great deal more sensible if I had done what I'd first intended,' he said, a little breathlessly.

'What were you going to do to me, Griff?' Maddy's breath caught in her throat as she tilted her head to look up at him in an unconsciously seductive gesture, her heavy lids reducing her eyes to golden, glittering almonds, her mouth darkly full, throbbing from his cavalier treatment.

He released her waist so rapidly that she would have staggered, perhaps fallen but for her hands about his neck. But he cruelly disengaged them, stepping quickly back to put some distance between them. 'I should have put you over my knee and spanked you the first moment you looked at me like that,' Griff said, his voice like a rasp on wood. 'You are positively dangerous.'

Dangerous? He was blaming her for what happened? Maddy snapped instantly out of the languid state that had pervaded her limbs so thoroughly that she'd hardly known what she was doing or saying. 'Dangerous?' she demanded on a sharp, angry breath. 'Lay one finger on me again, "Griff will do",' she flared up at him, 'and I promise you'll find out just how dangerous I am.' Her voice caught painfully in her throat, but she didn't stop. 'I'll see you in court.'

For one long, terrible moment his dark eyes regarded her with contempt, then he looked pointedly around. 'Why don't you call a policeman?' he said. With that he turned and walked swiftly away, as if he couldn't bear to be near her, clambering over the rocks at the far end of the beach and disappearing from sight.

Maddy groaned and dropped to the sand as her legs refused to support her any longer; she laid her forehead upon her knees and rocked from side to side. He couldn't have made his point clearer. They were alone, she had encouraged him quite shockingly and but for his restraint they would even now be lying on the foreshore locked in... It was awful—the most truly awful thing that had ever happened to her. The man had kissed her not from desire; if he had wanted to make love to her that might have excused her wanton response. But he despised her, had been punishing her.

Not that he was entirely immune, but then it would have taken a block of wood not to respond to the way she had thrown herself at him, and his arousal had been palpable. Yet he had still walked away. Gone fishing. And his invitation to join him had clearly been withdrawn. Nevertheless, she was going to have to bite the bullet, face his contempt and apologise for that stupid remark about taking him to court. It was clearly her week for eating humble pie.

'Oh, Zoe!' she murmured painfully. 'Why on earth did you get involved...?'

She stifled a moan and, tearing off her T-shirt, she threw it to one side and flung herself into the sea. She would have liked to have stripped away the swimsuit too and let the cool, sharp sea-water scrub her naked body clean as she swam the length of the lagoon and back in a fierce overarm. But she didn't dare. She had already exposed far too much. Griff had known she desired him even before she'd known it herself, had accused her of flirting with him. Even now, as she powered through the water trying to rid herself of the taste of him, the scent of his skin, the feel of his hands on her body, she didn't understand why she did desire him. She had been hurt—desperately hurt—by a man who'd wanted nothing but her money. Maybe she was flawed in some way, drawn to that cruel streak. . .

As she tired, she rolled onto her back and floated, drifting where the water would take her, staring up at a totally blue sky. Maybe it was simpler than that, more basic. Perhaps her young body longed for fulfilment and had recognised and reached out to the attractions of Griff's untamed, almost barbaric masculinity. And, trapped in paradise, she had no escape from her feelings.

Maddy finally staggered back up the beach, collapsed in a heap by the dying remains of her fire and poked at it in a desultory fashion. She'd seen nothing to excite her interest other than a yacht on the horizon, too far away to notice them, and the only aircraft that had passed overhead had been high-flying intercontinental jets. Paradise Island seemed to be just off the well-beaten inter-island air and sea lanes.

She sighed, retrieved the panama from the sand where it had fallen and fanned herself with it. It was hot and it would be getting hotter. It was probably better to relax and wait for rescue like Griff. No doubt by tomorrow Zoe would have worked up enough steam for both of them and got everyone running around in circles as she organised a search for her missing god-daughter. Griff's last radio contact had been at the approach to Paradise Island so the search would certainly begin there. She would just have to be patient. And very polite.

She shifted as the heat dried and tightened her skin. Despite her fiery colouring Maddy had been blessed with the delicate olive skin of her French mother, but that still didn't mean that she could sit all day in the fierce tropical sun. She gathered up her T-shirt and slipped it over her shoulders and applied more sunblock to her legs and arms and neck. Then she didn't know what to do with herself.

She was feeling confused and angry and very stupid—emotions totally alien to her forthright nature. Wrapping her arms about her knees and propping her chin on her hands, Maddy looked uncertainly in the direction that Griff had taken.

She ought to go after him, tell him that she didn't mean what she had said in the heat of the moment. It would be difficult to face him, but she knew it was always a mistake to let misunderstandings fester.

Maddy jammed her hat back on her damp, unruly hair and hid her eyes behind dark glasses, telling herself that it was the sun she was protecting herself from, not Griff's scornful eyes. Nevertheless, she rose with extreme reluctance to her feet and began to follow the footprints he had impressed upon the sand.

Scrambling over the rocks at the far end of the beach, she found herself in another, much smaller cove, but it was as deserted as the one she had left, with only a few tell-tale footprints leading to the water's edge.

Her heartbeat raised a fraction. She had been so certain that Griff would be propped lazily against a rock with a fishing line trailing out into the water that the total emptiness of the beach came as a shock

'Griff?' she called uncertainly, and was horrified by the little waver of doubt that had crept into her voice. Impatient with herself, she lifted her hand to shade her eyes, slowly sweeping the surface of the bay in expectation that he had taken to the water. But only the gentle ruffling of the breeze disturbed the palest turquoise water near the shore. Further out the colour deepened patchily to jade, celadon, heart of emerald, and for a moment she anxiously searched the shadows, looking for him beneath the water.

Then she snapped her fingers at her own gullibility. He had almost certainly swum into the next bay and was probably at this moment laughing into his beard. And she had come crawling after him intent on apology. Well, he could sit and stew for all she cared; she was perfectly happy with her own company.

She settled in the inviting shade of a huge rock and dabbled her feet in a pool left by the retreating tide. A small crab scuttled out of sight in a cloud of sand and Maddy leaned forward to examine the pool a little more closely, stirring the sandy bottom with her toe, watching the tiny tell-tale flurries with a thoughtful expression. He could keep his rotten fish, too. She would force him to acknowledge that she wasn't the helpless bimbo he so obviously took her for.

Maddy returned to the aircraft. Her cosmetic bag yielded a small pair of scissors and she sacrificed a pair of black silk stockings to provide herself with a shrimping net. It took a while to fashion a plaited vine into a hoop to keep it open at the neck, but time was the one thing she wasn't short of, she reminded herself as she

cut herself a cane and bound the net to it with the leg
of her stocking.

'Move over, Tarzan,' she said, with a soft laugh as
she whipped the finished net back and forth and discovered to her considerable satisfaction that everything
held together. 'This Jane is about to catch her own
lunch.'

She wasted no time but with great concentration
began to trawl her makeshift net just beneath the
surface of the sand and prod about under the rocks,
scooping up the transparent, barely visible little shrimps
as they scuttled for cover, shaking them carefully from
her net into the shell of a coconut. There was something
pleasurably atavistic in the process of hunting for her
own food, she discovered, focusing on her task with the
same earnestness that she would have applied to a new
business proposition. It was the way she did everything—all or nothing.

'Enjoying yourself?' So intent was she upon her
labours that the unexpected sound of Griff's voice
above her made her whole body jump. He was standing
behind one of the larger rocks, his arms folded upon it,
his chin propped upon his hands, watching her. She had
the impression that he had been there for some time.
The bronzed skin of his shoulders was already dry, his
recent immersion in the sea betrayed only by the tiny
drops of water that swooped along the dark, tangled
mop of his hair, to fall and trickle in tiny rivulets down
his strongly corded neck. For a moment she watched
them, mesmerised, then she straightened abruptly,
hoping he wouldn't notice the warmth that flooded into
her cheeks.

As it happened, he wasn't looking at her at all but
regarding her catch with considerable interest. 'Tasty

little things,' he observed. 'How are you going to cook them?'

'Cook them?' She had been so intent upon catching her potful of shrimps that she hadn't given a thought to what came next. Her previous experience of shrimps had been of the pink, cooked variety, from the fishmonger. But she wasn't going to admit that. 'I'll think of something,' she said.

'You certainly seem to have a gift for improvisation,' he agreed genially, reaching out one long arm and taking the net from her unresisting hand to examine it more closely. Then he raised those taunting eyes of his and she had the uncomfortable suspicion that somewhere, deep inside, he was laughing at her. 'Tell me, Miss Madeleine Osborne, do you *really* wear black silk stockings?'

Maddy flushed as deeply as if she had been caught parading in them for his titillation. 'Never on the beach,' she replied stiffly, and snatched the betraying net out of his hand.

He tilted his eyebrows tormentingly. 'What a pity,' he said, but before she could erupt he lifted a couple of bright red fish threaded onto a line for her inspection. 'You won't be wanting one of these, I take it?'

'I'm sure you can manage them both,' she replied, investing her voice with all the chill she could muster. 'Please don't feel you have to wait for me.'

He inclined his head in the direction of her proposed meal. 'Oh, I won't,' he said. 'It'll be nightfall before you've caught enough of those to fill a tooth.'

'I've caught dozens of the things,' she protested.

'All shell and head, though. I'll see you later.' He finally gave in to the temptation to grin. 'Much later.'

'Damn,' she muttered under her breath as he disappeared from sight, but she wasn't absolutely certain why.

The delicious scent, a little while later, of fish grilling over an open fire reminded her that it was a considerable time since breakfast, and she eyed her catch doubtfully. The shrimps wriggling in the dark recesses of the coconut husk looked very much alive...and suddenly very unappetising. But she had decided to make a point, prove she didn't have to rely upon a mere male for her food, and she would have to go through with it. Abandoning her net by the pool, unwilling to parade her mutilated stockings for Griff's further amusement, and holding the husk containing her reluctant lunch very carefully, she clambered back over the rocks to the larger beach.

Griff had speared his catch on a long cane which he had propped across two flat rocks placed either side of the hot embers of the fire and he was laid back on the sand, relaxing while they cooked, his hands clasped behind his head, his eyes closed. He accomplished his objectives with such economy of effort, she thought a little enviously, removing her hat and using it as a fan. 'Do you think you've finally caught enough?' he asked without opening his eyes.

'Yes, thank you,' she said, giving him a wide berth as she walked to the far side of the fire and sank to her knees. She regarded the shrimps with foreboding. They were still very much alive and kicking in their temporary home.

Griff rolled up into a sitting position and offered her a sliver of cane. 'I thought you might like to follow my example,' he said, indicating his own lunch. 'They shouldn't take long to cook.'

Maddy looked up, a little surprised that he should

bother to take so much trouble after the way she had threatened him. 'Thank you,' she said. The cane was long and sharp and the idea of using it to spear her helpless captives made her feel suddenly quite sick.

'My pleasure, Miss Osborne.' The brackets at the corners of his mouth deepened slightly. It wasn't quite a smile—she didn't know precisely what it was—but it disturbed her and she wished he wouldn't do it.

'Whatever happened to Maddy Rufus?' she asked, putting off the moment when she had to tackle the lunch.

'It no longer annoys you,' he said tormentingly. Besides, since I've been threatened with the law, a little more formality is called for.' It was clear that the threat did not concern him greatly.

'You—' she flared, then stopped. It was not what Griff had done that had caused the problem but her own unexpectedly wanton response. . . Her pulse began to thump at the still vivid memory of the way he had kissed her, the way she had kissed him back. Stupid conversation. 'I didn't mean it,' she said, quickly looking away from the steady regard of eyes masked behind tinted lenses that filtered out his expression and the colour that seemed to vibrate with his feelings. She knew it was the moment to apologise, but the words seemed to stick in her throat.

Embarrassed by her own shortcomings, Maddy dropped her gaze to the coconut husk and the wriggling shrimps that were destined to be her lunch and suddenly knew that she would never eat another shrimp in her entire life. But, aware of Griff's mocking scrutiny, she felt unable to back down and admit defeat. With a small gulp, she caught one of the creatures between her fingers and held it to the point of the cane. It was all legs and waving feelers and Maddy could see its tiny organs pulsating through its transparent body. A convulsive shiver ran through her body and suddenly Griff's hand was clasped about her wrist, steadying the tell-tale shake.

'Do you require assistance, Miss Osborne?'

'No!' She dropped the cane. 'I just think I'd prefer a banana for my lunch.'

She had expected him to gloat but he didn't. 'No need for that, Maddy Rufus. The snapper's just about done,' he said, taking the shrimp from her trembling fingers and dropping it back into the husk with its companions and finally meeting her eyes. 'But you're beginning to get the hang of things. I'll certainly give you ten for effort. Nil for execution.'

'I don't want anything from you.'

'No?'

'No! But what about. . .?' She looked guiltily at her catch; it seemed even worse to deprive them of life and then not eat them out of squeamishness.

'Come on,' he said, taking her elbow and drawing her to her feet, his touch mercifully brief as he bent to pick up the shrimps and hand them to her. 'You can put them back in the pool.'

'Do you think they'll survive?' she asked, suddenly as anxious as if they were a tankful of pet goldfish.

'They've a better chance there than on a skewer,' he pointed out somewhat wryly, and she shuddered, lifting one hand to cover her mouth at the thought, swallowing hard.

'I'm afraid I lack the killer instinct,' Maddy said as she released her lunch to live another day, watching thankfully as the shrimps immediately buried themselves in a flurry of sand that clouded the water.

'Oh, don't underrate yourself,' Griff said. 'Like most women, I'm sure you're more at home in the drawing room, stalking larger game.'

In the sheer relief of returning her captives to the freedom of the water, Maddy had momentarily forgotten his hostility. Now she turned on him, determined once and for all to clear up any misunderstanding, but, confronted with the expressionless stare of his dark glasses, the hard line of his mouth, she suddenly felt it safer to leave things as they were. Hostile.

'I'm sorry to disappoint you, Griff, but I don't have much time to waste swanning about drawing rooms.' Maddy pushed past him, gritting her teeth as her shoulder brushed against his arm and sent a dangerous flutter of desire shivering down her spine, her body determined on a perilous course of its own.

'I'd better go and get some fresh water,' she said as they returned in silence to the fire, anxious to put some distance between them and get a grip on herself.

'It's done.' And he scooped out a half-shell of fresh, clean water and handed it to her. She hesitated, unwilling to take it and risk the dangerous touch of his fingers. 'I thought you wanted this,' he prompted, and she was certain he knew, understood her fear. She took the shell quickly, spilling a little, drinking it quickly so that she could retreat to a safer distance, but he continued, impersonally enough, 'I thought you were going to man your signal fire day and night until you were rescued,' he said, sinking back onto the sand. 'Why did you abandon it?'

'Simple logistics,' she said, happy enough to change the subject.

He raised a brow. 'Are logistics ever simple?'

'In this case, indisputable. Not a single aircraft has

passed overhead since we've been here, apart from high-flying jets. But then you undoubtedly already knew that we are off the inter-island air routes. And if the local fishermen simply think we're having a barbecue there isn't a great deal of point in trying to attract their attention that way.'

He shrugged. 'They're used to seeing me here.'

'Are they?' She frowned. 'Why?'

'I like it here.' She waited, but he didn't elaborate.

'In that case, why did you ask me to build a fire in the first place?'

'It seemed a good idea to keep you occupied,' he admitted. 'Despite that rather—' he paused to consider his words '—*spirited* manner, I was afraid you might fall apart at the seams when you realised the island was deserted. Mercifully you didn't.'

'If that was meant to be a compliment, Griff, I have to tell you that your technique leaves something to be desired. Perhaps you should consider taking lessons.'

'You wouldn't want me to say something I didn't mean, would you?' His voice trailed a challenge.

'There doesn't seem to be any danger of that,' she snapped back.

'None whatever,' he affirmed, leaning forward to take the fish from the fire, carefully transferring them to the waiting banana-leaf plates. Then he looked at her. 'I never say anything I don't mean, Maddy. Remember that.'

'Very commendable,' she said quickly as his direct gaze brought a fierce blush to her cheeks. 'What a pity your honesty doesn't extend in other directions.' He glanced up, tilting his brow at a questioning angle, and Maddy wondered just how many hearts he had broken with that one look. Was Zoe merely the latest in a long line? 'You're obviously in the habit of taking advantage of the owner's frequent absences to use this island as if it were your own,' she said.

'Am I?' The lines at the corners of his mouth deepened suspiciously. 'Well, I'm sure he doesn't miss a few coconuts, or the odd pineapple.'

His amusement was even more infuriating than his rudeness and demonstrated his lack of scruples very adequately. 'Whether he misses them or not is hardly the point, they aren't yours to take.'

'You didn't object at breakfast,' he pointed out, with some justification. 'In fact, I would say you didn't give the matter a moment's thought.'

'This is an emergency,' she blustered. 'Altogether different. I'm not sneaking about taking advantage of his unwitting hospitality and I shall make a point of writing and thanking him as soon as we're picked up.'

'Don't expect him to be overwhelmed by your finishing-school manners,' he warned. 'He's not the type.'

'Whilst I hate to disabuse you of one of your prejudices about me,' she said carefully, 'it might interest you to know that I cycled to the local comprehensive school every day, come rain or sun, until I was eighteen years old and my "finishing" consisted of a course in Business Studies at the nearest technical college.' She had refused to move away from her friends and go to the fancy boarding-school her father had favoured when he'd finally reached the point at which he stopped chasing banks and they started chasing him. 'And I'm fluent in French not because of some expensive tuition but because my mother came from France and had an aversion to everything English, particularly the language.' Griff was regarding her with a puzzled, questioning look. 'Don't you believe me?' she demanded.

He shrugged, carelessly. 'Why shouldn't I? If you say your mother is French—'

'Was. I said she *was* French. I no longer have a mother; her aversion to everything English included my father. But I didn't mean that—I meant about my schooling, my life.'

He lifted heavy lids to probe her face and suddenly Maddy regretted her outburst about her mother, certain that she had rather foolishly overreacted to his torments. 'It matters to you what I believe?' he asked.

Did it? Oddly she found that it mattered rather more than she would have believed possible. 'I don't tell lies,' she said. Then, because she had said far more than she'd intended, she quite deliberately changed the subject. 'Why don't you tell me about the mysterious owner of Paradise Island?'

'There's nothing mysterious about him. Except. . .' He paused, a tiny light dancing in his eyes.

'Yes?'

'Except that the locals call him the Dragon Man.'

'The Dragon Man?' Maddy's eyes widened slightly. 'Good lord, does he breathe fire?'

He laughed softly. 'On occasion. . .'

'But. . .who is he really?'

'I'm sorry, Maddy; you'll have to ask Zoe that.'

'He's a friend of Zoe's?'

'He's very fond of her.'

Fond enough to help her godmother out of the mess she seemed to be in? Fond enough to send 'Griff will do' packing? 'What's he like?'

'What do you want to know, Maddy Rufus?'

'Everything you can tell me. You can't be too careful

and I wouldn't want Zoe getting mixed up with the wrong type of man. . .' Her hint made no impression on him.

'Oh, I'm sure *you'd* approve. Gossip says that he's loaded.'

'Well, that's a good start,' she said brightly.

'I understand that it's the start and the end as far as you are concerned,' he said.

'Understand? More gossip?' He gave her a sharp glance and she had the oddest impression that she had caught him on a raw spot. 'It's really so wide of the mark that I'm tempted to ask you to repeat it,' she continued, enjoying for once the feeling of having gained the upper hand. 'I enjoy a good joke. But I realise it would be miles beneath you to repeat unsubstantiated tittle-tattle.'

'Unsubstantiated?'

'Obviously. I'm not looking for a husband, and even if I were money wouldn't be a consideration—'

'Then it's not true that your father is thinking of setting up a charitable trust with the majority of his fortune? Won't that leave you a little short?' Maddy's brows drew down sharply at this. The trust was far beyond the thinking stage and for her own reasons she had encouraged and supported her father every step of the way, but it was still highly confidential—certainly not the subject for poolside gossip. Had her father told Zoe? 'Before you answer,' Griff continued unwaveringly, 'I refer you to the statement you made earlier about never telling lies.'

'No comment,' she snapped. 'And, to return to the subject of this conversation, I was thinking about Zoe, not myself. I wouldn't want her to get hurt by some ruthless fortune-hunter. How long have *you* known her,

Griff?' For a moment her amber eyes challenged him, but he merely frowned a little, his eyes all question, and, suddenly flustered, she indicated the fish. 'Are we going to eat these, or study them as works of art?'

CHAPTER SIX

Griff gave her an old-fashioned look as he handed her one of the snappers. 'They should be cool enough to handle,' he remarked.

She tried a piece. 'It's delicious,' she said quickly.

'I hope you still feel the same way in a week,' he replied, a little wryly.

'A week!' Her voice rose to an uncharacteristic squeak and Griff's eyes gleamed wickedly. 'Oh, very funny!'

'I'm glad it amused you. I wonder if you'll still find it funny seven days from now?'

'I'll swim for it long before then,' she declared fervently, then added quickly, 'Tell me some more about the Dragon Man. And I'd already worked out for myself that anyone who can afford to keep a Caribbean island all to himself must have more money than he knows what to do with.' A sudden thought struck her. 'It was his yacht Zoe was on the other night, wasn't it?'

'That's very quick of you.'

'The name is something of a give-away,' she said, thinking hard. Griff, it seemed, had competition. 'He must have tons of money,' she said with considerable satisfaction. 'Did he inherit it, or did he earn it by the sweat of his brow?'

'Does it matter how he came by his money?'

'It would to me. But then, I'm picky.'

'So I noticed.' He shrugged as if he'd expected nothing better. 'I'm sorry to disappoint you, Maddy, but the owner of this island is not one of your pretty aristocrats with a family fortune to play with. Ten years ago he had nothing but enthusiasm and an idea. He's your original fourteen-hour-day, sweat-of-the-brow man.'

'He actually earned enough to buy this island?' she asked, astonished. 'That fabulous yacht?'

'I believe he even has a little to spare for the necessities of life,' he replied.

'Honestly?' Maddy demanded, suddenly suspicious.

He laid his hand upon his heart. 'Scout's honour.'

'I didn't doubt what you said, Griff. I meant. . .' His eyes sparked dangerously and she gave an awkward little shrug. 'Well, you know what I meant.'

'Yes, I know what you meant,' he said almost angrily. 'But he's not a crook.' As if aware that he had overreacted, he turned away and looked towards the plane pulled up on the shoreline, swinging a little on the high tide. 'Actually, he started the Inter-Island Transport Group ten years ago with that aircraft.'

She followed his glance towards the single-engined seaplane lifting gently on the high tide and stared at the fierce little red dragon on its tail—a dragon now borne by a large fleet of modern aircraft and ferry boats that plied the islands.

'So that's why he's called the Dragon Man,' she said. 'And he sold his first plane to you?' She was astonished. 'How on earth could he bear to part with it? If it had been mine I would have parked it outside my office and polished it once a week just for luck.'

'Would you?' For a moment his face softened. 'Well, as you can see, I take good care of it for him.'

'On the outside,' she agreed. It was quite beautiful in fact. 'But if you're planning to follow his example and build a transport empire you'll need to give a little attention to maintenance,' she said, half joking, then turned and stared at him. Was that how he had managed to extract so much money from Zoe? Had he spun her some tale about wanting to start a business of his own? What secrets did his eyes conceal in their ocean depths? She turned quickly away before she drowned and never found the answers. 'I suppose it takes that kind of ruthlessness to build an empire,' she said quickly, and laughed to cover the shake in her voice. 'I'll have to try a little harder not to be sentimental. . .'

'I would never have put you down as sentimental, Maddy. Except of course, about shrimps. . .' he teased, his eyes creasing at the corners.

Maddy swallowed. 'Oh, I'm hopeless,' she rattled on. 'I still have a dreadful old machine I learned to type on. It's practically a museum piece, but I wouldn't part with it for the world.'

'And you do a lot of typing?' He took one of her hands and examined it. 'I don't think so. Not with those nails.' For a moment her fingers lay in his and she stared at them, briefly held by the contrast of the pale, polished ovals of her nails against his hand.

Abruptly she pulled away. 'Not a lot,' she declared. 'My secretary takes most of the strain these days.'

'You have a secretary?' This seemed to surprise him. 'Zoe said you have some little agency—a hobby to keep you busy. I didn't get the impression it rated a secretary. But then I suppose you wouldn't want to be tied down to an office; it would seriously cut down the time you could spend on tropical beaches.'

'A month isn't much out of three years—' she began, then stopped. She had no reason to justify herself to this man. 'It sounds as if you and Zoe spent a considerable amount of time discussing me,' she said with just a hint of exasperation.

He didn't flinch from her accusing eyes. 'Perhaps she did run on a little. . .she was somewhat upset the other night.' 'Upset'? Zoe had spoken her mind, but 'upset' overstated the case a little. 'And I'm a good listener.'

Part of the stock-in-trade of a conman, no doubt, she thought caustically. 'Zoe made her feelings perfectly clear at the time. There was no need for her to discuss it with you.'

'I think it was your reaction to her talk with you that so upset her.'

'But I thought she understood. . .' Then she sighed. Maybe not. She loved Zoe, but her godmother had a very personal way of looking at things, which made her just a little exasperating at times. 'I swear if I told her that I was planning to open a branch in Paris she would just assume it was to make it simpler to get to the spring and autumn collections,' she muttered, half to herself.

'And are you? Planning to open a branch in Paris?' His hearing was clearly acute, his insolent amusement wounding. Maddy had worked hard for her success and didn't like being mocked. But she wasn't about to let it show.

She laid the tips of her fingers against her breast. '*Moi?*' she said, opening her eyes very wide, apparently incredulous that he could possibly have taken her seriously.

Griff's eyes narrowed as he regarded her with a thoughtful expression and Maddy had the uncomfortable feeling that she had gone just a little too far. Heaven alone knew what nonsense her godmother had filled Griff's head with, and he'd seen enough to colour his own opinion a very nasty shade of disapproval; now she seemed hell-bent on making it worse. Why couldn't she just have said yes, for heaven's sake? It's none of your business. Mr 'Griff will do', but my 'little hobby' is so successful that I've decided to expand into Europe.

What on earth was it about the man that made her react like that? Maybe because he's the first man you've come across that you can't control, can't run away from, and it frightens you to death, her subconscious prompted helpfully.

Maddy felt her sun-warmed cheeks flush a shade darker. Rubbish, she thought, consigning her subconscious to the dustbin. Absolute rubbish. This conversation had nothing to do with her. It was Zoe who mattered.

'What is it?'

Maddy's glance collided with the clear, penetrating stare of her fellow castaway. 'Nothing,' she said, with an unconvincing little laugh as she quickly attempted to turn the conversation and her thoughts to less dangerous channels. 'I've just realised why no planes fly over the island, that's all.'

'Oh?' His voice was soft as thistledown, yet insistent, not to be ignored.

'Your Dragon Man has obviously arranged it that way,' she said, making a brave attempt to ignore the ripple of goose-flesh on her skin. 'I don't suppose he wants to be reminded of work when he's on a back-to-nature kick.'

'You could be right,' Griff agreed, his eyes still holding hers.

'And I'm glad he's got his island,' she continued a little desperately. 'Even if he doesn't have much time to visit it. Anyone who has earned his money the *hard* way knows how to appreciate what he's got.'

'He appreciates it,' he said intently. Then, as he turned to stare out to sea, his eyes finally released her.

Relief mingled with an almost palpable sense of loss and she wrapped her arms about her legs and laid her chin on her knees. 'Not too often, I hope, for your sake. I can quite see that it wouldn't suit you to have the owner in residence,' Maddy said, then added a wicked little afterthought. 'Of course, if he marries Zoe he might build a home here. She was very taken with the villa on Mustique. That would put your fishing trips on permanent hold.' He began to choke and Maddy leapt to her feet and scrambled behind him, clasping him under the ribs, but before she could do more he grabbed her hands and stopped her.

'No,' he said, a little huskily, looking over his shoulder, his face so close to hers that she could almost feel the faint stubble that darkened his jaw. For a second neither of them moved, his hands upon hers locking them together, her arms about him holding her body close to the warmth of his back, her cheek touching the pulse of his strongly corded neck, her lips within reach of the chiselled line of his jaw. Her mouth parted slightly and she moistened it with the tip of her tongue. Abruptly he released her. 'I'm fine,' he said curtly.

Maddy sat back on her heels, her face scarlet. I'm sorry. I thought you were choking on a fishbone. . .' she mumbled, covering her embarrassment by scooping him some water from the bucket, but unable to meet his eyes as she passed it to him. 'I did this first-aid course. . .'

'You must have passed with flying colours if the speed of your reaction is anything to go by,' he said; his voice was gentler than she'd expected. 'But I think it was just shock.'

'Shock?' Her brows drew together in a little frown and he gave an odd little shrug. 'Do you mean at the idea of building a vast villa on Paradise Island?'

'There's no danger of that,' he said.

'Oh.'

'You sound disappointed.'

'I'd like Zoe to find someone who will make her happy. . .someone kind. . .'

'I don't think she'd be happy on an uninhabited island for very long.'

'With the right man, who'd be unhappy?'

He reached out and touched her lips warningly with the tip of one finger. 'Have a care, Maddy; you're beginning to sound almost human. . .'

Maddy pulled back, jolted by that touch. 'Nonsense. I wasn't talking about me.' His eyes refused to believe her. 'Of course, you're right about the villa,' she said briskly, not wanting to probe the reasons for such unlooked for wistfulness. 'Paradise Island needs something less theatrical, something to blend into the surroundings so that, flying over the island, you would never know anyone had ever set foot upon it.' He smiled and shook his head, clearly amused. 'What?' she demanded.

'Nothing, nothing. . . Tell me, Maddy, what would you build here, if the island belonged to you?'

'Me?' Relieved to be on safer ground, she rolled over onto her stomach and propped her chin on her hands, staring up at the island rising steeply away from the beach, thinking how wonderful it would be to come here to your own hide-away whenever you wanted to. But lonely too. She glanced at Griff; then away again

quickly. He couldn't be the right man. He was a
conman, a thief of hearts. But not hers. Hers was safely
under lock and key. Then why isn't the burglar alarm
ringing?

'Well?' She jumped as he interrupted the taunt of her
subconscious and gratefully she gave her undivided
attention to this much safer topic.

'Well,' she said quickly, 'I think I'd want to use thatch
or wooden shingles for the roof—'

'What about rot?' he interrupted. 'It can be very
humid at certain times of the year.'

'I didn't realise this exercise had anything to do with
reality,' she objected.

'And if it had?'

'I...well...' For a moment she almost believed he
meant... No! This was all pure fantasy. A game. 'If
you're going to worry about such mundane details, I'm
sure it wouldn't be a problem with modern preserva-
tives,' she said, airily dismissing his concern.

'All right,' he said, laughing, and the sound pleased
her; it was rich and warm—something he should do
more often. Maddy waved a hand to take in the curve
of the beach.

'It should be set back from the beach, a little way up
the hill to take advantage of the shade.' And she began
to see it in her mind. 'Hardly what you could call a
house—more a series of rooms, very open to catch the
sea breezes, the water could easily be piped down...
Solar power...' She caught herself as she saw him smile
and she realised that her enthusiasm was running away
with her—a fault her accountant was always trying to
curb. But then what was life without enthusiasm?

'And when it rains?'

'What a pessimist you are,' she chided. 'I'd have wide verandas.'

'Wide verandas? I'd never have thought of that,' he teased. 'How wide?' It was a game, she reminded herself, and buried the feeling that there was something else happening beneath the surface.

She took a deep breath. 'Absolutely vast,' she declared fervently. 'Shaped to carry away the rainwater to a small pool where I'd keep pet shrimps that must never, ever be eaten, on pain of life banishment.'

'Even if you were starving?'

'On Paradise Island? With its endless supply of fish and coconuts and bananas and who knows what else if you were to look?' She raised her hand solemnly. 'I hereby declare I shall never eat another shrimp in my entire life.'

Griff lifted his hand and placed his palm against hers, matching her fingers against his own. 'I can live with that.' For a moment neither of them moved, while the air shimmered with something unspoken, undreamed of, and Maddy's insides seemed to roll over like a puppy inviting play. Griff abruptly dropped his hand. 'You obviously have a talent for this sort of thing,' he said. 'Rather more sympathy with your surroundings than Zoe.'

Mention of her godmother brought Maddy crashing back to the present and her immediate predicament. 'I wonder if she's phoned Dad and told him what's happened?' she mused anxiously. 'He'll be worried to death.'

Griff looked away. 'She won't worry him unnecessarily. How was the fish?' he asked, changing the subject.

She looked at the heap of bones on the banana leaf.

'It was quite delicious.' She hesitated. 'Thank you for saving me from the shrimps.'

'I was thinking of myself,' he said briskly, as if regretting that moment when they had come close to something unimaginable. 'You looked as if you were about to be sick.'

'Oh.' Well, that was that.

'Would you like some coconut milk?' he offered politely.

'Only if it means you have to climb a palm tree to pick a nut.'

His mouth twisted into a lopsided grin that did something crazy to her insides. 'I'm afraid not.'

'In that case water will do just fine.' She picked up a coconut husk, but he overturned the bucket before she could dip it in.

'Warm. Very nasty. It's better straight from the stream.' He stood up and held out his hand. Maddy hesitated, remembering their earlier encounter at the waterfall certain that it would be foolhardy to venture there again in his company. There was something drawing her to him—a recognition that she had at last met a man strong enough to take her, if he chose. And, despite his attempts to cover his feelings, resist them, Griff felt it too, she was sure.

'I'm not that thirsty,' she said abruptly. 'Besides, someone might come by.'

'No one is going to come by, Maddy, and it's time to get out of the sun for a while.' He didn't sound as if he was about to take no for an answer. 'I'm sure Jack would be pleased to see you.'

'Well, that will make a nice change,' she said crisply, and was rewarded with the ironical lift of a dark brow. Nevertheless the lure of the cool green forest was very enticing, but she ignored his hand, rising slowly, brushing the sand from her legs. Then she bent to pick up the bucket.

'Leave that.'

'But water-carrying is women's work, remember?'

He grinned broadly, revealing strong white teeth. 'You can fetch some later,' he promised, and Maddy only just managed to bite back the angry retort that flew to her lips. Griff always seemed to be able to top her, no matter what she said. It was time she put her mind to the problem, because no one treated her the way that he did and got away with it. Not for ever.

'How do you know he's called Jack?' she asked as she followed him up the narrow path. Griff halted suddenly, turning his head to stare over his shoulder at her, and Maddy only just managed to prevent herself from bumping into him. 'The parrot,' she explained a little breathlessly. 'How do you know his name?'

His eyes narrowed momentarily, then he gave the smallest shrug and the deepening clefts in his cheeks betrayed just the hint of a smile. 'He told me, of course. That's the advantage of a talking bird.'

She tapped her forehead with the flat of her palm. 'Now why didn't I think of that?'

'There are clearly some glaring gaps in your education,' he replied with perfect seriousness. For a moment Maddy didn't know whether to hit him or laugh. Her sense of the ridiculous won hands down and, unable to help herself, she giggled. It must have been infectious because Griff's smile deepened until there was no doubt that he too found the idea quite ridiculous.

'You should try and find him a mate,' she suggested. 'It doesn't seem right that he's on his own in paradise.'

'You're an unlikely romantic, Maddy.'

'Am I?' She lifted her shoulders a fraction. Not romantic, not sentimental—just how did he see her? She didn't care, she told herself, but she wasn't entirely convinced. 'Life's full of surprises.'

'Isn't it, though? And in fact you're quite right. The St Vincent parrot is an endangered species. Maybe I should catch him and send him to the breeding pro-gramme on St Vincent.'

'You? Wouldn't the Dragon Man object?'

'I. . .' For a moment she thought he was going to say something. Then he threw his arm about her shoulders, drawing her into his side so that they could squeeze up the path together. 'I'll ask him. Come on, Maddy. I believe it's time you saw a little more of Paradise Island than the beach.'

There was a delicious warmth that had nothing to do with the ambient temperature, Maddy discovered, tucked against his firm body as they walked up the path to the pool. Griff stopped to point out a flurry of tiny hummingbirds drinking nectar from the huge scarlet hibiscus flowers, their plumage copper-green in the filtered sunlight. While she watched, he plucked a stem of creamy orchids and, removing her hat, threaded it through her hair.

'Now you look more like a dusky island maiden,' he said. 'The hair's something of a give-away, though.' He pushed a wayward tendril from her brow and tucked it behind her ear.

'It's the humidity,' Maddy said, not quite in control of her voice. 'I've gone rusty.' Then, to cover her blushing confusion, she quickly went on, 'It's almost as if this was once a garden that's gone to seed,' she said, looking about her. Looking anywhere but at Griff.

He followed her gaze. 'Nature's own. Seeds have been brought by the sea and by birds, or on the feet of travellers, and they've found a niche. Everything fits.'

'Except Jack?'

He glanced down at her. 'He's survived. He's made a place for himself. If the wind or chance brings him a mate, then he and his kind will become a part of the island.'

'Even if they push out something else?'

'That's how it's always been.'

'The strong preying on the weak?' she asked pointedly, pulling away from the dangerously seductive circle of his arm.

His brows closed in a frown. 'Yes, Maddy. Since the dawn of time.'

But not if she could help it. She had to get hold of that cheque somehow and send it back to Zoe. Not now. He'd miss it. But when someone came to take them off the island. She'd find a way. They stopped at the pool to drink from water that splashed over the waterfall into their cupped hands. Then Griff climbed onto the rocks and extended his hand to pull her up after him into the cascade of water. 'Come on.'

For a moment she hesitated. 'I know it's ridiculous, but I feel as if I'm trespassing,' she objected.

'This was once a bare volcanic outcrop, Maddy. Everything on it was a trespasser once.'

'But I haven't found my niche.'

'You will.'

'And if I change something?' There was a hint of challenge in her voice. 'Irrevocably?'

'It's a risk we take by being alive. We change places, places change us.

'Do they?' But she knew the answer. She had already

changed. She didn't quite know how or in what way. She just felt different. 'You're quite the philosopher, Griff.'

'No. Just your average man wondering what's over the rainbow.' Griff turned to where a single ray of sunlight angling through the canopy high above them caught and split in the spray and a miniature rainbow arched tantalisingly across the cascade, calling her, inviting her to step beyond it and discover some glorious secret. Then he turned back to stare down at her. 'Come with me, Maddy.'

For a moment they remained, poised between earth and sky. Then Maddy reached up to clasp his hand, gasping as he pulled her up through the spray. It showered her face and throat and soaked her T-shirt so that it clung to her, deliciously cooling, outlining her body as she clutched at him unsteadily before finding her footing.

She propped her panama on an overhanging branch, pushed her sunglasses up into her hair and in a gesture of sheer pleasure tilted her head back so that her face caught the sun and her vivid hair hung in the shaft of sunlight, vying with the rainbow for glory. For just a moment Griff held her there, his arm looped about her waist as they balanced on the edge of the waterfall, their bodies almost, not quite, touching. It was primitive and glorious and she saw from Griff's darkening eyes that it was dangerous too. But then, what was paradise without forbidden fruit?

She was dragged back from the brink of some madness by a piercing wolf-whistle, the flash of orange and yellow banding a pair of brown wings, then Jack settled on the branch above them. She stepped free of the almost drugging pleasure of Griff's touch and looked up, anywhere but at his eyes.

'Hello, Jack,' she said a little breathlessly.

'Hello, Jack,' the bird repeated, and put his head on one side in a conspiratorial little movement that brought a smile to her lips.

'We're exploring; care to show us the sights?' she invited with a careless little gesture as she tried desperately to cover the palpitating confusion of her own thoughts. The bird flew down onto a nearby tree and then hopped away to the right, as if leading the way. 'I do believe he is,' Maddy laughed, making a move to follow him, but Griff caught her arm.

'Not that way, Maddy, the ground falls away rather steeply.'

'But there's a path,' she objected. 'It looks quite well-worn.'

'Appearances can be deceptive. And if you slip and hurt yourself—'

'I won't be much use to you as a drawer of water and hewer of wood? I remember.'

'I'm glad you do,' he said, steering her firmly over the stream via a series of well-placed rocks. 'This way takes us to the top of the island. The view is well worth the effort.'

'Perhaps we should have lit our fire up there,' Maddy said a little scratchily as she glanced back at the beckoning path and caught the faint but unmistakable scent of frangipani blossom.

'No, nothing to spoil the perfection...' His hand upon her arm stopped her. 'But I should warn you that there is a risk involved.'

'A risk?'

'Once you've been to the summit of paradise, you may never want to come down.'

Startled by the intensity of his voice, she turned and looked up into his face. 'You really love this place, don't you, Griff?'

For a moment, the space of a heartbeat, she saw something in his eyes, a feeling of great intensity too fleeting to capture, to interpret. Then, as if he realised that he was in danger of exposing some deep personal feeling, he looked away. 'The fishing's great,' he agreed, with a careless gesture that quite definitely put an end to the subject, but Maddy knew that for him it was a great deal more than just a handy place to catch fish. And she wondered how he felt about someone else owning it, but his face betrayed no secrets as he held back a branch that dipped across the path. 'This way, Miss Osborne,' he invited, sketching a bow with mock formality.

She took a tentative step forward and he extended his hand to her. It was square and darkly tanned, with long, strong fingers that bore the scars of a hard life. It didn't look like the hand of a man who spent his life robbing gullible women of their money when there were worlds to conquer. On the contrary, it looked like the hand of a man you could trust with your life. And she had already done just that, she thought, and shivered a little at the recollection of the way he had landed the seaplane. He had not let her down. She met his eyes and was suddenly quite sure that he would never let her down.

Maddy wondered idly if perhaps she had had rather too much sun; she certainly didn't appear to be behaving quite rationally. But then, this wasn't a very rational situation. The poised, efficient Miss Osborne had been cast away on a desert island with the kind of man most girls dreamed about. Not her of course. She was far too sensible to fall for such foolish dreams twice in one lifetime, wasn't she?

Maddy pushed back a strand of hair that had fallen across her forehead and her hand came into contact with the spray of orchids that Griff had tucked behind her ear... Oh sensible, Miss Osborne, Maddy's subconscious rose to mock her wickedly. With a tiny catch of her breath, as if she was taking some great, irretrievable step, Maddy consigned her subconscious to the dustbin, reached out and placed her hand in his. It looked so fragile, small and pale against his broad palm. Then he closed his hand over hers and she had the clearest feeling that she would never get it back, that Griff had claimed it as his own.

'Shall we go?'

'"The woods are lovely, dark and deep..."' she quoted huskily.

'"But I have promises to keep..."' he continued slowly, then his eyes shaded as if he had remembered something, and an odd little shiver rippled down Maddy's spine. 'What's the matter?' he asked as the tremor transmitted itself to him.

'Nothing.' She snapped her hand back to her side. 'I'm just a little wet from the waterfall, that's all. Shall we try and find the sun?'

He turned without a word and led the way up the path. For a moment Maddy stayed where she was, and knew that she was a fool for wishing her hand was still safely tucked up in his. Definitely too much sun. Jack gave a loud squawk from his perch some way above her and then fluttered from tree to tree, retracing the way they had come. She watched him for a moment and, as if aware of her scrutiny, he settled on a bush the other side of the stream near the path, and put his head on one side. Despite Griff's warning she was certain that the bird wanted her to follow him and she took a step towards him, then another.

'Maddy?' She started guiltily and spun round. 'Where are you going?'

'Nowhere,' she said, too quickly. 'Just daydreaming. Sorry.'

He stood back, indicating the path she should take, and she didn't linger, hurrying through the forest, no longer lulled by the incessant, hypnotic hum of insects, hardly even aware of the more strident calls of the mockingbirds. She was lost somewhere inside her head, where Griff's soft, insistent voice was repeating over and over, "Places change us." It was true. She was being changed irretrievably by the island. By him.

Then abruptly she burst through the thickly forested slopes and was on top of the world, surrounded on all sides by an ocean sparkling in the sunlight, the broken necklace of the Grenadines disappearing into the afternoon haze, the peaks of Union tantalisingly close, yet as far out of reach as if they were a thousand miles away.

The white wake of motor boats trailed teasingly in the distance and the snowy sails of a dozen yachts dipped under the breeze, one seeming almost close enough to hail. But it was an illusion, she knew. The wind would whip her voice away, and if anyone was looking in her direction and she was seen waving, who would suppose she could desire rescue? They would do just what Griff's passing fisherman had done and wave back.

It seemed impossible to be stranded so close to so

many people and Maddy knew that twenty-four hours ago she would have raged at her impotence. Now she settled on a smooth, sun-warmed rock, startling a tiny, basking lizard which disappeared in the flash of green. She leaned back on her hands, closed her eyes and lifted her face to drink in the fresh, cooling scent of the trade winds. Rescue would come when it came. There was no point in raging against anything. Right now she had nothing more important in the world to do than sit here.

Griff settled very quietly beside her on the stone. She could sense the warmth of his body, the sharp, musky, male scent of him. 'You're right, Griff,' she said, acknowledging his presence without opening her eyes. 'It's beautiful up here.'

'Do you still want to summon some gallant to your rescue?' She turned to him to deny it, but he was offering her a conch shell. 'Put it to your lips and blow,' he suggested. 'Someone might hear you.'

She took the shell between her hands. It was heavy, rough on the outside, but the inside shone with a beautiful peachy-pink lustre. She put it to her ear and listened to the sea for a moment. It was lulling, seductive. 'Not yet,' she said, with a sigh so small that she was hardly aware of it. And she put the shell down on the rock beside her. 'There isn't any rush.'

CHAPTER SEVEN

'MADDY?' Griff said her name softly—so softly that for a moment she wasn't certain she had really heard his voice. 'Maddy,' he repeated, as if he could not help himself, and under the soft, hypnotic sound of her name she raised her lids and turned to face him. It seemed almost as if he was moving in slow motion as he raised his hands to capture her face and draw her into his body.

She did not resist, could not—the moment was too perfect, too right. Her lips parted slightly over even white teeth as she waited, her face cradled in his hands, his long fingers threaded in her hair—waited for him to kiss her.

This time he did not crush her soft mouth beneath his, nor did he tease her with a taunting butterfly touch of his lips that left her longing pitifully for more. He bent his head to hers slowly—so slowly that she could see the thick dark fringe of lashes normally hidden behind dark glasses, the tiny flecks of blue in the sea-green of his eyes as he paused, his lips a bare inch from hers. Then his heavy lids closed as his mouth touched hers, and a strange longing, entirely new and yet instantly recognisable, sparked through her.

His lips began to move over hers in the most gentle exploration, greeting her lips, her teeth, the tip of her tongue with his own, as if committing the taste of her to his memory. Maddy remained very still, containing her fervent longing to respond to his caress. The kiss

was a gift, from Griff to her, and although her heart
was almost bursting with the aching need it stirred deep
within her some elemental instinct warned her to be
patient, to let him take the lead. When he lifted his
head a few moments later, with a shudder that betrayed
the intensity with which he had held himself in check,
she knew she had been right to hold back. The kiss had
been heart-rendingly sweet. A promise? Or, as he knew
that rescue must come soon, that they must leave the
island, was it simply goodbye?

But for a moment Griff said nothing and she was
content enough to lean her head against his shoulder,
content to enjoy the clear, fresh scent of the sea carried
on the breeze, overlaid with the elusive sweetness of
frangipani, content to enjoy the rattle of wind through
bamboo, and the poinsettia, a vivid splash of red in the
lush vegetation that spread below them—reminder that,
despite the heat, Christmas was nearly upon them—and
Griff beside her, his dark hair tousled by the breeze,
the hard edge of his profile shadowed against the sun.

She lifted her face to look up at him and for a blazing
second their eyes met and anything might have happened. Then Griff pulled back. 'I'm sorry, Maddy,' he
said, 'I shouldn't have done that.'

Maddy put out her hand, cradled his cheek lightly in
her hand. 'It's all right, Griff. I promise I'm not about
to summon the constabulary.' Her voice was a shy
husky murmur from deep in her throat. 'And I'm not
about to scream. Promise.'

'Don't!' He groaned and she withdrew her hand. 'I
didn't mean to kiss you, Maddy. Not like that. . . God
knows, I didn't mean to. It was wrong.' His sweeping
glance took in the island spread at their feet before he
turned to her, his eyes as dark as obsidian against the

brilliance of the sun, his face shadowed, and suddenly she remembered and guilt stabbed through her.

'Because of Zoe. . .'

Startled, he turned to her. 'You've guessed?'

So it was true. 'You were careless, Griff. . .'

'I knew I'd said too much. . . Maddy. . .'

How could she have ever forgotten? Zoe would be shattered to discover that she had made a fool of herself over a fortune-hunter. How much worse it would be if she discovered that her young lover had made a pass at her god-daughter before he'd even banked the proceeds. . .

'How could you do it?' she asked a little despairingly.

He stood up abruptly. 'I can't expect you to understand. You could never begin to understand how much I owe. . .'

He was in debt? Maddy felt a surge of hope. It was as simple as that? She could handle that. She would return Zoe's cheque, deal with Griff's problems. They would be expensive, no doubt, but she would do anything to save Zoe from the bitter disillusionment of knowing that a man had wanted her only for her money. She looked up into his face. Expensive and dangerous, but there was no other way. The tip of her tongue moistened her dry mouth.

'I want you to forget about Zoe, Griff.' He stiffened, but she ploughed on before she entirely lost her nerve. 'You don't need her. Just tell me what you want; I'll do anything—'

'Stop that!' He seized her arm and shook her. 'For a moment—for just a moment—I hoped, dreamed. . . But I should know better than to rely on a shooting star.' He jerked her close, so that his mouth was threatening hers. 'So, tell me, my beautiful little gold-digger, what is it that you do that drives men crazy? What tricks—?'

'What. . .what are you talking about?' Bewildered by this sudden change in his manner she tried to step back, but his hand tightened about her arm and she didn't make it.

'I'm cut from a different cloth from the men you play your teasing games with. What the Dragon Man wants—'

'Dragon Man?' Confusion was fogging her mind so that she could hardly think. The Dragon Man? What on earth was he talking about? The Dragon Man wasn't here. . .

'I've always thought, Maddy, that one day you would go too far. . .' And, seizing the hem of her T-shirt, he pulled it over her head in one smooth movement and tossed it aside. Before her stunned brain could react, he'd hooked his thumbs beneath the straps of her swimsuit and jerked them down over her arms, exposing the milky whiteness of breasts that she had never bared to the sun. There was a moment of shocked silence. 'What the Dragon Man wants,' he repeated, in a low, throaty growl that scorched her very soul, 'he takes. And since you're so generously offering. . .'

Maddy's mind cleared in a sudden flash of understanding, but even as she opened her mouth to demand an explanation he jerked her close, crushing her pitilessly against the iron wall of his chest. And this time his lips were without mercy.

For a moment she was too shocked to react. It was far too long a moment before her fists began raining blows against his shoulders and she began kicking out with her useless sandals that made not the slightest impression. He took everything she could throw at him and still his fingers bit into her shoulders and she had to endure that fierce, loveless kiss.

It was as if he was determined to wipe out every trace of his brief, tender embrace at the summit of paradise, overwrite his memory with something far earthier, more primitive than that most loving touch, reducing it from something splendid to man's most basic instinct.

And as the realisation of what he was doing finally penetrated the turmoil of her confused, bewildered brain Maddy stopped fighting. She accepted gladly the chance to eradicate that moment from her memory, welcoming the savage intrusion of his tongue in the knowledge that it would destroy for ever the sweet taste of his lips and offer her some kind of freedom. If he had wanted to make her hate him, he couldn't have chosen a more effective weapon. And, with all of her heart, she wanted to hate him.

When finally, after what might have been a lifetime, he raised his head and she saw that his eyes were hard, blanked of all expression, she lifted her hand and wiped the back of it across her burning mouth in a heartbreakingly vulnerable gesture that brought a soft oath to his lips.

'What have I ever done to you, Griff?' Maddy demanded, breathless but determined, her eyes blazing in her white face, taking on the question in his bottomless green eyes, flinging it back at him, and for a moment it seemed to shake him.

'Don't you know?' His voice was barely more than a breath. 'Have you no idea—?' He stopped abruptly, releasing her shoulders without warning so that she stumbled and her foot came sharply up against the root of a tree blown down by some tropical storm that had swept the island long ago. She cried out as she put out a hand to save herself, but with a swiftness of movement that seemed to defy gravity he was there, holding her, cursing under his breath at his own stupidity as he steadied her.

But she jerked away from him, from the burning touch of his hands upon her skin, staggering a little as she broke free, holding him at bay when he would have reached out to help—then blushing fiercely as she saw that his eyes were fixed upon her body. 'For pity's sake, cover yourself. . .' When, transfixed by embarrassment, she made no move to do so, he caught the straps of her swimsuit and pulled it up.

His touch was sufficient to break the spell that held her and she jerked back, holding her costume to her with her arm as a tiny, anguished moan escaped her lips. 'Don't touch me!' she said with desperate urgency, struggling with the straps. 'I don't want you to touch me ever again.' It was impossible for her to risk that longed-for caress.

How had she ever been stupid enough to believe she could forget his kiss, the extraordinary joy of that moment when she had believed he had meant it? She would try, but she knew it would be a lost cause. Nothing he could do to her would ever destroy that shimmering moment in time when she had been ready to believe. . .anything. She would always remember. If she lived to be ninety-two, the honeyed touch of his lips would still be the most bitter-sweet memory.

'Oh, God, Maddy.' He took a step towards her. 'This is a nightmare. I never meant—'

She held out an imperious hand to stop him. She didn't want to know what he meant. Locked in that maelstrom of passion and pain, she had worked out the bare bones of it for herself. Hugo Griffin was the

Dragon Man. The clue had been there in his name all
the time. Griffins and dragons were all cut from the
same dangerous cloth. Did he mean her to know, or
had it just slipped out?

How foolish she had been. How gullible. The dinghy
that hadn't stopped. The way he had delayed her when
she had tried to light the fire to attract a distant yacht. . .
the lighter that had conveniently refused to work until
it was too late. . .

'Maddy. . .' He reached out for her.

'It's my nightmare, not yours, Dragon Man,' she flung
at him. Griff bit down hard, his lips thinning as he
fought to keep inside whatever it was he wanted to say,
man enough to know that he could not apologise for
what he had done, that there were no words to cover it.
But it was precious little comfort. And, hand still
outstretched to keep him at a distance, she walked
slowly, carefully around him until she was between him
and the path that led back through the forest to the
beach. 'I'm going back to the beach,' she said. 'Alone.'

He retrieved her T-shirt, took a step towards her. 'I'd
better come with you—'

She snatched the shirt, pulled it over her, feeling too
naked in her demure swimsuit. 'Don't! Don't call me
Maddy,' she said, her voice oddly calm. This wasn't the
moment to scream. Her pain was an icy knot deep
inside her, contained too tightly for such an easy
release. She wasn't sure that she would ever be able to
raise her voice above a whisper again. 'Don't speak to
me at all, Hugo Griffin.' How hard it was to say his
name! 'From now on I don't want you to do anything
for me; I don't want you to come near me.' He didn't
say anything but remained perfectly still a foot away
from her. 'Is that perfectly clear?' she demanded.

'You wanted me to answer you?' he asked, his eyes glittering dangerously in that small, scented clearing high above the Caribbean. 'I understood I wasn't supposed to speak.' She snapped round, took a step towards the path, but his voice followed her. 'There's no way off this island without me,' he warned.

'Someone will come looking for me. Until they do, just stay away from me.' She turned and half stumbled onto the path.

'Will you be taking up shrimping again, Maddy Rufus?' he asked very softly, tempting her to a truce, and she faltered, glanced back. But she could never return to that state of armed neutrality that had governed their relationship until now. One tender kiss and she had been prepared to lay down her arms and surrender all too willingly. Dignity was all that remained and precious little of that, but if she stretched it thinly it might just save her.

'The shrimps are safe from me,' she said, with only a little shake in her voice. 'I can survive on water for the next twenty-four hours if I have to. Even Zoe should have got the message by then.'

'And if she hasn't?' He took another step towards her as if he sensed her vulnerability. She didn't wait to find out but stepped back onto the path before turning to run as fast as she dared down the steep, narrow track towards the space and safety of the beach. Once she glanced back—she couldn't see or hear him, but she didn't pause until she was brought to a breathless halt in the glade above the waterfall by the barrier of the stream. The stepping stones seemed further apart than she remembered, or maybe they were just more daunting without his strong arm to cling to as she leapt across.

As she stepped out onto the first stone she saw him

out of the corner of her eye, his face riven with concern. 'Maddy, wait!'

But she couldn't wait, mustn't wait. He remained where he was, afraid, perhaps, that any sudden move on his part would initiate disaster, and Maddy locked him out of her head, making the return journey with enormous concentration, determined that she should not slip on the wet stones, give him any excuse to come after her, touch her. Finally she stepped onto the opposite bank with a long sigh of relief and it took all her will-power not to look back.

Jack had disappeared from his perch above the falls, although she fancied she heard his squawk tempting her from somewhere below, down the forbidden path. Maddy did not even look; it held no attraction for her now. She just wanted to get back to the beach. She would be safer there in the bright sunlight, but first she had to negotiate the waterfall. From below, with Griff to pull her up, it had seemed simple enough, but, from above, the ground seemed far away, with the slippery rocks lying in wait to tear at her if she should make the slightest error.

The rattle of a stone warned her that Griff was close behind. 'There's only one way down,' he said, and before she could even register his presence at her side his arm was about her waist, pinning her tight against him. Startled, she glanced up, and he stared down into her face. 'Ready?' He didn't wait for her answer but leapt with her down through the cascading falls and into the dark water of the pool. It was much deeper than she had supposed and they sank, it seemed to Maddy, for ever, his arms and legs wrapped protectively around her, her hair streaming out above them.

For a moment they hung motionless in the water.

Griff's face was pale underwater, with dark shadows that made him seem both strange and beautiful, and Maddy thought her heart must break in two. Then he gave a fierce kick with his feet and they were speeding upwards, the water fizzing around them as they erupted, gasping, locked together, the water streaming down their faces. 'Shall we go back and do that again?' he invited, his eyes dark with some unfathomable mystery. And Maddy would have given anything in the world to be able to say yes.

Then she saw the spray of creamy orchids floating on the surface of the water—the flowers that he had picked and threaded through her hair—and a small cry escaped her lips before she clamped them shut on her pain.

She closed her eyes tightly. How could there be pain? She had known the Dragon Man for such a little time. For turbulent, difficult hours, it was true, but he had never hidden the way he felt about her. From the very first moment he had been consistent. Until he had kissed her and melted her heart.

Maddy put her hands against his chest and pushed, turning away from the heady challenge in his eyes, and swam swiftly to the side, where she hauled herself out of the pool. She had lost her sandals in that wild, breathless jump from the top of the falls and as she cast about for them Griff leapt down beside her, cutting her off from the path to the beach. A bubble of panic rose to her throat as he moved slowly towards her, then a flash of orange caught her eye. It was Jack showing her the way and she turned and plunged after him through the thick curtain of vegetation, ignoring Griff's urgent warning shout.

There was a path of sorts—the one she had seen from

the top of the falls. It was steep, damp beneath her bare feet, but she didn't care. As she heard Griff at her back she flew down it.

'Maddy, stop!' She half turned and missed the tangle of roots until it was too late and she was already falling and pain was spearing through her ankle. 'Oh, Maddy,' Griff said as he came to a halt beside her. 'What ever am I going to do with you?' he said, tucking down beside her on his haunches.

'Nothing! Stay away from me.' She made a move to stand and for a moment she thought it was going to be all right. She could ignore the pain, she told herself. Then she put her weight on her ankle and she was falling again, this time into Griff's waiting arms, but as everything went black it no longer seemed to matter.

Her faint could not have lasted more than a second or two. She was dimly aware of being carried swiftly along the path in Griff's arms, every step jarring her injured ankle. She gritted her teeth, refusing to cry out. And then, after a hundred yards or so, the elusive scent of the frangipani, which had seemed to haunt her all day, grew steadily stronger until quite suddenly the tree swam into focus beside her, its ugly grey bulbous branches laden with exquisite, scented blossoms.

And there was something else beyond the tree. For a moment she couldn't quite work out what she was looking at, so well was the house disguised from the casual observer. Then she stiffened in disbelief. A house! While she had been living in the most primitive conditions on the beach, civilisation had been a few hundred yards away with hot running water, beds without sand. . .

And not just any house. The wooden roof shingles seemed to mock her; the supporting posts that did nothing to interrupt the cooling breeze might almost have sprung from her own laughing words as she had accepted Griff's invitation to describe the kind of house she would build on this island if it were hers. For a moment the whole idea seemed so ridiculous that she wondered if she might be dreaming, or if the house was a mirage conjured up from a childish game of make-believe by her unconscious brain. She closed her eyes and opened them again. It was still there. And then she remembered his amusement at her description—restrained, under the circumstances.

Maddy looked up into Griff's concerned eyes, then looked away again quickly. 'Very funny,' she snapped.

'I'm not laughing, Maddy,' he said softly.

'Oh, please, don't hold back, Dragon Man, you might split something. . .' She caught her breath as he stepped up onto the veranda and hot pain jarred through her ankle.

'Don't move,' he said as he laid her carefully on a thickly upholstered sofa. 'I'll be right back.'

'Please don't rush,' she told his retreating back through gritted teeth. Then, as she lay back against the soft cushions, she added, 'I'm not going anywhere.'

She stared up at the veranda roof—a series of pyramid shapes supported on thick pillars, lined and crossed with sweetly scented native woods, each delineating a separate room open to the breeze blowing in from the sea. Her first impression of the Dragon Man's lair had been quite wrong. It went far beyond her own simple idea of a small beach house hidden from the world by the thick forest. This was a masterpiece of design and construction.

She lay on one of two huge sofas covered with dark green linen which were set on either side of a low, square mahogany table, very old and so thick that it must have taken four men to move. Cool rattan cairs were upholstered in tropical shades of green and yellow. And everywhere there were tall plants and beautiful *objets d'art*, in brilliant colours that began to merge into one.

Then the colour was gone and Griff's face swam above her and he gently pushed back the hair that was clinging limply to her forehead. 'I'm sorry, Maddy,' he said. 'But I'm afraid this is going to hurt.'

When Maddy opened her eyes the sky was white and she frowned. That couldn't be right. This was paradise and the sky was always blue.

She moved her head, but it wasn't lying on the sand. It was propped on a soft down pillow. She turned and was immediately aware of a pair of thighs inches from her face. Strong, tanned, impossible to ignore. She gave it her best shot, closing her eyes, but he didn't go away. Instead he laid his hand upon her forehead.

'How are you feeling?'

She stiffened at his touch. 'You really don't want to know that.'

'Sore? Well, I've brought you some painkillers for your ankle.'

'Ankle?' She glanced down at her feet; one of them had been expertly strapped. That wasn't pain. Not real pain.

'I was afraid you'd broken it, but it's just a sprain. Come on, I'll help you up.' Without waiting for her agreement, he hooked his arm under hers and lifted her into a sitting position, propping the pillows behind her. Then he held out a couple of tablets and a glass of water.

'Civilisation as we know it.' But two tablets could do nothing for the pain of treachery so deep that she knew she would rather have been lying on the beach than face the truth.

'Since you fainted on my doorstep, it was easier to bring you here than return you to the beach.'

'The dragon's lair?' For a moment she challenged him, but then stared down at herself, at the unfamiliar bathrobe. 'I was wearing a swimsuit when I fell.'

'A wet, somewhat muddy swimsuit,' he said, with a degree of matter-of-factness for which she knew she should be grateful, but wasn't. 'Would you like something to eat?'

'No. Thank you. I've quite gone off fish.'

His expression warned her that she was pushing her luck. 'What about a cup of tea and a lightly boiled egg?'

It sounded like bliss, but she refused to be so easily tempted. 'China tea?' she enquired, with just a hint of acid. 'And are the eggs free-range?'

His eyes sparked in the soft, cool light of the room. 'For a moment back there, Maddy Rufus, I almost thought you were human.'

For a moment back there, 'Griff will do', I almost believed it myself, Maddy thought, but said nothing.

'Whilst I am in fact a callous, gold-digging little brat who needs a serious lesson in manners?' she enquired. 'I mean why else would we be camping on the beach when you've got a perfectly. . .adequate. . .house?'

'Why else?' he murmured softly.

'Well, you've made your point, Dragon Man. Had your fun. Lesson learned. Now, will you get on the radio and call up someone to take me home, or will I?'

His jaw tightened ominously. 'I can't do that, I'm afraid.' She was almost convinced by that regretful little shrug. 'I've never bothered to install one. I've always used the one on the plane or—'

'Or the yacht?' she demanded. How much more was she going to have to bear? 'Where is it?'

'On charter for the next month. It's not a toy; it has to earn its keep. Sorry.'

'You're not in the least bit sorry,' she stormed. 'You're enjoying yourself. Just wait until I tell Zoe—'

His face darkened. 'I was beginning to enjoy myself,' he said tersely. 'The bathroom's through there, so if you don't need my help. . .?'

'I'm sure I can manage.' She stood up to demonstrate that she needed nothing from him. Absolutely nothing. 'My ankle isn't that bad.'

'Ah, well, you see, I did a first-aid course once. . . You never know when it might come in useful.' And he shut the door with a snap as he left the room.

Maddy blinked as tears stung at her lids. It would be ridiculous to cry. She never cried. At least, for years and years. She stared determinedly about her, trying very hard not to think about him undressing her. She was in an enormous room, the stark whiteness of the walls broken only by two very beautiful primitive paintings the brilliant colours of which vibrated against the dark masculine furniture.

And the bathroom was enormous, with simple blue and white tiles and dark mahogany fittings. There was a shower, a bath big enough for two and a pile of dark blue plush towels exactly like the one he had used on the beach. Not Zoe's, then. Had he come and collected it so that she would be more comfortable lying on the sand? 'Oh, Maddy, wake up, girl. It wasn't meant for you. You were meant to lie on the sand and suffer,' she told herself. If she hadn't had hysterics, she would undoubtedly have done just that instead of spending the night wrapped in the safety of his arms. She stared at her reflection in the mirror. Her tan had darkened a shade or two, her hair was, if anything even brighter after a couple of days spent outside, but nothing else had changed. Not on the outside.

She removed the robe and sponged herself all over with warm water and was drying herself when she heard the bedroom door open. Wrapping the towel around her like a sarong, she hopped to the bathroom door. 'Is this accommodation temporary,' she demanded, 'or can I have my bags?'

'Say please and anything's possible.'

'I'd rather sleep—'

'Say and it's a fact!' he warned.

'In my own nightdress,' she said, rapidly retreating from her threat, certain that he wasn't bluffing. 'And I need a toothbrush.'

'They'll wait. Come and have something to eat.'

'Dressed like this?'

'I promise you, Maddy, no one is about to call.' And he held the bedroom door wide, inviting her out onto the terrace.

She threw the end of the towel over her shoulder and made to sweep by him, for the moment forgetting her ankle. He caught her as the pain took her unawares, and picked her up.

'Keep your hands off me,' she demanded, trying to shake free of him.

'This is my house, Maddy Osborne, and I'm the only one who gives orders in it.'

'You are nothing but a. . .a. . .'

'Lost for words?' he enquired.

'I'm too much of a lady to utter them.'

'I know what I am, Maddy Rufus,' he told her. 'The
jury's still out on you.' Before she could reply he carried
her to the table, sitting her on one of the high-backed
chairs before which had been laid the promised eggs, a
pile of fresh toast and a pot of tea. Despite the fact that
the sun was already turning the sky pink and it was
hours since she had eaten, she ignored them, fixing her
gaze instead upon the table. It was cut from a single
cross-section of some richly dappled gold and brown
timber and supported on crossed legs of a much darker
wood.

'You have excellent taste in furniture,' she said,
studiously ignoring the eggs. 'Did some local craftsman
make this for you?'

'I made it and when you've got a spare month I'll tell
you about it. Right now I want you to eat.'

'I'm not hungry,' she said, regarding him with the
stubborn expression that had once made teachers
quake. Griff was unmoved.

He caught her wrist and put a spoon into her hand.
'Force yourself,' he said with quiet authority, and sank
to his haunches so that his eyes were on a level with
hers.

'I'm not hungry,' she insisted, trying to keep her own
voice on the same even keel as his, but she knew that
another minute of the tantalising smell of fresh toast
would drive her stomach to noisy reproach. She tugged
at her wrist, but although his grasp was light it was not
to be moved. Besides, his eyes were inescapable; they
pinned her to the chair like a butterfly to a card.

'Now,' he continued in the same quiet voice, 'I'm
going to fetch your bag from the plane. But just so you
don't misunderstand my determination I'm going to tell
you what I will do if you defy me.' Apprehension

cartwheeled beneath her ribs. There was something very ominous about his insistence.

'What?' Her voice caught drily in her throat, but she lifted her chin a little. 'What will you do?'

He lifted the towel where it was draped over her naked shoulder and ran the edge of his thumb along her collar-bone. She shivered convulsively and he nodded as if satisfied. 'If, when I return, you haven't eaten every scrap I shall remove this very fetching sarong and make love to you, Maddy. Right here.'

CHAPTER EIGHT

THERE was no emotion, no threatening gesture. The words were completely matter-of-fact. He might just as easily have said, I'll have a cup of tea and a biscuit. Yet she believed him. It was frightening how easy he was to believe. More terrifying still was the way her body kindled to his threat.

'On the dining table?'

'Whatever turns you on.'

'But. . .that would be rape,' she replied hoarsely.

'No.' He finally released her wrist and raised his hand to her face. The pad of his thumb grazed the hot flare of colour on her cheekbones and a little shock wave rippled beneath her skin, fanning out from the epicentre of his touch until her body felt consumed, her mind unravelling in her desire for him. He offered a sympathetic smile as if he understood. 'Not rape, Maddy. It would be much worse than that. We both know that you'd be begging for more.' He uncurled in one graceful movement and walked away.

Fear so raw that she could taste it rippled through her and she looked at the spoon still clasped in her hand. She wanted to smash the egg with it. Instead, she began to tap the egg, very gently, removing the shell in the slow, meticulous manner that she had once used to drive her mother to fury and that in some subtle way defied him. But nevertheless she ate it all, and every crumb of toast, although it practically stuck in her throat. Because, no matter how much she denied it to

herself, she knew she was in no position to call his bluff.
How could such a thing have happened? How could she
have fallen in love with him when she believed him to
be her worst nightmare? And there was still the cheque.

He had not returned by the time she finished and,
refusing to sit like a child waiting for permission to
leave the table, she gathered the dishes and hobbled
painfully to the kitchen with them.

The kitchen was decorated in an earthy mixture of
pale terracotta, soft creams and rich dark wood. Perfect,
like the rest of the house. But she didn't want to think
about the house, because that meant thinking about the
way he had deceived her. She quickly filled the sink
with warm water and washed up, leaning against the
edge of the unit to take the weight of her foot. It didn't
take long.

She made her way slowly back to the terrace, determined to put her foot up on one of the sofas, but then
it occurred to her that she would never have a better
opportunity to look around. Despite his casual denial
of a radio, it seemed unlikely that a man in Griff's
position would be so cavalier about communications.
He would surely have some backup? She grasped the
handle of a tantalisingly closed door and began to turn
it. Then she stopped. He'd had his fun at her expense.
It was over. Why on earth would he pretend?

'Griff?'

She found him contemplating the inlet a few yards
from the little seaplane. It was the first time she had
voluntarily spoken to him for three days—three long
days during which there had been no sign of a search
for them by air or sea and Maddy's nerves had been

stretched to breaking-point by the almost unbearable intimacy of sharing a house with him.

'Maddy?' he replied with a laconic lift of a brow, and she almost winced.

She had known it would not be easy, but she couldn't let things drift on like this and she had screwed herself to the sticking-point to face his amusement that she had finally been forced to beg. But it was as clear as day that Griff was content to continue as they were— swimming in the calm water of the inlet and idling their time away. It was as if he was waiting for something. And this was, after all, his home. He was doing precisely what he'd intended to do—fish a little, read, explore the reef with a snorkel. She had watched, wanting to accept his casual invitations to join him, but unwilling to risk the flare of damped-down passion that she was so intensely aware was just beneath the surface.

'We can't go on like this.'

'I can,' he assured her, but as her eyes pleaded with him to understand he relented and patted the sand beside him. 'Sit down. Tell me what's on your mind.'

'You know what's on my mind,' she said, ignoring his invitation to sit. 'I want to get off this island and go home.'

'Really? I thought it was imperative that you stay with Zoe?'

'That was Father's idea. He thought...' It didn't matter what he thought. Whatever Zoe's cheque was for, it clearly wasn't to support the Dragon Man in idleness. 'Once I'm off this island I'm getting the first available flight back to London. My father will be going frantic, not having heard from me.'

He looked up at her, shading his eyes from the sun. 'You do know, then, that people worry about you?'

She frowned slightly. 'Of course I do.'

'I didn't mean the fact that you are long overdue on your visit to Zoe's.'

'Didn't you?' What else could he mean? Then she brushed his interruption away with an irritable little twitch of her hand. 'Anyway, Zoe clearly hasn't been all that bothered. . .' She went suddenly cold as a shiver ran down her spine. 'Unless. . .' She looked at him. 'Unless they think we crashed into the sea. That we're. . .' She covered her hand with her mouth and sank onto the sand beside him, forgetting her anger with him in her anguish. 'That's it, isn't it? That's why the authorities aren't looking for us. They think we're dead.' She stuffed her fist into her mouth. 'Dad will have to go to Paris to tell my mother. . .' He wouldn't telephone and despite everything, he still loved her too much to let anyone else do it. She felt tears of pity for them both well up in her eyes. 'Oh, Griff. This is awful.'

He swore softly and put his arm around her, thumbing away the tears that had unaccountably welled onto her cheeks. 'Oh, come on; it isn't that bad.'

She looked up at him. Why wouldn't he understand? Griff, this is serious. . .'

'If anyone thought we were in trouble they'd be out looking for wreckage, Maddy. Zoe probably thinks I've tempted you to my lair and is being terribly discreet.'

'She would never think that!'

His brows rose sharply at her indignant denial. 'My mistake.' Then he frowned. 'I thought you said you didn't have a mother.'

Maddy remembered with painful clarity exactly what she had said to him: I no longer have a mother. She had thought it for so long that she hadn't realised how heartless, how cruel it was until this moment when she pictured her mother grieving for her. She had blamed her for so much. . .'My mother left, years ago.'

'Another man?'

She shook her head. 'No. She has her faults, but faithlessness isn't one of them.'

'Then what?'

'Money.'

'Ah, the Osborne family failing.'

'My mother certainly thought so. When she discovered that Dad had mortgaged the house for the fifth time to finance his latest venture she just walked out. She couldn't take the fear any more, I suppose. Dad had come close to disaster before and she'd lost her home when everything had had to be sold to pay men's wages and the creditors.'

'But you didn't go with her?'

'Someone had to stay and look after Dad. Perhaps daughters are less critical than wives.'

'But you blamed her?' He saw everything so clearly, so black and white. But he was right. She did blame her mother that she had been left to cook and clean and answer the telephone and be her father's unpaid secretary when she should have been working for her A levels. You didn't walk out on your responsibilities. She had scraped through her exams with the bare minimum, and instead of accomplishing her dream of reading English at Oxford she had ended up doing a year at a local college.

Maddy discovered that she was smiling at the irony of it. An English degree might just have got her a job in a publishing house. Business studies had given her the foundation to run a successful company of her own. Life had its own pattern. One door closed and another opened.

'Maddy?' She realised that he was waiting for an answer.

'Living with him must have been a nightmare for someone like my mother, who loves order and security. The pity of it was that after all those years of worrying whether she was going to be able to pay the electricity bill he had made his first million within a year of her leaving.'

'I'm surprised she didn't come back. Or perhaps she felt guilty about leaving you?'

Maddy hadn't thought about it clearly for a long time. Now she shook her head. 'If you only knew half the things she had to put up with. . .'

'Perhaps you should tell her how you feel.'

She looked at him then. 'Perhaps I should.' It was like a door opening in her heart and she smiled. 'And when I open the Paris branch I'll be able to spend a lot more time with her.'

'The Paris branch?' The irony was back.

She gave an apologetic little shrug. 'Like father, like daughter. I shall have to raise the money on my flat if I decide to go ahead. It must run in the blood.'

'Unless you can catch a rich husband in the meantime?'

Maddy met Griff's eye and gave a little shiver. 'That will do it every time,' she conceded sarcastically. Considering that she wasn't supposed to be talking to the man, it occurred to Maddy that this conversation seemed to have got rather out of hand. She had rehearsed what she was going to say to him. The bare minimum. How had they ever got so far off the subject? She disengaged herself from the comforting curve of his arm. 'But to snare the prize I have to get off this island.'

'You want me to build a raft?' he offered.

She remembered the table. 'Could you do that?'

'It would take a while,' he said with a shrug. 'Have you ever tried to saw up palm wood with your teeth?'

'No, I haven't,' she said, leaping to her feet, cross with herself for falling so easily for his teasing.

'You have something more practical in mind? A message in a bottle, perhaps?'

She glared at him. 'I'm not prepared to sit here any longer and do nothing.'

He linked his fingers behind his head, lay back on the sand and closed his eyes. 'You should try it once in a while, Maddy. You might enjoy it.'

She allowed her eyes to make a lingering journey down the strong column of his neck, across a pair of well-muscled shoulders and the deep chest with its scattering of body hair that arrowed to a fine dark line across his taut hips. He had confounded her theory that he lacked a bathing suit, but the black slip that hugged his hips did very little to disguise his manhood and the skin across her high cheekbones darkened. Oh, she could enjoy it. Despite her frantic attempts to keep busy with sketching, taking photographs, teaching Jack some new words—anything to occupy her mind—she knew that if things had been different between them she would have been more than happy to lie back and. . . She jerked her gaze away to find that he had opened his eyes and was watching her.

'It's time for the last resort, Griff. I want you to set fire to the plane,' she said, wanting to shock him, provoke some reaction other than a cool, teasing smile. He didn't move. 'I'll pay you if that's what it takes. How much is that old plane worth?' Not by one twitch of a muscle did he betray that he had understood what she was demanding. 'The smoke will be black, acrid,'

The words began to tumble out as he still made no response, but his eyes hardened. 'Not like a bonfire. It would be seen from the other islands. It couldn't be ignored.'

'No,' he agreed, 'it certainly couldn't be ignored. I'm sure we'd be descended upon by every environmental officer in the Grenadines and beyond, all demanding to know why we were polluting the atmosphere.'

'It's an emergency!'

'Really? You've been delayed a few days and it's a crisis? Everyone must jump to attention?'

'I want to get away from you, Griff. And you needn't pretend you'd be desolated to lose this particular Eve.'

'Maybe I would. After all, you have a certain entertainment value.'

'Entertainment value?' She could hardly believe her ears. 'I hardly dare ask. . .?'

'I particularly like the way you curl your tongue over your lip when you're concentrating very hard.'

'I don't!'

'You do, actually. And that little wriggle you give before you fling yourself into the sea.' He moved his hand to demonstrate. 'And those black stockings—'

'All right,' she said quickly. 'You can set me up as a public amusement and charge admittance if you'll just get me off this island!'

He shrugged. 'It's a lot to ask, Maddy.'

'Well, if you'd made more of an effort—' She stopped, began again a little more placatingly this time. 'I know it's probably your pride and joy, Griff, but—'

He lifted his head to look at her. 'You haven't much time for other people's feelings, have you, Maddy?'

She stared at him. 'And just what is that supposed to mean?'

'What do you think all this has been about?' She stared at him. 'Cast your mind back a few days and put yourself in the shoes of Mr Rupert Hartnoll.'

'Rupert?' she demanded. 'What on earth has he got to do with you? Are you life-long buddies or something?'

'I've never met the man.'

'I congratulate you,' she said.

'You told me yourself that he asked you to marry him. You're not suggesting you offered him no encouragement?'

'I'm not suggesting anything,' Maddy replied, as angry with herself for her uncharitable remark as with Griff for provoking it. Rupert had been the most charming companion until he had suddenly decided that she would make him the perfect wife. 'It was none of your business.'

'I made it my business. Tell me about "real" money, Maddy Rufus,' he said, recalling for her the jibe she'd made to Rupert at the villa. 'What would it take to buy your heart? Or have you got one?' He regarded her stonily. 'Or is it just a cash register that rings when a man with sufficient cash bears his soul?'

Once. Once she had had a heart and for the briefest moment in Griff's arms she'd begun to think that it might be resuscitated. 'I don't want to talk about it.'

His eyes gleamed coldly. 'If you want me to set fire to my plane, I'm afraid you're going to have to.'

'Damn you, Griff. I'll do it myself!' She turned to walk away but his hand snapped around her ankle strapping, detaining her. 'Let go of me,' she gasped, unable to pull away.

'I thought you'd need this.' He was turning the lighter between the fingers of his other hand. Maddy made a wild grab for it and collapsed to the sand as her foot gave beneath her.

'Give it to me,' she demanded, but he held it away from her.

'Not before you tell me all about your poor rejected lover.'

She was sprawled across him and his questing eyes were boring uncomfortably into her. She sat up quickly, putting a little space between them. 'Why should I tell you anything?' she asked, a little huskily. She wanted the lighter, but she didn't see why she should indulge his curiosity.

'Let's say I'm a student of human nature,' he said. 'And I'm giving you the opportunity to tell me your side of the story.'

Why was he so insistent? Why on earth did he care about one rejected suitor, a man he had never even met? 'Rupert Hartnoll isn't poor and he was never my lover. Just obsessed. . . I didn't realise quite how badly until he turned up in Mustique and persuaded my father to let him stay with us.'

'Not poor? Not rich enough for you, though—'

'*Real* money, for your information, Griff, is a family code, a joke between Dad and me. It's the kind of money you earn yourself. Like my father, like me. Like. . .like you. Two pounds or two million pounds. The amount is immaterial.'

She saw him frown as he digested this information. 'But surely it doesn't matter—?'

'Doesn't it? Since Dad's become successful we've met a lot of people with the unreal kind—people like Rupert. He has a whole bankful, inherited from generations of Hartnolls who never dirtied their hands with the stuff but employed clever people to make more and

more for them. People like my father. But he broke
free. . .took unbelievable risks to be his own man.' She
surged on before he could interrupt. 'Rupert is good-
looking, charming and, despite anything unkind I've
said, he can be great company when he isn't imagining
himself in love. But charm is not enough.'

'Not even charm and money?'

'A man has to have more than that, surely? If Rupert
lost all he had tomorrow he wouldn't know how to earn
the money to buy himself a loaf of bread. He certainly
wouldn't be able to live off the land.'

'I see.' Did he? Had she betrayed herself? She
glanced swiftly at him, wondering if he had caught her
unintentional reference to his ability to live at ease with
the world, but his eyes gave nothing away.

But Maddy had gone too far, exposed more of herself
than she had ever intended and she felt the need to
disguise her heart. 'Of course,' she said, with a little
toss of her head, 'his grandmother's ghastly ruby and
diamond cluster ring was the last straw. I mean, with
my colouring. . .'

He caught a wayward strand and wrapped it around
his fingers. 'I can see that he should have made the
effort to choose something more suitable,' he said
gravely. 'Something rare, individual—'

'It wouldn't have made any difference,' she said,
regaining control of her hair and tucking it firmly
behind her ears.

'Because of the money?'

'Because I didn't love him.' Silence greeted this reply.
Finally she had said something that he couldn't respond
to with some sarcastic remark. 'May I have the lighter,
Griff?' she asked, after an age.

He seemed to come from a long way off and snapped

his hand shut over the lighter. 'Some things in this world are beyond price. Rupert Hartnoll could not buy your love, Maddy,' he said. 'And not even *real* money can buy my plane.' As if to emphasise this, he tucked the lighter back in the top of his briefs, tantalisingly within reach, but far too dangerously placed to risk. . .

'I'll see you get another one,' she said urgently. 'At least as good. Better.'

'No, Maddy. You see, it's irreplaceable; it's part of what makes me what I am.'

'And what are you?' She jumped to her feet. 'You criticise me for being callous, but there'll be people out there grieving for you too. Haven't you got a thought in your head for them?'

'A wailing and a gnashing of pretty white teeth all over the Caribbean?' he offered, so perilously close to her own thoughts that she felt quite naked. He smiled as if he knew, and added, 'Just think of the party when I return from the dead.'

'Damn you!' She stamped. It was a mistake and before she could recover he was up and beside her, his arm about her waist, and she was so close to him that she could feel the hard shape of the lighter pressed against her waist.

'You once boasted that there was nothing wrong with your manners,' he said, with a savage little smile. 'My plane may not be for sale, but if you'd remembered to say please I might just have given it away.' The sensuous curve of his mouth was inches from her own, his thigh hard and warm against her own, and despite everything a tremor of desire warned her that this was a trap. He touched her cheek, grazing it lightly with his knuckles. 'Say please, Maddy, and you can take the lighter. . .if you dare.'

'Go to hell!' And she stepped back, pushing him away with the flat of her palms, and he made no effort to hold her as she hobbled away.

But that night she ignored the food he cooked for her. He could do what he wanted; she just wasn't hungry. She crawled miserably into bed and contemplated another night, another day in a paradise that seemed tantalisingly within reach, a paradise to which she was unable to find the key.

She slept fitfully, dreaming uneasily of her mother—that calm, serene woman who had rejected her husband's love because he had wanted excitement, risk. Maddy began to shout at her, tell her she was crazy, stupid, that nothing was perfect, that she must take what life offered. But her mother couldn't hear and she was drifting further and further away. 'No!' Maddy cried. 'No! Come back!'

'Maddy!' Griff was holding her, crushing her against his chest as she reached out for her mother. 'It was just a dream, my love. Hush now.' He captured her arms and turned her into him, rocking her gently, and gradually she stopped struggling, became aware of her surroundings, the large white bedroom. That he was holding her. That he had called her his love.

'A dream?' she murmured. What was dream and what was fact?

He brushed the hair back from her face. 'Do you want to talk about it?'

She shook her head, then realised what he meant. 'It was my mother. I haven't dreamed about her for a long time.'

'You'll see her soon.'

'Will I? It doesn't seem very likely.'

'I promise.' He regarded the tangled, damp ruin of her bed. 'Come on. You can't stay here. You can have my bed—'

'No, I'll be all right,' she said quickly, pulling back.

'Don't argue.'

'I can't. . .'

'I hadn't planned to share it with you, Maddy.'

'Why would you?' She shook her head. 'It's just that I don't want to go back to sleep. Dreams sometimes come back—'

'Then we'll go down to the beach and wait for the sunrise.' He lifted her from the bed and, cradling her in his arms, carried her down the path to the white crescent of the beach, settling beside her, cradling her head against his shoulder.

'Another day in paradise,' she said with a sigh.

'It could be.'

'Not for me.'

'Try a little harder. Listen.' The sea lapped gently against the shore to the counterpoint of tree frogs chirping in the forest and the occasional disgruntled chuntering of a bird disturbed on its perch. ' "A ship, an isle, a sickle moon—/With few but with how splendid stars/The mirrors of the sea are strewn/Between their silver bars!" '

Maddy turned to Griff, her cheek brushing against his shoulder as she looked up into his face. 'That's beautiful.'

In the moon's deep shadows he seemed to smile. 'It's a pity that the moon's full. Perhaps I could tempt you back when it's new.'

'Tempt me? Don't you know that if you wanted me, Griff, I'd never go away?'

'Want you?' He groaned softly. 'Maddy, don't you

know how much I want you? Why else would I care what you are, what you do—?'

It was enough. She laid a finger to his lips. 'Don't speak. Don't say anything.' And when she was sure that he would obey she took her hand away, replacing that light touch with her lips, kissing him, softly, gently as the sigh of the waves, and in that moment her body seemed as fragile as an eggshell—his to cradle gently in his hand, or to break.

'Oh, Maddy,' he breathed as her head fell back across his arm to expose her smooth white throat. 'You idiot. You crazy, beautiful little idiot.' Then he buried his face in her neck, his mouth firing a trail of kisses across that delicate arch, his tongue liquid fire as it traced the sensitive hollow of her collar-bone, and his hands slid beneath the baggy T-shirt she had worn for sleeping, to cradle her back, the pads of his fingers deliciously rough against her skin, sending tiny shivers of electricity charging through her veins.

Maddy reached out tentatively, to stroke her finger-tips through the rough hair of his naked chest, to graze small male nipples that hardened to her wondering touch, and she felt almost giddy with the heady sense of power as he trembled beneath her hands.

'Maddy!' He gasped an urgent warning. 'I'm not made of wood.' As if to demonstrate his all too potent humanity, he lifted up the T-shirt, drawing it over her head, dropping it to the sand. Maddy, her arms upraised as if in supplication to the moon, its rays shimmering her body with silver, felt only gratitude for her release, the glorious sense of freedom. The most gentle of breezes rippled from the inlet, stirring her hair, cooling her fevered skin, and she couldn't wait to be completely naked. She uncurled from the sand like a nymph, standing for one breathless second before Griff's kneeling figure.

'Help me, Griff,' she said from somewhere deep in her throat, in a voice she barely recognised as her own.

'Oh, dear God, Maddy,' he groaned, laying his cheek against the soft curve of her belly, his hands cupping the flare of her hips. 'You don't know what you're doing to me.'

She looked down and touched his face, traced the outline of his cheekbone, his jaw, the warm, soft curve of his lips that parted and caught her fingertips. In that moment when they were on the brink, when sanity was still—just—a possibility, she understood with an almost blinding clarity of vision that no matter what else she did with the rest of her life this was one moment that she would never regret.

'Show me.' Her voice quickened. 'Show me what I'm doing to you.'

Griff slipped his hands beneath the silk wisp of her panties and suddenly she was exultantly free, standing before him, ready for love as she had never been in her life. His lips touched the delicate white skin in the hollow of her hips and her whole body shivered with the shock of pleasure, her bones melting as his mouth, his tongue, his hands traversed her body, rising with almost agonising slowness across the plane of her stomach, exploring the indentation of her navel, the curve of her waist.

He rose to his feet then to wonder at the soft swell of her breast, drawing each firm tip into his mouth to tease it with the tip of his tongue, his teeth, until she was moaning softly deep in her throat, her nails digging into his shoulders as she thought she might pass out from the exquisite, almost agonising pleasure. Then he raised his head.

'Now it's your turn, Maddy,' he said, his voice scorching her skin.

Hardly knowing where to begin, she could only follow her instinct and the lead he had given, using her hands, her tongue to explore his body, wanting to give as much pleasure as he had given her, and taking it in the little involuntary shivers and moans of delight that her untutored touch provoked from him. And when she encountered the barrier of his shorts she did not hesitate but slipped the button at his waist. Then, with fingers that trembled as the velvet hardness of his need for her became demandingly apparent, she released him, shaking from head to toe as she eased the cloth over his hips. But her need was as strong as his and as his shorts fell away she slid her hands beneath his buttocks and pulled him against her.

'Love me, Griff,' she breathed, and there was a roaring in her ears that might have been some primeval male love call, or might have been her own fierce need pounding through her veins. Whatever. It didn't matter. His mouth was urgent as his lips claimed hers and they sank together onto the damp sand, and with only the warm night air to cover them and the waves lapping at their thighs he carried her with him to some glorious height from which they finally plunged in a wild, reckless fall that echoed that dizzy leap from the lip of the waterfall. For a moment she was utterly, gloriously breathless. Then, laughing at the sheer, unexpected glory of it, Maddy looked up at him. 'Would you like to go back and do that again?' she asked.

He stared down into her face, a little crease of concern drawing his brows together. 'Maddy. . .'

She raised her hand to touch the frown, smooth it away. 'Don't look so serious.'

'It's just that you took me by surprise. I didn't expect. . . It's been a while, since you've had a lover?'

She felt a little stab of pain. 'Did I disappoint you?'

'Don't you know?' he whispered.

'I thought. . .it seemed. . .' She tried to read his face, but it was all shadows. 'I know that I'm not very good. . .'

'Dear God, you don't know,' he murmured, and she felt foolish, unbearably young and inexperienced.

She struggled to sit up, attempting to move away from him, but his hands captured her, held her. 'I'm sorry if I disappointed you—'

'Disappointed? I feel. . .' Laughter bubbled from low in his throat. 'I feel like the first man on earth.' And he kissed her with such painful tenderness that she could not doubt him, and finally, when the need for air drove them apart, her breath caught on a little sob of happiness and tears spilled down her cheeks.

'Tell me, Maddy,' he demanded fiercely. She shook her head, not wanting to destroy the perfection of the moment with dark thoughts of the past. 'Tell me who hurt you that much.' When she would have pulled away, he refused to let her go. 'Don't let it poison your life, Maddy. Talk about it.'

'I wouldn't know where to start,' she mumbled into his chest. It was so long since she had allowed herself even to think about it.

'Start with his name.'

His name. 'Andrew.' Her voice was so faint that she could scarcely hear it herself. She met Griff's clear, penetrating eyes and drew strength from him. 'His name was Andrew,' she said, more bravely, and after that it seemed to pour out—the glamour of a man five years her senior, with a minor title, a job in the city and a sleek red sports car. And the family estate in Gloucestershire. Every young girl's dream.

'How old were you?'

'Just nineteen.' A very protected, rather native nineteen, fresh from a college course, with her heart and everything else intact and worlds to conquer. And her father's sudden wealth had meant that it was a much larger world than anything she had been used to. Without her mother to act as his hostess she had been pitchforked headlong into it. She plucked at the sand, unwilling to relive her humiliation.

CHAPTER NINE

'TELL me, Maddy.'

'I. . .I can't. I've never told anyone. . .'

He took her chin in his hand and turned her to face him. 'You will tell me.' His voice was gentle, but there was an insistence, a firmness about his mouth that could not be denied.

And Maddy discovered that despite the pain of recalling that dreadful awakening from innocence she did want to tell him. 'I was young enough to be bowled over by his eagerness to marry me. He'd actually got the licence in his pocket and wanted to whisk me away to the nearest register office.'

'What stopped him?'

'I was stubbornly dewy-eyed. I wanted a white wedding in church with a dozen bridesmaids and all my family and friends. That needed more than a few days to organise, and my father's cheque-book to pay for it. And Dad insisted we waited six months.' Although, being wise in the ways of the world, he'd suggested it would be a good idea to go on the Pill. 'In the meantime I was invited down to Gloucester to meet the family, get to know them.'

'No doubt they rolled out the red carpet.'

She felt a warmth at the fact that he had so quickly understood. 'Red carpet, antique crystal, grandmother's ring. . .' Her voice quavered on that.

'Rubies?'

'I scarcely noticed, I was so happy.'

155

'And with Grandma's ring on your finger Andrew decided it was high time to cement the relationship? I'm sure you had conveniently adjoining rooms?'

'Not adjoining. My bag was in his room. I was surprised, in his parents' home. . .but he said they would expect it. . . After all, we were engaged. . .and they were miles away on the other side of the house. . .'

'I'm sure he was very convincing.' Griff said abruptly, refusing to allow her to dwell on it. 'How did you find out that he was after your money?'

'We'd been out to lunch and afterwards he wanted to go back to his flat. . . I found his constant desire for me. . .reassuring. I knew I wasn't very good. . .'

Griff swore somewhere deep under his breath. 'You are breathtaking.'

She shook her head as if she still could not believe him. 'When we got in the light was flashing on the answering machine. He switched it on as he walked past and went across the room to fortify himself with a drink before the coming ordeal. . .' She faltered. 'Anyway, he was too far away to stop it when the first message was so obviously something I shouldn't hear. . . It was his father, wanting to know how much longer it was going to take his son to get one stupid girl pregnant.' She stared at the sand. 'Apparently they were one step away from the bankruptcy court and I had been elected for the privilege of bailing them out. I'd never heard such crude language. Although, I discovered very swiftly that it ran in the family. When I told Andrew that I had been taking the Pill he seemed to take great pleasure in explaining in graphic detail just how tedious I was in bed.'

'Nasty,' Griff said tightly.

She couldn't begin to describe how nasty it had been.

'It could have been a lot. . .nastier. If I hadn't found out. . .'

He lifted her hand to his lips. 'I'm deeply flattered that you trusted me enough. . . I still can't believe it. You're beautiful, so utterly desirable. . .'

'Don't stop,' she said, her voice shaking on a tiny hiccup.

He grinned. 'Provoking, irritating, impetuous. . .'

She flung herself across him. 'Has anyone ever told you that you talk too much?'

'You have the cure in your own hands—' He broke off to moan disjointedly as she took him at his word and began to torment him with delicate caresses. 'Maddy, please. . .please. . .'

'Hands don't seem to work,' she murmured then gave a little scream as he rolled over and pinned her beneath him.

'Perhaps you'd better leave it to me.'

'Please. . .' she begged. 'Once more before the moon goes down. We may be rescued tomorrow.'

'Don't you know, my darling, that tomorrow never comes?'

'If only that were true. . .'

'It is. You have my word.' And the reassurance of his lips was all the promise she would ever need.

They didn't see the moon set. But as the first rays of dawn blushed the edge of the sea Griff rose, pulling her up with him in one smooth movement from the sand, swinging her into his arms.

She put her arms about his neck and laid her cheek against his chest. 'Where are you taking me?'

'Wait, my darling. Just wait for the magic.'

It was still dark in the forest, but he was sure-footed

on the path and helped her up the waterfall, holding her close as they stood above the spray, listening to the songbirds call in the canopy high above them to a rising sun they could not see. Beside him, the milky moon flowers were still open, filling the air with their sweetness.

'Maddy.' He breathed her name and kissed her, too briefly. Then he turned her to face the morning as, without warning, the sky blushed, touching the spray from the waterfall, the moonflowers, the surface of the pool, until it seemed to Maddy that the whole world was the most delicate shade of pink. 'Now,' he said, and they leapt together off the end of the world.

When they surfaced, it was over. The early-morning light filtering through the trees was mint-fresh and clear. The droplets of water clung to Griff's hair as his arms slid about her waist and he drew her close.

'Dear heaven,' she whispered as her core turned to liquid desire and her arms linked around his neck, drawing him down to her. 'What have you done to me?' But as they slid together beneath the water, wrapped in each other's arms, there was no answer and Maddy no longer cared.

They exploded to the surface and she turned and ducked away from him, but her throaty laugh invited chase and they swam like a pair of young otters, hardly aware whether they were under the water or breathing air, their bodies teasing and touching, together, then apart. When Griff caught her, he held her close, possessing her with his lips, his hands, until they were forced upwards once more for air and once more she slipped away, eluding him as he searched for her in the dark water.

Laughing, she caught him from behind, gripping his

shoulders and forcing him under, but it had been far too easy. He rolled and took her down with him and this time when he held her prisoner against him there was no escape, nor did she seek one. They hung suspended in time and space, his lips on hers and his tongue exploring her mouth with an exquisite thoroughness until she thought she must dissolve, become a part of him, and Maddy knew that was what she desired most in the entire world.

Then he lifted her from the water and set her on the smooth ledge below the falls. 'Good morning, Maddy Rufus.'

'Good morning, "Griff will do",' she said shakily, scarcely able to believe what had happened to her in the space of one night. No. Not in one night. The fuse had been lit the moment they'd first set eyes on one another—a long, slow fuse that last night had finally detonated. He put his arm about her and they walked slowly back to the house

'I'd like to have a shower and wash my hair,' she said as they reached the bedroom door.

'On your own?'

'Do you mind?'

His eyes danced at her blush. 'I think I'm going to hate every moment you're out of my sight.' He kissed her briefly, as if to linger would make leaving too hard.

'Griff. . .' He glanced back at her, a question in his eyes. But she held back. She mustn't say anything stupid, do anything that would spoil the moment. He held out his arms and she went to him, because despite her need to be alone to take out all these new feelings and examine them she was suddenly afraid to let him go. 'Stay if you want to.'

He dropped a kiss on the top of her head. 'Goose.

Go and get under a hot shower; you're shivering.
There's something I have to do.' He turned her round,
gave her a little slap on the rump and closed the door
behind her.

She went into the bathroom and stepped under the
shower, but when she reached for the shampoo it was
empty. Griff would have some in his bathroom. She left
the water running and wrapped the towel around her
and stepped onto the veranda. She could smell coffee
brewing in the kitchen and smiled. No need to bother
him. She padded swiftly on bare feet to his room a few
doors away, but froze as she heard his voice raised
against the static of a radio... A radio.

'Zoe, my darling, I think I can guarantee that she's
got the message.' There was a pause. 'We'll fly out
today.' He laughed softly. 'I knew you would forgive
me; I only hope Maddy will be as generous when she
finds out that I faked that emergency landing...'

Zoe? Did she know? Was she part of the "lesson"?
And now he was chatting to her as if nothing had
happened beyond a few cold showers, a little discomfort. Her heart screamed out to her godmother, Don't
listen to him. He has betrayed you, betrayed us both.
But guilt kept her silent. It wasn't just Griff who had
betrayed Zoe. When she had been wrapped in his arms
she hadn't given her godmother a second thought. He
had stopped speaking, clearly interrupted, and his
shadow disappeared as he moved away from the shuttered window, and she heard the creak of cane as he
sank into a chair and when he spoke again his voice was
too low to hear what he was saying. But he had said
enough.

'One day you'll meet someone who won't take no for
an answer,' he had said. She had mocked him and he

had wreaked his revenge. All he had had to do was wait and she had fallen like a ripe plum into his lap. It was over. He had won and now he was going to fly her out. Fly her out!

Maddy, her hand still stopping the scream that was clamouring somewhere deep inside her, backed quietly away from the door. She didn't even bother to turn off the shower but dressed in the first thing that came into her hand, grabbed her handbag and fled.

She wasn't certain how she made it to the beach. She could never afterwards recall retracing her steps, only that she'd made it somehow.

Her trembling fingers struggled with the knot that fastened the guy-rope to the palm tree. It wouldn't budge and, terrified that he would discover she was missing and come looking for her, Maddy seized the machete and swung furiously at the rope, slicing it through. The tide was still coming in and she had to wait agonising moments until the seaplane rose on an incoming wave and drifted obligingly out into the bay. She waded after it and climbed on trembling legs into the cockpit. The keys, she knew, were still in the ignition—far the safest place; after all, no one was about to steal a plane that couldn't fly, were they? Certainly not a tease of a girl who needed a serious lesson in how to behave. . .

The engine caught first time, the propeller biting the air, spinning eagerly, flashing against the sun until it settled into an even rhythm, and suddenly the trembling stopped. She was back in control. The madness had passed and a blissful numbness was, for the moment, blocking the pain as she concentrated on the controls of a strange aircraft. Maddy turned the machine to face the sea, picking up the radio handset to call the tower at Mustique, doing the fastest preflight check in history.

That she had never flown a seaplane before didn't daunt her in the least. It was a simple machine, the controls, on inspection, proving almost identical to those of the plane on which she had learned to fly. In a kind of icy calm she taxied out into the bay and waited for her instructions on height and heading with every outward appearance of calm, concentrating totally on the machine, impervious to Griff's frantic calls as he pounded along the beach.

Her hand trembled slightly as he began to splash through the surf towards her, but she tightened her grip, and as clearance rattled through the static she opened the throttle and pulled back on the control stick, sending the little plane rocketing towards the open sea with the total indifference of someone who knew that nothing could ever get worse. Then, as she saw the white line of surf that betrayed the island's protective coral rim racing towards her, she suddenly realised what he had been shouting. 'The reef. You won't make the reef.'

She hung onto the control column for dear life and somehow the plane listed clear with only barest suggestion of a scrape against the treacherous coral. Perhaps the high tide or the difference in their weight had been enough to give her a chance. For a moment her mind went blank with relief, then the realisation that the sea was rushing by not more than a few feet below her jerked her back into action and training took over and she began to fly the plane, climbing to the height she had been given and turning onto the heading for Mustique.

As she banked and headed north she saw Griff, still

standing in the inlet, his hand shading his eyes as he followed her progress. A victory roll would have been a satisfying touch. Perhaps it was just as well she hadn't the faintest idea how to accomplish such a thing. Since she had met Hugo Griffin she had taken more than enough risks to last her for the rest of her life. And she still had to make her first ever landing on water.

It was perhaps more of a splash-down than a landing, but both Maddy and the aircraft survived the experience. Just. One of the floats had been damaged on take-off and as she taxied to the jetty she had the distinct sensation that they were getting heavier in the water. She climbed out and saw with a lurch of anguish that the little craft was listing. But there was nothing she could do. He would find it there. Or someone would tell him where it was. It no longer concerned her.

She was halfway down the jetty when she remembered the cheque. She retrieved the envelope and stuffed it into her bag and then walked up to the villa. Someone would drive her to the airport.

That afternoon, in Barbados, she spent the afternoon in her hotel defiantly indulging herself in all the things that she had been denied while on Paradise Island. Spoiling herself thoroughly. Taking a grim satisfaction in doing precisely what Griff would most despise her for.

But, despite having her hair and nails done, wallowing in the most expensive scented bath oils she could find and then spending a ridiculous amount of money on a dress to wear on the plane home, there was precious little satisfaction in the looks she attracted as she hesitated in the lobby of the hotel. She still had two hours to get through before leaving for the airport, but didn't want a drink, couldn't face food—she didn't think she would ever be hungry again. She wasn't anything. Just empty.

'Maddy?'

She swung around at the sound of her name, but it was too late to hide. 'Rupert,' she said unenthusiastically.

'What are you doing here? I thought you were with your aunt.'

'Godmother,' she corrected him, shaking her head. 'A change of plans. I'm going home tonight. In fact I really should go now and get my things together.' She made a move, but if she had hoped to be off-putting she had failed.

'On the BA flight?' Rupert asked, following her. 'I'm booked on that. Perhaps we could share a taxi out to the airport.'

'Rupert—' she protested helplessly.

'Maddy, please,' he begged. 'I know I behaved like an idiot and I'm sure I'm the last person in the whole world you want to be with, but frankly, if you don't mind my saying so, you look ghastly.'

'Thank you, Rupert,' she said, but with a flash of humour at his total inability to say the right thing.

'No,' he muttered, embarrassed. 'Lovely dress, everything perfect. Just—something about the eyes. Has something happened? Your father's all right? That isn't why you're—?'

'No,' she said quickly. 'It's nothing like that. Rupert, I know I apologised for the way I spoke to you, but—'

'Maddy, don't; you're making me feel worse than I already do... Oh, look, come and have a drink. You needn't tell me anything, but you don't look as if you should be on your own. And if you'll promise to forget what an idiot I made of myself I'll promise I won't embarrass you by proposing again.'

'Do I look *that* bad?' she asked, her sense of humour finally getting the better of her misery.

'You could never look that bad, Maddy. I made a fool of myself, not that that matters—I'm always doing it—but I upset you and I'm sorry for that. Put it down to these hot tropical nights. . .'

'Positively dangerous,' she agreed, with feeling. I don't deserve you to be so kind.'

'You deserve—' he began urgently, then stopped. 'Well, to be happier than you look.'

She gave a little sigh. Perhaps it would be better not to be alone. 'An orange juice, then.'

Rupert grinned like a pleased puppy and Maddy remembered why she had found him so charming the first time she had met him. He wasn't threatening or demanding, which was why his sudden change in character had taken her so utterly by surprise. And he was soon chattering happily about the test match he had just watched—nonsense to take her mind off her troubles. He was so kind that she was forced to make an effort to appear to be diverted.

'Would you like a drink, madam?' The stewardess said, beaming at her shortly after take-off.

Maddy forced herself to relax. It was ridiculous, she knew, but until the doors of the great jet had closed, shutting out the soft tropical night and the ripple of a steel band somewhere in the distance, she hadn't felt quite safe. Why on earth would Griff follow her, for heaven's sake? This morning he hadn't been able to wait to be rid of her. She found a smile for the stewardess. 'I'd like a mineral water, please.'

'Would you make that two, Susie?' Maddy felt her skin contract at the shock of his voice. She couldn't look, refused to look. It couldn't possibly be him.

'Sure thing, Mr Griffin. Nice to have you aboard,' Susie said and swung smoothly away.

'I'm afraid there seems to be some confusion over seating arrangements,' Griff continued, producing his boarding card and addressing Rupert. 'You appear to be sitting in my seat.'

Maddy, her eyes fixed firmly on the seat ahead of her, put her hand on Rupert's arm. 'Please stay where you are. I'm absolutely certain that Mr Griffin will be perfectly happy in the seat he occupied during take-off.'

'I boarded at the last moment and had to sit in Economy. I did, however, request this seat especially.'

'Did you? This seat? Is it special?' And Rupert, groomed from the nursery in the conduct of a gentleman, stood up and reached for the card in his top pocket to consult the number.

'Very special. You see, I suffer acutely from a fear of flying... Unless I sit next to a qualified pilot I'm inclined to panic.'

'Good Lord,' Rupert said; then, as he sensed the tension that sparked between them, saw Maddy's stark pallor, he suddenly realised that something was going on between the two of them that was far above his head. But he latched onto something he did understand. 'But Maddy isn't a qualified pilot,' he said, clearly hoping that this would settle the matter once and for all.

'Oh, yes, Maddy is,' Griff replied, with the absolute conviction of a man who knew what he was talking about, and he swung into Rupert's place alongside Maddy, stretching out his long legs as he settled in beside her.

'I say—' Rupert protested—at this cavalier hijacking of his seat, at the possessive manner in which Griff took Maddy's hand, apparently oblivious to the way she flinched away from him.

'The thing about Maddy,' he continued, his tone confidential as he directed his remarks to Rupert, 'is her remarkable shyness about her accomplishments, but friends at the West London Aero Club tell me that she has been the keenest student. She gained her licence after the minimum number of flying hours and was pronounced an exceptional student by her instructor.'

Griff had checked up on her? That easily? Maddy finally turned and stared at him and found herself drowning in the cool challenge of his eyes. Somehow she had expected him to look just as she had last seen him—bare-chested, wearing nothing but a pair of scruffy shorts and ancient leather flip-flops, a faint shadow on his chin where he hadn't shaved. But he was clean-shaven, wearing a well-cut, tropical-weight suit in cream linen, his shirt open-necked, but his tie was draped around his collar as if, in his rush to catch the plane, he hadn't had the time to knot it. It was silk, an extraordinary and very beautiful blend of the colours of the sea around Paradise Island.

And on the hand holding hers was a signet ring, plain gold, but in the clear light at thirty thousand feet she could see the tiny griffin engraved upon its surface. How could she have ever been so stupid not to have realised? He had walked Paradise Island like a god, not like some casual trespasser.

'Is that true, Maddy?' Rupert demanded from the aisle, jolting her from her reverie. 'Can you fly?' He was astonished but clearly very impressed.

Griff answered for her. 'Take my word for it. Everything is true, except the fact that she's an exceptional student.' His jaw tightened ominously. 'In my opinion she's reckless in the extreme, takes quite unnecessary risks, and any landing that needs a crane to rescue the plane from the sea. . .'

'I haven't yet learned your trick of doing it with the power turned off.'

'Come back to Paradise and I'll be happy to teach you.' He turned to Rupert. 'The thing about Maddy is that once she gets the hang of a thing she's such an enthusiastic student.'

'Maddy. . .' Rupert muttered as they began to attract the attention of the other passengers. 'I don't understand. Do you know this man?'

Maddy was quite unable to answer. The numbness had finally gone and she was hurting. He was toying with her like a child twisting unwanted spaghetti around a fork and the pain was so intense that it was impossible to give words to, but she couldn't take her eyes off Griff.

'Well, Maddy,' Griff encouraged her, 'answer the gentleman's question. Would you say that you *knew* me?'

Her cheeks were scorched by a fierce blush. How could he be so hateful? What on earth was he doing here anyway, tormenting her? He'd had his fun; what more could he possibly want from her?

But Rupert was waiting, agog at the barely sheathed hostility between them. 'We met briefly when I was flying to Zoe's,' she said, carelessly, because it was essential that Griff should never know how much he had hurt her.

Griff extended his strong, square-cut hand to Rupert. 'Hugo Griffin.'

'But Griff will do,' Maddy said cuttingly, and then wished she hadn't as he turned to face her and raised a brow in a tiny acknowledgement that her barb had found its mark and would be repaid with interest. Before he could say something outrageous she said, 'May I introduce my companion? Rupert Hartnoll.' Something happened to Griffs eyes. The green became slaty and despite the fact that there was not the slightest change in his expression the tightening of his grasp upon her fingers betrayed how much effort it took to keep his feelings under close restraint. The knowledge went to her head like a rocket and she added, 'You'll recall that he asked me to marry him. . .'

Out of the corner of her eye Maddy saw Rupert stiffen and hated herself for using him. But he didn't let her down. 'As soon as you say the word, old thing. . .'

'Covering all your options, Maddy?' Griff asked softly, and her whole body gave a little jerk as she realised what he was implying. 'But then the full moon is notoriously fecund.' Did he truly believe her capable of foisting another man's child on poor, unsuspecting Rupert? And yet, if he thought that, he would surely never bother her again? He would leave her alone to try and put her life back together, relieved no doubt to be rid of any responsibility. For a long moment he regarded her, his eyes scouring her face, ransacking her mind to discover the truth. She kept her face quite blank, walled up her heart against him. 'Don't even consider it, Maddy. I'll not allow another man to bring up a child that I have fathered.'

He wouldn't allow? What the Dragon Man wanted, he took? 'What will you do, Griff?' she demanded. 'Breathe fire?'

He didn't answer, but removed the signet ring from

his little finger and, taking her left hand firmly in his, slipped it onto her third finger and held it there. There was a terrifying finality about the gesture.

'Take it back,' she said, panic-stricken. 'I don't want it.' But when she tugged at the ring it wouldn't budge. 'It won't come off.'

'Anxiety makes the body swell,' he advised her. 'That's why small boys get their heads stuck in railings.'

'Then I'll summon the fire brigade and get it cut off,' she threw at him, a little wildly.

'No, you won't, Maddy. You're mine and you know it. There's no escape.'

Maddy felt herself being swept away on a rising tide of panic and she had to put a stop to it, do something before she did something really stupid like throw herself into his arms. 'If you don't go this minute and leave me alone, Griff, I'll scream,' she said very quietly. 'You were very impressed with my scream. It was convincing. . .you said.'

For a moment he continued to challenge her, then, clearly impressed with her determination to carry out her threat, he rose to his feet. 'You have a scream that could cause a riot. Not wise at thirty thousand feet. And I like flying with this airline.' He reached into the overhead locker for a blanket and draped it around her, tucking it in as if she were a child. Then he touched her cheek gently. 'You look tired, Maddy; try and get some sleep. I'll have a car waiting when we land. And once we're on the ground you can scream all you like, I promise.' He straightened, nodded briefly to Rupert and walked away, found a seat somewhere behind them where, thankfully, she couldn't see the way his hair curled into his neck, or the beautiful shape of his ear. . . A little sob escaped her lips.

'Maddy. . .?' Rupert asked as he resumed his seat, his voice so gentle that she flinched.

'Don't!' she begged, and beneath the blanket she gave a little tug at the ring that was a shackle holding her fast to the Dragon Man. It stubbornly refused to budge. Her stupid trick finger wouldn't let it go.

The stewardess returned with their drinks. 'Ah, you have all sorted out the problem with the seats? That's good.' She beamed, bearing Griff's mineral water away.

Maddy's glass rattled against her teeth as she swallowed her drink and she was grateful—deeply grateful—that Rupert chose not to say anything. Later she would try to explain. Later. But the tears were rolling down her cheeks and Rupert put his arm around her and drew her onto his shoulder. 'Maddy, love. . .' And without meaning to she found herself weeping silently into his lapel.

'Oh, Rupert, I'm sorry, so sorry to have involved you in that.'

'Don't fret. I'm sure it'll all sort itself out. . .and if it doesn't, if you really wanted me to marry you I dare say I could force myself,' he said, passing her his handkerchief with an encouraging smile. 'No matter what Griffin says.'

'Oh, don't,' she wailed unhappily into the soft linen. 'I couldn't feel any worse.' But as the hours passed and they drew closer to their destination she felt a great deal worse. And when she went to freshen up the fact that Griff was stretched out in his seat in the relaxed posture of someone deeply asleep did nothing to set her mind at rest. It suggested total confidence that he had everything under control.

'He can't make you go with him,' Rupert insisted. 'I'll take you home. Or wherever you want to go. You could stay with my mother if you like.' She shook her head, but when Rupert stood up she asked nervously, 'Where are you going?'

He smiled a trifle absently. 'Don't worry, I'll be back in a moment.' And when he returned to his seat beside her a few minutes later he would not be drawn, but when the plane taxied to a standstill, the stewardess, all concern, ushered Maddy to the exit ahead of the other passengers.

'How did you manage that?' Maddy demanded.

'I told her you were on your way to a clinic for a life-saving operation.'

'And she believed you?'

'Next time you pass a mirror, Maddy, look in it. You're so white under that tan that you look as if you're about to suffer from liver failure.'

'Oh.' Then, glancing nervously behind her, she added 'But it won't help; we'll have to wait for our luggage.'

But Griff, although hard on their heels as they approached Immigration, didn't appear in the luggage hall and, having reclaimed their bags, Rupert steered her firmly towards his waiting Rolls.

'But what could have happened to him?' Maddy demanded as they were whisked into London.

'Maybe his passport was out of date. Will you be all right?' he asked as he dropped her off at her flat.

'I'll be fine. I just need a little space and a good night's sleep.'

'Well, if you need me, you know where I am.' He paused, then said, with half a smile at his own foolishness, 'But you don't need me, do you, Maddy? You need him.'

CHAPTER TEN

DESPITE a restless night, Maddy decided to go into her office the day after her return. Anything had to be better than sitting at home dreading the ring of the bell in case it was Griff on her doorstep. Anything had to be better than sitting there longing for him to be there.

'Your holiday doesn't appear to have done you much good,' her father said, when he dropped by later that morning. 'Maybe you picked something up. Better see a doctor.'

'It's just jet lag. I didn't sleep very well last night. How did you know I was back?'

'Zoe telephoned to make sure you were home safely.' Maddy felt her whole body jolt. She would have to face Zoe, but right now she didn't feel strong enough. 'She said there was some kind of mix-up at the airport?'

'Mix-up?'

'Was someone supposed to give you a lift?' He didn't wait for her answer, impatient with such trivia. He propped himself on the corner of her desk. 'So, did you find out what's going on with Hugo Griffin?'

'Dad—'

'He can't be after her money. He owns an enormous transport company. Air, sea, car hire—you name it.'

'Yes, I discovered that for myself. Is it sound?'

'I wish I had a piece of it; the man has a genius for organisation apparently.' Then he realised that she was serious. 'Have you heard something?'

'No. But Zoe gave him a cheque.' She told him the

amount and he whistled. 'The thing is, I. . .I've got it. I don't know what to do with it.'

'How on earth. . .?' he began, then apparently thought better of it. 'Send it back to her. She's had time for second thoughts; it's more than most of us get. . .' He stood up to leave. 'Oh, by the way, she wanted me to give you a message. Apparently your phone was off the hook.'

'I didn't want to be disturbed.' Her father gave her a rather hard look. 'What was the message?'

'She said to tell you that she's sorry about what happened, that she'll explain when she sees you and that you mustn't, on any account, marry Rupert Hartnoll. For any reason.' The unasked question hovered in the air.

Sorry? Maddy felt like laughing at the inadequacy of the word, but it wasn't Zoe's fault that Maddy had lost her head in the moonlight. 'Well, you can tell her not to worry. I'm not going to marry Rupert. I'm not going to marry anyone,' she added, with a determined set to her jaw, and she gave the dragon ring a surreptitious twist, to no avail.

'No?' Her father tried hard to hide his disappointment. 'Well, of course, that's what I told her,' he said. 'But she seemed absolutely convinced. I believe the woman's wits are wandering. She should get married again; it would give her something to occupy her mind.'

'That's terribly chauvinist of you, Dad!'

'Well, that's me,' he said. 'I can't pretend. What you see is what you get.'

'Don't ever change,' she said, standing up quickly, turning to stare out of the window so he shouldn't see the tears that suddenly stung her lids.

Her father joined her at the window. 'I wish you

could find someone, Maddy—' Then, as she took a deep, shuddering breath, he asked, 'What is it?' He looked more closely at her. 'Hey, girl, come and sit down. What ever is the matter?' He settled her on the sofa where she conducted informal interviews and poured her a glass of water, but she shook her head. 'Tell me, sweetheart,' he said, sitting beside her, taking her hands.

'It's difficult.'

'I've never known you to back away from a problem.'

'Oh, this isn't like me at all.' She gathered herself, tried to hold in her mind that moment on the beach when she had recognised a moment of absolute truth, a moment she had promised herself she would never regret. Well, fate, it seemed, was determined to test her to new limits. She tried a smile and found that it wasn't as bad as she feared. 'The thing is. . .I wondered. . .since you want to be a grandfather so badly. . .would you mind if I managed it without actually getting married. . .?'

Her father looked at her, rather hard. 'That, I take it, is not a hypothetical question?'

'It's too soon to be sure.' And yet she knew, had no doubt that she was already nurturing a tiny life within her. 'No,' she said, with sudden conviction. 'Not hypothetical.'

'Was that what Zoe meant? That you shouldn't marry Rupert just because—'

'It wasn't Rupert,' she said quickly.

'Are you going to tell me who—?'

'It. . .it doesn't matter, not now. I shan't even tell him.'

'I see.' Her father frowned.

'You don't think I'm right?'

'It's your decision, I suppose, but. . .well, if it was me, I would want to know.' He patted her arm. 'I'll be here for you, you know that. . .I just wish you had your mother to advise you. . .' He paused. 'I had hoped you would see more of her if you decided to go ahead with the Paris office. I suppose that's on hold?'

'I hadn't thought about that, but I suppose so.' Then she gave his shoulder a little shake. 'Once I tell her my news, she won't be able to keep away. Perhaps it's a good thing. This way, you'll get to see more of her too.'

'Do you think so?' He covered her hand with his own. 'Look, you should still be on holiday; why don't we both go to Paris this afternoon and break the news to her? Maybe, if we can show her how much we need her, we can persuade her to come home with us.'

Maddy dropped her bag, closed the door of her flat and leaned back against it. It had been wonderful to make her peace with her mother, wonderful to see the spark between her parents rekindled, but it was a relief to be home and be able to stop smiling, stop putting on a brave face for the world.

Her hand was full of mail, mostly Christmas cards she had picked up from her box, and she flicked through them, but there were no envelopes with handwriting she didn't immediately recognise. Relief and pain in equal amounts assaulted her. Had he come to the flat while she had been away? Gone away when he realised she wasn't there, flown back to Paradise? Well, wasn't that what she wanted, why she had so eagerly grasped the escape her father had offered? She tossed the mail onto the hall table. She would look at it later; right now she needed a shower and a cup of tea, in that order.

She was under the shower when she heard the house

phone buzz and she decided to ignore it. But it rang again—an urgent little tattoo that demanded attention.

She wrapped herself in a towelling robe and pressed the button. 'Who is it?'

'Maddy? It's me, Zoe. Can I come up?'

Maddy held her breath for a fleeting second, wanting to refuse. But it was nearly Christmas. The season of goodwill. 'Of course,' she said, and pressed the front-door release, opened her own front door and then retired to wrap her dripping hair in a towel.

She heard the front door close. 'I'll be with you in a minute, Zoe,' she called. 'Can you put the kettle on? I've only just this minute got back from Paris.' There was no answer, but she heard the water being drawn in the kitchen. She walked back in. 'Mum came back with us. . .'

Griff was hunting through the kitchen cupboards and as her voice died away he turned to her. 'Where do you keep the tea?' he asked.

'Where is Zoe?' she demanded.

He produced a hand-held recorder from his pocket and pressed 'play'. 'Maddy? It's me, Zoe. Can I come up?'

'You—' He raised a warning finger and she bit off the insult that sprang to her lips, standing back from the door to leave the way clear. 'Go away. Get out of here, or I'll call the police.'

'Come on, Maddy, you've already pulled that one,' he said, without rancour. 'I've proved myself a pillar of society ten times over so it won't work again.' He turned back to the cupboard, opening a series of storage tins. 'Oh, here it is. Why is it in a tin marked. . .' he looked at it with a puzzled expression ". . .Tapioca"?'

'They both begin with T,' she said faintly.

'There's a somewhat baffling logic in that, I suppose. But why—?'

'What did you mean, I've already pulled that one?'

'Well, not the police. Customs. It was really very clever; I was impressed with your ingenuity.' He concentrated on pouring the boiling water onto the tea. 'They held me for twenty-four hours before I managed to convince them that I wasn't an international smuggler—'

'What?'

He turned to her. 'It wasn't you?'

'I couldn't have done that,' she whispered, horrified.

'But apparently you know a man who can. . .' He shook his head. 'Who would have thought Rupert Hartnoll had it in him?'

'Who indeed?'

'And when I had finally extricated myself you had bolted. To Paris, you said? With Hartnoll?'

'I went to Paris to see my mother. Why are you here, Griff?'

'You know why I'm here. To marry the mother of my child. The Christmas holidays will slow things down, but we shouldn't leave it too long. I have to get back—'

'Go back now, Griff. I don't need this. I don't need you.'

'And the baby? A child needs two parents—you know that.'

'I know what it's like to be deceived, deluded, lied to. . .'

'Don't be so hard on her, Maddy. Zoe thought she was doing something to help.'

'Zoe? I wasn't talking about Zoe. I was talking about

you!' Then she sank onto a kitchen chair. 'Oh, Zoe, what have you done?'

'She called in a favour. I once made her a promise that if I could ever do anything. . .if she needed anything. . .I would be there for her. . .'

Promises to keep. For a moment she was back in the cool forest, surrounded by flowers, and the scent of the frangipani was almost real. 'So, what did she ask you?' she demanded, jerking herself back to the present.

'To teach you a lesson. Make you think about other people.'

'And, having witnessed my rejection of poor Rupert, I can understand why you found it so easy to be unpleasant, rude, downright horrible to me. You thought I was a really nasty piece of work and you were going to teach me the lesson of my life.' But did you have to make me fall in love with you as well?

'Zoe was very convincing. You had been spoiled by money and now that your father had decided to put his fortune into a trust you had become a monster. She knew you, Maddy. I didn't. And, as you say, I had the evidence of my own eyes.'

'But she knew. . .'

'About Andrew? Yes, she admitted as much when I spoke to her. But Zoe had a hidden agenda. She was certain that if we were thrown together. . .that if there was no escape. . . She was right, Maddy. When I walked into the clearing that first morning and you were standing there under the shower I thought my heart would burst.'

'I would never have known.'

'You'll never know how hard it was to keep it up. I

tried to tell you how I felt. . .when we climbed to the top of the island.'

How could she ever forget that moment, that kiss? 'And what about afterwards?' she demanded.

'I thought you had guessed. You said. . . I don't know. . .something about Zoe and I was convinced you had realised who I was. And, having discovered that I was not just some penniless charter pilot but the Dragon Man, you threw yourself at me. Anything I wanted, you said, and I knew then that Zoe was right. I hated you for that. . .and I hated her. . . I lost my head. . .'

'I had no idea who you were. I thought you wanted money from Zoe, that you were going to hurt her. I'd been there, Griff. I wanted to save her from that.'

He face creased in a puzzled frown. 'But why on earth did you think that?'

'When you came to Mustique with Zoe, Dad and I. . .' She swallowed. It seemed so ridiculous now, in retrospect. 'We assumed that you were Zoe's lover.'

'Lover!'

'Zoe was asking Dad about selling stocks and he was suspicious. . .You were so much younger than her. . .And then I found the cheque.'

'You have it?' She nodded reluctantly and fetched her bag. The crumpled envelope was still where she had thrust it and she handed it to him. 'I'm about to launch a scholarship fund for the island children. Zoe wanted to be a part of it.'

'I see,' she said very softly.

He glanced sharply at her. 'Do you?'

'So no one else's mother will have to work themselves to death. . .' She couldn't go on. 'Well, that's it. You kept your promise, Griff. It's over now.'

'It will never be over, Maddy,' he said, and moved towards her.

'No,' she cried a little desperately as the warm scent of his body seemed to invade her spirit, weakening her resolve. She pushed him away, retreated to the sitting room. 'I don't want to hear this. I just want you to go away and never come back.'

'Why?'

'Why? Can't you understand how betrayed I felt?' She could hardly breathe with the pain of it. 'I stood on the veranda of a house that you told me didn't exist, listening to you talking to Zoe on a radio that could have had us off the island an hour after we landed. Except that was no part of your plan. After all, there was no emergency. There was nothing wrong with the plane; it had all been a clever little plot to teach Maddy Osborne to be a good girl. Well, you taught me, Griff.' She raised her chin and lashed him with her eyes. 'Tell me, how good was I?'

'Maddy—'

'Not that good, apparently, because you couldn't wait to get me off the island.'

'For pity's sake, Maddy, if I was so anxious to get rid of you why do you think I followed you? Why have I been kicking my heels around a cold, damp city when I could be in the sun?'

'Guilt?' she demanded.

He raked long fingers through his hair. 'Sit down, Maddy. Listen to me.'

Maddy, beyond arguing, sat down, ready to repulse him if he came too close, but Griff sat on the chair opposite her, leaned forward, his elbows on his knees, and began to speak. 'Have you any idea of the fright you gave me when you took off from the island?'

'I wasn't thinking about your feelings at the time,' she said. 'In fact I can guarantee that what you were suffering was very much at the bottom of my list of priorities.'

The muscles in his jaws tightened. 'I suppose I deserve that. But I had no idea that you could fly—you never said a word—and my head was full of pictures of your body mangled in the wreckage. I couldn't blot them out. I had no idea where you'd go, if you even knew where you were going... I put out a call and when I had word you had arrived in Mustique...'

'I'm sorry about your plane, Griff. I know how much it meant to you.' He didn't answer. For a moment it seemed as if he couldn't speak, and Maddy held out her hand halfway, but his eyes were closed and with a little gasp she snatched it back. 'I was going to tell you that I could fly,' she said crisply. 'If you hadn't been quite so rude I would have asked you if I could have taken the controls for a while... But you were so forbidding, so angry.'

'That, my dear girl, was because I was already half in love with you and yet I had to believe Zoe, do what she asked—'

'Why? Just what is it between you two?'

'I met Zoe when I flew her down to her villa ten years ago. All I had was that little seaplane and a dream.' He looked down at his hands. 'A dream,' he repeated, very softly. 'She encouraged me, helped me with contacts, introduced me to the right people—the people who could smooth the path—and when everything might have failed at the last minute she stepped in to guarantee my loan with the bank. Without her there would be no Dragonair, no Dragon Man.'

'There is no Dragon Man,' she said, accusingly. 'This

is a griffin.' She held out her hand. 'The head and wings of an eagle, the body of a lion. I've been living rather closely with it for the past few days.'

'When we were deciding on a name for the company Zoe suggested that a dragon sounded more exciting. Who has ever heard of a griffin?'

Maddy nodded. 'So you believed her.'

'Only with my head. My heart went its own way. . . Come back with me, Maddy. Come back with me to Paradise.' He knelt before her, his hands on her shoulders, forcing her to confront the pain in his eyes, the dark rings beneath them that were an echo of her own. It was unbearable. He could make those eyes tell lies as easily as his lips—First when he'd wanted her body, now when he wanted her child. No matter what Zoe had told him, he should never have agreed to do what she'd asked. It showed an arrogance, a blatant disregard for her rights as a human being.

'But you couldn't wait to ship me out once you'd. . .' Made love to me. She couldn't even say it; it was too painful.

'Zoe was going to come and fetch you on Sunday. That was the arrangement, but I couldn't carry on with the deception. Won't you try and understand?'

She shook her head. 'No, Griff. I will never understand. Not in a thousand years.' She stood up, walked away so that he shouldn't see her face. 'I think you'd better leave now,' she said stiffly.

'I won't let you go.'

'You can't force me to marry you simply because I'm expecting your child, Griff.'

'Then it is true?' His voice shook a little, but it took a moment for Maddy to realise what that meant. . . He had seemed so certain. . .

'It's far too soon to tell,' she said a little huskily. 'Please. . .please go, now.'

'But if you are really expecting my child—'

'It doesn't make any difference, Griff. You can't make me love you,' she said, a little desperately.

'You already love me. That's why you're finding it so hard to forgive me.' She could feel the warmth of his body at her back, but he didn't touch her. 'I could show you that now, Maddy. I could make you beg me to stay, we both know that,' he said as a convulsive tremor shivered her body. 'But I won't. We are one, you and I, for the rest of time. The moon was our witness.' He turned her gently, took both her hands in his and raised them to his lips. 'I love you, Maddy, and when you can find it in your heart to forgive me I'll be waiting for you. No time limit.'

'Maddy? It's Zoe. Can I come up?' Maddy hesitated before pushing the release. It had been a week since Griff had used a recording of Zoe's voice to gain entrance to her flat. A week in which she had heard nothing from him. He had disappeared, as he'd promised, leaving her to make up her own mind, but she wasn't taking any risks.

'Prove it,' she demanded suspiciously.

'If you don't let me in this minute, Maddy Rufus, I'll call everyone I know and let them know that your nickname has nothing to do with your hair but an incident with a tin of red paint. . .'

Maddy slumped against the wall. Lord, how she had wanted it to be him. Then, as the phone buzzed again, she realised that she still had not released the door. She pressed the button and a few moments later her godmother burst into the flat with a hug that said everything.

'What are you doing here, Zoe? If Griff sent you—'

Zoe held her finger to her lips in mock horror. 'Darling, if he knew I was here he would never speak to me again. He made me swear I wouldn't try and influence you.'

'So?'

'I've come to grovel for your forgiveness on my own behalf. I know that it's entirely my fault that you're pregnant—'

'Don't be ridiculous, Zoe. I have a mind of my own. Besides, I'm not even sure that I am pregnant. It's far too soon to be sure.'

'There's no need to be kind,' she replied, with a shiver. 'Is there any chance of a brandy? In your shoes I would be sulking too.'

'I'm not sulking!' Then, more gently, Maddy said, 'You don't understand—'

'How could I? I wasn't there. But I'm sure it was perfectly dreadful. It was *meant* to be dreadful. Washing under that freezing shower, camping on the beach. . . I wanted him to feel *sorry* for you, want to comfort you. . .' But Maddy hardly heard her. Mention of the pool sent her heart flying back there, to the touch of Griff's hands as he had washed her hair under the shower, the dizzy plunge at dawn when they had swum there after making love.

'Oh, Zoe, why did you do it?'

'I knew he was ready to fall in love with you. I saw the way he was looking at you the night we called on you in Mustique. The man's a born romantic. But you would have run away. . .'

A romantic? He had threaded flowers through her

hair and kissed her and made love to her beneath the moon. And he had felt sick when his imagination had tormented him with pictures of her mangled body in the wreck of the plane. And he loved her. He was waiting for her. No time limit.

'Good heavens, is that the time?' Zoe said, leaping up. The sky had grown dark and as Maddy moved to close the curtains she saw the slender curve of a sickle moon behind the stark outline of the plane trees in the square. 'I must be going, Maddy,' Zoe said, touching her shoulder. 'I'm going to the theatre this evening.'

'Yes, of course. It's lovely to see you.'

'Well, I wanted a little chat. I hope I've cleared your mind a little.'

'It's a long way to come for a chat,' Maddy said.

But Zoe was searching in her bag. 'I almost forgot this.' She produced a package from her bag. 'I bought you a little present. Nothing much. Happy Christmas, darling.' She kissed her god-daughter and held her for a moment, then she was gone.

For a moment Maddy held the beautifully gift-wrapped parcel. She carried it across to the sofa, sitting down before she pulled the ribbons and opened it. It was a small furry dragon, bright red with a brave tail and tiny eager wings. She lifted it up and then touched it against her cheek and when, a long time later, she held it away she couldn't understand why it was wet.

The launch skimmed across the bright, sparkling sea. Maddy had set out at dawn from St Vincent and now Paradise was coming towards her out of the horizon. Approaching from sea level, it seemed larger, the small, central peak higher than she remembered. But it was, if possible, even more beautiful than she remembered.

As the launch neared the jetty she could just make out the house, adjust to the scale of it, appreciate the ingenuity that had gone into the design and construction. There were no hard edges to jar against the forest; the only bright colours were supplied by the flowers that tumbled over the roof and the veranda rails and softened the gentle slope of the path that led down to the white curve of the beach.

And Griff was standing at the end of the jetty, feet planted wide, arms akimbo as the launch drifted into the little bay. Maddy's heart caught in her throat at the sight of him, but he turned away to catch the rope thrown to him by the boatman, not meeting her eyes. He made the launch fast but as she moved to step up onto the jetty he blocked her way.

'Why have you come, Maddy?' he demanded.

Maddy had not known quite what reception to expect. Maybe not quite to be swept into his arms. . .but this? Shaken, she withdrew slightly from the eager movement that had carried her towards him. Because you were right. Because I love you. The words stuck fast in her throat. 'It's Christmas. I came to bring a present for Jack,' she said.

'Jack?' At least she had managed to surprise him, buckle that unwavering self-assurance.

She turned to the cage standing on the floor of the cabin out of the sun. Griff jumped down into the boat to examine the small brown parrot hunched unhappily on her perch.

'I've called her Jill. Not very original.'

He grasped the cage in one hand and her elbow in the other. 'Come on. Let's introduce them.'

A few minutes later Griff set the cage very quietly on the veranda below Jack's favourite perch up in the roof.

'I think we'd better leave them to it for a while.' He glanced at her. 'It's hot; can I get you a drink?'

It was all so very stiff and formal. Despite his urgent declaration in her flat, it seemed that he had changed his mind.

'A glass of water?' she suggested. They retreated to the kitchen, where Griff opened an enormous refrigerator powered by the solar panels on the roof.

'It's odd being in the sun on Christmas Eve,' she said, propping herself onto a high stool, attempting to achieve some normality in their conversation.

He was leaning against the units, arms folded, and as she nervously sipped at her water Maddy was aware that Griff's penetrating eyes never left her. 'Why did you come back?' he asked again.

'I told you—'

'Don't fudge it, Maddy. Don't use borrowed wings. . .' He saw her confusion. 'You could have sent Jill by air freight with a Christmas card.'

She slipped down from the stool. 'I think I'd better go.'

'Won't you admit it, even now?'

'You're not making it easy. . .'

'I want you to be sure in your own mind that you want to stay here, with me, for the rest of your life. Despite everything I said, I don't want you to stay just because you're pregnant. I'll support you and I'll want to see my child. But I don't want you to have any illusions. Once I send the boat away there'll be no more choices to make. You'll be mine.' The lines that bit into his cheeks deepened. 'You must want to stay for no other reason than that. Anything else is impossible.'

'Do you want me to stay?' she asked.

He refused to give an inch. 'You know what I want, Maddy. I told you in London.'

A crash from the veranda, a flurry of wings took them through the door. The cage was lying on its side, the door open and Jill was sitting preening herself on top of it while Jack watched contentedly from the rail of the veranda. If only it was that easy for people, Maddy thought. No stupid pride, no need to hide your feelings in case you were hurt. She turned to Griff and he was looking down at her, waiting. It was that easy. Griff had bared his heart to her, had given her all the time in the world to make her decision and still she had lacked the courage... But she must find it from somewhere. It was too important.

'I love you, Griff,' she said. 'I came back because I wanted to be with you. I'm not even sure that I'm going to have your child... It's a little early to be sure...'

He seemed to be a little closer. 'If that's the only thing that's worrying you, my love, we could make absolutely certain...'

'Tell the boatman to go, Griff,' she said softly.

'What boatman?' She turned to the jetty, but the launch was already disappearing into the distance.

'You...' She turned back to him. 'You've already sent him away...'

'You didn't think I'd take the risk of losing you again? Welcome to Paradise, my love,' he said with a soft laugh, and she smiled as, very softly, he enfolded her in his arms, kissing her until she thought she must surely cry with happiness.

Emma Goldrick was born and raised in Puerto Rico, where she met and married her husband Bob, a career military man. Thirty years and four children later they retired and took up nursing and teaching. In 1980 they turned to collaborative writing. After sixty years of living in over half the world, and a full year of studying the Mills & Boon® style, their first submission was accepted. Between them they have written over forty books, which have been published all around the world. Goldrick hobbies include grandchildren, flower gardens, reading and travel.

THE GIRL HE
LEFT BEHIND
by
EMMA GOLDRICK

To Margaret and Jim, in the hope
that they might forgive us for
moving the village boundaries five
hundred yards farther west.

CHAPTER ONE

MOLLY PATTERSON came around the curve in the road in her old Nissan and looked happily at her own house, poised on the cliffs above the grey Atlantic Ocean. Although she had been born and raised in the old Steamboat Gothic mansion overlooking Kettle Cove on Cape Ann, it still tugged at her heart whenever she had been away for a time. There was a strange car parked in front of the steps, and a man was sitting comfortably on the top stair, waiting.

She blinked her eyes nervously, trying vainly to focus on him, as she took her glasses off. Excessive pride dictated that she not wear the gold-rimmed spectacles, even if she was somewhat near-sighted. In months past she would have blundered along and made any visitor welcome. But since she had won the Lottery some six weeks earlier, Molly Patterson had grown up quickly. Not the megabucks millions, of course, just the weekly pay-off. Enough money so she could afford to take a year's sabbatical from her teaching job. And just in time, too, in the light of the considerable mess she had made about Alfred! Seventy thousand dollars, minus the taxes. And the tax men took their bite out of the cheque before Molly had even seen it. Nevertheless, in a small community, sixty thousand was a substantial attraction. And she had been too stupid to realise that Alfred could count that high without using his fingers and toes!

'Molly?' The figure on the stairs stood up, seeming to stretch endlessly. There was something about the face, gaunt and tired and unshaven. Something about the untidy mass of brown hair, bleached by the sun in places, fluttering in the offshore breeze. Something about the dark blue eyes. Something about the tall thin frame, thin almost to emaciation, but loaded with cable-muscles, as well she knew!

She fumbled for the first step as her mind flashed back. Pictures crowded in on her, imposing themselves one on top of another, each not quite obliterating the scene in front of her.

Six-year-old Molly; he was eight. 'It won't hurt, Molly, honest. And we have to do it because we're friends, aren't we?'

'But I'm scared, Tim! The knife is sharp, and——'

'And then we put our fingers together and we're sealed in blood, Molly, and we'll be loyal friends forever!' But it did hurt, and she cried, and nothing could soothe her spirit until her mother covered it with two Band-aids. And then she could boast, because not many of her friends had a finger with a bandage that size. As for Tim, you couldn't put a bandage on the place where *he* hurt after his father found out about it!

Twelve-year-old Molly; he was fourteen, sitting at the foot of the apple tree where he had fallen, holding his broken arm with the other hand. She had screamed her head off and run, while he kept back the tears. He had worn a cast for six weeks that summer, just because she had demanded that he rescue her cat—who didn't need rescuing. The animal had spit and scratched at Tim until his hand slipped and he fell. And when Molly's mother heard all the details she had marched her daughter off to her room and—but that was not the sort of thing worth thinking about!

Thirteen-year-old Molly; he was fifteen. They were at

the bottom of the sea-cliff. The cold rock towered above them, with hardly a foothold to be seen.

'It's easy,' he coaxed. 'Just follow me. Put your hands where I put mine, and don't look down.' Blindly trusting, she had done so, until halfway up the sixty-foot cliff she'd lost her nerve and clung sobbing to the tiny ledge which provided just enough space for her toes to gain a hold.

'Come on,' he had teased gently, but she had not had the heart. He had cajoled for ten minutes, and then left her to her tears. She had thought the world was surely done with her, but then he was back with ropes and tackle, talking gently to her from the top of the cliff as he set his anchors. And he was beside her.

'Hold tight to me, Molly.' Of course she did. Despite all her fears she clung to him as he gradually brought them up the face of the cliff to safety.

'I shouldn't have done that,' said the suddenly mature Tim. 'I shouldn't have dared you to climb like that.' But all Molly could think of was that she had trusted him with her life, and he had not failed her.

Eighteen-year-old Molly; he was twenty, with his parents divorced and gone away. And that was the year that her cousin Susan came to spend the summer. A summer of sheer misery, because eighteen-year-old Molly was a woman grown, but tall, gawky and all bones, while nineteen-year-old Susan was petite, blonde, all curves and smiles. And that summer Molly found out that she was the fifth wheel on the cart, and it ended dismally when Susan said, 'And of course you'll be my bridesmaid, Molly.' Molly's mother had smiled sweetly and her father beamed, and there was hardly any time for Molly to say, 'No, I'd rather cut your heart out!'

With an artificial smile on her face she had gone to the bottom step with the rest of the wedding party, and had thrown confetti, wishing it were bombs. Susan had aimed her bouquet, and it landed in Molly's hand. So long ago. Every female at the wedding had either died of old age or was married, Molly reminded herself grimly. Even the flower-girl. Everybody except Molly Patterson!

So Susan took Tim away, and the house next door grew empty and started to fall down, and Molly had lost both her parents to the sea and won the lottery, and now she was twenty-eight, with an old dog, and a heart that ached only occasionally, and settled in her little niche in life, and —

'Tim?' Her voice was dry, raspy, fighting the emotion that stormed at her heart. Or rather a combination of emotions—love, hate, memory, anguish. Her body froze on that bottom stair. He came rumbling down and his arms were around her and it was warm, and the years peeled off like a patch being removed. She ducked her head into the heavy flannel shirt he was wearing, and closed her eyes. It almost seemed as if once again she was the girl next door—but then one can never go back, can one?

Molly sighed, broke away from him, and knuckled at the little tear that formed in her eye. It had been ten years since her last hug from Tim, and the cracked heart she thought had been repaired turned out to have been papered over rather than cemented.

But I'm not going to go through all that, she told herself fiercely. You had your share of Molly Patterson, Tim. And I'm not going to let you have another bite!

He crushed her close again, his face buried in her long straw-coloured hair. 'God, what a fool I've been, Molly!' he groaned in her ear. Silently, cool-headed, dependable Molly agreed with him.

* * *

'Tell me about it,' she prompted, as she brought the hot coffee over to the big kitchen table. Enough time had elapsed for her to control the wild beating of her heart, to salve the reopened wounds. Enough time so that she could act as a nonchalant friend. She had always been a good actress, going back to the shared days at Gloucester High School. But then so had he. Come on now, she told herself firmly, don't make a big thing out of this. He belongs to Susan!

Tim warmed his hands on the coffee-mug. November on the high sea cliffs north of Boston was always a chilly time. 'I don't know how to begin,' he sighed. 'I need help—so where else would I look but to Molly Patterson?' He stared into the black of his steaming coffee, then sipped, all without looking at her.

She slid into the chair across from him, feeling more than a little anger. 'After ten years, Tim? With never a word?' He had the grace to blush. Almost she could see the boy in the face of the man. Almost.

'Yeah, I'm probably as welcome as the tax-collector.' His deep voice was no longer smooth and suave. There were cracks in it, as there were on his forehead. And there was a trace of embarrassment. The Tim she had known could never have hesitated about asking for help—especially from Molly Patterson!

'That's not true.' She forced a chuckle, wondering if he could hear how false it was. 'You're always welcome here. Remember, we sealed a bond for life?' She grinned as she held up her thumb. 'And I've still got the scar to prove it!'

He reached across the table and took her wrist. A hard, callused hand, thin but muscled, with fingers that could outreach hers by half. He turned her palm over and traced the scar. 'God, there's no end to the trouble I've caused, is there?' he muttered.

Molly mustered up her best smile. 'Come on now, Tim, if we were to add up the scars and bruises we've each inflicted on the other it would come out even. So life has its drawbacks. Lay your problem on me. That's what friends are for.'

That managed to bring a little smile, a little upward quirk at the corners of his mouth, a tiny gleam in his sea-blue eyes.

'Nothing's hurt you. You haven't changed a bit. I'm glad for you, Moll.'

No, nothing's hurt me—lately—she thought to herself. How could anything else hurt me after your wedding, Tim? She ducked her head to hide the bitterness.

'Well, among other things it's the money,' he said flatly. Her head popped up and she stared at him.

'The money? The sole heir to the Holland millions? What are you doing, Tim? Teasing me?'

'Not a single tease,' he sighed. 'The money's practically all gone. It never amounted to millions anyway. There might have been *one* million, but if my father had spent twenty dollars we would have fallen out of the class. Then, when my mother split, she took him for considerably more than half of it. And Susan and I, we led each other a mad, mad chase. In Europe, mostly. She loved Paris, I did too, for a time. But, you know, the night life got to be pretty boring. I had a lot of acquaintances, Molly, but no friends. Susan had a lot of—friends.'

'Drink your coffee,' she nagged him, and got up to top up his mug. 'So all the money's gone?'

'Not all,' he told her. 'There's still the fishing fleet and the freezer plant, and a few pieces of real estate, and some other things here and there, but it's slipping out of my hands. I need to be able to settle in one place and concentrate on Holland Ocean Fisheries, Incorporated. If I work hard enough at it I'm sure I can re-establish things, and get over the hump.' He slammed his fist down on the table. Both coffee-mugs jumped, and Molly's spilled over. She gave a vague swipe at it with a paper napkin.

'But I—I don't understand,' she said softly. The situation was getting out of control. Where, but a moment ago, she had anticipated giving him a hard set-down, now all of a sudden she was unable to mask her interest. 'Of course I'll do anything I can to help, but what about Susan? Where is she?'

'I haven't the slightest idea,' he snapped, and she could see his fingernails biting into the palms of his hands. 'When I told her the money tap was shut off, so was she. I haven't seen Susan for well over seven years.'

'But I still don't understand, Tim. What do you want from me? Money?'

He pushed his chair back, rasping it across the old linoleum. 'Money?' he asked sarcastically as he struggled to his feet. 'God, I'm tired! We drove all the way up from Washington today. No, I don't need money from you, Molly. I thought you of all people would understand!'

She jumped to her feet too, anger lighting her green eyes. 'Well, I would if you'd only stop feeling sorry for yourself, Tim Holland, and explain to me exactly what's going on! Now you just sit down and shut up! I mean—start talking!'

He grinned at her, and for a moment the daredevil Tim was back. Across the table from her he rubbed a hand across the stubble on his face. 'Among other things, what I need, Molly, is a little straightforward honesty.'

'So sit,' she said. You'll get all the straightforward honesty you can stand, she thought grimly. And then some. He grinned again and dropped back into the chair. 'And now,' she said, following suit, 'you can start off by telling me just who the "we" are that drove all the way up here from Washington! If Susan's not with you, who is?'

Tim held his hands out in mock supplication. 'I keep forgetting you don't know all that much about me lately,' he grimaced. 'There's Moira to consider.'

Molly shook her head, trying to clear the cobwebs, and asked the obvious question.

'Moira's my daughter,' Tim told her apologetically.

'Well, where in the world is she?' She glared at him, and the sudden movement sent her long silky red-gold hair swinging across her face. She pushed it out of the way and re-tied the old pink ribbon that held everything in a ponytail.

'She's asleep,' he said. 'Out in the car. She talked all the way up to Boston, then she sort of keeled over and fell asleep. Moira's my problem, Molly. I need someone to look after her while I put my heart and soul into this rescue mission. A matter of two or three months, no more.'

Molly was not the dunce of the Patterson family. The whole story was revealed in three sentences, and despite her resolve, she accepted the burden. 'Well, you'd darn well better bring her in,' she ordered peremptorily. 'Imagine the nerve of the man, leaving a little girl out there all by herself!' She wanted desperately to be angry with him, but one look at that crooked smile, the head slightly cocked to one side, was more than her sobriety could stand. After all, he *was* Tim, and she was the girl next door. A tiny smile sneaked out from under her anger.

'Ah, that's my Molly,' said Tim as he got to his feet and headed for the door.

No, that's *not* your Molly, she thought as she watched

his broad back disappear through the door. He slammed
it behind him, of course. Hadn't he always? I'm *not* your
Molly. Dear God, I always wanted to *be* your Molly, but
I didn't make it, did I, Tim? Always cast as the best friend,
but never the lover. If I had any sense, Tim Holland, I'd
print me a sign that says 'Molly Loves Tim is Past
History,' and I'd put a tenpenny spike through it, and take
up my hammer and nail it right on to your forehead so the
words were forever in front of your eyes—your *damn*
eyes!

The clatter of feet snapped her out of her reverie, as the
door opened and Tim came in, his daughter close behind
him. His daughter! A tiny little thing with an elfin face
and long straight blonde hair, a pointed chin and a big
smile that came to an abrupt halt when the child saw
Molly. The little girl stepped behind her father, one hand
clutching his coat sleeve, effectively hiding as her father
made the introductions.

Molly was fastened to her chair. The little girl was all
Susan. Every inch of her was her mother—except—no,
the little girl had brown eyes, rather than the startlingly
violet orbs that Susan was so vain about. Molly shook
herself mentally, then stood up gracefully and smiled.
'Welcome to my home, Moira,' she said softly.

The child remained in hiding behind the huge bulk of
her father, her face poised between sun and rain. Luckily
Shag came wandering in at just that moment. A brown
and white St Bernard, grey-muzzled with age, a hundred
and fifty pounds of creaking overweight pure-bred, Shag
owned Molly, the house, and the acre of scrubland around
it, and he knew it. He wandered vaguely across the floor,
favouring his arthritic hindquarter, and sat down directly
in front of the little girl.

'Ooh,' said Moira, 'he's big for a dog!' The child's

voice had that flat quality, that lack of stable tone that Molly recognised immediately. And then the girl looked Molly up and down and added, 'So are you.'

'Moira!' Tim was still holding his daughter's hand. He gave it a shake and looked just a little displeased. The child peered up at him.

'I mean, the dog looks big for a dog and she looks big for a girl, Daddy.' With which she moved around behind him again, like a child trying to hide from a lightning blast.

'*Molly*,' her father insisted. 'Her name isn't *she*, it's Molly. And the dog's name is Shag.'

'You know the dog?' The little girl peered out from behind him, her curiosity overcoming her nervousness.

He ruffled her hair with a gentle hand. 'Of course I do,' he chuckled. 'He was just a pup. I gave him to Molly on her fourteenth birthday.'

'Fifteen,' Molly interjected in the interest of accuracy. It had been a lovely gift; the finest she was to receive for many a year. And now she and her dog were years older and decades out of touch.

'Yes,' Tim continued, 'Molly spent a week agonising over what to call him. Seems to me I remember a great many tears——'

'Well, girls of fifteen tend to be emotional,' she snapped at him as she blinked back another tear. Too many memories, all crowding in on her. They *must* be stuffed back in the storage bag! Cool, calm Molly Patterson. Pragmatic. Phlegmatic. She sniffed a couple of times.

'So at the end of the week, when she was still shilly-shallying,' Tim continued, 'I named the animal for her—Shaggy Dog. Which then gradually became Shag. Hey, old mutt?'

Shag lifted his huge head as if it were a burden, and his tail wagged, once to the right, once to the left, and then down on the floor with a massive thump. His jaw fell open, displaying an array of massive teeth, and the dark rough tongue licked at the extended hand.

'He remembers,' Tim said softly, looking over the child's bright head at Molly. She nodded slowly.

'Could I——?' The little girl looked up at Molly, the question big in her eyes.

'Of course,' said Molly. 'Put both your hands out very slowly. Don't touch him—just put your hands in front of him so he can smell.'

The child complied. The old dog cocked his head, sniffed for a second, and licked. Moira squeaked, her hands shaking, but did not pull back.

'Say his name, then scratch his ears,' Molly instructed.

'Shag? Shag?' The exquisitely formed little hands moved slowly, and the treat began. The huge drooping ears fluttered. Shag leaned forward to get the fingers in just the right place, and made a happy noise.

After a moment the child looked up at Molly again. 'Shag,' she said firmly. 'But what do I call you? It's not polite to call adults by their first name—my dad taught me that.'

'That's all right,' Molly soothed. 'I can be *she* if that's what you want. Or Molly, if you like that better. Or—well, I *am* your mother's cousin, Moira. That makes me a sort of aunt. Would that be better? Aunt Molly?'

The child bit at the bait, came out from her father's shadow, and moved over to the table. She talked to Molly, but her eyes were all on Shag, who sat making vague scratching motions with his hind paw, and missing what he was trying to reach, the corner behind his straggly left ear.

'Aunt Molly? You knew my mother?' There was an anxious look in her little face. 'Was she pretty?'

'The most beautiful girl in Magnolia,' Molly said solemnly.

'Magnolia? Where's that?'

'That's here,' said Molly. 'This whole place is a village called Magnolia. Are you hungry?'

'When is she not?' Tim interjected with a grin. 'She looks like a stick, but eats like a horse!'

'Daddy!' One little foot stamped imperiously on the floor as Moira glared up at him.

'Oh, excuse me,' he chuckled. 'I forgot that we're grown up now.'

'He can't help it,' the little girl apologised in a strangely adult way. 'He's only a man, you know.'

'Yes, I know.' Molly grinned down at the solemn little face. 'I've known your dad since he was a little boy, and he never did know how to deal with girls! Now, what would you like to eat?'

It was no surprise to discover that the child wanted a hamburger. Molly prepared the only patty she had unfrozen, and made an omelette for Tim and herself. And as she worked she wondered. Strange, that a child could seem so young, and yet act in so mature a manner! There was a mystery here, for sure.

'I don't keep much out of the freezer,' she explained as they gathered around the table. 'And I don't heat the house often, either, only the kitchen and the bathroom. But since Moira's going to stay a while, I'll get everything going.'

'Does that mean you're accepting the challenge?' he asked. She stared at the tentative look on his face. Not handsome, she remembered, but nice. And worried.

'Of course it does,' she returned. 'It's a very convenient

time. I don't happen to be teaching this semester, and have a lot of time on my hands. Why? Was there ever any doubt? What are friends for?'

He shook his head, smiling, acknowledging the debt with his eyes as he scanned the kitchen. 'Not home much?' He gave her a look that bespoke a thousand questions, which Molly had no intention of answering. 'Hey, I'm sorry.'

'No need to apologise,' she laughed. 'No, I'm not home much. Up until two weeks ago I was working as a Special Needs teacher for the Essex School District.'

'No longer?' He leaned both elbows on the table and stared at her. The single overhead pull-down light, right over the centre of the table, cast his face into planes and shadows, making him unreadable.

'No,' she sighed as she pushed back her chair and started to clear the table. 'No longer.' And I'm darned if I'm going to tell you about *that* fiasco, she thought. 'I had a thought that I might go back to get another degree, but—well, I've become a terrible procrastinator, Tim.'

'I doubt that, Molly.' He pulled back his chair and came to help. She waved him off.

'Moira and I can take care of this little bit.' Molly looked over at the little girl, who was still busy with the sponge cake dessert. The child was facing away from them and seemed totally oblivious to their conversation. Another clue fell into place as Molly considered. Throughout the last two hours, every time Tim wanted to speak to the child he had moved directly in front of her!

'Then I'll leave you two to it.' Tim broke into her thoughts, wiping his hands off on the apron she wore over her slacks. 'I've got to hustle down to Boston and find a place to rest my head.'

'What the devil are you talking about?' Molly slapped

gently at the masculine hand that was toying with her hair. 'And don't think you can get away with teasing me to change the subject. Times have changed.'

'So they have,' he laughed. 'But it's true. I have to find some little den close to the action, and——'

'*You* haven't changed a bit, Tim Holland,' she grumbled at him. 'Still the same arrogant, insensitive boy I've always known! I have a lot of bedrooms in this house, all unoccupied. I'm twenty-eight years old, for goodness' sake, and a spinster to boot. You're not going to damage my reputation by moving in with me for a few months, and you're *not* going to get away with just dumping your daughter on me while you run for the bright lights of the city. You'll make your headquarters right here; I've got plenty of room, you can be with your daughter, there's a telephone, and Highway 128 is hardly ten minutes from our door. And that's the way it's going to be!'

Moira had turned around to look at them, her face as bright as springtime. 'There, she told you off, Daddy. 'Bout time too!'

'She certainly did, poppet.' He plucked the little girl out of her chair and hugged her before whirling her around in a circle over his head. She screamed in excitement, and was laughing deliriously as he gently lowered her to her feet.

'Aren't you going to whirl Molly?' The child looked at both of them expectantly. Molly put up both hands in self-defence and backed away.

'I don't think she wants to play,' sighed Tim. 'And that being the case, suppose I drive back to Gloucester and pick up all our gear. I dropped it off at the Cape Ann Motor Inn, figuring that might have to be our home for a while. It won't take long. You'll be all right, Moira?'

The child was all solemnity again as she smoothed

down her little dress and looked at the floor. 'I think so,' she said. 'Only you have to promise to come right back. I like your friend—Aunt Molly—but——'

Aunt Molly backed up against the solid support of the kitchen sink and watched as the pair of them made communion. He knelt down in front of the child and offered both hands. The girl took them, then squealed in laughter and received a kiss on her cheek as her father winked at her and stood up. There seemed to be no place for a third party in this closed community; Molly felt a little lump in her throat and turned away to hide the tiny droplet that seemed intent on escaping from her left eye. *She could have been my daughter!*

Tim started for the door. His little daughter coughed conspicuously and tapped her foot. He caught himself in mid-stride, turned and came back to where Molly was standing. 'Thank you again for everything, Moll,' he said. 'A fellow doesn't realise who his friends are until he really gets in a bind.' As he had with his daughter, he reached out both hands to take and squeeze hers, and kissed her gently on her forehead.

Molly didn't dare to answer. How could she possibly yell at the man, with his daughter watching? How could she possibly tell him that a kiss on the forehead would just *not* do? How could she tell him that she didn't want to be his *old friend* any more? Instead of words she tendered a tiny smile, and finally started breathing again when she heard the motor in his car start up.

'Now then, Miss Moira Holland,' she said. 'How about you?'

'How about me what?' The little girl went rigid and stood her ground.

'Well, for one thing,' Molly smiled, 'who's been buying your dresses lately? That one you're wearing is short enough to— give you a considerable chill this winter. Are all your dresses the same?'

Moira looked down at the little gingham thing that clung to her bodice and ended three inches above her knees. 'My dad buys all my clothes,' she said. Again that solemnity that rules when a child has lived most of her life with adults instead of other children. But then her head shook, her little tongue protruded for a moment. 'He don't know much about girl clothes. That's why I wear a lot of jeans. He thinks I like them.'

'And how come he thinks you like them?'

''Cause I tell him so. It's the only way I can keep my bottom warm!'

Now don't start off trying to reform some other person's children, Molly told herself sternly. Mind your own business! But if he's placing the child in *my* care I think we'll go down on Lexington Avenue and have a shopping afternoon. And then there's school, and we need more groceries, and I'd better see about milk delivery, and I need to have the oil tank filled for the furnace, and—good lord, I thought I'd spend the winter in splendid isolation!

The bathroom was a comfortable seventy degrees when she managed to coax Moira upstairs some time later. The little girl was a silent shadow, doubts registering on her face at every step. Without her clothing she was a chunky little thing, big for her age, splashing gently away in the huge old-fashioned tub, at times relaxed enough to show the child through the adult veneer.

As Molly carefully contained the long blonde hair in a plastic shower-cap, the little girl fumbled with her right ear and put something on the chair beside the tub. Conversation seemed to cease after that. She would make a statement or ask a question, then duck under the water and come up in a spray of water. Molly rolled up her sleeves and scrubbed Moira's back. The game went on until the water in the tub began to cool.

'You'd better climb out now,' Molly said quietly. She was kneeling down by the tub at Moira's side. The child stilled instantly, and turned to stare at her.

And that's the final clue, Molly told herself grimly. Slowly, without actually making a sound, she mouthed the same words. Moira nodded, and scrambled to her feet. She's reading my lips, Molly sighed to herself. Not yet eight, and she's reading my lips! She struggled to mask her emotions as she pulled a big bath towel from the rack and wrapped the little girl within it.

The first thing that Moira did when her feet hit the rug outside the tub was to rub her right ear with the towel, and reach over to re-insert the little hearing aid. 'That's nice,' she said. 'I love splashing baths. Mrs Morriset, she didn't like splashing.'

'I don't mind a little splash,' Molly responded. 'I was champion splasher in this house at one time. Did you know that?'

'Really truly?'

'Really truly. And do you know something else? My mother told me that your dad and I often had baths together in this very tub—of course we were little then.' And how about *that* for a way to get to a child's heart, Molly chided herself. She absolutely adores her father. What a lucky man!

Molly talked on as her hands scrubbed at the child with the towel. 'You have a lovely name—Moira. I like that. It's an old Irish name, you know.'

'Is it?' With her head barely visible among the folds of the towel, the little girl finally managed a grin. 'Do you know what it means?'

'Well, yes and no,' Molly chuckled as she pulled one of her old linen shirts over the child's head to serve as a nightgown. 'Actually it's the same name as mine, deep down. It's the same as Mame, Molly, Polly—oh, there are a dozen nicknames that go with it. But essentially it means Mary. And that's from the Hebrew—and that's all I'm going to tell you tonight. Come on now, hop into bed.'

The corridor outside the bathroom was cooler. They ran the length of it, holding hands, and Moira vaulted into the canopied bed and was under the covers before Molly could catch her breath. Moira sat up, with the quilt pulled up to her chin.

'Aunt Molly,' she said, squirming, but never taking her eyes from Molly's face, 'you haven't said a word.'

'About what, dear?'

'About my hearing aid. Mrs Morriset said it made me look ugly.'

Molly's anger, always on a quick fuse anyway, almost burst through the top of her head. 'She lied, my dear,' she said forcefully. 'You're beautiful. Who was this woman?'

'She was our—housekeeper, I guess. She was one of those friends of Daddy's. Why would you want to know?'

Because I'm related to Lizzie Borden, Molly wanted to shout, but didn't. And I'd like to get out my little axe and give that fool woman forty whacks—or more, for that matter! 'Oh, I was just curious,' she said. 'I suppose your dad had a lot of woman friends?'

'There were plenty,' sighed Moira. 'Daddy didn't seem to keep girlfriends long. Some day we oughta talk to him about that, don't you think? You being such an old friend of his and all?'

'Well, perhaps we might,' Molly responded carefully. 'Your dad is a fine man. He's big and strong and intelligent and——'

'Good-looking,' his daughter prompted drowsily, just before she fell off to sleep.

'Yes, and good-looking,' Molly whispered softly. 'And dumb, dumb, dumb, dumb! Damn the man!'

She heard the noise as his car drove up outside. Not quite wanting to leave the little girl alone on her first night in a strange bed and house, she backed out to the open door of the hallway and waited.

Tim joined her in a moment, bringing with him the chill of the November night. His cheeks were red, he was puffing from the exertion, but the devil gleamed in his eye.

'If she's asleep now, she'll sleep till morning,' he whispered. Molly nodded and led him to the room next door, the one he had always used when he stayed over, those long years before. Ten minutes later he joined her downstairs.

'There are drinks in the cabinet.' She waved towards the old mahogany sideboard that had been her father's favourite piece of furniture. 'There's not much of a choice, but you're welcome.'

He walked across the room, inspected, and made his choice. 'You're not having any?'

'No,' she said, sitting down primly on the edge of the couch. 'I—don't drink alcohol any more. And I wanted to ask you a question.'

'Only one? You're a paragon, Molly!'

'Only one,' she sighed. 'Tell me about her hearing.'

Tim sank back in the overstuffed chair opposite her, took a sip that half emptied his glass, then considered.

'I suppose you think that's none of my business, asking a question like that?' she asked warily.

'No, not at all,' he returned. 'It's something Moira and

I have come to accept—and Susan would not. And you need to know if we're going to spend the winter together.

'Good God!' Molly cried. 'Susan abandoned her because she's hard of hearing?'

'Not entirely,' he answered bitterly. 'By the time Moira was six months old the doctors had determined that she suffered from a degenerative congenital hearing loss. She can't hear at all in her left ear; her right ear is gradually losing its response. The doctors say that by the time she reaches puberty she'll be totally deaf.' His shoulders seemed to sag at the end of the statement. 'And that *and* the money were too much for Susan. She bugged out one night—cleaned out her closet and my bank account, and that's the last we've seen of her.'

'Hearing problems are a hard thing to face,' Molly said quietly. 'I've been doing a great deal of work with special interest children at school. Moira has years ahead of her; she can learn all the other communications means. She can already read lips, and I can teach her sign language. And by the time she's twelve, who knows what the world of medicine might have learned to cure!'

'You don't understand, Molly.' Tim stood up, gulped down the remainder of his drink, and set the glass down hard on the end table by his chair.

'Don't give me that *you don't understand* business,' she snapped as she stood up to face him. Her height was her advantage. Although he was over six feet, she was five foot eleven herself, in her bare feet, and could glare back at him almost on an even keel. 'I'm Molly Patterson, not some floozie you picked up in the village. If you think I don't understand, then tell me!'

His glare gradually faded, but the pain did not. 'I said she had congenital hearing loss,' he sighed, his face distorted with pain. 'It has something to do with her inherited genes. It doesn't run in *my* family, and it doesn't run in *Susan's* family. Dear God, Molly, I love that child with all my heart. Susan is her mother, I'm positive of that. I was there when she was born. But I wish the hell I knew who her father was!'

An hour later, snug in bed, Molly wrestled with the problem. He didn't come back because I'm pretty, she told herself. And he didn't come back because I'm rich—I think. He came back because of the money, and because he needed help with his daughter. And that's the way I have to play it. Best friend, that's my role again. Don't be too sombre, girl, and for heaven's sake don't weep over him! Be cool, be calm, be normal. Argue with him, fight with him, laugh with him—but don't ever let him know how much you love him!

And as for the little girl—whose daughter was she? Had Susan become that much of a tramp that a man wouldn't know his own child? A dear lovable little girl with a handicap. So how to approach the problem? First of all, accept the idea that Moira *is* his daughter. Secondly, make no great show about her handicap. Treat her as a normal healthy child. Avoid embarrassing her. Speak slowly, clearly but unobtrusively. And do everything you can to build up the child's confidence against the impending wall of silence that threatens her!

And with all her thoughts thought, all her plans planned, Molly turned over on her side and tried to sleep. It was difficult. Just on the other side of that wall is Tim Holland, she told herself fiercely, the man that I'm not going to give another emotional thought to. And oh, how I want him!

CHAPTER TWO

MOLLY was busy at her dressing-table at seven the next morning, brushing her shining hair, when little Moira knocked and walked in. 'How about that?' smiled Molly. She was wearing a pink flannel nightgown which stretched from high-buttoned neckline to her ankles, caressing her curves as it fell. Moira, wearing one of Molly's old shirts over her stick-figure, managed to achieve the same general appearance, the tails of the shirt reaching down to her ankles. The child climbed up on to the bench beside Molly, squirmed a bit, and looked into the mirror.

'Whatcha doing?' she queried.

'Braiding my hair. I prefer to keep it out of the way, and yet I don't have the courage to get it cut. Don't you braid yours? It's certainly long enough.'

'No.'

'Just no?' Molly put her brush down and looked at the child's mirror-reflection. A very stubborn little chin was tilted slightly upward to emphasise her determination.

'Just no. I don't like to show my ears.'

'But you have very pretty ears, Moira.'

'Kids laugh at me when they see my hearing aid. Ears ain't pretty when you have to stuff them with 'lectric.'

Oh my, Molly sighed to herself. Here we go! A child's peers can be the most cruel people in the world. Anybody *different* is to be mocked! And now what, Miss Patterson?

'Look at me, Moira,' she ordered. The child responded, looking straight ahead into the mirror. Molly leaned to

28

one side and opened a drawer. Her gold wire-rimmed glasses came to hand. She took them out, cleaned them casually with a Kleenex, and slipped them on. 'There,' she said in a very satisfied tone. 'Don't they look nice?'

'They do,' the child returned. 'But you wasn't wearing them last night. How come?'

'That's because I was too stupid,' Molly explained. 'I think they look ugly. But if I don't wear them, I can't see.'

'You can't see?' The child's interest was immense. 'Nothing?'

'Well, I can see shapes,' Molly admitted. 'And when people stand really close I can make them out. But only just barely.'

'That's stupid all right,' Moira agreed. 'You *hafta* see. Only a dummy wouldn't wear glasses when she can't see. And besides, they're kind of cute!'

'Yes, well, maybe they are,' Molly said reflectively. 'And of course, people who can't hear are dummies if they don't wear their hearing aids, and besides, I think they look cute!'

'Why, I——' The little girl stammered to a stop and then sat quietly for a moment. 'That was a trick, wasn't it?' she said softly. Molly looked down at her. The child had disappeared, to be replaced by the tiny adult again. How old could she really be?

'Not exactly. I was thinking more of a bargain.'

Silence. And then, very cautiously, 'What kind of bargain?'

'I figure that I'll wear my glasses just as long as you wear your hearing aid, and we'll both be proud of ourselves no matter what anybody says, because we'll both know we're cute!'

And now let's see if the fish will bite at the lure, Molly thought, as she continued her braiding. I *want* her to bite.

I want very much to see this little girl happy. I want to help her to know as she goes down the tunnel into silence that there are many other ways to communicate with the world. I *want* her to be happy! I've only known her for twenty-four hours, and I don't understand why I should care so much, but I do!

'How do you do this braiding stuff?' Moira interrupted her train of thought. The child was twisting her hair as best she could, with no good result. Two pairs of eyes met in the mirror, and a conspiratorial smile was exchanged.

Tim was the last one down for breakfast, but after all, it was Saturday. Sleep had erased the haunted look from his face. His daughter was a ray of sunshine, her hair in two proud braids down her back as she helped Molly with the breakfast preparations. Which was fortunate, because the weather was all fog and grey outside the windows.

'But it can't get in!' Moira said shrilly. Now that Molly was aware, she noticed the occasional flatness of tone when the girl spoke, a sure indication that the child could not clearly hear herself.

'No, it can't get in.' Molly smiled gently at Tim and automatically reached for the eggs. He was a big man, she remembered. He favoured ham and eggs and toast and coffee and orange juice, and could occasionally be tempted towards steak and eggs. But he burned it off as fast as he took it in.

Molly searched him out surreptitiously as she worked. His thatch-coloured hair had receded just the tiniest bit on the right side of his head, where he combed it. It was as unruly as always, but he had taken the time to shave and comb and wash, and looked very much as he had years ago. Except for the two deep furrows on his forehead, and a tiny scar just at the side of his patrician nose. There might be just a fleck of white in his hair—just the tiniest speck. It gave him a more distinguished look, she thought as she rescued the eggs and slid them on to a plate. His blue eyes were clear and warm this morning, his oval face considerably thinner than once it had been. But, altogether Tim. She sighed a gusty appreciation as she filled the plate and put it on the table in front of him.

'How come *you* make the breakfast here?' Moira looked up at her with a happy grin on her face. 'My dad makes breakfast at home, you know.'

'Not when there's a woman around,' Tim teased.

'That's the way it is, Moira,' Molly sighed sombrely. 'Woman's work is never done. You should have been born a boy.'

'Not me,' the child responded quickly. 'Girls are nicer. Boys are all whiskers and dirty shoes and toads!'

'Funny,' laughed Molly as she took her own plate to the table and sat down, 'it took me twenty-five years to discover that, and here you know it all already? When's your birthday?' The child must be nearly eight, she was so grown up.

'Mapril,' Moira pronounced solemnly.

'That's certainly a nice month for a birthday,' Molly agreed cautiously.

'Yes. It's flexible,' her father interjected. 'We're always moved around a great deal, and——'

'I understand,' Molly returned. Vagabonds, she thought sympathetically. They may have had a happy life, but they have no roots! 'My, we have a lot of things to do today,' she added.

'We have?' They both spoke in startled unison.

'We have,' she maintained firmly. 'There's going to be a great deal of running around, what with this new arrangement. I need to get a better car.'

'But you ain't got no——'

'Don't have a——' her father corrected quickly. 'This child doesn't quite have a speaking acquaintance with English.' He patted the little girl on her head, then softened the blow. 'But her French is pretty good, and her Spanish is excellent.' His hand played lovingly with Moira's braids.

'But you don't have a car.' Moira re-stated her proposition. 'I looked outside. All you got—all you have is a bicycle.'

'You just didn't look in the barn behind the house,' Molly chided. 'I have a car. Well, maybe that's too strong a word—it's not much of a car. But that makes it all the easier for me to buy a better car, doesn't it?' She sniffed disdainfully as the pair of them stared at her.

'Female logic,' Tim declaimed pompously. 'Come to think of it, your Aunt Molly always did follow a twisted path in reasoning.'

'I don't understand, Daddy.'

'Chauvinist,' Molly muttered under her breath.

'That's what I said,' he chuckled. 'Eat your breakfast. What kind of a car do you want, Molly?'

'A two-door red one,' she replied, toying with her own eggs. Over the course of the last years she had become a non-breakfast eater, subsisting on innumerable cups of coffee until lunchtime, but now she felt the need to share.

'That's all your requirement?'

She glared at his grin, feeling more at home now that she and Tim were off in one of their continuing arguments.

'Of course that's all,' she said slowly, accentuating every word so even the stupid might hear. 'What more would I want? I like a two-door car because you can put little people in the back without worrying that they'll get out of the doors. I want a red one so people can see me coming. What else?'

'What about horse-power and brakes and steering?'

'What about it?' She got up to clear the dishes. 'I only want it to go. I don't care how *much* it goes. If it stops going I'll just find some man who knows all about things like that and I'll bat my eyes at him, and he'll fix it. You taking notes, Moira? Like this.'

She knelt down beside the girl's chair and slowly fluttered her eyelids. The little girl chortled and tried an imitation.

'All right now,' Tim objected, 'Don't start teaching my daughter that sort of thing!'

Molly dissolved in laughter, and almost dropped the plates. Luckily they were ironware, the sort that just won't break when dropped. Moira followed her over to the sink with a couple of saucers. One slipped out of her hand and splattered into a thousand pieces. Shag, who had been lying in the corner, got up slowly and stalked indignantly out of the way.

'Oh my!' said the child, and ducked her head. Molly tilted her chin back up with one finger.

'I never did like that saucer anyway,' she said distinctly. Moira smiled back up at her. Beamed, rather. A connection had been established.

The rain had stopped and the fog had cleared by the time they started out on their shopping trip. A little weather warning, Molly explained to the child. 'Yesterday it was chilly, today started out with rain—before we know it we'll be up to our briskets in snow. Cape Ann is not the kindest place in the winter world.'

'Where's my brisket?' She knows and she's teasing me, Molly decided. Score one for our side. She's more like her dad than ever I thought!

'Oh, that's the place just above the part that you sit on,' she explained solemnly, then stole a look and caught the little smile as she drove down through the village and along Hesperus Avenue, heading for the big city. This child is older and smarter than she ought to be, Molly thought. Seven and a half, going on eight? All her front adult teeth are in; she understands a great deal more than her father gives her credit for. This is getting to be like a Dorothy L. Sayers novel; there are mysteries within mysteries, and I'd better pay some attention to my driving!

There was not much need to choose a subject for conversation. Hesperus Avenue ran just inland from the coast, through an avenue of trees, most of them stripped of their leaves. But there was enough green cover to fill out a beautiful bucolic picture. That was, until Moira, peering out of the window to her right, spotted the twin towers of Hammond Castle. The sight shook her out of her reserve.

'A real castle, Aunt Molly!' she gasped in surprise.

'Well, not exactly real,' laughed Molly. 'Not if you mean as in knights in armour and medieval maidens, and all that. It was built by John Hammond as his home, back in the late 1920s. Mr Hammond was the inventor of FM radio. We'll come and see round it some day.'

'That's a promise?' the little girl asked wistfully. She sounded as if promises were not much kept in her short life, Molly thought, and a little pain struck her at the thought. She was quiet as they turned into Western Avenue, and thus around the western harbour and down into the centre of Gloucester.

Molly might have had some trouble buying the car she wanted. Two salesmen were prepared to give her some

argument until she mustered the magic words, 'For cash.'
So she and Moira drove away in less than an hour in a
little red four-wheel-drive Bronco 11, heading back
towards Magnolia.

'And here we are,' she smiled as she parked on
Lexington Avenue in the village.

'Yes,' the child returned doubtfully as she squirmed out
of the high seat and looked cautiously up and down the
single block of stores that marked the village centre. 'I
thought you said we were going to the shopping area.'

'Believe it,' grinned Molly as she slid out on to the
pavement. 'This is it—the finest block of stores in
Magnolia. In fact, the *only* block of stores in Magnolia.
Shag, guard the car!'

The dog made a magnificent defender as he sat up on
the front seat and let his heavy muzzle hang over the side
of the open window. Strangers walking down the road
veered away at the sight of him, not knowing that he was
a spiritual brother of Ferdinand the Bull.

And so the two went, hand in hand, like the best of
friends, down to Ina's to find something to suit the child.
Another surprise for Molly: little Miss Holland knew
exactly what she wanted, and got it. Jeans that met the
modern style; dresses that both fitted and were attractive.
And underwear. And how Moira revelled in the
underwear department!

The last stop on the trip was the Star Market, out on
Route 1A, where numberless sacks of groceries required
the help of one of the bag boys, and the little car was
comfortably full.

'It must of cost a lot,' Moira commented ruefully as
she tried to find a space to sit.

'You don't want to know,' Molly answered firmly.
'Sufficient unto the day is the evil thereof. That's from

the Bible. I'm not sure what it means.'

'You know what it means,' the little girl—suddenly adult again—said. 'You know everything. You can fool my daddy, but you can't fool me.' Her little head cocked to one side as she studied her new aunt solemnly.

'Have you been in love with him for a long time?'

'In love with whom?' asked Molly, stalling for time.

'With my dad,' the girl sighed in exasperation.

'Bite your tongue,' Molly muttered savagely, and ground the gears as she headed back to the house.

He was waiting for them outside under the grape arbour when they drove up. Proud of herself and her car, Molly applied the brakes a little too strongly, and skidded to a halt in a cloud of dust and pebbles.

'Hiyo, Silver.' Tim touched a finger to the brim of his hat in a sort of salute as he leaned over into the car. 'Red. It certainly is red!'

'Unnecessarily smart remarks will leave you without lunch,' Molly snapped. 'There are packages to be carried.'

'And I suppose I'm the *carrier*?' He tilted his hat back on his head and grinned.

'Was there any doubt?' she answered primly. 'Why else would any sensible woman want a man around the house?'

'Why indeed?' he agreed as he lifted his daughter out from between all the packages.

'Don't forget carrying out the garbage,' the young lady interjected. 'That's another thing men are good for.'

'I can see this is going to be a hard winter,' Tim laughed as he set the girl down on the ground, pointed her towards the house, and patted her bottom to urge her on.

They both watched as the child skipped towards the

house. Shag, ambling along beside her, looked to be twice as large as Moira, and his ancient tail was wagging in time with her gabbing. Molly stiffened as Tim's arm came around her shoulder, then she forced herself to relax. He hardly seemed to notice.

'Buy anything besides the car?' he teased.

'Groceries,' she said very firmly. 'We have to eat.'

'Yes, and I expect to pay for the eating,' he replied.

'I don't——' she started.

'But I do,' he interrupted. His strong hand squeezed her shoulder, and a little shiver ran up her spine. 'How much do you think you'll need for a month?'

His hand moved away as he fished in the pocket of his jeans for his wallet. She missed the warmth of it instantly. 'I haven't the faintest idea, Tim. I've never budgeted for a fam—for a group, before. I've got plenty of money. Let's let it run for a month and then we can square accounts.'

'You're sure?' Those dark blue eyes stared into her green ones. 'This place doesn't look all *that* prosperous.'

'I'm not a charity case,' she snapped. 'Don't judge by the amount of painting that needs to be done. That's because you can't hire a house-painter for any amount of money these days!'

'Hey, whoa!' Both hands were back on her indignant shoulders. 'I'm not trying to insult you, Molly. So you're doing well. I'm glad for you. And whatever it is you want, we'll do it *your* way.'

She came back down to earth with a thump. Why in the world should I get angry with Tim about money? she thought. Or about anything, for that matter? He's a good man. Just because he can't see beyond the end of his nose there's no reason for me to cloud up and storm all over him! And his daughter is a lovely child, and it's going to be a long cold winter, and I'm lucky to have the company, aren't I?

'Yes, well—I'm sorry I snapped at you,' she sighed. 'And I can't ever remember you giving up an argument so easily. Now, how about moving the groceries?'

'After we have a small talk, away from prying ears,' he coaxed. That warm arm came around her shoulders again. But it's only friendship, she warned herself. He doesn't really think about me as a—female. She gritted her teeth and moved at his urging, out under the grape arbour that hugged the south side of the house.

'Picked every single grape, I see,' mused Tim, and her temper flared. This wasn't what she wanted to talk about!

'No such thing,' she snapped, then relented. Dear lord, he was Tim, not some bum like Alfred DeMoins. So maybe he was blind, but—the thought brought a little smile to her face as she readjusted her glasses. 'No,' she said more softly. 'I left everything on the vine until after the first frost. That's what the Germans do, you know. It improves the wine. They call it *spätlese*. Only a flock of starlings ganged up on me. There must have been over a hundred of them, and they stripped the arbour in two days, before the frost could come. Now, what was it you wanted to talk about?'

'Over here,' he said, and guided her to the end of the arbour, and the crooked-legged old bench that *he* had built for her when she was eleven years old. He patted it affectionately. Molly pulled her coat closer around her and settled back.

'It's about Moira and you and me,' he said, joining her on the rough planks. The short leg dipped under his weight and she slid the inch or two down the incline that put her thigh hard up against his. Not a bad start, she told herself as she made an effort to move an inch away. Moira first, and I'm second. Or better still, I'm in the middle, between Moira and Tim. That's nice. But it's only a dream.

'I'm listening,' she urged. The sun was up and full, shining every bit of power it had on the south side of the house. But still, it was late November, and although old Sol was doing its best it was a bleak effort. A little shiver ran down her spine as Tim draped one arm casually around her shoulders.

'I want you to understand,' he said softly. 'In everything I do, Moira comes first. I need a great deal of money to be sure that *she* goes first-class. If I can't buy her a cure, I *can* buy her a comfortable life.'

'I understand, Tim.' Almost unconsciously her head tilted sideways and landed on his broad shoulder.

'So, for the next three or four months I'm going to play shark in the money sea, Molly. It'll take me all hours of the day and night. I expect it will throw me in with some strange bedfellows, and I know I'll have to skirt the edges of some laws—from your viewpoint, I suppose it might even occasionally look like a dirty pool. But I'm going to do it.'

It was a great deal to think about, and Molly could hardly reason past 'strange bedfellows'. Only a cliché, of course, but it struck her at a vulnerable point. 'You mustn't go so far that she won't recognise who you are,' she returned. 'It wouldn't be much fun discovering that your father is a shark—even if a civilised one.'

'You object?' Cold, bitter words, almost as if he had bitten each one before he spat it out.

'I don't object, Tim,' she said firmly. 'I don't have the right to object. Just tell me what you want me to do about Moira.'

'A great deal,' he offered, squeezing her shoulder. 'I

want you to mother her for me until springtime.'

'Mother her? Almost any woman could do that.'

'That's not true,' he grumbled. 'Lord knows I've tried enough different types of women to do just that, and none of them was a success. Moira's been battered from pillar to post—mentally, that is—from the number of substitute mothers she's had.'

And there I go, Molly told herself glumly. Just the current substitute, in a long line of women. I'd like to hit him right on his nose—if I dared.

'I think I can tell you your biggest mistake,' she said cautiously. He cocked his head and looked down at her. 'If you'd selected a woman *just* to be Moira's mother you wouldn't have had all those problems. But I'll bet you couldn't leave it at that, Tim. You had to drag them into your bed, didn't you!'

'Hey,' he objected, 'cool down!' He had a temper of his own, as well she remembered. Molly moved away from him an inch or two. 'No, I didn't *drag* any of them into my bed. But I sure had a tough time keeping them *out* of it.' One of his fists banged into the other as he took out his frustration on himself. 'What I need is a motherly person who doesn't look at me as a sex object!' Again that fist slapping into the palm of his hand. Molly's heart fell clear through her boots.

'But you don't really know anything about me, Tim,' she protested weakly. 'I haven't been sitting here on this bench for all those years just waiting for you to pop up!'

'Hey, I know all about you,' he grinned. 'All about how you grew up—and out—and got your degree, and won the state's Teacher of the Year Award for being the best Special Education teacher——'

'Twice in a row,' she interjected, thinking, well, it's not often that a girl gets to blow her own horn!

'Twice in a row?' He squeezed her gently. 'Aunt Gerda forgot that part.'

'Ah, Aunt Gerda.' Molly grinned. 'The Great Seer, who sees all, knows all, tells all—and the only decent human being in the Holland family!'

'You've got the lady just right,' he agreed. 'She's been writing to me once a month, through all these years. And in fact she——' He stopped, looking like a man whose tongue has just overrun his common sense.

'In fact she what?' she demanded.

He shrugged his shoulders and gave her that lopsided grin which, she knew from experience, signified that he didn't intend to say another word on *that* subject.

'Funny,' Molly mused, 'I've heard a lot from your aunt Gerda too. In fact, I've been down to her place in Framingham a few times, when I needed a refuge.'

'Oh? Refuge? That's something she never mentioned.'

'Well, thank the lord for that!' sighed Molly. 'But anyway, you were talking to Aunt Gerda, and she said something, and that's when you thought about Molly Patterson,' she stated challengingly.

'And that's when I thought of Molly Patterson,' he agreed. 'Will you fill in for me until springtime?'

Yes, certainly, she wanted to say. I'll be glad to mother your daughter. But I'm not saying that, some time in the dark of winter, I might not poison you, Tim Holland. Or dump you in boiling oil, or push you off the cliffs! Damn you, man, can't you see what's in front of your eyes?

She struggled with herself, her back turned quickly in his direction to mask the anguish. Her voice was perceptibly weaker as she turned around again. 'And after springtime, then what?' It was a question she *had* to ask, but didn't want to. Or rather it was the *answer* that she didn't want to hear.

'After that, I suppose we'll have to reassess the situation,' Tim said sombrely. 'Is that asking too much, friend Molly?'

'No, lord, no.' She hurried her answer, wanting to get it in before he had a change of mind. 'But you know that in every family there has to be discipline?'

'I'll take care of that part,' he said grimly. 'You just do the happiness bit; I'll do the rest. And I pay all the expenses. You won't be able to do whatever you usually do for a living.'

'I'm a schoolteacher by trade,' she reminded him. 'But, as they say in the theatre, I'm resting at the moment.'

'So I'll throw in a salary too,' he insisted. Molly squirmed around on the seat, reached up, and pulled his stubborn chin around.

'I'm doing this for friendship, Tim Holland,' she declared angrily. 'If I were doing it for money, you couldn't afford me.'

'Hey, take it easy, Moll! I just thought——'

'Remember the time you and Jackie ruined my best doll?' she asked ominously as she struggled out of his grasp and stood up in front of him.

'Well now,' he drawled, a big smile on his face, 'as I remember, you got Jackie down and kicked one of his teeth out, and then you——'

'How would you like *another* black eye, Timothy Holland?' she interrupted, balling up her fist in front of his nose.

He was up, locking her fist in one capable hand, before she could catch a breath. Somehow or another both his hands moved to her shoulders, then around her back as he pulled her hard up against him. 'And do *you* remember what happened right after that?' he whispered in her ear.

'I don't recall,' she maintained angrily as she struggled

to escape his grasp.

'Try this on for size,' he muttered, and his warm, moist lips were on hers, drawing her out from herself. His tongue probed at her, and she could feel the surge of tingling emotion that spread out from her midriff into every portion of her body. For a long minute Tim crushed her to him, as eager as any swain could be. For a long moment the sky behind her closed eyelids flashed with rocket explosions. Then he put her gently away.

'I—don't remember anything like that,' she gasped as she leaned her head under his chin.

'No,' he agreed, and there was an odd tone to his voice, 'I don't remember it being just exactly that way either.' Molly couldn't see his face, or the puzzled expression that flitted across his brow.

'What was you two doing out there all that time?' Moira enquired as her father brought in the last of the groceries.

'Talking,' Tim returned. 'Grown-up talk.'

'It sure didn't look like talking,' his daughter giggled. 'Although it was pretty hard to see clearly from the kitchen window. I had to climb up on a chair to see out the top part! Aunt Molly, did you know your windows were that dirty?'

'How would you like to clean them all?' her father threatened. 'All we need around these parts is a little snoop! Help your aunt put the groceries away!'

'You gotta help,' the little girl laughed as she dodged him by running around the table. 'Molly's making lunch, and I can't reach all the shelves, so you'll——'

'Oh, great,' he grumbled as he set to work. The pair of them made a game of it. Molly, whipping up an egg salad for luncheon sandwiches, followed them with her eyes and felt just a little twinge of jealousy.

Moira should have been *my* daughter, she told herself as she took down a can of soup and began warming it. What a fine family we'd make! There, I said it—well, at least I thought it. Family! But why am I getting so—angry? I've been a day late and a dollar short all through my life. I wonder if I'm too late to strangle Susan? Come to think of it, he never mentioned if they were divorced!

As a result of her little conversation with herself she thumped the plates down on the table in front of the pair of them, and managed to spill more than a little of the mushroom soup on to Tim's lap.

'Hey, that's hot!' he protested. His daughter glared at him, and probably kicked him under the table, Molly thought, because he swallowed the rest of his protests, manufactured an injured smile, and picked up his spoon.

'My fault,' Molly admitted. 'I was thinking about something, and——'

'Something bad?' Moira squirmed in her seat, those brown eyes tracking Molly's every move.

'Well, for a fact,' said Molly, 'it was something rather nice. I thought I was strangling my worst enemy!'

'Ooh——'

'Hush up, baby,' her father interjected. 'It might have been me she was thinking about. Or you.'

'Never you, Moira.' But Molly was not about to offer any soothing for Tim, and his quick mind caught it up instantly. The rest of the meal passed in comparative safety, as Moira told him, in excruciating detail, about their morning shopping trip.

'And then there was this castle, Dad.' The little girl was full of life as she did her best to describe it all. Until, at the end, 'Aunt Molly, did you ever dream about bein' a princess and livin' in a castle?'

Caught unawares, Molly blushed. What to answer? Certainly not the truth. Tell her yes, but my knight ran off with the other woman? 'I hadn't given it much thought,' she lied brightly. But Tim's eyes were following her, staring, questioning. She shrugged her shoulders.

'Your aunt Molly was always a practical person,' Tim told his daughter. 'She didn't have much time for that romantic stuff.'

'And you believe that . . .?' his daughter sighed.

Tim waited around downstairs, remembering that little remark, until the two females went up 'to make the beds', Molly had said. When he was sure they were out of sight he picked up the telephone. The Framingham number was engraved on his mind, so he had no need for a book. And his aunt Gerda answered on the second ring.

'Tim? I hadn't expected to hear from you so quickly, nephew. Well?'

'I'm not sure that it's all that well, Gerda,' he replied softly. 'We're in—the pair of them are upstairs housekeeping. Molly has taken to Moira, I can see that.'

'I told you she would,' the chief schemer of the Holland family told him. 'A real softy, Molly Patterson is.'

'Maybe,' he sighed. 'About kids and dogs and lost causes. But I'm not so sure that Tim Holland rates on her list any more. I've tried a couple of—well, they didn't work out at all. She's bound and determined to be my best friend—and that's all. I can see that written all over her face every time I try to get too close.'

'Early days yet,' his aunt advised. 'You can't expect to recover all the ground you've lost in ten years, Timothy. I told you and told you what a fool you were being, but you wouldn't listen, would you? Well, now you'll just have to play it my way.'

'I wish I were as sure as you are,' he admitted. 'She's

just as lovely and desirable and warm as ever she was before, and I'm having a hard time *not* telling her—or keeping my hands off her. Are you sure, Aunt Gerda?'

'I'm sure,' his aunt replied. 'Just remember all the experience I've had.' For the life of him, Tim had trouble recalling. His aunt Gerda had contracted a young and foolish marriage, and only the quick death of the man she had chosen had kept him from running through her entire inheritance. Two years of wedded non-bliss. Did that qualify her as an expert? But then, considering how poorly he had done for himself, Tim shrugged his shoulders. Anybody in the world could know more about love and marriage than Tim Holland did. His one encounter with Susan had shaken his confidence about women completely.

'Well, all right,' he agreed reluctantly. 'I'll keep it up. Slow and easy wins the race?'

'Propinquity, that's what does it,' his aunt assured him. 'Keep your mouth shut and your ears open, and be noticeable. Got it? Now hang up before she gets suspicious! And next time, call me from a phone booth. When she gets her monthly bill she'll see this call listed, idiot!'

'Yes—yes, ma'am,' he replied, but his aunt had already hung up. He put the instrument down, feeling about as unsure a conspirator as Brutus must have been the night before Julius Caesar was murdered!

CHAPTER THREE

GLOUCESTER, with some twenty-seven thousand inhabitants, is neither the largest nor the oldest city in Massachusetts, yet it has always had an important place in the scheme of things. It huddles around the shallow waters of Gloucester harbour, protected from the harsh Atlantic by Eastern Point. Like many Yankee cities, it is surrounded by others: Essex, Rockport, Manchester-by-the-Sea. And it incorporates the tiny village of Magnolia, like bait at the end of a long fishing line. The city sits by the sea, and draws its life from the fishing fleet. Not a deepwater fleet, such as home ports like New Bedford, but rather the inshore fleet, the smaller boats. Fishing is an industry that has been sick for years, and Gloucester looks it.

The two of them, Moira and Molly, had made the short trip up the shore road again, wandered through the maze of streets in the centre, and finally parked illegally on Pleasant Street, across from St Agnes. The church and the parish school, that was. For some reason it all looks smaller than it did, Molly thought as she scanned the old building. And older. Can it really be twenty years since Tim and I both went to school here? Dear lord!

'It's sort of scary.' Moira, her happy chatter overawed, clutched at Molly's hand and moved closer. 'I wish my dad could of come.'

'Could have,' Molly agreed. 'And your dad was up and out of the house by seven o'clock. You have to keep up your self-confidence, Moira. All the people in this

47

building are nice people, and they all want to help. Besides, your dad is down in Beantown now, wrestling with the bears of Wall Street.'

'Bears? I thought he was in the fishing business?' The little head cocked to one side as the child looked up at her. Watch your tongue, Molly warned herself. She's smarter than you are!

'It's just an old phrase people use when they talk about the Stock Market.' She fumbled for a better explanation as she led Moira in through the double doors and down the corridor to the Principal's office. 'You should have seen how scared *I* was when my mother brought me here. But Tim—your father—was already enrolled, so——'

'And so you were both the nicest students in the school?'

Molly almost choked. 'Er—yes, of course,' she lied heartily. 'We—were the very model of outstanding students. Yes, your father and I—well!'

Sister Alice was standing at her open door as they came around the corner. The elderly lady, barely five feet tall, plump, spry, with the marks of forty years of teaching on her face, was dressed in a serviceable brown street dress, with a wooden cross suspended around her neck on a leather thong. She put out both her hands towards Molly.

'I'm sure you don't remember me,' Molly started to say, when the nun began to laugh, then covered her mouth with one hand as she waved them both into her office.

'Molly Patterson,' Sister mused as she settled into the big chair behind the desk. 'I knew it had to be Molly Patterson. I was looking out of the window when you got out of your car, and the moment I saw that hair——Well, little Molly, all grown up, and bringing your daughter to us?'

'Er—not exactly,' Molly sputtered. 'I—I don't

suppose you remember Timmy Holland? I——'

'Of course,' the nun chuckled. 'The Terrible Duo. How could I forget?'

'You knew my dad?' Moira's reserve was overcome by the magic word—dad. She wriggled off her chair and went over to the desk. 'He came to this school too?'

'So—Tim Holland's girl. Come around here to the light and let me get a good look at you.' Sister Alice swivelled her chair around and took Moira's little face between her hands. 'Why, of course. I knew your dad, and——'

'Aunt Molly,' the child prompted.

'Aunt Molly, is it?' Sister Alice suppressed a sigh. 'I would have bet a fortune that Tim and Molly would have married. Lucky I'm not a betting woman!' The old hands gently caressed the child's blonde hair. 'Always in trouble, that pair. Your father was the ringleader, but he never re-alised that Molly's hair stood out a mile in any direction. Any time there was a commotion that head of red-gold hair could be seen, standing out in the crowd like a light-house. We always knew right away who the culprits were!'

'Trouble?' Moira looked astonished. 'Molly said they was—they were perfect students!'

Sister Alice rang a little hand-bell on her desk and squirmed back in her chair, her tiny feet dangling, unable to reach the floor. 'I've always meant to get this chair lowered,' the nun commented. 'But then I thought it was a temporary job, so—yes, of course,' she agreed amiably. 'Perfect students, your father and your aunt. Yes, I recall that now.'

A senior girl student came in from the Administrative office. 'Althea,' the Principal said gently, 'this is——' she looked down at the paper that Molly had placed in the middle of the desk '——Moira Holland, who is considering entering our school. Would you show her around the building while her mother—I beg your pardon—while her aunt and I have a talk?'

Moira went reluctantly, holding the hand of her preceptor, and looking back over her shoulder appealingly at Molly. 'Now then,' Sister Alice said briskly, 'to business. You said on the telephone that she was a special interest child?'

'She has a hearing problem,' said Molly. 'One ear is totally deaf, in the other she requires a hearing aid about which she's very sensitive. She reads lips excellently.' All that was said gently, and then, unable to control her thoughts, 'It's a degenerative disease, Sister. I'm afraid there's no cure. I hope we can—damn! Excuse me, Sister, I seem to have gotten something in my eye.'

'Yes, I can see that,' the nun replied. 'I seem to have a problem myself. Degenerative?'

'Yes. Hereditary.'

'Does she know?'

'Yes, she knows. And seems so light-hearted about it all that I suspect she's all bundled up inside.'

'And may break down or out at any time,' the Principal mused.

'She might,' Molly sighed, 'but before it all happens, she needs to mix with others, to build up a larger vocabulary, to become adjusted to her peers. And I intend to teach her sign language!'

'And who better?' Sister commented. 'Now that I recall, there was something in the newspapers a year or more ago about you, Molly Patterson. Would you tell me something if I ask an impertinent question?'

'I suppose I would,' Molly said softly. Even though I don't know anything more about Moira, I suppose there may be something I forgot! But when the question came, it left her completely off course.

'Why is it that you and Timmy never married?'

'I——' Molly stood up stiffly, stared out of the windows and around the room before coming back to the smooth sweet face of the nun. 'I suppose,' she stammered, 'because he never asked me!'

'Well, I don't see Moira as a problem,' Sister replied after a long pause for reflection. 'Of course, we expect the parents to interest themselves in the school's work——'

'Timmy—oh dear,' Molly sighed. 'She hasn't a mother, you see——'

'I see perfectly,' the old nun chuckled. 'So Timmy Holland just brought her home and dumped her on you? Times haven't changed a bit!'

'It's not *exactly* like that,' Molly objected, then shrugged her shoulders as Sister Alice stared her down. 'Well yes, it's exactly like that. And there are more problems. They've been living in France, and the child has been educated——' She fumbled for the right word.

'Haphazardly?'

'The very word.' The two women smiled at each other. 'There aren't any school records. I have no idea what grade she would fit into. She's going to be eight very soon, but I——'

'No problem,' Sister assured her. 'We'll test her, then make an assignment. She's a lovely child. Behaviour problems?'

'Not that I know of,' Molly answered, then added, 'Well, she's very reserved. That's a tendency of children who are hard of hearing. And then you have to remember that she *is* Timmy's daughter, you know. I would suppose she——'

The Principal swung back and forth in her chair for a

moment, to work up momentum, then got to her feet, laughing. 'I understand entirely,' she smiled. 'She's Tim Holland's daughter and Molly Patterson is her aunt, and everyone knows that *they* were perfect students! But there is a price to pay, you know.'

'The tuition? I—Sister Alice, Tim doesn't know that I've brought Moira here, and I don't think he has—well, I suspect he has money problems. I'll pay for everything.'

'Of course there's that,' Sister sighed. 'And it gets more expensive every day. But that's not exactly what I meant, you know.'

'Then what?' Molly's brain raced through all the things she knew about St Agnes, and none of them added up to extremely high fees. The smile on the Sister Superior's face was too broad to be passed up.

'No, no,' Sister said. 'We require parents to participate in the school's activities. Usually it turns out to be the mother—or the aunt, if that applies. Especially if the aunt is the best Special Needs teacher in Massachusetts. It would be wonderful, Molly, if you might see your way clear to teach a class in sign language once a week?'

'Why, I—I didn't know you had that many handicapped,' Molly started to say, but the Principal held up a hand to stop her.

'If you mean physically handicapped,' she said softly, 'we have our share. But that's not what I have in mind. We need to sensitise our non-handicapped children to the needs of others, and learning sign language would be the ideal way. We can't afford to pay for a teacher of your calibre, Molly. Could you see your way clear to——'

'Of course,' Molly interrupted. 'Of course I could.' Soft-hearted Molly, she told herself. Everybody walks on Molly. But then when she looked up, Sister Alice was smiling so broadly, so warmly, that she realised immediately that one hour a week could hardly compare with the sacrifices that this tiny nun was making in *her* life.

Molly was still blushing as she drove home, leaving Moira behind for the day. A skein of high thin clouds had closed over the area, shutting out the sun. With that, the temperature was dropping fast. She detoured through the waterfront. Gulls were coming ashore to roost on the flat roofs of buildings, a sure sign that a storm was coming. A pair of fishing boats, their rigging heavily hung with ice, were doggedly ploughing up the channel. Molly shook her head. A hard way to make a living, fishing.

They were both home at Magnolia at six o'clock. Moira camped out on the living-room floor for a cartoon session in front of the television set. But Molly had the need for fresh air, for solitude, a chance to think. She slipped on her Fair Isle sweater under her heavy coat and strolled out in the twilight to the edge of the bluff.

Some long-ago Patterson had built a little wooden gazebo here at the edge of the cliff. With rails instead of walls, and a roof to keep off the weather, it provided the perfect observation post. From its north side a pair of haphazardly constructed wooden stairs zig-zagged their way down the cliff to the little patch of sandy beach where one or two boats could be tied up. Directly at her feet to the east, looking out over the Atlantic Ocean, were the three rocky islands that marked the entrance to Kettle Cove. A tiny boat, no longer than thirty feet, was re-setting lobster-pots in the cover itself, rushing to beat the knell of darkness.

Two immense stone crocks which once had held flowers guarded each side of the landward entrance to the gazebo. The flowers had long since gone and now the crocks served as outdoor garbage collectors. Molly patted the side of one of them with a cold hand. Her adventurous great-uncle Bill had brought them both back from Egypt at great cost as mementoes of the great Pharaonic culture, only to discover they had been manufactured in Brooklyn. But the Patterson family had always been like that; enthusiastic after causes, with perhaps too much warm-heartedness.

The skyscraper lights of Boston splashed a brilliant fluorescence into the darkling sky in competition with the cool winter moon that sat on the sea-horizon. With the coming of sunset the wind was preparing to shift, and for a moment a quiet calm lay over the bay and the headlands. The headlights of the Porsche outlined Molly as Tim drove up to the house. In a moment he was at her side.

Molly turned slightly to welcome him. He smiled back as he came up alongside and laid an arm around her shoulders. She barely suppressed the sigh of contentment, and leaned back against him, enjoying the clean warmth and strength. 'There's been a shortage of men for leaning on in these parts lately.' She rubbed her head gently into his shoulder, and the sigh escaped.

'Aha!' he laughed. 'I knew you missed me! Where's Moira?'

And that's all the attention I'm going to get, Molly told herself as she folded her arms across her stomach and moved an inch or two away. 'In the house, watching the tube. A black and white movie. I think it's called *Godzilla Eats the World*.'

'Hey, don't knock it!' His arm pulled her so that her back was against his chest, and now one of his arms rested on each shoulder, hugging her gently. 'I think we saw that flick ourselves a good many years ago, didn't we? You were always a sucker for horror movies! How did the day go?'

Molly needed a moment to fight back all the errant little

impulses that ran up and down her spine as she relaxed against him and his hands moved down to her waist and covered her own. 'Funny you should ask,' she said primly. 'Why didn't you tell me?'

'Why didn't I tell you what?'

'That Moira has never ever been to *any* school before?'

He was so close that she could feel his warm breath at her ear, and for a second she hoped he was going to nibble on the lobe. One of her fetishes, earlobe-nibbling. A girl could hardly expect to hang around for ten years without *some* experimenting. With regret, Molly acknowledged to herself that that was as far as it ever had got. But this was Tim, and he wasn't in a nibbling mood! Which earned him another sigh.

'You enrolled her in school? It never crossed my mind to say,' he admitted. There was just the slightest bit of apology in his voice, but no interest in her sighs. 'She's had a tutor all this time. Why? What happened?'

'Well, the guidance counsellor down at St Agnes gave her a battery of tests to decide in which grade they should start her, and her reading level is already at the ninth grade, Tim! And her other scores would make you stand up and cheer. I told Sister Alice she was almost eight years old, just about right for the third grade, but they put her in the fifth! I just hope it doesn't cause her any problems.' The silence of the sea enfolded them for a moment. 'Tim?'

'I heard.' He sounded so distant that she turned slightly in his arms, but his face was masked by the rapidly gathering night. He seemed to shake himself. 'I think she'll be OK. She's not only older than you think, but she's also older than the average child of her age. I'm more concerned about how *you* got along with her, Molly.'

'Me?' She twisted out of his arms and moved away, kicking at a pebble. 'I—we get along fine,' she said. 'It's getting chilly. Maybe we'd better go have some supper?'

'Good idea.' Tim took a step or two in her direction, blocking out the moonlight. Both his hands fell on her shoulders again as he pulled her close. Mesmerised, she watched his head move closer, blocking out more and more of the sky. The light was dim, but the little scar on his nose seemed to increase the closer it came. He's going to kiss me, she reasoned with alarm, and then I'm going to fall into little pieces, and heaven knows what I'll do!

He *did* kiss her—on the tip of her patrician little nose. 'Thanks, buddy,' he murmured. He was off towards the house in a loping run before she could muster up a word. Which was probably just as well, because all the words she could think of were hardly ladylike at all.

'Buddy,' she muttered under her breath as she regained her control. 'Boy, you've got something coming to you, Tim Holland! And you're going to get it any day soon, you just watch and see!' She was still nibbling on her full lower lip when she came up the stairs and into the house.

The pair of them were sitting on the floor in front of her twenty-six inch television screen when she banged the door behind her, stopped long enough to hang her sweater on the old coat rack by the door, and went straight into the kitchen. A few minutes later the music on the television programme swelled to a finale, and the pair of them tumbled into the kitchen like a pair of frolicking bear-cubs.

'What's for supper?' Moira carolled as she appropriated the best chair. Her father took the adjoining chair and both sat looking up expectantly at Molly.

When she turned around from the serving counter with two plates in her hand, and a grim expression on her face, all the smiles disappeared. 'Cornflakes,' she muttered as she slammed a plate down in front of each of them.

'But that's breakfast——' The little girl jumped as if someone might have kicked her ankle under the table. 'I—just love cornflakes,' she added timorously. 'Don't you, Dad?'

'Love them,' he agreed nervously. 'I really love—er—cornflakes.'

'I'm glad,' muttered Molly. But then the tension grew too high, and her right eye sprang a leak. She glared at the two of them and ran for the stairs.

She slammed into her room, stalked around its perimeter while she stanched the floodtide, then threw herself down on her bed, hands clasped under her head. She stared at the ceiling with her eyes closed. Funny, that. She could still see the crack that ran across the room from corner to corner, even with her eyes closed. Superimposed on the almost white background was Tim's laughing head, with both Molly's hands wrapped around his throat as she gleefully strangled him.

Her eyes snapped open. Don't stay here, she warned herself, and bounced to her feet. You'll only feel sorry for yourself, and you know how useless a thing *that* is. Her unguided feet carried her over to the little bench in front of her vanity table. One quick hand tore loose her braids; the other snatched up her hairbrush as she punished her scalp for its—and her—transgressions. Fifty slashing strokes, until her hair sparkled and her scalp tingled. Then she put the brush down, stared into the mirror, and thought.

Pure nonsense, she lectured herself. Pure unadulterated nonsense. He caught you off guard, and there you were trying to make a mountain out of a molehill. He didn't love you ten years ago, and he doesn't love you now. He laid

it all out on the line, but you, Little Miss Stupid, you have
to create the world's greatest romance out of a hug, and
then presume he's broken your heart just because you only
got kissed on the nose! Stupid!

It's gong to be a long winter. Either you help him out,
Girl Friday, according to *his* rules, or you might just as
well pack up, take your money out of the bank, and go to
Florida for the winter, just the way you'd originally
planned. Now what's it going to be?

Out of the maze of pains all Molly's pragmatic
attributes began to reassemble. She measured them one
by one. So you're still stuck on Tim Holland. Poor girl.
But if you play it his way, at least you'll know where he
is, won't you? You'll get to see him every day, right?
That's something you've not done lately. And maybe now
and again he might give you a brotherly little kiss? No,
don't think like that, Molly Patterson. That's a very
sarcastic approach to the problem.

Think, girl! What is it that you really want? Tim
Holland? Then stop being a drip, and start hunting him!
Gradually, of course. Give him a little time to adjust.
Then—then what? she asked herself angrily. So hunting
is the female approach. It's the lioness that makes the kill,
right. Just because you haven't any experience at hunting,
it doesn't mean you can't learn. There are hundreds of
books on the subject! Do a little better with your clothing;
make him notice that you're female. Then make him
jealous—how about that! Find some other man you can
flaunt in Tim's face. Someone like—oh, God, Alfred?

Shaking her head, Molly leaned forward towards the
mirror and inspected what she had to work with. Bright
golden hair with a red tinge to it, that curled when she
failed to discipline it. Midway down her back it ran riot.
Hardly anything to attract a man. Green eyes that always

seemed slightly out of focus. With a start she pulled her
spare pair of glasses out of the vanity drawer and put them
on. The thin, gamine face became instantly clearer, more
dignified. And the bridge of the spectacles covered the
line of freckles that were strung out across the base of her
nose. Strange how thin her face had become; at eighteen
her cheeks had been chubby, and the two dimples popped
in at the merest smile!

She pushed the glasses back up her nose with one
finger, then brought the finger down across her full red
lips, her sharp chin, as she leaned back. A short neck,
nothing to boast about there. Clear white skin, and
shoulders that sloped slightly, small breasts. Pert, Alfred
had said on that mad night, before she'd hit him. A good
handful, he had said, and she had hit him again and run!

Good legs, she assured herself as she stood up. Good
for running, that is. Slim thighs, swelling hips, a narrow
waist. Good lord, here I am going into the most important
battle of my life, weaponless!

She made a face at herself. Pull yourself together,
Molly Patterson, she ordered. Stop all this mooning, and
go downstairs and eat a little supper!

Getting away from the vanity mirror was the most
difficult of her many problems. She suddenly felt like an
old lady, fumbling to make her legs perform to command.
But after that difficulty, the rest was easy. She let her
shining hair hang free down her back, and went to check
her wardrobe.

As with almost any schoolteacher, her closet was filled
with dark slacks and replaceable blouses. Two
businesslike dresses, of course, for Parents' Night. One
slinky knee-length, just for devilry. One evening gown,
in case Sir Lancelot took a wrong turn off Highway 128.
Which didn't leave much choice.

With trembling hands she replaced her skirt and blouse with the very slinky dress, and walked slowly down the stairs.

The Hollands were still at the table in the kitchen, holding a family conference—which ceased the moment the door-hinge squeaked and Molly came in. She coughed a couple of times to clear her throat. It was hard to keep the colour from flooding her cheeks.

'I made a mistake in the menu,' she said gruffly. 'The cornflakes were for tomorrow. Tonight we have steak.' She had her back to them as she fumbled in the refrigerator. One quick look in the mirror over the sink showed that they were all smiles, although they said nothing. Neither of them noticed her slinky dress. So much for hunting the male, she told herself disgustedly. She bit her lip as she went on with the work.

Moments later, with the steaks in the broiler, she went back into the refrigerator again for her own meal.

'You're not having steak, Aunt Molly?' Moira had jumped down from the table and came over to her side. 'What's that?'

'Cornish hen,' muttered Molly as she set the little bird in a microwave dish and covered it.

'Cornish hen? I don't understand.'

Molly stopped her preparation and knelt to look the little girl squarely in the eye.

'It's a bird,' she explained slowly. 'It's as close as I can get.'

'To what?' Moira insisted. Her quick-witted father was making choking noises from his place at the table. When he finally managed to swallow and clear his throat he tapped the table a couple of times.

'Don't ask your aunt any more questions,' he managed to gasp. 'Come and sit down, Moira, before Molly burns the steaks!'

The steaks had not burned, although the rock-hen was somewhat underdone. Moira chattered away about school, and by the time the meal was over Molly was feeling just a little more normal. They all helped with the washing up, then decamped to the living-room. Moira already had homework, but it seemed more joke than labour, if one could judge from the giggles emanating from the corner where she was at work.

'And how was *your* day?' Molly asked softly. Tim looked over at her, sitting in her usual deep-cushioned chair, her knitting bag at her side.

'Always busy, Moll?' he replied. 'I remember that well. No matter what was going on, your hands were always busy.'

'And I remember well,' she chuckled, 'how skilful you were at evading questions! How was your day?'

'You're going to catch cold wearing that dress,' he commented.

'Timmy!'

'My day? Somewhere between awful and catastrophic,' he admitted ruefully. 'The freezer plant is working at half capacity, four of our boats are laid up, and there are all sorts of creditors snapping at my—feet.'

Molly coiled her feet up under her in the chair and picked up her needlepoint. Sympathy was one thing he didn't need at the moment, she told herself. 'About par for the course, then?' She gave him a wicked grin, which served to dispel his frown. He leaned back in his chair and winked at her.

'About par for the course,' he agreed. 'There's plenty of material to work with. All I need to do is stave off the creditors with one hand, and push the efficiency button with the other. Easy!'

'Well, I'm glad that's settled.' Her needle clicked as she followed the pattern with half her mind. 'Now we can deal with the important stuff, like Moira has to have some school uniform, and tell me something more about how your aunt Gerda is getting along, and is Captain Francis still aboard the *Ocean Princess*?'

In the lamplight Tim's face was half shadowed, but Molly would have sworn he hesitated and took a deep breath before he answered. 'Yes, of course she has to have school uniform,' he agreed pleasantly. 'So you order it!'

'I did.' It was hard to hide the laugh. Molly turned sideways in her chair to observe more fully. She had him in a corner, and had always loved to watch him try to wriggle out. 'And your aunt?'

'Well—er——' he hedged, 'I think Captain Francis has retired. In fact, so has *Ocean Princess*. We ought to look him up some time, I suppose.'

'Yes, I suppose so.' Molly manufactured an artificial sigh. 'He's such a good man. And he has a nice little house over in the village, on Flume Street, near the church. Now, about Aunt Gerda?'

'Well,' blustered Tim, 'if you knew all that, why were you asking me?' Typical Timmy, she thought. The best defence is a good offence. 'We really should go and visit him—you're right.'

'Best fleet manager in Gloucester,' Molly insisted. 'If *I* owned a fleet that was badly off I'd sure go ask for advice from someone who knows. Now, about Aunt Gerda?'

'I—advice. What a good idea, Molly! Captain Francis—why didn't I think of him! Don't you think it's time for Moira to get to bed?'

'Yes, right after we mention Aunt Gerda,' she

chuckled. 'Come on, Tim. You never *could* fool me with those evasive tactics. So she kept you informed about me during all those years. And then what?'

'Why would you want to know about her?' he demanded truculently.

'Because she's the finest relative you have, and the closest, and I always admired her, and she loves children, so why didn't you go to your aunt with Moira and your problem?'

'I couldn't,' he said solemnly. 'Aunt Gerda is suffering from a terminal disease that's completely incapacitated her. She's totally unable to take care of a little child. Especially a little handicapped child.' He turned his head in Molly's direction, flashed a solemn but soft smile, and looked her straight in the eye—a sure indication that he was lying like a sailor in a foreign port!

'She must have an active ghost.' Molly stabbed her needle into the work in front of her and set it down in her lap. 'She's sent me a birthday card every year, including this one.'

'Birthday——' Tim muttered, then recovered. 'Oh, of course! She arranged for that sort of thing through her lawyer, you know. I get one too. Lovely thought.'

'Lovely,' Molly agreed. 'Her lawyer must be a lovely lady. Her voice on the telephone sounded just like Aunt Gerda. She called me tonight, faker, wanting to know if I had any idea where you were!'

Tim collapsed in his chair, nonplussed. 'My aunt called you?'

'About five o'clock, Timothy. From her home in Framingham.'

'Oh, boy,' he grumbled, shaking his head in disgust. 'Nothing ever goes right, does it? Whom can you trust?'

'She tells me she offered you some—advice—a month ago.'

'Gave me some orders, you mean,' he groaned. 'Knocked me down, turned me inside out, and gave me some instructions.'

'Such as?'

'I—can't tell you that, Moll. It's her secret, and you know I wouldn't betray someone else's secret, would I?'

'No, of course not.' Molly managed another artificial sigh. 'But I suppose I can get it out of her in time. I invited her to come and spend the winter with us. She'll be along next week some time. And *now* I suppose it's time for little girls to hit the sack. Come on, Moira.'

As she walked out of the door she managed to catch one moment when Tim's face was directly in the lamplight. He wore the sombre frown of a boy who had stolen two apples and found them both green.

'You was teasing my dad,' the little girl accused Molly as they went up the stairs hand in hand.

'Guilty, Your Honour,' Molly admitted with a grin. 'I love to do that. Your father sometimes becomes pompous. He fills himself with ideas that he can't share with mere females. Obviously your great-aunt twisted his tail.'

'Did what?'

'Gave him a bad time,' Molly translated. 'Into the tub, love. Cleanliness is next to—I forget what.'

'You do not,' Moira answered solemnly. 'I don't think you ever forgot nothin' at all. Sister Alice said you was the best rememberer in the whole school in all her years of teaching. And that must be a lot, 'cause she taught you when you was a kid, and you're very old now.'

'Wash behind your ears,' her aunt Molly directed in very chilling tones. 'Very old, indeed!'

CHAPTER FOUR

AUNT GERDA arrived on Thanksgiving morning, the last Thursday in November, a national holiday in the United States, where feasting sometimes prevailed over thanks. She came early. Molly and Shag were waiting on the front porch, bundled against the threat of snow. Tim was still in bed; so was Moira.

The little lady, on the shady side of sixty, climbed out of her ancient limousine as if all her bones ached. She was no stranger to Cape Ann. Tim's aunt Gerda had been making this trip three or four times a year for, as she proclaimed, 'A weekend in the country.' Molly had repaid in kind by making an equal number of trips in the other direction each year. She and Gerda Messier were two of a kind, and on a first-name basis.

William, the seventy-year-old chauffeur, remained in his seat as was their custom when the little lady travelled. 'You go for your vacation now, Will,' Aunt Gerda lectured. 'Florida. I left you plenty of money. And put some of that eucalyptus oil on your arm. You hear me?'

'Aye,' the old man replied, even though they all knew he would almost certainly never comply. 'That stuff stinks, Gerda.'

'Stink or not, you put it on, or I'll—oh, good morning, Molly. I have to give Will his orders or he won't take care of himself.'

'Yes,' Molly agreed. 'And I'll just get your luggage while you do.'

The four suitcases in the boot were heavy. Molly,

despite her size, found she could not move their weight, hide her laughter, or sympathise properly as Gerda required with every tenth word. So instead she piled all the cases up just beside the porch step.

'And don't you dare forget to wear your flannels, Will!'

'In Florida?'

'Even in Florida. You have a weak chest.' And with that parting shot Aunt Gerda fluttered away from the car and waved. Will set the car in motion and zoomed away.

'I have such a hard time with Will,' sighed Gerda as she came over to Molly and stood on tiptoe to kiss her cheek. 'He needs managing, you know.'

'Doesn't everyone?' Molly laughed softly as she slipped her arm around her favourite visitor.

'Yes, I think you're right,' Gerda replied as she looked around with an estimating eye. 'Now, let me see what I have to do to get things organised around here!'

By now Molly was looking down at the little lady with a big grin on her face. There was no doubt about it, Aunt Gerda, flighty as a hive of honey bees with no queen, was filled with the compulsion to manage everything and everyone about her. And yet she looked such a gentle soul in her deep blue cloth coat, her little pillbox hat—and yes, even a muff!

'Now where's that good-for-nothing nephew of mine?' the little lady asked.

'Well, I honestly don't know,' said Molly. 'When last I heard, he was snoring away in bed. Come on in, Aunt Gerda, and let's have breakfast, shall we?'

'I didn't get this round by saying no to a good meal,' Aunt Gerda replied, patting herself amidships. 'And then we'll get that man out of bed and he can carry my luggage!'

'That's where I got that idea,' Molly told her. 'Men are meant for carrying things, right?'

'You never said a truer word,' Aunt Gerda replied solemnly. The pair of them marched up the stairs and paraded across to the kitchen. 'But I never expected *him* to move in on you, Molly. Shameful!'

'Oh, I don't mind,' Molly replied gently. 'It seems to me, over the years, that Tim was always moving in on someone!'

'If I'd known, Molly Patterson, I would have been down here like a shot! Imagine the gall of the man, alone in this house with you for weeks! Oh, for breakfast, I'd like something light, of course,' the little lady continued. 'I had toast and tea in Framingham, I do so hate to eat before a trip, especially a long trip. A weak stomach, you know. A family trait.'

'Of course,' Molly agreed, knowing from past experience that the Holland family was equipped with cast-iron stomachs. 'It must be all of twenty-five miles from here to Framingham. How about bacon and eggs, toast, coffee, orange juice?'

'Nice. But where's that great-niece of mine? I've never met the child.'

'You've never met the child?' Molly turned away from the coffee-pot and stared. Tim had hinted that Aunt Gerda knew everything there was to know about Moira. He had also taken evasive tactics when the subject came up again. To be specific, he had almost swallowed his Adam's apple trying to keep her from meeting Aunt Gerda again. Why? Obviously because the dear woman knows something that he doesn't want *me* to know, Molly thought. Which is why I invited her to come and stay with us! Two can play at this game, friend Timothy! And if I get out my shovel and dig deep enough, I'll find out!

Unfortunately for Molly, it was some time later before she found out that there were *more* than two players at the board.

Geared up to peer and pry, she had barely managed to get her mouth open when Moira came strolling into the kitchen, swinging an old tired Raggedy Ann doll by one arm. The little girl was combed and washed and neat, but still in one of the long nightgowns Molly had found for her on one of their many shopping expeditions. 'Look what I found!' the girl chirped.

'My goodness!' said Molly. And then, because in more than a week of hard work the child had mastered more than two hundred words and constructions in American Sign language, she clapped her hands for attention and signed, 'My favourite doll, love. And this is your great-aunt Gerda.'

'May I play with her?' the child signed back. Molly, half of whose mind was on the bacon, was startled into speech.

'Play with Aunt Gerda?'

'No, silly,' Moira laughed, 'with the doll!'

'What's going on here?' A baritone rumble. Tim was at the door, unshaven, hair not brushed, rubbing at his eyes with one knuckle. He looked them all over as if he had stumbled into a bunch of strangers.

Moira giggled. 'I love you,' she signed. Not to be outdone, Molly signed, 'I love you too,' and grinned at him expectantly.

He stretched, touching the top of the door with his upswept hands. 'Well, I can see you've both been studying hard,' he rumbled. 'And I suppose that little bit of fingering means good morning? Show me how you do it.'

'You guessed!' Molly jumped in first, before Moira

could give the right translation, and very solemnly demonstrated to his satisfaction. 'Breakfast?'

'Yeah, I——' he yawned, but Aunt Gerda had outwaited her patience.

'First things first,' she ordered. 'Timothy——' He made a face at the formality of it all. 'Timothy,' his aunt repeated firmly, 'Molly is making my breakfast. And she's making the Thanksgiving dinner too. So I think it only proper that you go outside and bring in my luggage before the snow starts.'

'But——'

'Good morning, Daddy,' his daughter grinned. He looked down at the child, then around the circle of feminine faces.

'Hooked, by God,' he muttered, and stumbled out of the room.

Aunt Gerda stared after him, shaking her head from side to side. 'What that man needs is a shave and a haircut and a good woman to take him in hand,' she said.

'That's true,' Moira commented solemnly.

'I believe you're right,' Molly said under her breath, but two pairs of eyes staring at her announced that they had heard. With a very self-satisfied look on her face Aunt Gerda assaulted her plate of bacon and eggs. Moira pulled up a chair beside her and watched her neat, gentle, but efficient dispatch of the food.

'Are you really my aunt?'

'Only one in existence,' Gerda announced between mouthfuls, and then, dating herself, 'You bet your bippie, kid!'

Molly, feeling a greater warmth in the room than she had first noticed, looked at the two of them carefully inspecting each other, feeling each other out, and smiled. Not just for them, but for herself too. In a place where joy is shared, there are often crumbs of happiness, even for outsiders. And who knows, she asked herself, how many members the Holland family might yet count?

Thanksgiving dinner was typically off schedule. They finally sat down to eat at three in the afternoon, 'Because that leaves more time for snacking later,' Aunt Gerda insisted. Molly, swept up in the tide of being managed, even in her own home, just laughed and agreed. Roast stuffed turkey was, of course, the entrée, done to a turn, surrounded by mashed potatoes, mashed turnips, carrots, peas, green salad, and cranberry sauce. And then three kinds of pie: blueberry, pumpkin, and apple, with real whipped cream. 'An' you have to eat it, Daddy,' Moira insisted. 'I whipped it all by myself!'

'So there's hope for you yet,' he laughed as he ruffled her hair. 'For the longest time I thought you were going to grow up to be a boy!'

'Oh, Daddy!' Accompanied by a long disgusted sigh, such as only a youngster could manage.

But with almost everything eaten, he had the colossal nerve to escape into the living-room with his daughter. 'To play chess,' he announced grandly. Molly sat at table, both elbows on it, looking around at the mass of left-overs, the mountains of dirty dishes, the oceans of pots and pans in the kitchen, and she sighed too. 'At least he might have offered to help with the dishes,' she grumbled.

Aunt Gerda, equally full, shook her head and grinned. 'A man?' she asked cynically. 'Doing dishes on Thanksgiving Day? You expect too much, Molly. Maybe in fifty years or so— but not in my lifetime. Come on, I'll give you a hand.'

Molly came wearily to her feet. In order to stuff and

slow-roast the turkey she had been up at six in the
morning. The pies had been made the night before. 'I
wonder how they managed on the first Thanksgiving,'
she mused.

'Wooden platters,' Gerda suggested. 'Everybody
brought something to the feast.'

'Yeah, but the women had to cook it,' Molly chided.
'Aunt Gerda, why did Tim come back home?'

'Why?' Hidden behind a big apron, Aunt Gerda
hesitated. 'Because he remembered the girl he left
behind?' she asked brightly.

'Oh, come on now. After all that time? I doubt if he
even remembered what I looked like. He said he talked
to you?'

'Big mouth, he is,' his aunt replied. 'Talks a lot. He's
continually running around with shoe-prints on his
tongue! Where does this go?'

'Right into the dishwasher,' Molly directed. 'Now, you
were saying?'

'I don't believe I was, was I?' the older woman asked
vaguely.

'But you were going to,' Molly insisted. She stopped
to wipe a drop of water from her eye, and so missed the
frantic expression on Aunt Gerda's face, as that lady
started out on one of the biggest lies of her life.

'Yes, of course, Molly. Well now.' Gerda pulled out a
kitchen chair and sat down. 'Yes. Tim telephoned me as
soon as he arrived back in the States. That would be
about—oh—three months ago.'

'That long ago?'

'Well, maybe not. You know, I'm not much good with
figures.'

'Funny,' Molly mused, 'I somehow had the idea that
he was just back from Europe, and came directly—I

guess I must have been mistaken. Go on.'

'Well, he explained about Moira's problems and asked my advice, and I remembered your write-up in the papers, about how good you were with deaf kids, so I mentioned your name and he decided to come and—and that's all I know.'

'And about the money, of course?' Molly prodded. Aunt Gerda looked startled, but quickly recovered.

'Oh—yes, of course. About the money. Did you want to freeze the rest of the turkey meat, or leave it out for snacks?'

Even a girl as dumb as I am can recognise that she's slammed the information door shut, Molly sighed to herself. 'Just leave it,' she said. 'It will all get eaten before nightfall, I suppose. Shall we join the others?'

Late that night, with Gerda and Moira both in bed, Molly came back downstairs. Tim was in the living-room, struggling with the sports section of the *Globe*. He looked up when she came in.

'Looks like the Red Sox are headed for last place next year,' he commented. Molly tendered a smile as she swept her skirts under her and sat down opposite him. As with all followers of the New England professional baseball team, it was always 'Wait till next year!' in the hot-stove league. But the Sox were not her major interest.

'I had a long talk with Gerda,' she announced. Tim winced and ducked behind his newspaper. She leaned forward and tugged at the bottom of it until he relented.

'Now,' Molly settled back in her chair, 'Gerda tells me that you asked for her advice about Moira and her problem, and that your aunt referred you to me. How come, Timmy, when we talked, you and I, it didn't come out quite that way?'

'I don't think I understand,' he sighed, setting his paper aside. 'What are you suggesting?'

'You gave me the impression that all this effort was because you'd lost all your money——'

'Well, not all of it,' he interrupted. 'Be fair! I didn't say all of it, Molly.'

She sniffed at him, but her eyes were blinded by that aura that had always affected her whenever she found herself within yards of Tim Holland. 'I suppose you didn't,' she continued firmly. 'But your aunt tells me that you came back from Europe, and you came up here, principally because of Moira's handicap.'

'Just speaking theoretically,' he asked cautiously, 'suppose that were true?'

'Oh, Tim! ' Molly was up out of her chair like a shot, settling in beside him on the couch. 'Don't you really see? You tell me it's all a money problem, when actually it's much more high-principled than that! Knowing that you've put that little girl first—that's important! It gives things a patina of morality that I can appreciate so much better!' It also earned a quick kiss for his cheek, which he in no way tried to avoid.

'Higher morality?' he mumbled. 'Yes, of course. I was——'

'Trying to hide it all behind a macho approach about dirty money,' she interjected. 'I like you better when you take the high road!'

'On the other hand,' he sighed, 'that just might be Molly Patterson, striving to think better about her friends than they deserve. Do you really like Moira?'

'Don't spoil my day,' she lectured. 'Yes, I really like Moira. It's not hard to love her, you know. It's my privilege to have her here—and you too, of course!' She blushed at the omission.

'Thanks for the enthusiasm,' he retorted wryly. 'What is that language you're teaching her?'

'American Sign language,' Molly explained. 'There are two types of sign used in the United Sates. The most popular one is called Signed English. It consists of a series of signs that support the standard English language, vocabulary and syntax. That's what you see on television, when somebody is speaking the words and making signs at the same time. But American Sign is different. It's a complete language with its own grammar, making an integrated whole. A person using Signed English has to know the spoken language beforehand—know it well, and that's hard if you're born deaf to begin with. With ASL you get the whole ball of wax, and can express yourself better.'

'And just how do you know all this?'

'Schools, practice—and more practice,' she teased. 'I'm not the same little girl you left, Tim. Time has passed for me too.'

'I know,' he said seriously, reaching out for one of her hands. 'But it's hard to accept the change. I guess I thought we could come home, you know, and everything could be as it was. Instead—maybe it's better!'

'Why, what a nice thing to say!' she laughed. 'Now *that's* something I'll have trouble getting accustomed to—gallant Timothy!'

'Try it, you'll love it,' he chuckled. He might have said something more, but at that moment Shag blundered into the room. The big dog, moving slowly as was his wont, carefully skirted the coffee-table, sat down in front of Molly, and whined.

'You need to go out?' Molly managed to free herself from Tim's grasp, and stood up. I wonder what else he might have said if we weren't interrupted, she reflected as she patted the dog's head. 'Out?'

Ordinarily Shag would have been at the back door instantly, but not this time. He pawed at her leg and whined again. It was not his regular drill, and Molly was worried. 'Out?' she repeated.

Shag sat back on his haunches and gave an exasperated little bark, then whined again. 'Trouble?' Molly asked. 'Go, Shag.'

It was the right command. The old dog yapped and headed towards the stairs, pausing at the door to be sure she was following. 'Back in a minute,' Molly tossed over her shoulder to Tim, and padded up the stairs behind the animal. The trail led them down the second-floor corridor to the very back of the house, and Moira's room. The door was closed.

Through the thickness of the old walls came the sound of someone crying. Molly grasped the knob of the door and walked into the darkness, Shag hard on her heels. Two strikes on me already, Molly told herself as she fumbled in the dark. No bell-lights, so the child can know someone wants to come in. And no night-lights. For a person with hearing handicaps, the lack of light means the lack of *any* communication.

The sobs were coming from the bed. Molly managed to find the reading lamp on the table beside the big four-poster, and snapped it on. Little Moira was sitting up, her hands clasped around her knees, crying her heart out.

The pain struck at Molly again. This little bundle of child, who had more burdens to bear than most, had completely stolen her heart. She knelt by the bed, crooning softly. The little girl might not have heard, but she toppled to one side in Molly's direction, until she fell straight into the warm arms which were reaching out a welcome.

'Aunt Molly?' Racked with sobs, the words barely came out.

'I'm here,' Molly whispered. 'I'm here.'

'Aunt Molly?' No explanation, no other words. With a sigh the tears came to an end, the little warm body wriggled closer, the little head rested on Molly's shoulder, and Moira went back to sleep.

But five minutes of kneeling in an awkward position put an unusual strain on Molly's back and shoulder. She tried to move to an easier position, but every change brought a whimper from Moira. Finally she gave up. In one quick move she stood up, picked up the warm little body, and settled it and herself down in the middle of the bed. The whimpers trailed off as the child slept. Molly, worn by a long day at hard labour, had intended to rest there only for a moment. Her eyelids were heavy, and when she let them drop, just for a minute, she was unable to recover.

Some twenty minutes later Tim came up the stairs, looking for the comfort and conversation he had expected. Two steps into the room demonstrated to him just how much of an outsider *he* was. Child and woman, they slept together, arms around each other, oblivious to the world.

'Molly?' he whispered tentatively. No answer.

'Molly,' he said softly, 'I wish you could love me as much as you love my daughter.' His face set in stern lines, he went back downstairs to test the quality of the brandy he had brought home from Boston.

CHAPTER FIVE

WINTER seized New England by the throat after Thanksgiving, and shook it until life almost came to a halt. Some eighteen inches of snow fell, in three different storms. By the time the city and the county had dug themselves out there were six-foot drifts along the sides of roads, and piled in odd corners. On the Wednesday before Christmas, the beginning of the school holidays, Molly had put in four hours of hard labour at St Agnes School. Three more partially deaf students had enrolled, and the entire school body was clamouring for sign-language instruction.

'I don't mind, if you think it will do some good,' Molly told Sister Alice.

'It's doing a great deal of good,' the Principal replied. 'Not only are they learning something practical, but they're also becoming more sensitive about other people's problems. I approve, Father Mulcahey approves——'

'And the Bishop?' Molly teased.

'And the Bishop *would* approve if someone ever told him about it,' Sister Alice said primly. 'Now, how can you go about it?'

'Very simply,' Molly explained. 'We'll use the old Mexican system, called Each one Teach one. I'll present classes to some of the seniors, they in turn will scatter, and each one will teach one of the other students.'

So for the first three weeks of December the scheme was applied. It raised the very devil with schedules, but none of the other teachers complained—in fact, most of them were learning for themselves. And then, on the Wednesday half-day, things had ground to a halt for the ten-day holidays.

'We're lucky,' said Moira cheerfully as she and Molly waded through the drifts and piled into the Bronco.

'Of course we are,' Molly agreed as she stepped into one drift deeper than her boots were high. 'Why?'

'Why? Well, because——' Moira laughed. 'Because we have four-wheel drive, among other things. And because it's Christmas—and because I'm famous! Oh, Aunt Molly!' She threw herself across the bench seat and wrapped her arms around her adopted aunt. Startled, Molly looked down. There were two tiny tears in the child's eyes.

'Crying?' She peeled off her thick mitten and pulled back the hood of the girl's heavy coat. 'Tears?'

'Happy tears,' Moira explained, wiping them away with the sleeve of her coat. 'Happy tears. I don't remember ever bein' so happy waiting for Christmas to come. And it's all your fault, Aunt Molly!'

'You're so happy you're crying, and it's all my fault?'

'So maybe I don't got—maybe I don't have the right words,' Moira sniffled. 'I didn't mean it was your *fault*, exactly. I meant you were the cause of it all, like. I mean——'

'I know,' Molly laughed. 'Don't try to explain it any further; ideas like that tend to get caught up in a mess. Leave it. But I *am* intrigued by the other part. You're famous?'

Moira flashed her patented wide-angle grin. 'I'm famous,' she averred. 'All over the school, everybody knows me—an' likes me, Aunt Molly. Would you believe that? I never knew so many kids before, and they all like me! I used to think that if a kid had one friend she was doing OK, you know, but there's hundreds of kids in that school——' the little girl paused to take a deep breath. '—and every one of them likes me!'

Molly started the engine, and waited for it to warm up before commenting. 'I think that's wonderful,' she said. 'You must have worked hard to gain their trust and all——'

Moira laughed. 'Me?' she gasped as she caught her breath. 'Not me! I'm famous because you're my aunt Molly! You're the one who's teaching lip-reading and sign language, and they like that, especially because to fit that in Sister Alice has had to cut down the spelling and the music classes!'

'Oh, me!' groaned Molly as she shifted into gear and started down Pleasant Street. 'You're famous because I've cut in on spelling!'

'Don't knock it,' the child said. 'You adults wouldn't really know about spelling and such.'

'Hey,' Molly objected as she swung the car down towards the docks. 'I was a kid once myself, you know. And in this very same school!' For the next few minutes she concentrated on her driving, but out of the corner of her eye she could see Moira solemnly shaking her head from side to side, as if denying that any present-day adult could ever really have been a child! But there was one thing very apparent. In the course of the last few weeks Moira had gradually lost some of her reserve—some of that shyness that followed handicapped children through their days.

Out of habit Molly drove down around the Harbour loop, then along the shore to the docks where the Holland Ocean Fisheries warehouses stood. As usual at the beginning of the Christmas season, most of the fleet was tied up. All eight boats of the Holland company were—eight? Molly brought the Bronco to a slipshod stop and counted again. Eight boats, thirty to fifty feet long, their decks covered with snow, their rigging a solid mass of ice. And only three weeks ago there had only been four Holland boats.

And there, coming along the sidewalk in his fisherman's rolling walk, was Captain Francis! Molly leaned across Moira and rolled the window down.

'Captain Ahab!' she called. Another local joke, calling the elderly captain by the name of the ship captain in the novel *Moby Dick*. He recognised her, made his way to the side of the car, and leaned in the open window. 'Well, I do declare,' the old man chuckled. 'Nobody's called me Ahab since——'

'I'm sorry,' Molly apologised. 'It's just an old bad habit. Have you met Moira Holland?'

'Ah!' One of his giant arms came through the window, and a rough sea-reddened hand swallowed up Moira's little paw. 'Tim's girl, hey?' After many years at sea, the Captain's conversational voice was just a little short of hurricane force. Moira nervously moved closer to Molly, but she said not a word as her hand was vigorously massaged.

'Yup,' the old man continued, 'ain't nobody called me Ahab since I took over the direction of the whole Holland fleet. Smart young man, your father, little miss.'

'You're scaring her half to death,' Molly told him. 'Took over the entire fleet, did you? When was that?'

'Ayup. About a month 'fore Thanksgiving, it were. Got me a call from Washington, from that young whippersnapper Tim Holland. Git your—oops, I can't say them words. Get yourself in gear, he sez to me, right on the telephone, and git over to the boats. I want to know how come we got more crew than fish! Mighty forceful, that man of yours, Miss Molly!'

A month before Thanksgiving? Long before I suggested the idea, he'd already taken steps. Suddenly deflated, Molly said defensively, 'He's not *my* man. But I'm glad you got the job. Couldn't happen to a smarter man!'

'Ayup.'

Doing her best not to giggle, Molly worked around to what she really wanted to know. 'So how come you have so many boats now?'

'Oh, them?' He waved a casual hand towards the fishing craft, tied up alongside each other. 'Ain't the half of it,' he chuckled. 'The *Barbara Anne*'s over on the other side. Just unloaded forty-three thousand pounds of mixed. And the *Theresa Marie*'s standing by to unload. They got about forty thousand pounds aboard!'

'But—I thought the company was——'

'Ain't never been in better shape,' Captain Francis chuckled. 'That Tim, he's about as sharp as his grandpa was, and tough as a nail. They don't make them kind no more!'

'No, they don't,' Molly commented as she rolled the window up and started off again. No, they don't. It's almost impossible to find a man with such a slippery tongue as Tim Holland's. The money's gone. Hah! Bankruptcy stares us in the face! Yeah! And we've put four more boats to sea, at least. Four boats!

'What did you say?' Moira was looking up at her, curiosity written in every pore.

'Nothing.' Molly shrugged. 'Starting to snow again. What say, shall we dash for home, or find a restaurant and have some lunch?'

'I vote for the restaurant,' Moira squealed. 'Then I

won't have to do the dishes!'

'What a lovely sentiment!' Molly chided. 'And instead we leave Aunt Gerda all alone in the house!'

'Only for a little while,' begged Moira. Molly found it impossible to avoid that lovely begging little face.

'All right,' she agreed. 'I'll call her from the restaurant.'

The car skidded as they turned back to East Main Street. In typical Yankee fashion there was no West Main Street. Instead, at the five points where East Main, Commercial, Rogers, and Washington Streets met up, the artery going westward was known as Western Avenue, a suitable compromise.

Because of the snow and the threat of more, half of Main Street was closed, but the sign on the Down-East Restaurant and its associated Oyster Bar was still lit. Molly managed to squeeze her car into a parking space someone else had shovelled—a terrible crime in Massachusetts—and hurried Moira inside. The sudden warmth, the homey atmosphere, struck them like a solid blow. They struggled out of their winter gear, then followed the manager to an empty table in the far corner.

'Now you see what you want to order,' Molly dictated, 'while I go and make that call to Aunt Gerda.'

'I *know* what I want,' Moira replied. But Molly was halfway across the room, heading for the telephone booths. There was some difficulty with the lines. Molly remembered driving north from Magnolia barely five hours earlier, and seeing the cables alongside the road bowing under the weight of snow and ice. Eventually, with the help of an operator, she made the contact.

'Don't worry about me' Aunt Gerda responded cheerfully. 'I've got my novel, and the house is nice and warm, and Shag is here to look after me. So you both stay and have a good time.'

All of which sent Molly back to the table in good spirits, only to find that the child had accumulated a pair of adult companions. The room was not brightly lit, and her glasses were fogged over, so it was not until she reached the table that Molly recognised Tim, carrying on a casual conversation with his daughter. He rose to greet Molly, and held her chair.

'This *is* a surprise,' he commented as he sat down between Molly and Moira. 'I thought surely the weather would keep you both home.'

'Not a chance,' his daughter said in a very subdued voice. 'There's always school, you know. And Aunt Molly is the best teacher there is!'

'Why, of course she is,' said the little woman sitting on Molly's other side. 'Always dependable Molly. Hello, Moll.'

By that time Molly had managed to get her eyes focused and her glasses off the ridge of her nose. Which was probably the best thing she could do as she stared—and felt her world fall into little pieces, like the snow melting off her coat collar. Her worst fear had come true.

'Hello, Susan,' she answered bleakly, and turned to stare at Tim with a haunted expression in her eyes.

'Susan and I have a family problem to work out,' Tim said cautiously.

'That's nice,' Molly said vaguely. 'That's nice. I——'

'Why, I haven't seen you since my wedding day,' Susan offered. There was all the comfort of a cobra about to strike, wrapped in her sharp soprano voice. 'Moira, did you know that Molly was my bridesmaid?' She might just as well have reached over and stabbed Molly in the back. And the little girl was not too comfortable either. She shifted and rocked in her chair for a moment, and then tried unobtrusively to slide it farther in her father's direction.

'Moira, your mother is talking to you,' Tim prodded gently. The child flared up.

'I don't have any mother,' the child snapped. 'I only got Aunt Molly!'

'That's enough of that,' her father reprimanded. 'Now, what would you two like for lunch?'

'I ain't hungry,' Moira said stubbornly, and looked an appeal across the table towards Molly.

'Come to think of it, I'm not hungry either,' Molly asserted. 'And it's beginning to snow very hard, and Aunt Gerda is all alone in the house, and I think we'd better——'

Tim's big hand caught her as she pushed her chair back. 'I know you're a lot of crazy things, but I've never known you to be a coward, Molly,' he said in an undertone. She shook her hand free.

'Then you haven't known me as well as you thought,' she muttered. 'I'm not going to sit here and—well, I'm not.' And then, in a tone of exaggerated deference, 'Would you wish your daughter to stay with you, or shall I take her along?'

'Oh, God,' Tim moaned. 'Why me, God?'

'So we'll have that cosy tête-à-tête after all,' Susan interrupted. 'But I did want to talk to my daughter, Timothy, love.'

'I'm gonna go with Molly,' said Moira, shoving her chair back abruptly. 'Why did you have to come and spoil everything?'

'Moira!' Tim commanded.

'Well, really, this doesn't boost your case at all!' snapped Susan. 'Such disgusting manners! She didn't behave like that in *my* care.'

'I don't think she could, seeing that you abandoned her before she could talk,' Tim said bitterly.

'Now, now, Timmy, we mustn't make nasty statements like that. Especially since *we* want something from Susan so very badly,' Susan retorted. 'I've changed my mind. Run along, Moira. Run along with your aunt Molly. And Molly, you really must do something with that hair. Even spinsters have to have some minimum care about their looks! Nothing to say?'

'Nothing,' seethed Molly. 'Nothing at all. Drink your coffee. It'll be good for you.' She stalked out of the room, struggling with her coat and scarf, with Moira close behind her.

The wind howled down the street, driving snowflakes in front of it. The car was cold, and gave trouble starting. Molly was cold, deep down inside her, where she stored all the cherished things of her life. Not a crowded place, but an important one. Susan back, she told herself as she waited for the motor to warm up. Susan back, and Tim has her. Even my life is back to re-runs. I might as well become a TV soap opera: *The Ten Loves of Molly Patterson*. Isn't it strange that they're all with the same man, and have the same ending? Is God trying to tell me something?

'Couldn't we go?' Moira interrupted. 'I'm cold!'

The trip along Western Avenue was nerve-racking. The roads had been ploughed twice in the last four days, but the falling snow was accumulating again, faster than the local Department of Public Works could move it. The Bronco, with its four-wheel drive engaged, held the crown of the road fairly well, and only an occasional vehicle coming in the other direction forced them off to one side. Magnolia looked like a winter postcard, with nothing stirring, as they switched to Hesperus Avenue and rumbled through the centre of the village and out the other side.

But the wandering road on the other side of Kettle Cove was a different matter entirely. Serving as it did only six or seven houses, it had received only one visit from the snow-ploughs. Their little car bucked and swerved and jumped, and for a time it looked as if they would never make it over the wooden bridge that spanned Colkers Creek, but they did.

'I've never seen anything so beautiful,' Moira commented as they pulled to a stop.

'Anything what?' Molly searched the area, and found nothing particular to note.

'I can't hear you so good.' Moira twisted around in her seat and stared directly at her. 'When I'm like in a car, or someplace where there's noise, my hearing aid picks up all the noises at once, and they sort of drown each other out.'

'That's ridiculous,' said Molly. 'There are half a dozen designs that filter out crowd noises. Expensive, but if your dad is running ten boats, he can afford them.'

'Well, don't get mad at me,' the child said in an injured tone. 'It's not my fault!'

'No indeed, it's not your fault, Moira. Now, what was the something that seemed so beautiful?'

'The house, silly. For the last two miles I was sure we were going to end up in a ditch. Even if the roof blows off, the house looks wonderful!'

'Oh, ye of little faith,' Molly laughed. 'Get in the house, kid!'

Shag met them at the door, followed at length by a startled Aunt Gerda, with a fried chicken leg in her hand. 'I thought you weren't coming,' the elderly lady said questioningly. She waved her chicken leg around like a conductor in the middle of *Messiah*.

'Well, we changed our minds,' Molly reported glumly. 'It was a——'

'They had something on the menu that we couldn't stomach,' Moira interrupted. 'Both of us. I mean, neither of us.'

'Whatever,' Molly concluded for her. 'Any more of that chicken left?'

'Comes frozen, in a package,' Aunt Gerda reported. 'All you have to do is slide a piece or two in the microwave. What do you think?' She waved vaguely in the direction of the Great Outdoors.

'I think we're working up to a blizzard,' said Molly. 'Have you been listening to the radio?'

'Funny you should ask.' Gerda led the way into the warm kitchen. 'Station WEEI claims a nor'easter is building up. They're predicting twelve to twenty inches of snow on top of what we already have.'

'What's that mean—a nor'easter?' Moira demanded to know.

'Just a big storm,' Molly explained. 'One that blows in out of the north-east, and has plenty of moisture picked up from the ocean. The worst kind of storm along these shores. And if their prediction is right, we could be snowed in.'

'Lucky that we stocked up the pantry yesterday,' Aunt Gerda said. 'Isn't there something else we——?'

'Several somethings,' Molly agreed morosely. 'Gerda, you check out the emergency lanterns and candles. Moira, you hop up to the bathroom and fill the tub with cold water—as high as you can, love. And I'll go around the house and get the shutters closed. We may have trouble with the electricity, and we could possibly have a problem with the wind. Scoot, Moira!'

The little girl ran off gleefully, glad to have something to do. Shag meandered along behind her, barely making the stairs. 'So now,' Aunt Gerda said quietly, 'the child is out of the way. What happened?'

Molly shrugged her shoulders. 'Something that's just par for the course for me,' she sighed. 'Every time I locate the tracks that the gravy train runs on, somebody cancels the schedule. We stopped in at the Down East Restaurant, and Tim walked in—you wouldn't believe.'

'I'd believe,' his aunt said grimly. 'I'd believe almost anything about that idiot nephew of mine. He was with someone?'

'He was with his wife,' Molly reported dolefully. 'Susan's back.'

'Oh, my God!'

'My thoughts exactly,' said Molly. 'You wouldn't believe how many fairy-tales I've been dreaming the past few weeks. I thought that pair were divorced!'

'Well, if it's any help to you, they are. You'd better get the shutters, Molly Patterson.'

By three o'clock that afternoon the old Patterson house was battened down, ready for almost anything. Almost, that was the word Molly used to herself, when the big yellow DPW snowplough made an unexpected visit, swiped a circle in front of the house, stopped long enough to let two figures out into the drifts, then ploughed its way back down to Route 127.

'Now what?' Moira came to the door and joined Molly, trying to peer out into the blowing snow. 'I can't believe any sane person would come calling at this hour of the day!'

'No, I guess you're right,' said Molly in stiff unbelief.

'It's your father. And he has someone with him!'

'I don't want to know,' the little girl groaned. 'Shag and I, we're going to go hide in your room, Aunt Molly. Please?' The appealing look again, wistful, begging. Almost Molly agreed, but then had second thoughts.

'Not in *my* room, young lady,' she admonished. 'I've got your Christmas present hidden in my room. If you *have* to be a coward, you——'

'Who's the coward?' Aunt Gerda came up behind them. The figures outside had united somehow or another, and were struggling up the steps to the porch, arm in arm, carrying a couple of suitcases.

'Nobody,' Moira answered glumly. Gerda moved to the door and swung it open. A blast of arctic air, smothered by more than a few snowflakes, flooded the living-room. Propelled by the wind, the pair stumbled in through the door, and it was immediately slammed shut behind them.

'Good lord!' Tim gasped. 'I haven't seen anything like this since the blizzard of '68!' He turned his companion around and began to brush the snow off her coat, and out of her hair. As she revolved under his caring hand, Susan giggled.

'Why, hello, Auntie Gerda,' she trilled. 'I haven't seen you in years! Do you remember me? Susan?'

'I should be so lucky,' muttered Gerda, and then more forcefully, 'Wipe your feet!'

'Well,' the little soprano voice said gleefully, 'not a thing's changed, Tim. Not a thing! And what a warm welcome. Tell them about us!'

Tim had shaken himself down, and was out of his heavy overcoat. 'It's Molly's house,' he said. 'We ask, not tell.'

'Oh, of course. Pardon me.' Divested of her outerwear, Susan was encased in a form-fitting scarlet cat-suit. She twirled around to give them all a good look. Tim's eyes seemed to follow the woman's every movement, Molly noted fiercely. Sickening, she told herself, as she struggled to maintain an outward calm. Sickening. Acts like a twelve-year-old, and wonders why people get angry. Listen to her gush! And why in the name of everything that's holy does she have to be so overwhelmingly beautiful!

Gerda directed Moira in the collection of coats and boots and scarves, while Tim brushed back his hair nervously and came over to where Molly waited, like some frozen statue.

'Susan just came in from Boston a couple of hours ago,' he explained. 'There doesn't seem to be any motel space available. Some sort of mini-convention is going on at the Marina Motor Inn, and all the rest of the motels seem to have accumulated stranded honeymooners and travelling salesmen. So I said to myself——'

'So you said to yourself, why not take her along to good old Molly's place,' Molly interrupted, forcing her voice to sound hospitable. 'And why not, Tim? Any friend of yours is a friend of mine, right?' She waved her finger in front of his nose, the finger with the scar from so long ago.

'Just so.' He broke out his number one grin, from ear to ear. 'So I said to Susan, I'm sure Molly would be happy to put you up for a few days—at least until after the Christmas season.'

Molly, who had never been very good at maths, did a quick study. Two days until Christmas, and then the twelve days to follow? Fourteen days? Two weeks? What was it her very Catholic mother used to say? *Sometimes God acts like a Protestant*! How can I stand it for that length of time? she thought.

But her New England conscience was not about to let her get away with such gibberish. Susan Holland is a guest in your house. It's the season to be merry! And stop moaning and groaning, Molly Patterson. Just because you came in second in the two-woman race for Tim Holland, it doesn't mean you can spend the rest of your life mooning around!

'Yes, of course,' she sighed. 'Of course, she's welcome for as long as she cares to stay. Come along into the kitchen, you two. It's warmer there, and we can have a cup of hot coffee——'

'Tea,' Susan insisted.

'——yes, tea,' Molly amended her statement. *What the devil was that stuff they poured in Socrates' cup*? She shook her head and led the way out into the other room, where Aunt Gerda, who only *looked* like a flighty woman, had made all the arrangements.

The wind seemed to be whistling louder and stronger around the house as they huddled around the kitchen table and watched while Gerda poured the coffee and tea from the same kettle spout. Instant miracles, with instant coffee and now instant tea as well. Susan made a face as she sipped at her mug, but evidently thought better of complaining when she saw Tim staring her down.

'I think we need a council of war,' he commented as he grounded his mug. 'We're in a pretty exposed situation up here on the bluff. What does the weatherman have to say?'

'Before our television antenna blew away, the Channel Four man predicted that the storm could last through the night and perhaps well into tomorrow,' said Gerda.

'And from the looks of things as we drove down from Gloucester,' Molly added, 'we're likely to be snowed in for three or four days.'

'Right through Christmas,' grumbled Moira, feeling sorry for herself.

'How else is St Nicholas going to get here?' her father teased.

'Phoo, who believes in *that*?' The child scraped back her chair and stomped over to the window. At barely four in the afternoon it was already dark outside.

'I'm glad to hear nobody believes,' Aunt Gerda chuckled. 'I can take the presents I bought back to Framingham when I go home.'

'I believe,' Tim said quietly. His daughter stared at him from the window seat, sniffed back a couple of tears, and ran from the room.

'Another display of bad manners,' Susan pointed out maliciously. 'There's no doubt about it, Tim, you haven't done a very good job of raising my daughter.'

He stared at her thoughtfully, as if carefully choosing his words. 'You shouldn't complain, Susan. You can't afford to.'

Whatever the words meant to the others, they struck Susan close to her heart. If she has one, Molly thought. The original ice-maiden!

'How about going on with our inventory?' said Tim. 'How are we fixed for food?'

'Plenty,' Molly reported. 'Perhaps not too fancy, but plenty. If everyone helps out in the kitchen we'll do well.'

'I'm afraid that's something beyond me,' Susan said. 'You'll have to do without me.'

'We can't all be gourmet cooks,' Tim informed her gently. 'So I guess that leaves you with the dishes. Moira can help. What else, Molly?'

'Water,' she said immediately. 'We don't have city water. Everything comes from our well, and the pump is electrical.'

'So then our problem is the electric lines,' Tim mused. 'Didn't you have an emergency power plant?'

'In the barn, Tim,' Molly reported. 'But I haven't used it in a hatful of years. I don't really know if it will start. There's plenty of fuel, but——'

'OK, that will be the first thing for us to look at,' he replied. 'In the meantime, no baths, no showers, minimum water-use starting at once.'

'Oh, no!' Susan stood up so quickly that her chair fell over backwards. 'I can't put up with that!'

'There are lots of things you can put up with if you have to,' Tim growled. 'And now you have to. Anything else, Molly?' He might have considered the subject closed, but Susan certainly did not. With a muffled moan she ran out of the kitchen and up the stairs. Molly moved as if to go after her, but Tim put up a warning hand.

'She—doesn't know the house very well,' Molly protested. 'It's been a pile of years since she's been here.'

'She'll survive. Now, what else?' This is the old Tim, Molly thought. Straight to the point, forceful—male! Where did that idea come from?

'Molly?'

Caught thinking when she should have been listening, she ducked her head to hide her give-away eyes, and fumbled. 'I—think the house has no defects,' she stammered. 'All the shutters are closed. In over two hundred years an Atlantic storm has yet to blow us down. We have plenty of lanterns and candles, if need be, but we must be careful of fire. There's no way the Fire Department could get out here to help. No way. I have an old CB radio someplace or other. I suppose we might rig that up just in case the phone line goes dead. No, I guess that's all, Tim. I'll get out all the stored blankets and sheets, and see everyone gets comfortable.' For everyone read Susan Holland, and I don't care if she's ever comfortable again. And don't tell me, God—I know that's not the Christian way!

'I'd better get moving,' she said. 'I didn't expect Susan. I suppose we——' Her faced turned brick red as she came to an abrupt halt. 'I—suppose she'll—be sharing a room, Tim?'

'I don't know why you'd suppose that,' he laughed, 'unless you mean to take her in with you?' Unable to find the right words, Molly crimsoned again, and strode purposefully for the stairs.

'Now that was mean,' Aunt Gerda lectured him. 'Just plain mean. What are you up to, young man?'

'The same thing I was up to a week ago,' he muttered. 'And don't tell me you don't understand, you scheming old witch.'

'And what kind of way is that for you to talk to your aunt?' Gerda asked cautiously. 'No, wait, don't answer that question. There are a number of things going on in this house, and I'm sure I'd sleep better tonight if I didn't know what they were. But why Susan?'

'I know,' he sighed, scraping at the side of his face with one finger. 'She wasn't in the cards, not by any means. Would you believe I haven't seen her in years? She just popped out of the woodwork today.'

'I believe you,' his aunt said grimly. 'Many wouldn't, but when I was a young girl I used to practise—you know, thinking up one absolutely unbelievable subject every week, and convincing myself it was true!'

'Aunt Gerda!'

'Don't turn up your nose at me, Tim Holland. I know you from a long way back. How do you suppose Molly is going to believe that story? And what exactly does Susan want?'

'For the first question, Susan seems to think she's found a loophole in my divorce settlement. She seems to think she can prove I'm an unsuitable parent, and custody of the child should be given to her,' he sighed.

'And do you think she has a chance of proving that?'

'Who knows, these days?' He shrugged. 'Besides, I think that's only her *stated* goal. What she's really after is a cash settlement. Somehow she's heard that Holland Ocean Fisheries is far from being on its last legs. She wants a bigger cut!'

'And what about what Molly thinks?' His aunt glared at him, demanding an answer he didn't want to give.

'I thought it would all be so easy,' he sighed. 'You know, I'd *seen the light*, so how could it be possible that Molly wouldn't have, too? We were just made for each other, Molly and I. But the way things are going on around here, she's become the relentless best friend, and doesn't mean to stir one centimetre off centre! Whatever happened to *absence makes the heart grow fonder*?'

'Well, I did warn you,' his aunt mused. 'More than once I warned you that you were putting things off to the point of danger!'

'Dammit, you know I couldn't come,' he grumbled. 'There was always that one last chance, just over the hill, that one of those famous European surgeons might be able to cure Moira's problems. I *couldn't* come—not until I got the last negative report.'

'You should have come,' Gerda insisted gently. 'Molly is the kind of woman who would have understood. Or you could have written—or even telephoned.'

'Yeah, sure.' It was a nervous affliction, this running his hands through his hair as he frowned. 'Yeah, sure. What would I have said? Hello, Molly, I'm sorry I picked the wrong woman, but would you mind if I came back and married you?'

'A little abrupt, perhaps,' his aunt commented. 'But it would certainly have been better than this brouhaha that you've thought up. She was down at the docks this morning, counting all the Holland boats, you know. Want to try again about that poverty-stricken act?'

'Oh, God!' he muttered.

'Yes, well, maybe He could help if you asked.' Aunt Gerda, who knew that Tim had not seen the inside of a church since his wedding day, threw in the barbed comment just to see him squirm. After all, she thought, it's all bound to come out right in the end, and in the meantime, nephew or not, he deserved to suffer.

'So you think Susan will involve you in a custody battle?' she repeated.

'I don't really know,' he replied. 'More money, I suppose, might settle the deal. On the other hand, blackmailers never stop. If I gave her money this year she'd probably want more next year, and I'm not about to let her leech on to me like that! On the other hand,' he said worriedly, 'I can't afford to take a chance, can I? Moira's too precious to me for that.'

Gerda's eyes lit up for battle. 'There's no chance of that, Timmy. Even the dumbest judge in the state, and lord knows there are a lot of them, couldn't rule against you. You think she means it?'

'I don't know.' He slammed his fist down on the table for emphasis. 'I don't think so. I think the game is to get me on edge, and try to use Moira as a hostage—something like that. If I could get Molly on my side, there's no court in the world would rule against me. Only I don't understand where Molly's coming from. Is there some other man hiding in the woodwork?'

Gerda leaned back in her chair and nibbled at her lip.

'Well,' she drawled, 'there *was* a name she mentioned a few months ago—in the middle of the summer when she came down to Framingham to visit. Now what was that ridiculous name? Alfred, that's it. Alfred DeMoins.'

'Alfred?' Tim half-closed his eyes as he ran the name through his mental computer. 'Alfred DeMoins? I've heard that name before, but I can't remember where! What are you grinning at?'

'Walter Scott,' his aunt said, and her grin spread all the way across her face. Tim sat up straight and watched his only dear relative, his co-schemer, looking at him like a cat watching a saucer of milk cool.

'Well, don't leave me hanging in mid-air,' he rasped.

'No, of course not.' Gerda, stretching upward to the full limit of her very tiny frame, seemed to overawe him. 'Walter Scott,' she repeated meaningfully. He shrugged defeat. 'Oh what a tangled web we weave, when first we practise to deceive!'

What with one thing and another, Tim knew he would sleep poorly that night. There were half a dozen pills left in his bottle, the palliative for a small accident he had suffered months before. Shrugging his shoulders, he swallowed one, gave life a considered thought, and had another on top of the first.

CHAPTER SIX

IT WAS a night of storm and bluster. The old house creaked
and groaned as the wind buffeted it from all sides and
whistled at the double chimneys. Molly huddled deep in
her bed, her electric blanket no proof against a power
failure. She was unable to sleep. Her mind worried at her
problem, like a dog worrying a bone. What to do? Tell
Tim that she loved him? Don't tell him, and suffer as he
played with Susan? And what about Moira? The child
needed a woman in her life, but was that sufficient reason
to marry Tim? And what about her? Could she survive,
needing Tim and not having him; or needing Moira and
not having her? Love is a complicated passage, and Molly
Patterson had hardly the experience to solve the puzzle.

But Tim was—not exactly the boy she had grown up
with. A little too slippery for a country girl to hang on to,
a little too ambitious, a little too—free with the truth?
There were tears on her pillow and her mind was as untidy
as an unmade bed, when the winds came to a sudden halt
along about midnight.

The stillness was almost as bad as the storm sounds
had been. The house settled down. Feet pattered up and
down the hall outside her room. Doors closed
surreptitiously. Distressed by her thoughts, Molly pulled
herself up in bed and sat there, listening. There were
strange additions to all the night noises she remembered.
Her Christmas gift to Moira lay in a little basket under
her bed and whined. Shag, outside in the corridor,
scratched at her door, his nose telling him what his

mistress would not.

Like a spider in my web, Molly thought. Tim's room on my right hand, Susan on my left, Moira across the hall, and Gerda at the other end of the corridor. Shag whined again; the little bundle under her bed whimpered, and faintly, from across the hall, Moira started muttering in her sleep.

Molly slipped out of bed, snatched up her warm winter robe and slippers, and made for the door. As soon as the knob turned Shag threw his considerable weight against the panel and forced his way in. 'Well, thank you very much,' Molly whispered sarcastically, but the big dog went straight for his objective. Moira was rambling again.

Stopping just long enough to make sure Shag was not about to create an international incident, Molly padded across the hall and into the little girl's room. The night-light showed the child tossing and turning in her bed. Molly sat down on the edge of the mattress and ran a hand through the girl's lovely hair. 'Easy now,' she crooned, 'Aunt Molly's here.'

One of those beautiful eyes opened, and then the other. 'I don't want you,' the girl muttered. 'I want my dad. I can't trust nobody else! Go away!'

'I couldn't sleep either,' Molly sighed. 'It must be the atmospheric pressure, or something.' The child sat up, resting her head against Molly's breast.

'It was gonna be a wonderful Christmas,' she sighed. 'Why did *she* have to come?'

'She?'

'You know who. Susan!'

'She's your mother, sweetheart. People always love their mothers.'

'No, they don't,' the little rebel said firmly. 'And she's not my mother. She gave up the job a long time ago. I hate her! I thought——' Tears interrupted, and refused to be stanched.

'I want my dad. I want my dad!' The appeal caught at Molly's heart, but there was no solace she could offer. So much bitterness caught up in such a tiny body! So much anger.

'All right,' she said. 'Lie down here. I'll go and call your dad.'

Luckily, at just that moment, Shag wandered into the room behind them. The little girl wanted Molly to go, but refused to release her. Molly urged the big old dog up to the bed where, because of his size, he could lay his muzzle on top of the covers without straining. For a moment the child hesitated then transferred her hold. Shag endured it all patiently.

With knees almost as stiff and strained as her heart, Molly managed to get up. The pair of them, the dog and the girl, remained unmoved. From the doorway Molly looked back. Poor kid, she thought. She can't trust anybody—not yet. Anybody except her father and my dog. For just one bleak second Molly felt the pain at being shut out. She wheeled and went out into the hall on her errand.

Tim's door was shut, but it opened quietly. The room was in total darkness. He had pulled the heavy curtains, and there were no lights left on. Careful to avoid stubbing her toe on something, Molly felt her way across the room in the general direction of the bed. 'Tim?' she whispered. She could hear him breathing heavily. 'Tim?'

There was no change in his breathing. Holding both hands out in front of her as a warning device, Molly continued her wandering. The breathing was coming closer. So was the bed.

Her knees struck the bed-rail before her hands found

any opposition. Although she had been moving slowly she wavered back and forth for a second, lost her balance, and sprawled across the mattress, hands outstretched, landing flat out on top of Tim. 'Oh, God!' she groaned.

He might have been a heavy sleeper, but he had instantaneous male reactions. Both his arms came up and grabbed at her, holding her struggling form down against his naked chest. 'Oh, God,' she muttered again. 'Tim?'

No answer. Instead he rolled over, taking her with him, until they were lying side by side, nose to nose, his hands in total possession. Fight? she asked herself. Scream? Reason with him? Forget it and just lie there in the warmth? Her body was willing, but her Puritan mind rebelled. 'Tim,' she whispered as she struggled to get one hand free. 'Tim!'

'I hate women who come to bed to talk,' he murmured drowsily into her free ear.

'Damn you, Tim Holland,' she whispered. It was terribly hard to conduct a screaming operation when there was a need for silence. 'Tim Holland, turn me loose!' She might have said more, but he closed her mouth effectively by sealing it up with his own lips.

Stunned, Molly relaxed for just that fatal moment that allowed him to penetrate her mouth. And from that point on, it was 'Kate bar the door.' Staid, pragmatic Molly Patterson disappeared in a cloud of dust, to be replaced by a squirming, moaning minx who could just not get close enough. His hands went sensuously down her back, stirring every passion, arousing every nerve-ending. And when he rolled her over, flat on her back, and one of his practised hands easily found the combination to both robe and nightgown, all her tactile senses exploded. His fingers found the stiffened bronze tip of her breast, his mouth teased at her earlobes, then shifted lower. Molly gave up thinking. It seemed the appropriate thing to do. Someone was murmuring in the night, 'Tim, Tim, Tim!' Luckily that's not me, the tiny segment of her brain still in action reported. But of course it was. And it was only that tiny conduit of thought that allowed her to hear Moira's sobs, and remember. With a gigantic effort she tore herself free, rolled again to her right, and landed with her knees on the floor, her nose pressed up against his.

'Tim,' she hissed, 'it's Molly, not Susan!'

'I know who it is,' he answered. 'I never go to bed with strangers, Molly.'

'Oh! You—monster!' she screamed, then clapped her hand over her mouth. 'You—you——!' It was impossible to find the right words. She bolted towards the door, and out into the hall. In the pale light of the hall windows Susan was standing at her own half-opened door, grinning.

'Sweet innocent Molly?' she laughed. 'Bed-hopping, Molly? Won't that look nice in court?' Susan was still laughing as she went back into her room. Molly, shaking, gathered her robe around her and hurried back to Moira's room. The bed was empty. But across the hall, from Molly's own bedroom, there was a little squeal of delight. She followed the sound.

Moira and Shag had transferred from one room to the other, but in the doing the little girl had knocked over the wicker basket by the side of Molly's bed, and disturbed the squirming little bundle that staggered over to huddle up against the big warm dog. The bundle began to whimper.

'Aunt Molly? Who's that?'

Molly grinned in the dark and shook her head. There was no way out of the tangle. She reached over and snapped on the bedside lamp. There, almost lost in Shag's heavy fur, was a wriggling bundle of puppy barely past the weaning stage.

'That,' Molly announced grandly, 'is your Christmas present.'

Moira squealed in delight and swung herself off the bed. 'A puppy? My own?' There was no sign of tears, or of panic. This was pure childhood joy, and the thoughts of a moment earlier were gone whistling down the wind. And I wish I could do that, Molly told herself. Either forget that strange passage of arms—Tim's arms—or preserve it forever, pressed hard against my heart!

'Your very own,' she said. 'Quiet down, love. It's all yours. Of course, if you'd waited until tomorrow, I would have wrapped him up in a tasty package. But what you see is what you get.'

Moira squealed again, and swept the little brown bundle up in her arms. 'I'm gonna call him—Bertie,' she said. 'My friend Nicole had a dog that she called Bertie, and he was the nicest friend, and that's why I'm gonna call him that!' Molly grinned. The puppy squirmed restlessly and then accepted the new warmth, yawned, and went back to sleep. 'Oh, Aunt Molly,' the little girl sighed, 'how wonderful you are!'

'Yes, aren't I,' Molly returned sceptically. 'Now, get into bed, chum, before you freeze your—little toes off!'

Moira complied with enthusiasm, jumping into Molly's slot in the bed, still cradling the puppy in her arms.

'That animal isn't house-broken,' Molly cautioned in a whisper. 'For heaven's sake calm him down. The whole house needs sleep this night!' The pair, the little girl and the dog, nuzzled each other, and almost instantly fell asleep. The child doesn't know any better, Molly told herself as she watched. Angels, the pair of them. Too bad they have to grow up!

The puppy and the child might not have known that dogs didn't sleep in beds, but Shag did. Nevertheless the big dog whined a couple of times and then, by a gallant effort, elevated himself into all the rest of the bed.

'Shag, you monster!' Molly hissed. The animal buried his head in the blankets and played out of sight, out of mind. 'And thank you all,' Molly muttered as she stole the duvet off the foot of the bed, switched off the bedside lamp, and coiled herself up in the lounge chair by the window.

Tim came down late, as usual. Not the last, but late. Aunt Gerda was at the stove, busy with a pile of wheat-cakes. Moira was at table, one hand on her fork, the other on her puppy. Shag lay on the floor at her feet, hoping for titbits. Molly, nursing a mug of hot coffee, sat in the corner on the window-seat, an island of glumness in a sea of good cheer.

'Good morning, all,' said Tim. Molly winced and ducked her head, expecting him to make some comment about the previous night.

His daughter smiled up at him and signed, 'I love you.' He turned expectantly to Molly, who conspicuously turned her back.

'You didn't sleep well?' Tim walked across the floor to Molly's side and laid one hand gently on her shoulder. She flinched away from him. He snatched the hand away as if it had been burned.

'Your wheat-cakes are ready, Tim,' Aunt Gerda announced.

'Look what Aunt Molly gave me for Christmas!' His daughter was unable to contain herself further. She held the puppy up in both hands and extended it towards her father.

'A dog?' He shook his head, a rueful look on his face. 'That's all we need, baby. With all our travelling from pillar to post, we need a dog like we need a hole in the head!' Moira looked as if she were about to cry, while Aunt Gerda made 'tut-tutting' noises.

But Molly, worn, tired, angry, lost her temper. She swung around on the window seat and glared at him. 'That's it, Tim Holland!' she snapped. 'Think only about yourself, as usual! Damn you!'

'What the devil have *I* done?' he replied forcefully. 'All I did was to say good morning. I even shaved before I came down. Do I have bad breath or something? My lord, when I first came back to Magnolia I thought you hadn't changed a bit, Molly Patterson, but now I see how wrong I was. You were a young grouch in the good old days. Now you're an *old* grouch!'

She jumped to her feet, hands on hips, ready to be the worst of fishwives. 'That's the way!' she shouted angrily. 'Change the subject. Bluster. Do anything but face the truth. That little puppy is a pure-bred German Shepherd. He'll stay with Moira for six months, so that they know each other well, and then we'll send him off to be trained as a Hearing Ear dog!'

'A what?' They were all staring at her now, and there was no way to back out.

'A Hearing Ear dog,' she said very firmly, her voice rising as she spoke from a soft whisper to a shout. 'You know that blind people use Seeing Eye dogs? Well, deaf people have the same sort of problem. They need something or someone to tell them about noises or people behind them, or sirens, or traffic noises. Especially at night, when most hard-of-hearing people take off their hearing aids. And that's when they need a Hearing Ear dog, to alert them to intruders or dangers that they can't hear. To guard them against all comers. And they have them. Hearing Ear dogs, trained to respond to unusual noises, and to alert their owners. Alert and guard them. And that's what this little fellow is. A year from now he'll be a blessing. And I don't give a darn about the inconvenience it might cause you, moving up and down and around Robin Hood's barn!'

'Hey!' protested Tim, a shocked expression on his face. 'Hey, I plead ignorance, Molly. I've never heard of such a thing! But now that you explain, it makes a wonderful amount of sense. I'm sorry, Molly.'

'Yes, I'll bet you are,' she said grimly, unwilling to be conciliated. Best friend Patterson, she snarled at herself, and loathed the thought of it. Right at the moment she was fully prepared to murder her 'best friend'.

'Hey now!' Tim protested as he moved closer, close enough to put an arm around her shoulders. 'Hey now, Moll. You really *didn't* get enough sleep last night, did you?' And then, trying to make a joke of it, 'I finally had to seek help for myself. I haven't slept better in months!'

'I'll bet you did,' she muttered at him. 'I've heard tell that that sort of thing relaxes a man.' Sharply focused in her mind was the picture of Susan watching as she had come out of Tim's room the night before, and the self-satisfied smile on Susan's face.

'Yeah,' he chuckled, 'you're right. It was so good that I tried it twice!'

'Oh, God,' she muttered as tears, rage, and frustration all rose at the same time. With a strength she never knew she possessed she brushed him aside and went running out of the kitchen, her eyes awash. He had just confirmed her worst suspicion. After *she* had left Tim's room, Susan had gone in! And certainly the pair of them hadn't stopped at a handshake! She stopped just long enough at the door to yell a final defiance at him. 'Timothy Holland,' she screamed, 'you are an insensitive, impossibly stupid—oaf!' And with that outburst she shouldered Susan to one side and went charging up the stairs and into her room.

'Well, what was *that* all about?' Petite Susan managed to regain her balance and sauntered into the room, looking the height of fashion in her flouncy semi-transparent négligé.

'I'm damned if I know,' Tim sighed. 'All I did was mention that I took two sleeping pills last night, and she blew her top! That's not like good old Molly! Maybe I'd better——'

'Maybe,' Aunt Gerda suggested pithily, 'you'd better sit down at the table and use your mouth for eating. My lord! You're the smartest Holland of your generation. You're the only male Holland left alive in the world! The rest of them died from terminal stupidity, Timothy—and you'd better see if you can't get an inoculation to save yourself.' At which point Gerda grounded a stack of wheat-cakes in front of him, sniffed in a very superior fashion, and marched smartly out of the room herself.

'I really need some breakfast,' whined Susan.

'Get it yourself,' Tim roared.

'You know I can't cook,' she protested.

'I'll make you some toast,' her daughter promised in a disgusted voice. When she delivered it, each piece was burned on the bottom, but Susan, completely out of her depth but hoping for the best, dared not protest.

Molly came out of hiding at noon. She was thoroughly cried out, and totally ashamed of herself. A short nap had improved her appearance, and now she contemplated the

ruin she had created all around her. What a mess! she
lectured herself. The only thing you salvaged from the
wreckage is that at least you didn't go around blabbing
that you loved him! Everything's spoiled. Well, there's
no hope for loving, but perhaps—just perhaps—I might
work my way back up to friend? With that thought in
mind she bundled herself up in workmanlike ski-pants
and heavy woollen shirt, and went back downstairs again.

Moira was at the window of the living-room, her nose
glued to the glass, watching the snow swirl in the clutches
of a rising wind. Gerda sat in the rocking chair, knitting.
'I'm—sorry I made such a fuss,' Molly said.

'No need to apologise,' Aunt Gerda replied. 'He
deserved it. If not for what he did last night, then for
whatever he's done in the past nine years. I say it
again—my nephew is an idiot!

'But that's not important,' Gerda continued. 'What's
important is that it's Christmas Eve tonight, and we don't
even——' Her voice broke as she waved a hand around
the undecorated room.

'Of course,' said Molly. 'You're right. And we
have—where's your father, Moira?'

'My nephew is out in the barn trying to do something
with that emergency power plant,' Gerda snapped
angrily. 'So far today he's managed to shovel a path to
the barn, another to the road, and a third to the gazebo on
the cliffs. Why would we want a path to the cliffs?'

'Maybe he plans to jump off,' Moira suggested
morosely.

'Or perhaps push somebody off,' added Molly, equally
glum.

'I don't understand how he could be so brilliant as to
make a million—as to make so few mistakes in business,'
Gerda complained. 'Why don't you get a baseball bat and

go reason with him, Molly.'

'I—might not be welcome,' she stammered. 'Where's—why don't we get Susan to go?'

'Her Royal Pain in the Backside has retired to her room,' Gerda continued. 'It would seem that eating breakfast was just too much for her. Or maybe it was having to wash her own dishes. Any objections?'

'I washed her dishes,' Moira complained. 'Me!'

'No,' laughed Molly, relieved to get out from under all the gloom. 'Well, maybe one. I don't own a bat!'

Aunt Gerda gave her a long glare, snatched up her work and started for the stairs. 'If there's one thing more we don't need,' the older woman announced to her great-niece, 'it's another female smart-mouth! Call me for dinner!'

Moira and Molly stood side by side at the window, looking out, wondering what to do next. The sun was rapidly disappearing, masked by more clouds marching in from the north-east. With a start, Molly looked down to see the child's fingers signing with speed.

'Do you think we'll ever live long enough to have dinner?' the girl signed.

'Never a doubt,' Molly returned. 'Even if it's only K-rations. I'll do it.'

'Do what?'

'I'll go and beard the lion in his den—I mean, in my barn!'

'I don't understand that middle sign,' the child said. 'Board?'

'Beard,' smiled Molly, and repeated the sign for instruction.

'I still don't understand,' Moira sighed. 'Beard the lion?'

'Yes. It's an archaic English expression,' Molly said

with a perfectly straight face. 'It means I'm going to go
out there and beat up your father.'

'I could help?'

'No, you stay here. You can be Florence Nightingale.'

'Sure,' Moira agreed. And then, 'You must be awful
old, Aunt Molly. What movie did Florence Nightingale
play in?'

'Watch my lips,' Molly said solemnly. 'I'm going to
teach you to speak a few Italian words. *Shut uppa you
mouth, kid!* Got it?'

'Spoilsport!' The girl ducked to avoid the round-house
swing which never would have reached her in the first
place, and laughed helplessly as her aunt struggled into
her outdoor gear.

Tim was bent over the frame of the big Elsen-Gorman
generator when Molly stamped into the barn. The one
electric light bulb made hardly a dent in the darkness. It
was an old barn, with cracks in the walls big enough to
let the cold wind squeeze through, and crowded with the
haphazard parking of two cars. Now and again he would
yell a couple of four-letter words and bang at the power
plant with his fist, but he did not realise that Molly had
arrived until she touched his shoulder. At that point he
swallowed a couple more words, and dropped his
screwdriver.

'What the devil are you doing out here?' he yelled at
her.

'Looking for you,' she replied. 'Did you know that the
wind-chill factor is down to minus twenty degrees?'

'No, I didn't know,' he shouted back over the steady
roar of the wind. 'Is there something else I should guess
at to win a prize?'

'Don't Tim.' She moved up close to make conversation

possible. 'Don't be sarcastic. All we seem to do is wind each other up these days. At this temperature if you touch that cold metal you'll lose some skin. Please? And tonight's Christmas Eve.'

'That's true, Molly.' He grabbed at an old rag and made a half-hearted attempt to wipe his hands off before he touched her. 'And somehow I get the impression that I've done something I shouldn't?'

'T'other way around,' she said ruefully. 'We both haven't done something we should have. The Christmas tree is over there in the corner.'

'I knew it,' he chuckled. 'I just knew it! Give me another few minutes here and we'll go decorate the tree.'

'Moira would like that,' Molly told him. 'Why don't you leave this old clunker alone?'

'Don't be insulting,' he teased. 'Machines are sensitive to criticism. The engine part here is almost a duplicate of the motors we have on our boats, and I'm sure I can fix it. Another repetition of last night's storm and we'll lose the city power for sure. What the devil is that?'

'That' was a large grumbling noise from outside. Molly went to the door and peered through a crack. 'Well, I'll be darned!' she called. 'A snow-plough! I don't know what to make of that. Usually the DPW doesn't get to us until five or six days after a——'

'After what?' probed Tim, still tinkering at the generator. She walked slowly back to him, hands clasped behind her back.

'Would you believe,' she sighed, 'it was a big blue snow-plough, with Holland Ocean Fisheries printed on the side?'

'I believe,' he grinned, and checked his wrist watch. 'I told them to get it done by three o'clock this afternoon. The power of positive persuasion!'

'You just *suggested* they come plough our street?' she asked softly.

'That's right, Molly Patterson,' he said. 'I called them on the telephone, oh, so politely, and *suggested* they come plough our street.'

'And they did,' she said glumly as she cleared a space on top of an old barrel and sat down. 'Sometimes, Tim, I wish I were rich. You know, real rich. With money to burn, and all that.'

'Well, it *is* the Christmas season,' he said solemnly. 'Here.' He folded something into the palm of her hand. She took a second adjusting to what she held. One small book of paper matches, and one genuine twenty-dollar bill.

'What——' she gasped.

'Hell, live it up,' he growled. 'Lord knows you've been put upon often enough in your young life, Molly. Light the thing up. You've got money to burn!'

'Tim, don't be silly!'

'I'm not being silly,' he insisted. 'Light it up. I'll hold the other end of the bill for you.'

'I couldn't, Tim. Honest, I couldn't!'

'Yes, you can,' he urged. 'Relax. Let it all out. Burn, baby, burn!'

Driven by her own devils, her eyes gleaming in the semi-dark barn, Molly lit a match. Her fingers trembled as she moved the flame closer to the bill. When it flared into fire she yelped so suddenly that Tim almost dropped the burning bill. The pair of them stood and watched until the last fragment was consumed. And they stared at the point where the flame had blossomed, long after it had gone out. Until finally, with a deep sigh, Molly said, 'Lord, that was a wonderful feeling!'

'Do it once a day for two weeks,' he ordered as he bent

over the power plant again.

'Don't be silly,' she muttered, but was attracted to the idea in spite of her New England conscience. And just at that moment the old generator snorted, rumbled, belched, and ran.

Tim watched the fly-wheel turn, a happy smile on his face. He had not for many years looked so boyish, so proud, so sure of himself. Anything that's machinery, she reminded herself. If you tell Tim what it's supposed to do, he'll make it do it!

'Now how about that?' he said in wonder as he reached for her, twirled her around in the air a couple of times, and kissed her most profoundly. It was a very nice kiss, and Molly had been without adult kissing for some time—not counting that wild attack in his bed the night before—since Alfred had cornered her at the Amateur Theatrical Group and done his best for the Sabine women!

'There,' said Tim as he set her down on her feet and inspected her in a very self-satisfied manner.

'There indeed,' Molly whispered, finding it difficult to shake herself back to reality. She wanted to hurry. There would, of course, be a second and a third kiss like that first one, and if she were properly appreciative, maybe a fourth! Despite her high-flying feelings of female independence, she was prepared to grovel just the *slightest* bit to get those extra kisses.

Unfortunately, Tim came down with foot-in-mouth disease at the very moment when he should have been charging forward. 'Let's go get that tree trimmed,' he said.

Moira was standing at the window, her nose hard up against the cold pane, her back turned very firmly towards the only other occupant of the room, her mother. Her puppy was cuddled up in her arms, snoring away with enthusiasm. Snow was beginning to spit again; it looked to be a white Christmas for sure, if only her did and Aunt Molly would come back from the barn.

'Moira, how would you like to come and live with me in New York?' The little girl heard, even though her hearing aid was turned down low, but made no move—gave no indication.

'See here, girl, don't give me *that* nonsense!' Susan had padded across the room, seized her by the shoulder, and whirled her around. They were almost of a size, with Moira shorter by perhaps three inches. 'I said something to you!' Susan snapped.

'I can't hear you,' Moira answered stolidly. 'Did you say something? I'm deaf, you know.'

'I don't know any such a thing,' her mother said shrilly as she shook the child a couple of times, as hard as she could. Moira glared at her.

'I don't know what you want.' She spat the words out one at a time. 'I know you don't want *me*. How would your friends feel if they knew you had a deaf daughter, Mama?'

'Why, you little—monster!' Susan pulled back her open hand, intending to slap the child, when Aunt Gerda bumbled into the room. All three of them froze, like sculptured ice-statues.

'I'm sure I'm not seeing what I'm seeing,' the round little elderly lady said coldly. 'I wouldn't want to see anyone lay a hand on that child. Anyone!'

'I can do what I like with my daughter,' Susan snapped.

'And I can tell Tim all about it,' Gerda added gently. 'Can you imagine what he'd do? Why, look, here they come now.'

'And they're dragging a Christmas tree,' Moira said excitedly. 'I didn't think——'

'Your aunt Molly would never forget the Christmas tree,' Gerda laughed. 'A very well-organised woman, your aunt. Very—pragmatic, I think the word is. And full of love.'

Susan tugged at Moira's arm. 'We'll talk again,' she whispered. 'Don't forget. It would be a shame for anything to happen to your sweet little dog. Ugh! Get that animal out of my face!'

Torn between pain and passion, Moira brushed her mother aside and ran for the back door. The pair outside had stopped for a moment for a snowball fight. One of them had terrible aim; the missile missed Tim, and came sailing up to bang off the open door just above Moira's head. 'Hey, you two,' the child yelled, 'if that's the best you can do, I'll beat you both!'

'Not a chance,' gasped Molly as she stumbled up on to the porch, leaving Tim to struggle with the tree. 'We have to get this decorated before supper. All the ornaments are in the hall closet, love. Why don't you start bringing them out while your father—not there, Tim! For goodness' sake, you know very well we *always* put the tree in the corner of the living-room!'

The rest of the afternoon was filled with noises, movement, laughter, teasing and love, as Tim and Molly did the high decorations, Gerda supervised, and Moira tied the light-strings around the lower branches. Shag even added to the excitement. He came in, thumped down beside Gerda, and took over as the puppy's nanny. Of Susan there was no sign.

At five o'clock it was dark outside. The storm still threatened, but had not yet delivered. The old snow, twelve to fourteen inches deep in flat areas, four to five feet high in drifts against the windward sides of the houses, was enough to keep everyone in Magnolia house-locked. 'WBZ Radio says more snow,' Moira reported as she came back in from the kitchen with a handful of pretzels 'to hold me over until suppertime'.

'I couldn't lift a finger if it did,' Tim reported. He was sprawled out, half in and half out of the big armchair that once had been Molly's father's favourite possession. 'I have digged all I intend to dig.'

'Dug,' Molly signed to Moira, who laughed. 'He speaks English poorly!'

'Cut that out,' Tim ordered. 'We'll have no more of those finger-painting conversations.'

'You only have to learn the language yourself to be up to date,' Molly teased. 'Your daughter is learning like a house on fire. Here, learn this one.' She walked over in front of him and smiled while she signed, 'I love you.'

'I remember that,' he chuckled. 'That's good day, right?'

'Right,' Molly and Moira chimed in at the same time. Gerda, who knew a little better than that, started to giggle. With painful slowness, looking directly at Molly, Tim repeated the signs. *So there*, Molly told herself. *I got him to say it, after all these years. Too bad he doesn't mean it, or even understand what he said!*

Tim sank back in his chair. 'The tree looks wonderful,' he commented. 'Just like it used to. Did you know, Moira, that I spent most of my Christmases over here with Molly when I was your age?'

'It must have been fun,' his daughter said. 'Did your mum and dad come too?'

'Not exactly,' he sighed. 'My mother—wasn't with us too often at Christmas, and my dad, he—do you remember the story I told you in Paris about Ebenezer

Scrooge?'

'Bah, humbug,' Moira laughed.

'That's the very man,' Molly encouraged her.

'That was your grandfather to a T,' Tim added solemnly. 'Bah, humbug! He didn't believe in Christmas.'

'I know he was my brother,' Aunt Gerda interjected, 'but he didn't even believe in people, God rest him. Well, suppose we eat? I don't know any ceremony that can't be improved by a good meal!'

'I'll call Susan,' Molly offered, then looked down at the child, busy trying to appear invisible. 'While Moira gets washed, right?'

'I'm gonna wear away,' the little girl complained. 'Every time I turn around somebody wants me to get washed. My skin is going to peel away and turn into gills or something!'

'*Git,*' her father commanded. She got, snatching up her puppy as she went by Shag, and taking the stairs two at a time.

'We really need another bathroom,' Molly sighed as she watched.

'Well, that certainly fits into the conversation,' laughed Tim, as Molly started up the stairs, much more slowly. She found Susan sitting by the telephone in the upstairs hall. The woman had a smirk on her face as she concluded her conversation and restored the instrument to its cradle.

'Just a minute, Molly,' she called as her cousin started to turn into her own bedroom. She rose gracefully and took the two steps that brought them face to face. What big teeth you have, Grandmother, Molly thought apropos nothing. More like a shark than a grandmother!

'I'm sure Tim told you why I came all the way up here,' Susan said blandly.

'I can't say that he did,' Molly replied. 'I suppose he thought it was none of my business.'

'Perhaps. But there is a part of it that concerns you.'

'Oh, yes?'

'Yes, cousin.' There was the tiniest barb on that last word, or perhaps a calling in of favours due to a relative? Molly cocked her head to one side and prepared for the storm. 'I came up here to talk over Moira's position in the world,' Susan continued. 'That was something not settled by the divorce decree. Usually the mother gets custody, especially when it's a daughter, you know.'

'Oh?' A very weak *oh* at that, Molly chided herself. The whole idea was a surprise to her. Susan might get custody of the child? Good lord! She was so astonished that she missed the next few words of the one-way conversation.

'—and we'd scheduled a meeting with my lawyer,' Susan was saying, 'only of course with travelling so difficult and all—well, it's almost impossible for us to go to his office. But we're lucky.'

'Yes, of course we are,' Molly sighed, still not sure where the conversation was headed. 'Why are we lucky?'

'Because he lives up here in Manchester,' Susan explained. 'Isn't that nice? Now he's agreed to drive over here tonight, you see, and Tim and I and the lawyer can sit down together and iron the whole thing out. Wouldn't that be nice?'

'Yes, of course,' Molly repeated, still feeling fuzzy about the whole affair, and wondering what in the world was going on.

'But with the storm coming in again,' Susan said hurriedly, 'he might not be able to drive back to Manchester, so we would have to invite him to stay the night.'

Relieved to have finally arrived at some sensible point, Molly nodded her head, managed a half-smile, and said, 'Certainly. Did you invite him?'

'Well, to tell the truth I did.' Susan was displaying that little feline smile that meant trouble. Molly had seen it many times before, but people from downstairs were calling, something about the supper being on the table, and she missed the cue.

'Come on.' She held out her hand to Susan. After all, it was Christmas Eve, the woman *was* her cousin, and forgive and forget, wasn't that what Christianity was all about? On their way back down the stairs they scooped up Moira, looking just the slightest bit more neat than when she had come up, and the three of them walked into the kitchen together.

CHAPTER SEVEN

IT WAS a pick-up supper. Molly contributed spaghetti and meatballs and a bottled tomato sauce. Aunt Gerda added a Jello dessert, stuffed with canned fruits, and a home-made loaf of garlic bread. Tim brought a large appetite to the dining-room table; Moira provided an excess of excitement. And Susan sat in the middle of all the action, doing nothing, but smiling that weird smile—like a vampire waiting for the clock to strike, Molly told herself.

What really nagged her was that Tim was devoting most of his time to his ex-wife. 'He should be giving some attention to his daughter,' she muttered to Gerda as they passed each other on the way to the stove. What she meant was, he should be giving *me* some attention! She didn't have to tell Gerda that. The elderly lady seemed to be the only one in the room who understood all the players and all the rules.

When Molly staggered into the dining-room with the huge platter of spaghetti, Tim came to the door to help. 'You got him!' Moira yelled.

'Got who?' asked Molly puzzled. Tim had both hands on one end of the platter, while Molly had her hands on the other.

'The mistletoe!' Moira shrieked excitedly. Both Tim and Molly looked up at the same time. Some misguided soul had hung a sprig of holly and mistletoe above them in the middle of the doorway. Molly did her best to back up, but her fingers held fast to the plate, and Tim refused to give ground. In fact, egged on by cheering from the table, he pulled the platter in his direction, and before Molly could gather her flustered senses, his warm moist lips were on her own. For a moment she felt the pure bliss of it all. A small triumph, surely, but for a girl whose triumphs were few and far between, this kiss was an overwhelming success.

'Yeah man, go!' yelled Moira.

'How lovely,' Aunt Gerda commented as she inched Shag away from the table with the toe of her shoe.

'Don't drop the spaghetti,' Susan warned disgustedly.

It was that last comment that shocked Molly back to sensibility. 'Don't Tim,' she objected, pulling her head back.

'You never used to object to a mistletoe kiss,' he murmured.

No, Molly thought, but in those days I hadn't dreamed of Susan coming out of your bedroom, nor heard you boasting about *doing it twice,* for heaven's sake! Even a best friend has to be sensible about some things. Especially sex. 'Take the platter to the table,' she told him firmly, and turned back to the kitchen for the sauce.

Determined not to put a damper on the Christmas Eve celebration, when Molly came out of the kitchen on her last trip she came with a smile and a joke. There was no argument about who had what place; the table was round, and big enough to hold half a dozen additional people.

Aunt Gerda was at her best too, recalling a dozen or more stories about the 'old days,' when Molly and Tim had been known as the Disaster Duo. Moira hung on her every word. Susan could hardly keep from yawning. And the two alleged participants ducked and dodged and blushed—but could hardly deny the truth of most of the tales.

So the meal ended in good spirits. As they transferred
to the living-room they could hear a car driving up
outside. Moira ran to the door. The incipient storm was
only a threat, but it was still a difficult driving time. The
visitor was receiving a warm welcome. There was a
suitable delay to allow the discarding of boots and
overcoat, then Moira danced into the living-room, hand
in hand with—Captain Josiah Francis!

'I didn't think I'd make it,' the Captain said as he
walked directly across to the fireplace and rubbed his
hands in front of the gas-blaze. 'Comin' up to storm again.
Did I miss anything?'

'Spaghetti, Captain Ahab,' Moira chimed in. He turned
and laughed down at her.

'You're the cute little piece I met with Molly, aren't
you. Molly?'

'Right here, Captain. It's wonderful to see you on
Christmas Eve, but did I forget I'd invited you?'

'*I* invited him,' said Gerda, moving up to take the
Captain's arm. 'I couldn't bear to think of the poor man
all alone on a night like this.'

'Besides, we've been sharing Christmas for years,' the
Captain chuckled. 'Did I spoil something? Make the
numbers wrong?'

'Nothing like that,' Molly said cheerfully. 'And we
were about to be hopelessly short of men around these
parts. Have you eaten?'

'Done that already,' he told her. 'Do I put these presents
under the tree?'

'I'll take them, Josiah,' said Tim. The two men shook
hands in a bone-breaking clasp that illustrated a
considerable friendship. The Captain unloaded his
pockets, then spied Susan.

'I don't believe I've had the pleasure,' he said.

'Ah. Susan, this is Captain Francis, the Commodore of our fleet.'

'And I'm Tim's wife,' Susan announced as she came around the table.

'So.' The Captain looked quickly at Gerda, and evidently received some signal. He nodded his head and said, 'And what brings you to these parts, little lady?'

Susan took his other arm. 'I think I was cheated on the division of the spoils,' she told him. 'My lawyer and I are looking into the situation. And of course, I just *had* to see my daughter, you know. Mother love is a strong urge!'

'I wouldn't know much about that,' the Captain said gruffly as he turned around to Molly. 'I don't know that I'll be able to drive back tonight, Miss Molly,' he continued. 'Would it be inconvenient for me to stay over?'

'Of course it wouldn't' said Aunt Gerda, and gave Molly a guilty look.

'Of course it wouldn't,' Molly repeated. 'Sit over here, Josiah. Are you sure we couldn't offer you something to eat?'

'Nope,' he declined. 'Had me a big supper earlier, up to Gloucester. Never go on a trip without a good meal beforehand, that's my motto. Who in the world is *that* comin' up?' Another car motor had sounded outside, a horn tooted, and brakes squealed.

Tim pulled back the lace curtain and peered out into the gloom. 'Can't see a thing,' he reported. 'The snow's out to make a record for itself. Coming straight down, and big flakes.'

'I'll go,' Susan announced, to everyone's surprise. 'I'm expecting my lawyer, Molly, if you remember?'

'Oh—yes,' Molly replied. 'I'd almost forgotten.' Round and round in her mind a little equation was playing. Seven people, probably to spend the night, and only six bedrooms free. Oh, wow! She looked around the room in desperation. Tim and Moira were eyeing each other, and making some small talk over Bertie. Aunt Gerda and Captain Francis were exchanging messages like long-lost lovers. *Lovers*? *At their age*? *And why not*! Which left Molly and Shag to stare at each other, listening faintly to the very effusive welcome Susan was offering to the latecomer.

It took longer for this newest guest to shed his outer garments. Or maybe Susan had to have a private consultation? Molly asked herself. None of this makes sense. Susan wants—what? Custody of Moira? That was what the verbal communication indicated, but underneath all the words there was something different at stake. What Susan wanted, Molly thought, beyond any doubt, was more money. Or could it be—oh, lord! Molly took a deep breath to try to assuage the sudden pain that had struck her just under her heart. Could it be that Susan wanted it all—wanted Tim back again? If so, she would use *any* manoeuvre to achieve her goal!

So by the time Susan came back into the dining-room, her lawyer behind her, Molly had set her face in an uncompromising judgemental frown, which was almost instantly knocked off.

'People,' Susan said as she walked in, 'I want you to meet my lawyer, Alfred DeMoins!'

Oh, my God, Molly screamed at herself. Oh, my God! And while Susan was leading the lawyer around the room, making introductions, Molly was struggling with her stomach, trying to keep from the final social disgrace. Al DeMoins! The one man in all the millions who lived along the North Shore whom she not only never wanted to meet again, but had fervently prayed that their original meeting might be washed off the records by the Recording Angel!

'Well now, whom have we here?' Al DeMoins. As handsome as a girl's dream, his little individual defects swallowed up in the whole. Five foot ten or so, a little more rotund than he had been during their high-school days, a full head of brown hair that might possibly not be entirely his own. Alfred DeMoins, the man Molly had finally concluded could be the one with whom she might share her first sexual adventure, until, at the last minute, she had discovered just what sort of barracuda he was!

'Hello, Alfred.' Tim's head snapped up as he heard Molly make that dismally discouraging greeting.

'Molly Patterson, I do declare!' Alfred's lips were just a little too full, his tones a little too ripe. 'Our newest heiress! Did you know I've been looking all over Cape Ann for you?'

'No, I didn't know.' Molly clamped her mouth shut. It hadn't been easy, keeping out of Al's way. Not only had she given up all her local friendships, but she had also withdrawn from the job she really loved, teaching. And all because Al DeMoins thought that Molly Patterson owed him something!

'Heiress?' queried Tim, coming around the table to stand at Molly's side.

'Yes,' Alfred replied. 'Won a bundle in the State Lottery, started out to be the Playgirl of the Western World, then disappeared. Dropped completely out of sight! Well, am I glad I found you again, Moll. You owe me.'

'Don't call me that,' she snapped. 'Only my friends call me that.'

'Ah. Of course,' he chuckled. 'And I'm more than a friend, aren't I, Molly P?'

'And don't call her *that* either,' Tim said flatly as he
put one arm around Molly's shoulder. It was the nicest
thing that had happened to Molly in a month of Sundays.
She leaned back against Tim's solid frame and found her
courage instantly restored.

'Yeah, Molly and I had some interesting nights,' Alfred
boasted.

'*One* interesting night,' Molly stated. 'And I was lucky
I had enough mad money to get me home, Mr DeMoins.'

'We'll just have to pick things up where we left off,'
he commented.

'I don't think so,' said Tim, and there was something
in his voice that caused the lawyer to blink his eyes and
look twice.

Alfred licked his dry lips, and tried another attack.
'Staking a claim?' he asked. 'I saw her first.'

'The hell you did!' Tim retorted angrily. 'Molly's been
my girl since she was in her cradle. You're not making a
social call, DeMoins. You're here on sufferance as
Susan's lawyer. Now why don't you and your client come
along to the den with me, and we can get down to
business. Maybe you can be back to town in an hour or
so.'

'I don't think so,' Susan interrupted. 'The snow is
really piling up out there. In another few minutes nobody
will be able to drive. I think Al will have to spend the
night.'

Tim shrugged his shoulders. 'Maybe,' he grated. 'That
will be Molly's decision; it's her house. Come on!'

He led the way out of the dining-room, with Alfred
hard to his heels. But Susan delayed long enough to glare
at Molly. Moira, her puppy in her arms, went over to stand
beside her adopted aunt. 'Listen,' Susan hissed, 'don't
think a couple of odd remarks have won you any prize,

Molly. You may be my cousin, but Tim is my husband! You couldn't keep him all those years ago, and there's no way I'm going to let you have him now!' And then, turning to her daughter, 'Get that dirty animal away from me, girl! Don't you know anything about hygiene?' With which she shared a glare equally among all the members still standing in the dining-room, and followed her lawyer out into the hall.

'Well!' Aunt Gerda managed a weak little laugh as she moved a few inches closer to the Captain.

'She's mean,' said Moira. 'How could Bertie be dirty? I gave him a bath just this afternoon!'

'Not to worry,' Molly replied. 'There are some people who can't tell clean from dirty, physically or mentally! How about let's finish up our dessert, and then we'll turn on the tree lights, and then——'

'And then we'll all go to bed and wait for Santa Claus to come,' Moira said happily. ''Course, I don't believe in Santa Claus, 'cause I know he's my dad, but——'

'I know,' Molly agreed. 'But on the odd chance that there might be a present or two, you're willing to suspend your disbelief for just one night?'

'Aunt Molly,' the child said suspiciously, 'sometimes you sound more like a kid than a grown-up!'

Eleven o'clock, Christmas Eve. Moira had given up the ghost at ten, worn out by the events of the day. Captain Francis had volunteered to carry her upstairs, where Aunt Gerda had slipped her into her winter nightgown and tucked her in.

Molly had managed to do the dishes and clean up the kitchen, and now she was back in the living-room, her feet drawn up beneath her on the sofa. The wind had risen again, until a glimpse outside indicated that it was snowing sideways. The house rattled and groaned, like an old ship riding the high seas.

The Christmas tree, almost touching the high ceiling, and fastened into its corner in three directions, seemed to rock with every attack of the gale outside. The two dozen little fairy lights blinked, and the angel perched at the very top was dancing. But it had done its duty. The child had been enchanted by the whole affair. When Tim came back from his conference, with Susan and her lawyer close behind, Molly told him about it.

He dropped on to the sofa at her side, which was another plus. The sofa was one of those two-person love-seats. But Tim was somewhat more than one person, and, as a result, he crowded next to her very comfortably. Susan sneered at them both as she sank into one of the armchairs, leaving Alfred to struggle with one of the straight-backs.

'I wouldn't be surprised,' mused Tim. 'We've been a pair of wandering gypsies, with no real place to call our home. I mean to make that up to her.'

And I'll help, Molly thought, but kept her mouth shut. Best friends don't go around making statements like that. Tim was so obviously gun-shy that a single wifely remark like that might send him off and running again!

'Strange child,' Alfred chimed in. 'I never thought, years ago, when I first met Susan, that she would have a child like that.'

'Oh? You knew Susan years ago?' Tim was about as casual as a man could be, which meant, Molly told herself, that there's something in the wind here. That casual *bon vivant* role was his best act! She sat up a little straighter to follow the conversation.

'Yes indeed,' Alfred rambled on. 'I knew Susan back in her salad days, so to speak.' The man was just far enough away from the little blonde so that her attempt to kick his ankle failed. Molly marked that down and filed it in her capacious memory.

Tim got up and refilled the lawyer's brandy glass. It wasn't for the first time, and Alfred was showing evidence of having been to the well too often. Susan, giving every evidence of a woman about to have a screaming fit, just could not get his attention.

'And deafness too,' the lawyer wandered on. 'Isn't that funny? We have a lot of that in my family. My aunt and my sister both came down with it. Some sort of congenital defect, I understand. All in the female side, it seems. Luckily it skipped me.'

'You surely are lucky,' Tim agreed affably. 'It would be pretty hard lawyering if you were deaf. What do you think about that, Susan?'

'I think I'm going to bed,' she hissed at them, her face red with fury. 'Did you find a bed for Alfred?'

'Yes, indeed,' Molly told her. 'Moira and I are doubling up in my big bed, and Mr DeMoins can have her room. Would you show him, Susan?'

'I'll show him *something*,' Susan retorted. For the first time Al realised that he had his foot in his mouth. He followed the other woman out, his face red as a beet.

'Now what do you suppose *that* was all about,' asked Tim as he came back to the sofa and squeezed in beside her. He was wearing his most innocent expression, but Molly had been down that route too many times in the past.

'Tell me about it,' she murmured. His arm came around her shoulders and settled in. 'You know darned well what. Al DeMoins knew Susan a long time ago. Al DeMoins comes from a family that has hereditary problems with deafness. Two and two make———'

'Five,' he interrupted, laying a finger across her lips. 'Listen to me carefully, friend Molly, because this is the first and last time I expect the subject to come up. Moira is *my* daughter, and I shall love and cherish her as long as I live—no matter who her natural father is. Got that, have you?'

Molly gulped. The pressure of his finger on her lips was the lightest of touches; the pressure of his look, gleaming out of a pale determined face, bore all the weight of years. 'Yes,' she whispered, 'I've got that!'

They sat silently for a while, savouring the warmth, the brightness of the Christmas lights, the soft sound from radio station WBZ, broadcasting carols. The wind dropped off, but the snow continued, piling flake on flake in its inexorable attempt to shut off human life. Finally she stirred.

'Early morning, Tim. Remember? Moira will be up at the crack of dawn, ready to open her presents. Everything's in the hall closet. How about bringing the packages out while I hang the stockings?'

'Mrs Kringle, I take it,' he chuckled. 'OK. And while I'm at it, I'll shake out a little hay for the reindeer.'

'Don't you dare!' She shuddered in mock fear. 'All the hay's in the barn. If you try to go out there tonight we'll need two St Bernard dogs just to *find* you.'

'I'll be careful,' he promised jokingly. 'St Bernards were the dogs that carried the brandy casks around their necks to sustain the lonely traveller, weren't they?'

'Don't look at *me* like that. I don't have anything around my neck for you, Tim Holland!'

'Well, you could have fooled me.' And me too, Molly told herself. For there was something around her neck—both his hands, gently caressing, pulling her forward until her breasts flattened against his shirt-front, her nose buried at about the third button of his shirt. Her arms stole around his waist—well, as far around as they could reach.

The hug was gentle, as brotherly as one might expect. But when he tilted her chin up and kissed her there was nothing brotherly about that. Nothing at all. For what seemed like hours he punished her with delight, until she clung desperately, breathless.

'And just what was that all about?' she gasped at last as he relented and set her an inch or two away from him.

'For old times' sake,' he murmured.

Please don't tell me that, Molly thought wildly. Not anything about the good old days. *These* are the good old days, Tim Holland. I've never had it so good. I've never been kissed with such—enthusiasm. I've never dreamed such dreams as now. And then he lowered the boom.

'You have to help me, Molly.'

'With what?' Barely a whisper, that. She was still caught up in his magic.

'With Susan and her stupid lawyer,' he sighed. 'I think I have everything fixed up. I have a French divorce, and an absolute settlement in writing. But I suppose an American lawyer could pick some little hole in the structure. I mind losing money, just for the principle of the thing, but I could live with a money loss. What I can't live with is the idea that she might be able to take Moira away from me.'

'You know that I'll do anything I can,' Molly answered. 'I love that little girl—' *almost as much as I love her father*! '—but I don't know just what I can do.'

'There are two things,' he suggested hesitantly. 'For the short term, just be nice to the pair of them. As nice as you can possibly be?'

'I guess I could do that. It won't be the easiest thing in

the world, but if I can just keep my temper—What else?'

'Well,' he stammered, as if the words were stuck in his throat, 'the biggest problem is that a court generally tends to give custody to the mother, especially if the father hasn't remarried. It's that bit about how much better a mother can raise a daughter than a father can.'

'So?' Molly swallowed. Her throat was dry, and her mind tingled with anticipation. 'You plan to get married, Tim?'

'Yeah,' he grunted. 'For Moira's sake, of course.'

'Of course. Do I know the lucky woman?'

'Molly?' He took a step or two away from her, then came back, his face under stern control. 'Molly, you don't sound as if you think she'd be all that lucky.'

'How can I tell, Tim? Maybe she's hard up.' *Like me, you fool*! 'Maybe she's nursed a secret passion for you since she was ten years old?' *Or perhaps even six*? 'Or on the other hand, maybe she's waiting around for some words like love and devotion and happy ever after. Has she given you any hope?'

'Not directly,' he muttered. 'But Aunt Gerda says——'

'Aha! A conspiracy? Tell me about it, Tim.'

He took a deep breath and stared down at her with an unfathomable look. 'No,' he sighed, 'I guess I'd better not. I don't think you're ready to hear what I've got to say. Where did you say those presents were?'

'In the hall closet,' she replied, and turned abruptly away from him so he could not see the tears in her eyes.

Luckily her bed was wide. Moira was coiled up on the far side, next to the wall, with little Bertie beside her on her pillow. Shag complained when he was shooed off the other side of the bed. He clumped his way over to the door and stretched out on the throw-rug there. Moira's night-light had been moved to Molly's room. It cast a ruby sheen over everything.

Molly coiled up in her armchair by the window and stared out. Although it was dark outside, it was the reflective darkness of a snowfield, just enough light to show the big flakes drifting down. Behind her, she could hear Shag's heavy breathing. We're getting old, my dog and I, she thought. For a moment there tonight I thought I had a hand on the brass ring. But close is a measure only good while playing horseshoes.

Poor dumb, beautiful Tim! How can such an intelligent, lovable man be so stupid about women? I wonder, is it a *new* woman he's talking about, or can he be so foolish as to take up with Susan again? How in heaven's name could Alfred DeMoins be Moira's father? Al was in law-school when Tim and Susan were married, and he didn't graduate until two years later. Which left practically no time for him to zoom over to Europe and do the dirty deed! And Aunt Gerda! I was almost positive she was on *my* side, but no, that pair—the Captain and Gerda—are deep in a conspiracy to—to whatever. If I were in my right mind I go down the hall and wake Gerda up right now, and demand an answer!

Putting action to words, Molly slipped into her heavy winter robe and her fur-lined slippers. Shag protested at the opening of the door. So much disturbed was the old dog that he padded down the hall after her, breathing heavily. A few chains to rattle, and he'd make a great ghost, Molly thought as she gently turned the doorknob and opened Gerda's door.

There was practically no light at all in Aunt Gerda's room. Molly stumbled across the rug by the bed, and shook the covers. 'Gerda?' No response. 'Gerda!' Still no answer.

Determined to have her way, Molly felt across the top blanket, ready to shake a shoulder—or whatever else she came across. She leaned so far across the bed that eventually she slipped and fell flat on her face. But her nose, her hands, questing, returned the same message. Aunt Gerda was not in her bed. A moment later when Molly managed to turn on the bedlamp the conclusion was unavoidable. Aunt Gerda was not in her room!

Nonplussed, Molly sat down on the edge of the bed. 'Here's a how-de-do?' she whispered. Only W.S. Gilbert could provide the words for her present situation. Aunt Gerda was—perhaps sixty years old? Not too old, of course. Not too old for what? her conscience demanded. Maybe she's in the bathroom? Not too old for Captain Francis, who was about the same age, and as spry an elderly man as could ever be seen!

Being a true optimist, and stuffed to the gills with curiosity, Molly stopped off to inspect the empty bathroom, and almost fell over Shag, who was sitting patiently outside the door. So Aunt Gerda was missing, in the middle of the wildest snowstorm since the blizzard of '88. 1888, that was.

I can't spot-check the house, Molly told herself. Besides, everyone except Moira is an adult, and if they all want to play at adultery, what business is that of mine? Nevertheless, when she went by Susan's door, she stuck out her determined chin and tried again. There was a little light in Susan's room, a reflection from the hall lights. And once again an empty bed.

A hysterical little giggle rose in her throat. I worried about having enough beds for everyone, she told herself, and here I already have two empties! Quit while you're ahead, kid! She pulled her robe more tightly around her and headed for her own room. Shag had beaten her to the bed; she had to shoo him off again. He went reluctantly.

Molly slid gently under the sheets, trying not to disturb the little girl. Warmth enveloped her, and she became drowsy. I wonder, she thought, if Tim is still in *his* assigned bed? For a moment she thought to check, but when she moved one toe out from under the covers the cold shocked her, and she changed her mind. 'Besides,' she whispered, 'I don't really want to know. Well, I really do, but I don't dare to know. It's Christmas morning, and I have to wake up early to be with Moira.' With which thought she fell into a troubled sleep.

CHAPTER EIGHT

THERE was no dawn on Christmas Day. Heavy clouds hung over all the north shore of Massachussetts, but the snow had stopped. As expected, Moira was up at the first sign of light, and Molly, sharing the bed, was forced to join her in the mad dash downstairs. The house rang with the child's excited shouts, and not all the householders were pleased.

'Can't you keep that kid quiet?' grumbled Alfred as he came downstairs, bleary-eyed, at seven in the morning. By that time Moira had picked over the pile of presents under the tree, shredded the paper on those marked for her, and was marching up and down with her puppy tagging along behind, and a huge Snoopy doll in her arms. It was amazing to see how her shyness and reserve had vanished under a landslide of love.

'I'm sure we could,' Molly responded coldly, 'but who wants to?'

'I do,' Alfred snapped. 'If I were her father I'd slap her bottom good!'

'If you were her father,' Molly replied tersely, 'she'd deserve it. There's coffee on the stove, toast on the table, and scrambled eggs on the sideboard.'

'I have croissants with my coffee,' he complained as he sat down.

'Tough,' Aunt Gerda said sarcastically.

'You don't look too bad,' Molly told the elderly lady as the pair of them turned their backs on the lawyer. He gave them a disgusted look and walked out into the living-room.

'Too bad for what?'

'Well, I went looking for you just after midnight,' Molly chuckled, and Aunt Gerda blushed.

'I'm a little old,' she replied, 'but I'm not dead. Not yet, Miss Prude. Why did you want me?'

'It doesn't matter now,' Molly sighed. 'I'd been talking to Tim. He seemed to suggest that you and he were involved in a conspiracy to get him married again. He didn't appear too enthusiastic, and it didn't concern me, so——'

'Conspiracy?' Gerda interrupted her. 'And it didn't concern you?' Molly shook her head. 'I can see why you would think things are confused,' Aunt Gerda said. 'But it that's all the explaining Tim is ready to do, I'm sure I ought to keep my mouth shut about it. Did you know that Captain Francis comes to spend the holidays with me at Christmas, Easter, and the Fourth of July?'

'Does he really?' smiled Molly. 'Have a good time, do you?'

Aunt Gerda grinned broadly. 'The best,' she chuckled. 'Celibacy isn't all it's cracked up to be.'

'I wouldn't know,' sighed Molly. 'Somehow or another I just seemed to be too busy to—well, to find out.'

'You couldn't find a better time,' Gerda teased. 'Snowbound like this? Now's your chance. Hop upstairs and make your selection.'

'I couldn't do it,' Molly replied glumly. 'Yours wasn't the only bed I checked on last night. Although I didn't run into anyone, it seems to me that the traffic up and down that hall must have been something fierce. If I could have sold toll tickets, I might have made a bundle. But my courage failed, and I went back to my own bed.'

'Poor baby,' the older woman said. 'Pass me the

coffee-pot again.'

Tim chose that moment to poke his head in from the living-room, where he had been sharing Christmas with his daughter. 'Ho, ho, ho,' he chortled. 'Why do I see gloomy faces in the kitchen?'

'Bah, humbug,' Molly told him. 'Did you have enough breakfast?'

'I did,' he reported. 'Who gave me this—astounding—necktie?'

'The one with the yellow dragon breathing fire? I thought it was most appropriate,' Molly said primly. 'It about matches the green shawl you gave me, the one with the three can-can dancers on it.'

'Hey, the bell has sounded. That's the end of round one,' Gerda laughed. 'Back to your corners. Alfred, did you eat all the toast?'

'Who, me?' the lawyer looked up at them all through bleary eyes. Plainly he had nipped at the brandy bottle after he had gone up to bed as well as before. 'We need to talk some more, Holland.'

'No, I don't think so,' Tim answered nonchalantly. 'After thinking it over I think my answer is not only no, but hell, no! Not a penny more. And the first person who makes any threat about *my daughter*——' the words hung explosively in the air between them '——will find it very detrimental to his health. Or hers, as the case may be. Now, how about some more toast, Aunt Gerda?'

About a mile north of the house, at just that moment, in the middle of Norman Avenue, Billy Sunderson was making a stupidly gallant effort to deliver a late Christmas present. As he came up to the crossroads at Ocean Avenue a dog ran out into his path. He slammed on his brakes, skidded across the intersection, turned around twice, and smashed the back end of his truck into the power pole on the corner. The pole shifted, the hot wires at its peak snapped, and half the village of Magnolia lost its power. Including the old house on the bluff overlooking Kettle Cove.

'Oh, damn!' grumbled Tim. Everyone in the kitchen waited. There was an automatic switch out in the barn which was supposed to turn on the emergency generator when the main power went off. Nothing happened.

'Oh, damn,' Tim repeated as he got up and searched for his work clothes among the heap of jackets by the back door. 'I'll have to shovel my way to the barn and turn the thing on by hand.'

'I'll help,' Molly offered. Alfred came back into the kitchen and sat down stolidly in his chair, with never a thought of helping.

'I can't shovel. My back, you know, but the Captain can,' Aunt Gerda volunteered. 'I'll call him.'

'No, don't wake him up,' Tim objected. 'Molly and I can handle this. Why don't you recruit some help and check on the lanterns, the gas fires—things like that. Will the furnace run without electricity, Molly?'

'I hope so,' she groaned. 'It's supposed to. But then the emergency power is supposed to work too. Come on.'

'Papa, can I come too?' Little Moira, ready to give up the warmth for a romp outside.

He was about to say no when Molly nudged him in the back. 'Yes, of course you can,' he agreed. 'But get bundled up. And you have to leave your dog inside, you know. Puppies aren't quite ready for sub-zero snowstorms. Aunt Gerda will help you.'

'That was a good thing to do,' Molly told him after she caught her first breath of frozen air. 'I think I'll just wrap this scarf around my nose too.'

'What, even with the can-can girls on it?' he laughed.

'Don't be indelicate,' she told him gloomily. 'Take up thy shovel and walk, man.'

'And where are you going to start?'

'I'm directing,' she chuckled. 'Me chief, you Indian. Get with it!'

'Well, you just said the magic word.' He handed her his shovel, tipped his fur cap jauntily over one eye, and stepped off the back porch.

'Tim Holland, you dirty rat,' she screamed at him with her best James Cagney imitation. 'You come back here and shovel!'

'You're not supposed to shout at daddies like that,' Moira said from behind her back. The little girl was swaddled in every conceivable kind of warm clothing, and clutched a toy shovel in her mittened hands.

'He's not *my* daddy,' Molly grumbled. 'Tim Holland, you come back here!'

'I'm doing just what you said,' he called. 'Walk! It's power we want, not paths. The snow's only at my knees along here. You two shovel while I just plough my way over and get the generator started!'

'Now why didn't I think of that?' Molly asked her partner in shovelling.

'I dunno,' said Moira. 'How can you talk sign language with mittens on?'

'You can't,' Molly laughed. 'It won't work in the dark, either. C'mon, let's shovel like good little girls.'

'You're not,' the child said as she started to work.

'I'm not what?' Molly was already out of breath, and the path was exactly four inches wide—and not likely to get any wider.

'You're not little, and you're not a girl,' Moira teased. 'I dunno about bein' good. My daddy says you're the goodest person in the world.'

'Well,' drawled Molly, her shovel moving the slighest bit faster. 'Tell me more! What else does your daddy say?'

'No, sirree,' Moira giggled. 'I'm no blabbermouth. What's that noise?'

Molly stood up to rest her aching back. 'I must be getting old,' she muttered. 'That noise, young lady, is your smart-guy father getting the generator going.'

'So we don't hafta shovel any further?'

'Farther,' Molly corrected. 'No, we don't have to shovel any farther. He can come back the same way he went out—Shanks's pony.'

'Well, in that case,' warned Moira, 'you'd better duck!'

Molly smiled to herself. Another crack had appeared in the child's wall. And where there was tolerance there could be love?

The snowball war lasted about ten minutes before Tim appeared on the horizon like an invading army of Huns, and swept the field. The three of them tumbled into the kitchen moments later, cheeks as red as MacIntoshe apples, their breath steaming in the warmth.

'Dear God,' Susan shrieked, 'shut that door! I don't want to freeze! What in the world were you doing out there in the snow, Tim?'

'And a good morning to you too,' he said grandly, hugging his two helpers. 'I had to turn the electricity back on. Molly forgot to pay the bill!'

'I don't doubt that,' the little blonde sneered. 'What a sloppy house this is! They ought to tear it down and construct a slum on the site.'

She's looking for a fight, Molly warned herself as she struggled out of her mackinaw. And she won't get it from me. Tim wants me to treat her nicely—but not too nicely, of course. 'I *have* had offers,' she said wryly. 'Bettencourt Construction offered me half-a-million just for the site—and offered to move the house for me, if I could find someplace to move it to.'

'And you turned the offer down,' gasped Susan, almost dropping her coffee-mug.

'There wasn't much choice,' Molly sighed. 'You have no idea what land is selling for these days, and I've seven acres up here, right on the edge of the bluffs. But you just try to find a plot available at a reasonable price to which I could have the house moved! Impossible. And I have to live somewhere!'

'But you could live in Paris, New York——'

'Not me,' said Molly. 'I'm a small-town person. Did you get something for breakfast?'

'No. For some reason Aunt Gerda stormed off when I came down. I only asked for croissants, you know, and she blew up as if I'd ordered something out of the ordinary. As far as I can tell, she's upstairs telling that Captain person all about it. And that's another thing, Molly Patterson. How *could* you allow someone like that to spend the night with us? Why, I quivered in my bed all night!'

Why you're a thoroughly disgusting person, Molly assessed to herself as she turned back to the stove. Only Tim was close enough, though, to hear her mutter, 'In *whose* bed?'

'Count to ten,' he murmured in Molly's ear as he helped Moira to shed her outer gear.

'I've done that twice,' she muttered in return. 'Susan, would you like some wheat-cakes? Or more toast? Or a grapefruit? I have a couple of grapefruit in the refrigerator.'

'Nothing.' The blonde seemed to contain more bad temper than could be explained by a simple hangover. After all, it *was* Christmas Day. 'A piece of dry toast,' she ordered. 'Trim the crusts, and please don't burn it!'

Ten, eleven, twelve, Molly counted to herself as she prepared the bread. And no crusts? Well, she has enough crust for both herself *and* the bread. Fifteen, sixteen, seventeen—— She looked down at Moira, standing at her side, fingers busy. Eighteen, nineteen, twenty, the child signed, and grinned up at Molly as she did so.

'You cut that out,' Molly signed back to her. 'She's your mother.'

Moira shook her head from side to side as she signed, 'No! No! Never!'

'And would you two stop that stupid finger exercising,' Susan grumbled. 'Isn't it bad. enough that we're snowbound up here in the wilderness, without having that idiot mumbo-jumbo being flashed in our faces?'

'I don't mind,' Tim interjected mildly. 'It's sort of attractive, knowing that they can communicate as well as they can. But why now, Moira?'

The little girl looked up at him with an innocent expression on her face. 'Because the battery in my hearing aid has gone dead,' she said very solemnly. 'So until I get a replacement I'll just have to struggle along with lip-reading and sign language. Would your friends in Paris like to see that, *Mama*?'

There was a gargling sound from the table as Susan almost choked herself to death on her coffee. Tim hurried over and pounded her on the back—which did nothing to help her cause.

That's the first time I've heard her call Susan *Mother*, Molly thought. Does that mean the child is reaching out to her parent? But then look at the gleam in the girl's eyes. It's more as if she called her that as a challenge! And feel the tension! The air is so thick you could cut it with a knife!

Little Bertie, the puppy, took that moment to wander across the kitchen threshold. Moira dropped to her knees and tried to coax him forward. The puppy wagged its tail madly, and began to wobble across the highly polished linoleum floor. Twice his legs slipped out from under him and he landed flat on his belly, with an astonished look on his face. When he scrabbled to his feet he was facing the wrong direction, and his first few steps bounced him off Susan's leg.

'Get that filthy beast away from me!' she screamed. Her foot drew back, and had not Tim's intervening hand caught at her ankle, she would have kicked the little bundle of fur. Moira dived forward across the floor, snatched up her pet, and rolled away from the table.

'Don't you *ever* touch my dog,' the child said threateningly. 'Not ever!'

'Have your fun,' grated Susan. 'Your father has refused all my offers, my lawyer tells me, so I shall go into court in January to get custody. And then we'll see, young lady, about dogs and wild language and rudeness—won't we?'

'No, we won't,' Moira muttered, moving behind her father for protection. 'No, we won't neither. I'd druther run away than live with you, you—Daddy, tell her!'

'Yes, perhaps I must,' Tim responded softly. He looked over the heads of the pair close to him, straight into Molly's eyes. From long practice she could read his hurt, his pleading, and she knew he was about to pose a whopper of a statement. 'There won't be any question about custody, Susan,' he continued. 'In case you didn't read your mail several years ago, I not only have a custody award from the French court, but I also have an adoption award from an English court. I'm sure you wouldn't want to have to explain an American court about blood-tests and things like that, would you? Especially with Mr

DeMoins as your lawyer?'

'You devil,' muttered Susan as she scraped her chair back. 'You damn devil! Maybe I will anyway, just to prove—and maybe I'll tell your darling little Moira all about it too. How would you like that, to be held up as a bachelor non-father?'

Tim's face turned chillingly cold. Susan backed away from him, her hand over her mouth as if to block the words that could not be recalled.

'Go ahead,' he said softly. 'Moira and I have talked at great length about this. She knows everything there is to know, except for an actual name. I'm sure you'd be happy to have all that splashed over the front pages of the *Globe*? And I mean—everything, Susan.' He stopped talking for just a moment, and a slow smile spread across his face. 'And while we're at it, I want you to be the first to know that Molly and I are getting married!'

His ex-wife backed up a couple more steps, until she was against the wall. She nibbled nervously at her fist, fire in her eyes. 'You think you've won everything, don't you,' she muttered. 'You and Miss Goody Two-Shoes there. Well, I could tell *her* a thing or two, believe me! I'm not finished with you, Tim Holland, not by a long shot!' At which she turned and ran from the room.

'Well,' Moira drawled, 'isn't life full of surprises! Is that true, Dad, that you and Aunt Molly are going to——'

'Maybe I spoke a little prematurely,' he told the child. 'Why don't you go play with your puppy while your aunt and I have a long talk?'

'Yes, why don't you do that?' Molly seconded grimly. Her mind was in a whirl of confusion. Everything she had ever wanted was within her grasp, and to her surprise she wasn't quite sure she wanted it. Not this way, like a sudden announcement from on high, with no explanation, no solicitation. As if Molly Patterson had nothing better to do than hang around until Tim Holland should—damn the tears!

'Molly, I'm sorry to break it to you that way.' Tim moved to her side and put a hand on her shoulder. She shook it off. A very concerned young man took one step backwards. 'Molly? It's something I had to do. Susan knows she hasn't a chance in court if I'm engaged to be married to you. No judge on the North Shore would consider *her* over *you*. Molly?'

'I don't want to talk to you right now,' she told him bitterly, turning her back. 'I've lots of work to do—and I just don't want to talk to you, Tim Holland. Go away—please!'

'All right.' She heard the footsteps retreating, the sound of the kitchen door closing, and then she went at the dishes, at the supper plans, at almost anything she could find to do, just to keep her hands busy.

As the day passed things returned to normal, but Molly felt walled away from everything and everybody. Aunt Gerda came down to help with the meal preparation. She had a great deal to say, but it all sounded as if she were on the other side of a wall. Moira bounced in and out, and almost penetrated the shield, but even the child knew something was wrong, and made no attempt to push. Captain Francis wandered in, received a quiet signal from Gerda, and announced that he 'had better get out and do some shovelling.'

Tim was already outside, shovel in hand. He had expanded the path out of the back door eastward to the barn, and had cleared enough space so that the doors could be swung open. He stopped long enough to have lunch, eaten in complete silence in the kitchen, then started on a path from the front door to the look-out point on the bluffs.

'That's pretty silly,' Aunt Gerda insisted as she came out for a momentary breath of air. 'Who the devil wants to walk out there?'

'Nobody, I suppose,' Tim replied glumly. 'It's just something that Molly's father always did—he was in love with the sea, and always wanted access to the point. So to me it's habit. And it won't hurt anybody, will it?'

'I don't suppose so,' said Gerda. 'Only we'd be better off if we had a path down to the road.'

'That comes next,' he sighed, grounding his shovel. 'But I don't think the road will be passable until it's ploughed again, and that won't happen for another couple of days. What does the radio say?'

'Just that,' Gerda informed him. 'They look for the skies to clear tonight or tomorrow, the DPW crews are out ploughing the main streets at the moment, they expect to get to Magnolia in a couple of days, and don't go out on the roads unless you have to. And we don't have to!'

'The devil we don't,' Tim said angrily. 'Another two days penned up in a house with *that* pair? God knows what they'll think of. The only sure thing is that they'll try *something*.'

'Well, you really blew it, I hear. How is it that a man as smart as you can act so stupidly, nephew?'

'Just practice, I suppose. If I could add up all the times I've really screwed things up where Molly is concerned—but I honestly thought she'd be willing to go along with an engagement to help me with Moira.'

'Yes,' his aunt commented sarcastically. 'And I heard that's just the way you put it, right? Or wasn't there something about "and, Susan, you'll be the first to know that Molly and I are to be married"?'

'I—seem to remember words like that,' he said

cautiously.

'And she was, wasn't she? Susan? She was the first to know?'

'I—go ahead, twist the knife,' he snapped. 'So I had my foot in my mouth again, didn't I? Yes, it's all true. I should have told Molly first—asked Molly first. But it did seem like a fine time to go so cautiously with Molly that I don't seem to be going anywhere at all! What do I do now?'

'You ask me?' His aunt dismissed him with a shrug of her shoulders. 'I never knew a man to have so much trouble getting a girl who already loves him to marry him! Never!'

'You really believe that?'

'Of course I believe it. Molly Patterson has been in love with you for a hundred years or more. Now if we can only keep you out of the way while I try to patch things up—why don't you go ahead and dig that other path down to the road? And when you're done with that, how about a scenic walk along the cliffs, or maybe you could start on the road? It's only two miles from here to the intersection, right?'

'Boy, you really know how to make a guy feel wanted,' he grumbled.

'Tell me about it,' his aunt told him as she turned and went back to the house.

Inside, still busy as a bee, Molly had arrived at the point where tears stopped flowing because there was no liquid left to flow. The fact that her brain was no longer working hardly seemed important. When Gerda bustled in, cheeks red with the cold, Molly paid no attention, but went on with her unnecessary tasks.

But when her adopted aunt began to rattle pans and

make a commotion in the work-areas which Molly had just polished, she did essay a small protest. 'Well, I can't help that,' Aunt Gerda insisted. 'Tomorrow is Tim's birthday, and he *has* to have a cake.'

'He *is* a cake,' muttered Molly. 'You're making——?'

'Strawberry shortcake,' Gerda interrupted. 'His favourite. With the old New England recipe, and plenty of whipped cream——'

'All I have is the canned whip,' said Molly. 'Whipped cream, strawberries—do you know what I'd like to do with——'

'No,' Gerda interrupted again. 'And I'd rather you didn't tell me. Why don't you go give Moira a language lesson, or go upstairs and mope in your own room?'

'Maybe I should go out and help Tim shovel snow,' Molly offered tentatively.

'No, that's a terrible idea, love. Leave him alone to his misery.'

'*His* misery? He should catch cold and die from *his* misery,' Molly snapped. 'Do you know what that nephew of yours said to me?'

'No, I don't think I do, and I'm too busy to listen,' the older woman said. 'Get out of my kitchen.'

'*My* kitchen,' Molly returned, but her heart wasn't in the argument. Obviously Gerda rated Tim's birthday cake higher than Molly's peace of mind. She fiddled with her apron for a moment, then gave up and stalked out into the living-room where Moira was busy with a colouring book and crayons.

'Christmas Day is always tough,' Molly commented, sinking into an armchair.

'I hadn't noticed,' the little girl said. 'I've had such a good time that—lordy, Aunt Molly, I've never had such a nice day in all my life! Not ever!'

Surprised that someone could be cheerful on such a terrible day, Molly turned on her side to examine the little face. It was alight from an inner glow, there was no doubt about that. 'Presents?' she probed.

'Oh, they were nice,' Moira answered, 'but there's so much more to Christmas than presents, isn't there? There's so much lovin' and things like that—and then you and Daddy are going to get married—and what more could a girl ask?'

'That—really isn't all that important—your dad and I are getting married, is it?'

Moira squirmed around and gave her a startled look. 'Not that important? That's crazy! It's the very most important thing of the whole day, that's what!' Her little hand stole across the space separating them and caught up Molly's.

'I didn't realise,' Molly whispered.

'Well—it is,' the child reported.

Molly took a grip on herself; shook herself by the imagination, reorganised her priorities, re-established goals, all in a fraction of a second, then returned to the fray a little more lighthearted. 'For a girl with no battery in her hearing aid, you hear pretty good,' she commented drily.

'Pretty well,' Moira corrected. 'You got lousy grammar. Did Sister Alice really teach you?'

'Yes, she did. What about the battery?'

'There's nothing wrong with my battery,' the child announced in a very self-satisfied tone. 'It must have been a loose connection or something. Every time that—that woman comes near me my battery seems to go on the blink.'

'Yes, I can see that,' her aunt declared. 'Or something. Where's your dog?'

'Well, they were tired from getting up so early, so Shag went into my room to rest, and Bertie went along with him, and I thought that was a good idea. I shut the door so that—woman—couldn't get at them.'

'That's a nice idea.'

'When are you two going to get married—and can I be in the wedding?' Moira wanted to know.

'I—don't think your father is quite ready for a wedding,' Molly answered. 'First there has to be an engagement period, you know. A time when we have a chance to think things over.' Molly took a quick peep to see how that line of argument was going. Moira had indeed got up too early. Her eyes were blinking steadily, and as Molly watched, both eyelids came down and stayed there. 'And I don't think I'm going to marry your father,' Molly whispered. 'Although I may kill him.'

'That's nice,' Moira mumbled.

Molly watched for a moment; the child was completely out. And how long has it been since I could do that? Molly asked herself. Fall asleep on a hardwood floor; have so much confidence in my elders that all they had to say was taken with complete trust? How long has it taken me to become a sceptical spinster? Ten years—fifteen? Why is it that every time I think the world is looking better, Tim Holland can come along and upset my applecart? Well, he won't get away with it this time. I don't know how I'm going to do it, but I have a revenge list a mile long, and I mean to get even with all of them. Susan Holland, for stealing my man, Alfred DeMoins, for almost stealing my—well, enough said about that. And Tim Holland, for—for letting me love him all those years under false pretences. There's only one restriction. When I get even with Tim, it must be in such a manner that Moira doesn't suffer as well!

From behind the closed kitchen door she heard a murmur of voices. Captain Francis had reappeared, and he and Aunt Gerda were talking. And that's a strange pair, Molly smiled to herself. Whoever would have thought, at their age! Love must be wonderful, when it comes from both sides. But there now. If the Captain is downstairs, maybe I could hustle up and get a couple of the bedrooms straightened out!

The word was mother to the deed. Alfred and Susan were still not accounted for, so she stole up the stairs in stockinged feet and began to work in the Captain's room. The big wide bed was a terrible mess. Molly grinned as she replaced the sheets from the hall closet, made everything up as pretty as could be, straightened and picked up, and was still smiling as she stepped out into the corridor.

Gerda's room needed hardly a lick and a promise. The bed was as unused as it had been before the holidays. Molly was laughing as she came out into the corridor and ran smack into Alfred.

'Well, what have we here?' he said, in that oily voice that sent shivers up her spine.

'What we have here is the ordinary garden-variety room maid,' she told him. 'And if you would kindly get out of my way I could get about it.'

'Now, now, Molly,' he said, reaching out both arms in her direction. 'Everyone seems to be busy——'

'Except for Susan,' Molly interrupted. 'And if you think I add two and two and can't get four, you're sadly mistaken, Mr DeMoins.'

'Mr DeMoins? My, how formal we've become! It wasn't like this the last time we met. Besides, Susan is fast asleep—the strain, you understand. All her problems. Of which you are but one, Moll. Why don't we sneak into your bedroom and see if we can't take up where we left off all those weeks ago?'

'I don't sneak into bedrooms,' she snarled at him, more furious than she had been in years. Sweet Molly Patterson, she thought, the girl who wouldn't hurt a flea. And here I am ready to kill this man!

Unfortunately, while she was thinking he was moving. With the skill of much practice, he trapped her, bundled her down the hall to her own room, and opened the door. 'Inside, love,' he laughed softly.

'I'll scream,' she threatened.

'Now, now,' he teased, but she could hear the iron behind the soft words. Here's a man with rape on his mind, she told herself as she let him push her into the room. He followed close behind, keeping her wrapped up in his arms, until he stumbled over Shag's recumbent form. The old dog stirred, waddled to his feet, and took a good look at the couple. Alfred, not sure of himself in the face of the gargantuan animal, stepped back half a pace. And there, Molly told herself dispassionately, is the opening. Her mind running cold and clear and totally unexcited, she moved in his direction. His hands came up again, reaching for her shoulders. Thankful that she was wearing slacks instead of a dress, Molly waited until he had reached optimum range, then slammed her knee viciously up into his groin.

Everything happened in just the way her instructor at the martial arts class had explained. Alfred seemed to draw in a shrieking breath, clutched madly at himself, and collapsed on the floor, his feet kicking in agony. Shag came over to watch, neither pleased nor angry—as befitting a dog who has known dozens of crazy humans. The thud and the groans must have carried down the stairs. Feet pounded, and Captain Francis crashed through the door, ready for almost anything.

'Did I kill him?' Molly asked hopefully.

'No, but you surely put a dent in his future prospects for heirs,' the Captain chuckled as he made a cursory examination. 'Say something impolite, did he? He'll be out of action for a long time. It was an accident, no doubt?'

'I don't think so,' Molly said solemnly. 'That's number one.'

Shag, deciding finally which side he was on, moved up to Alfred's perspiring forehead and began to lick with that huge rough tongue of his. The Captain, obviously an unrepentant sinner on his own, asked no further questions. 'He'll need ice-cubes,' he mused.

'Ice-cubes?' queried Molly in surprise.

'Well, I don't think a couple of Band-aids will do him any good,' the Captain chuckled as he took her arm, helped her step over Alfred's recumbent form, and led her out of the room.

CHAPTER NINE

MORNING, December the twenty-sixth. It *had* to be morning; all the clocks said so, even though the sun had failed to make an appearance. The snow had ceased, but leaden clouds reigned from horizon to horizon. All the lights were on at Logan International Airport to her west, and the towers of Boston sparkled in the distance. Molly took a deep breath of the damp cold air and gave thanks for the path which Tim had shovelled to no purpose. From her vantage point on the observation platform in the gazebo, no matter which way she looked, the world was mantled in white. Soberly she walked back to the house and into the kitchen.

'We have enough fuel for the generator for another twenty-four hours,' she announced as she bent to pry off her boots.

'Well, thank God for that,' Gerda returned. 'Now are you ready for breakfast?'

'Yes, I'm ready. No sign of our other—people?'

'Moira's up and about. The Captain is shaving. Mr DeMoins, I'm given to understand, isn't feeling well and won't be down.'

'And Susan?'

'You said *people*,' Aunt Gerda grumbled. 'I don't consider Susan to be in that category—good morning, Tim.'

'Good morning,' he groaned as he limped in from the hall. Molly took a deep breath to settle her nerves. Just the seeing of him was bothering her these days. Not as handsome as usual, he looked just a little frayed around the edges, and was not quite standing straight.

'I ache,' he announced grandly.

'All that stupid snow-shovelling yesterday,' his aunt told him, without the slightest bit of sympathy in her voice. 'Here are your sausages, Molly dear.'

Molly dear did her best to hide the grin as she settled into a chair and admired her breakfast. Sausages, scrambled eggs, toast, coffee, orange juice. Typically American. And dear Tim—still grumbling as he tried to fit himself into the chair opposite. Getting even with people like Tim was difficult; things seemed to slide off his back without leaving a mark. Slide off his back!

'After I finish my breakfast I know just the thing to make you feel better,' she said innocently. Perhaps too innocently? He's staring at me as if he were the cobra and I the mongoose!

'How kind of you, Miss Patterson,' he replied cautiously. 'Perhaps you could tell me how I am to be done good to?'

'Your syntax leaves a little something to be desired,' she chuckled. 'I'm going to massage your back——'

'Why do I get the feeling I won't like this?' he interrupted. 'With what?'

'Why, eucalyptus oil, of course. My mother swore by it for backaches!'

'The very thing,' Aunt Gerda contributed.

'Not on your life!' Tim managed to work up enough energy to protest, but the two women paid him no attention. 'I don't intend to become a human stink-pile,' he added.

'There's nothing wrong with eucalyptus,' Molly said firmly a few minutes later as she bullied him into lying down on the sofa in the living-room, an old towel beneath him. 'According to the *Geographic*, koalas eat nothing but eucalyptus leaf. Don't wriggle so!' With practised skill her fingers dug into his tortured muscles.

'That feels good,' he murmured. 'I *really* thought you planned to murder or maim me.'

'That comes tomorrow,' she promised, applying more power to her seeking fingers.

'And you'll smell of eucalyptus for days,' he chuckled. 'Didn't you know that koalas are famous for bad breath? That oil is so penetrating that you'll be days trying to wash if off!'

'Not me,' Molly told him. 'You may—you probably will, Tim Holland, but I'm wearing rubber gloves!'

'What in the world is that awful smell!' Susan appeared at the living-room door then walked in. 'Timmy? How could you stand—what is that woman doing to you?'

'You needn't worry, Susan,' he said cheerfully. 'Anyone willing to marry me is authorised to use whatever rubbing oil she wants. Eucalyptus oil. I'm thinking of importing it from Australia!'

'That's nonsense,' his former wife sniffed. 'Alfred wants to talk to you, Timmy. He has an idea——'

'But maybe I don't want to talk to him,' Tim stated flatly. 'I understand that he's—incapacitated.' He rolled over and sat up, the better to watch Susan's face. 'Captain Francis told me all about his little escapade. And when he gets well enough to have visitors, I'm going to pound him to a pulp.'

'You don't have to become so damn macho,' Susan snapped. 'I want to get out of this rats' nest as fast as I can, but I'm——'

'Why, you wouldn't want to rush off and miss my birthday party?' Tim, at his sarcastic best, was almost believable. To everyone except Molly, who knew him better than he knew himself. He's really angry, she thought. Boiling underneath. If Susan and her Alfred don't watch out, they're going to get badly burned!

'Oh—well,' Susan stammered, 'I guess we wouldn't do that——'

'And besides,' he continued inexorably, 'your lawyer's car is under an eight-foot snowdrift. Why don't you get him out of bed so he can start shovelling?'

'Tim,' Susan said, exasperated, 'it doesn't have to end like this. Regardless of how you feel now, we *did* have something going for us. Talk to Alfred, please.' It was the sort of appeal that Tim could understand.

'All right,' he sighed, 'I'll talk to your lawyer, Susan, but I can't promise you anything. My mind is pretty well locked in concrete. Is lover-boy awake?'

'He's still in bed,' Susan replied, 'but he's able to talk. I told him I'd ask you to go right up.'

'I'll need a few minutes,' said Tim as he stretched to get up from the sofa. The low coffee-table was between him and his former wife, and Molly had just set the opened bottle of oil down on it. But Susan, filled with a sudden exultation, crowded against the table and tried to throw her arms around Tim's neck.

'Watch out for the oil!' Molly and Tim both shouted at the same time. Susan looked down to see the bottle tottering, and grabbed at it, but a moment too late. Instead of getting both hands around the neck of the bottle, the little blonde managed to get both hands into the flow of oil spilling out over the table. Molly, her hands swathed in the rubber gloves, snatched the bottle out of the way, but not before the other woman's hands were soaked by the aromatic mixture. Tim snatched up the towel on which he had been lying, and managed to sop up the oil before it ran off the coffee table on to the rug.

'Damn! Damn! Damn!' With tears in her eyes, Susan stood helplessly in the middle of the room, with both hands elevated to eye-level.

'Here.' Molly offered the use of her apron.

'My best clothes,' Susan muttered. 'God, everything I touch in this house turns to manure! It's all your fault, Molly Patterson! I think you do it all on purpose! Damn you!'

'Now you know better than that.' Tim came around the coffee-table and tried to help in the drying-up. 'It was all an accident. Now, if you want me to talk to that—to your lawyer, you'd better go wash your hands and come with me.'

The enticement was strong enough to shut off the tears, but as Tim escorted Susan out of the room she looked back over her shoulder and gave Molly a glare that the Medusa would have cherished.

'Why, she hates me,' Molly murmured as the pair of them disappeared. 'She really *hates* me! *She's* had all the good life, but she——' For a home-body like Molly, who had never really felt a measure of pure hatred before, it was a startling revelation.

'Who hates you?' Moira bubbled into the room, her face covered with chocolate and her arms full of puppy.

'Good lord,' Molly exclaimed. 'What are you? An accident looking for a place to happen?'

'I was just helping out,' Moira said defensively. 'Auntie Gerda is making the strawberry shortcake, and a dozen cupcakes as well.'

'Chocolate cupcakes?' Molly tried to suppress the grin, but had no luck at it. Moira's puppy was squirming around in the child's arms, trying to lick off some of the excess around her mouth.

'Who hates you?' the child asked again.

'Oh—nobody, I suppose. It was all a misunderstanding.' Yes, Molly told herself as she watched the two in front of her enjoying each other. I've never had anyone who *hated* me before. What a terrifying experience it is to discover that my very own cousin hates me! I wonder how long, and why?

'Oh, I forgot,' Moira interrupted her thoughts. 'Auntie Gerda says if you're going to make the supper you'll have to get busy pretty quick, because there's only Cornish game hen left, and somebody has to stuff them all and like that——'

'I get the picture,' Molly chuckled. 'And in the meantime, young lady, I want you to put your puppy down in his box over there while you scoot upstairs and get a real bath. Cleanliness is next to godliness.'

'Good lord, where do you get all those *ucky* sayings?' Moira queried.

'Get lost, or I'll *ucky* you,' Molly threatened as she made her way out to the kitchen.

The two women in the kitchen were going all out on an international dinner for Tim's birthday celebration. Stuffed Cornish rock hen, asparagus flown in from Mexico, Idaho potatoes, *petits pois* from California, and a chocolate mousse—the latter Moira's choice as she wandered through the kitchen at one o'clock, looking for her puppy.

'He's probably just wandering,' Aunt Gerda told the worried child. 'Look for Shag. They're always together.' Molly kept one eye on the girl for a moment. The puppy's disappearance was but one of several odd interruptions. Tim had appeared at eleven-thirty, shaking his head as he snatched up a cup of coffee.

'They want the world,' he reported dismally. 'I got so

mad I told them both I wouldn't give them another cent. Not a damn penny. And that damn DeMoins! Imagine the nerve of the man! He said something wild about you, Molly, and I was forced to make him eat his words.'

'Oh, Tim,' the peace-loving Molly chided. And then, 'Did you hurt your knuckles?'

'All in a good cause,' he answered cheerily, rubbing his right hand gently. 'You and I have to talk, Molly.'

'Talking won't stuff the chicken,' she told him.

He shook his head dolefully. 'I'll be in the den,' he said. 'Paperwork, you know.'

'I just don't understand him any more,' Molly told Gerda. 'Sometimes he's good, and sometimes he's—bad, and——'

'And when he's bad he's very, very bad,' Gerda chuckled. 'Where the devil is the poison princess going?' She gestured out of the kitchen window. Susan, dressed in her high-fashion clothing, and obviously shivering in the cold, was out probing around Alfred's big Cadillac.

'She'll never get that car out of the drifts,' Molly commented. A few moments later Susan came storming through the kitchen, using a great many four-letter words—some of which Molly had never heard before.

'Very impressive vocabulary,' Aunt Gerda said drily as the kitchen door slammed. Moira appeared again, crestfallen.

'I still can't find Bertie,' the child reported. 'Is there another chocolate cupcake?'

'Lunch is in twenty minutes,' Molly cautioned. 'Rouse Shag. He'll help you.'

'Well, I dunno,' sighed Moira. 'Shag's such a lot of dog it's hard to wake him up.'

'You'll never know until you try,' Molly chided, and promptly burned her finger on the oven door. So what

with one thing and another time passed, it was two
o'clock, the luncheon table was set, and a general call
went out. Susan came, looking daggers at the world.
Alfred declined; it seemed he had some problem with his
mouth. Captain Francis came in like a hurricane; Timmy
drifted along a moment later.

'And where's Moira?' Heads around the table turned.

'The last I heard she was looking for Bertie,' Molly
reported.

'The pup is missing?' asked Tim. Yes, the pup is
missing, Molly lectured herself. And the girl was worried.
Why the devil couldn't I stop what I was doing and help?
There's a lot more to living than getting the right stuffing
for rock hen!

'I—think we'd better have a look around the house,'
she suggested. 'Those cellar stairs are a problem, and I'm
not sure I locked the door this morning.'

'I'll check the cellar,' Tim said, suddenly serious.
'Captain?'

'Let me scoot around upstairs,' the older man
proposed.

'Susan? You can check the downstairs rooms.'

'Not me,' Susan muttered. 'I'm here for lunch, not for
a house-to-house search.'

'I'll do it,' Aunt Gerda volunteered bitterly. 'I don't feel
like eating next to somebody like you, Susan Holland. I
hope you plan to drop your married name soon. It's a drain
on my Christian sensibilities.'

What Susan had to say in return went unheard as the
search party set out, leaving Molly alone with Susan. A
restless, worried Molly, and a stolid Susan, chewing at
her food like a robot.

'I've got a funny feeling,' Molly said quietly.

'That's not all you've got that's funny!' Susan snarled.

'I intend to get out of this house as soon as I can, Molly Patterson. And I don't intend to come back ever. Sweet little nauseating Molly! God, how sick you've made me feel. Did it hurt when I stole Tim out from under your nose? If I hadn't found Europe so great I would have loved to be here to watch you squirm after the wedding.'

'I'm sorry you feel that way,' Molly told her cousin, 'but right at the moment—did you hear that?'

'Hear what? All I've heard lately is the damn house rattling. When is it going to fall down?'

Molly shook her head in disgust. 'You really are a rotten person, aren't you, Susan!' And at that moment she heard the noise again—from outside. Panic edged up into her throat. Without thinking she grabbed up her boots, stuffed her feet into them, and went dashing out into the snow without a coat. Clear of the house and all its miscellaneous sounds, it became easier to spot the source of her worries. From far beyond the house, over by the bluff, Shag was whining, scratching at something on the ground.

'Oh lord!' Molly screamed, and started running. Slaloming might have been a better term for it, as, with knees pulled high, she cut a path around the house in the direction of the path dug towards the observation platform. Shag, hearing her come, began to bark. The old animal came down the path a few paces, barked again, and turned back. Without her glasses, Molly could hardly see what the trouble was, but there seemed to be a bundle lying on the ground just at the edge of the bluff. She kept her legs pumping, but a slight glaze that had formed over the snow made it slippery going. From behind her she could hear the sounds of pursuit.

The observation platform had been cleared clean down to the wood. When her foot hit the platform Molly's foot slipped and she went crashing down. At this close a range she could see that the bundle already there was Moira. The little girl had obviously slipped, knocked off her hat against one of the wooden stanchions, and slashed a cut across her forehead. Her eyes were closed, her legs were extended below the railing out into empty air, but in her arms was the struggling Bertie.

'Oh, God, sweetheart,' Molly muttered as she fumbled herself to a sitting position and tugged the child's head into her lap. 'Moira, love! Moira!'

The child moaned, but did not move. Fighting down her anxiety, Molly made a quick check. Arms and legs seemed solid; only the child's head, where she had smashed into the pole, showed evidence of damage. And then Tim was there.

'You forgot your coat,' he growled as he dropped the heavy mackinaw on Molly's shoulders and reached down to take charge of his daughter. Molly, pushed back out of the way, struggled into the coat, all the while watching while Tim checked his daughter in almost a professional manner.

'Take the pup,' he instructed her. Molly grabbed at the struggling bundle of fur and clutched it tightly up under her chin. Tim stood, picking Moira up with him. 'Hospital,' he commanded. 'A concussion, perhaps.'

'My truck,' Molly said tersely. 'Four-wheel drive. I'll drive. I can handle it better.'

'You're probably right,' he told her as he padded down the slippery path and began to cut across towards the barn. 'But since it's going to be a murderous drive, and I'm the one with all the muscles, we'll do it my way.' Molly was almost ready to object, when the common sense of it all intervened. Of course he was the stronger. And more experienced. And wasn't it just a taste of wonder to have a man take charge like that?

With his long legs he gradually pulled away from her, making protest academic. In the clear cold of winter something teased at Molly's nostrils. Tim, of course, smelled to high heaven of eucalyptus oil. But now he was far enough away from her, and her nose was still being bothered by that overwhelming smell. She slowed for a moment and sniffed again. From the puppy, no less. Little Bertie smelled as if he had had liberal contact with Australia's strongest export!

Tim needed help with the barn door by that time. In his spurt of shovelling the previous day he had cleared a path for the door to swing out, and dug a couple of ruts down to the road. But the old doors were heavy, and with his daughter still in his arms, he was handicapped.

Molly bent to release the pup in a cleared space, and set her shoulder to the door. At about that moment Captain Francis came puffing up from the house and added his weight. The doors groaned, but swung clear.

'The lawyer,' Tim called. 'Get him out here. We'll take him to the hospital too. Tell him he's got two minutes!' The Captain started back to the house to pass the word. Molly swung around the far side of the Bronco, climbed up into the high seat, and fished for the emergency keys, held by a magnet to the underside of the driver's seat. Tim moved in beside her and took over. The motor was reluctant to start, but once coaxed it burst into a roar of power. Molly moved into the back seat and took Moira's head in her lap.

'I'll take it easy,' Tim advised. 'Let me know if there's any change in her breathing. I think she's just knocked out, but we can't be too careful. What damn foolishness took her running out into the snow like that?'

Before Molly could think of an answer Alfred was at

the car, protesting all the way. 'I can't leave all my—luggage,' the lawyer complained. 'And it's dangerous riding in this kind of weather.'

'Shut up and get in,' Tim commanded coldly. 'You're doubly a fool if you think I'm going to leave a skunk like you back here.' The lawyer took one look at him, and complied.

'We'll try the Addison,' Molly called out of the back window at Captain Francis, who nodded and waved an arm, then ducked out of the way as Tim backed the truck out of the garage, wheeled it around in the cleared area, shifted into four-wheel drive, and took them bumpily down the track that led to the road.

The little truck ploughed along, slipping and sliding from side to side, groaning over each hillock of snow, but never actually stopping. When it vaulted over the ridge piled up by the snowploughs it almost seemed that it was blowing its heart away, but the four-wheel drive and Tim's skilled handling sustained it. They dropped with a mighty clangour into the middle of the street, where the earlier ploughing had partially cleared the way.

'I don't think I want to go,' Alfred complained.

'I think you do,' Tim snarled at him. 'We might get stuck along the way, and you're a prime candidate to help push us out. In the meantime, shut up and save your breath!'

They rolled down the narrow access road at something like four miles an hour, the truck swaying from side to side, and bouncing up and down front to back. 'Worse than that lobster boat you were going to make our fortune with,' Molly called to Tim. 'Remember? The one that sank just off Normans Woe when you were sixteen?'

'It was a good idea,' he replied. 'I was just unlucky. That's been the story of my life, Molly Patterson. What road shall we take?'

'I wouldn't dare go through the village,' she called back at him. 'That's Route 127 up ahead, Western Avenue. Why don't you give it a try?'

Tim leaned forward and peered out through the windscreen. 'It looks as if they've tried to plough it,' he agreed. 'As usual, we're in God's hands, love.'

That had such a nice sound to it that Molly travelled the next two miles cushioned above the seat by some force—some power, that sustained her against all attacks. It must have been all mental, for as far as she could note out of the corner of her eyes, Alfred was showing definite signs of seasickness. And the shifting and rocking and swaying as the little truck battled the snow was making a terrible mess out of the cabin of the vehicle. Still, with a strength she did not know she had, she held Moira's comatose body against her, held her breath as Tim was called upon for more skill than she had expected, and managed to survive until they reached the bridge where Western Avenue passed over the Blynmon Canal. There, to her absolute joy, two ploughs were moving eastward ahead of them in tandem, clearing the roadway, sending plumes of snow high in the air towards either side. And Moira stirred in her arms and opened her eyes.

'Thank you, God,' Molly whispered as they came up to the Clifford Avenue turn-off, where Tim regretfully saluted the ploughs and turned north. 'Just a few blocks,' he announced in as calm a voice as he could muster.

'Moira's holding on,' she reassured him. 'Go carefully.'

Her comment brought him back to his senses. He lifted his foot slightly off the accelerator and let the vehicle slow down. Clifford had been cleaned, a surprise in itself, and when they came to the corner where Emerson branched left he took it cautiously, and made the two short blocks that brought them into the entrance to the emergency room at the Addison-Gilbert Hospital. When she climbed down from the high cab on trembling legs she took a deep breath and laid a hand on Tim's arm.

'I'll say one thing for it,' she confessed, 'I never could have made it myself, Tim.' He smiled at her as he lifted his daughter out of the back seat.

'And knowing how much that kind of admission costs you, Moll,' he chuckled, 'I'll treasure that statement forever and ever.'

'Alfred,' Molly said in her most exasperated voice, 'I really don't care *what* you do.' The pair of them were in the lounge of the hospital, waiting. Tim, as a father might, had gone through the emergency procedures with his daughter, and Molly had no room for anything except her anxieties. It had been almost two hours since their arrival, and so far she had heard not a word. Alfred, after a brief patchwork exam in the emergency room, had been turned loose to go where he would.

'I saw a couple of cabs moving,' she suggested to the worried lawyer. 'Why don't you call one of them, and go over to the Cape Ann Motor Inn. I'm sure they'd make room for you. Or the alternative, why don't you let a doctor admit you to the hospital? You don't exactly look healthy, you know.'

'If I don't it's all your fault,' he whined. 'All your fault.'

'Probably,' she retorted, not the least bit like the old sympathetic Molly Patterson. 'And I'd do it again if the occasion warranted!'

He backed away from her, both hands up in front of himself, protectively. 'What in the world did I ever see in you anyway?' she asked rhetorically. 'Or Susan. What in the world did Susan ever see in you? You don't have the backbone of a jellyfish! Maybe what I need now is to give you a knuckle sandwich.' She balled up her fist and whacked it into the palm of her other hand as she took a couple of steps in Alfred's direction.

'You can't do that,' he blustered. 'You might hurt me!'

'Yes,' she agreed, 'but think how nice that would make me feel, Alfred!' Two more steps and Alfred struck his colours. No arguments from him about the weaker sex; not after that wild ride through the snow. No sooner did her foot hit the ground than he turned and fled through the double doors.

So Molly was laughing when Tim came through those same doors a moment or two later, a surprised look on his face. 'Something funny?' he asked.

'Not really,' she sighed. 'Lack of the true Christian impulse. I was picking on a lesser mortal. How's Moira?'

'Moira's all right—the doctor thinks,' he assured her. 'But she won't tell me anything about what happened. She wants *you*!'

Tim was silent as he hurried her down the hall and into a cubicle. Dr Hanscomb was standing by the curtained door. 'Why, Molly,' the doctor smiled, 'I didn't know you were married. The little yike says she won't talk to anyone except her mother.'

'*Pro tempore*,' she said solemnly, using up exactly one half of all her Latin education. The doctor grinned and stepped aside. His own Latin was limited to prescription-writing these days.

Moira was lying on a plain examination couch, covered by a sheet. Molly stopped at the entrance and wiped the fog off her glasses and took a good look. The child might not be Tim's natural child, but her little narrow face was firmly set, just the way Tim's had been once when he was on one of his stubborn streaks. When the child saw Molly she sat up on the table and began to cry.

Weeping herself, Molly hurried over and wrapped her arms around the little girl. 'There now,' she comforted, but her words had no effect. Moira, in all the confusion, had lost her hearing aid, and with her head firmly buried in Molly's shoulder she was cut off from communication. Body language was left. Molly hugged her tightly, used one hand to smooth down the hair at the nape of the child's neck, patted her gently in the middle of her back, and waited until the outburst was over. When Moira drew back slightly, far enough to read her lips, she mouthed the words, 'What happened?'

'I don't want Daddy to hear,' the little girl repeated in the same mode as she held up her hands. 'She stole my dog,' Moira signed slowly. 'Took my dog outside and dumped him in the garbage can at the bluff. She isn't real. Nobody could act as mean as that. She *can't* be my mother, can she?'

Molly looked down at the pleading tear-stained cheeks, gave about a tenth of a second to logic and pain and history and Tim, and made up her mind. 'No, of course not,' she signed back. 'How could she be when *I'm* your mother!' The pair of them stared at each other, then broke out into big smiles.

'Well, that's better,' said Dr Hanscomb as he pushed in past the curtain. 'What's been going on, Tim?'

'How would I know?' Tim responded. 'It's some kind of hen party, and evidently mere men are not to know! What's the damage report?'

'The X-rays are clear,' the doctor said. 'No sign of a fracture. Her eyes are clear. There's always a chance of a slight concussion, but that's something only time can tell.

Look, I hear that they're ploughing Route 127 now. Why don't you take the little lady home and put her to bed? Keep her there for twenty-four hours. If she shows any signs of pain or dizziness——'

'I know,' Tim sighed. 'You ex-Army doctors are all the same. Take two aspirins and call you in the morning, right?'

'You needn't get huffy about it,' the doctor chuckled. 'I've been here since Christmas Eve!'

'Do I go home now?' Moira was already halfway off the couch when the doctor put out a restraining arm.

'Not yet,' he laughed. 'You can't come into hospital without having something to show for it all, can you? Now let me disinfect those scratches on your cheek, and we'll add a little bandage—like so. There now, isn't that better?'

The attending nurse held up a little hand mirror. Moira checked herself out, then looked questioningly at Molly. 'It looks very—professional,' Molly responded. 'Very—patientish.'

'There's no such word.' Her newly acquired daughter, showing typical childhood disgust at the limited vocabulary of adults, slid off on to the floor and proceeded to hug her new mother. 'Now I'm ready to go home,' she announced.

There was another little argument at the door. 'Nobody goes to the door except in a wheelchair,' the nurse insisted. 'It's the rule. And I have to drive you by the admissions desk to see if everything is—well, you know—about the bill and all.'

Which resulted in another fifteen-minute delay before they were back in the Bronco again. 'And I'll drive us back,' Tim insisted. It was Molly's car, and practically Molly's road—since she used to drive it every day—and

she was about to make a protest when she was smitten
with an attack of common sense. After all, he *was* a very
attractive male, with a very sensitive ego, who had
already told her she was going to marry him. She was still
perturbed about that *told her* business, but out in a little
truck with snow up to her—well, at least that high—why
give him a chance to change his mind?

The drive home was easier and sweeter than the drive
to the hospital. The three of them shared the front seat,
Tim with both hands on the wheel, Molly with one arm
around Moira. The little girl was in some strange shape.
Every now and again she would shiver; a moment later
she would be laughing. Confused, Molly just hung on.

The doctor was only partly right. The pair of
snowploughs were about to start for Magnolia. After all
the summertime complaints from the village about
potholes, and the city's absolute neglect of same, it
seemed that the Mayor of Gloucester had raised the
priority for Magnolia's streets. But the four crewmen,
being civil servants, were sitting in the cabs of their
vehicles, consulting maps, drinking coffee, and doing
other things that civil servants are wont to do in almost
every country.

'So what do we do now?' Molly asked impatiently.

'We wait,' laughed Tim. 'Turn on the radio.' She did,
switching to the FM band, watching for the classical
music of WVCA-FM.

'I'd do better with a little country music,' Tim
suggested.

'Well, I wouldn't,' she protested. 'This is the only
one-man radio station left in the United States. You surely
remember Mr Geller, Tim?'

'Good lord, is he still operating?'

'As you hear,' she laughed. 'Owner, technician,

salesman, disc-jockey, he still does it all, right from his own living-room.'

'And the only time the station goes off the air is when he has to go out on an errand,' Tim recalled, watching the ploughs steadily. 'Well, that did the trick. Maybe they don't like Mozart? Here we go: Canticle for two snowploughs and a Bronco, in C Minor!'

'And the first thing we have to do when we get home,' Molly decided, 'is to find Moira's hearing aid.'

'No need to make a problem out of it,' Tim replied. 'She has two spares in her luggage, and a boxful of spare batteries.' Tapping Moira on the shoulder, Molly repeated the conversation by signs. The little girl giggled. 'I really don't need them,' she signed in return. 'You don't need batteries for signing, and my dad says we have to keep down the expenses.'

'Why did he say that?' Molly signed.

'Because he said weddings are expensive,' the child returned.

'Would you two cut that out,' Tim challenged. 'It isn't polite to whisper when other people are present.' As he spoke, Molly was translating into sign.

'Yes, sir,' his daughter said dutifully.

'Yes, sir indeed,' his future wife responded, but the two pairs of fingers kept up the conversation, and, after all, he had to keep his eyes on the road!

They followed the ploughs in lonely convoy until they reached the turn-off for Hesperus, and since that was the way the DPW was going, they followed right along. As a result they edged their way down to Norman Avenue, where two trucks from the electric company were doing their best to replace a pole, and out to Magnolia Avenue, where the ploughs made a great circle and turned back the way they had come. The great stormclouds had finally gathered up their skirts and departed. A three-quarter moon displayed a smile, and the myriad stars of winter sparkled like cold lights in the heavens.

Tim stopped the car at that point and went over to have a few words with the drivers. Watching through the cleared windshield, Molly smiled as she saw Tim's hand dive into a pocket and pass something to the older driver. As he sauntered back she could see he was whistling, and the plough was reversing its direction.

'They volunteered to plough all the way up to the house,' he grinned as he slid into the warmth of the truck. 'My lord, it's cold out there! They say that the storm wasn't so bad just to the south of us, and the routes through to Boston are all ploughed already. How's that for efficiency?'

'Only you could do it, Tim,' Molly teased him solemnly.

'How true!' That grin was back again, boyish, cheerful, memory-provoking, as he shifted into gear and followed the spume of snow from the plough.

CHAPTER TEN

THE plough made a great deal of noise as it roared almost to the edge of the bluff, where it turned around and clanked back towards the village centre. The old house was lit up from end to end, a signal that power had been restored in the neighbourhood. Gerda was waiting for them at the front door as the three walked through the crunchy dry snow.

'You were so late we didn't know when to expect you,' said Gerda. 'How's my baby?'

'Where's my Bertie?' Moira interrupted urgently, not realising the others were talking. 'I want my puppy!'

'Of course you do,' Aunt Gerda said gently. 'I moved the box into the hallway. Here he is, the tired little darling.'

Molly took over the sleeping puppy, displayed him to Moira, then explained to Gerda, 'She's fine, but she's lost her hearing aid. I'll take her up and get her settled, then——'

'I didn't know when to expect you, so I thought we'd go ahead with the meal,' Aunt Gerda explained. 'But we've only just sat down.'

'In which case, since you've done all the work so far, Tim, why don't you go in and start your meal? I'll take this little miss up and then come join you when she's comfortable.'

'I can take her up, Molly.' Tim had lost all his sophisticated appearance; it was a harried father speaking.

'So can I. And I want to.' Molly dropped a protective arm around Moira's shoulder, and the little girl snuggled up at her side. Tim, tired, perturbed, saw quickly that she was not to be stirred.

'Go ahead in,' he told Aunt Gerda. 'I'll wash up in the kitchen and join you.' Molly encouraged Moira to walk up the stairs, moving slowly. She could hear the clatter of dishes and conversation from the dining-room, and it gave her a little stab of pain. Poor pale Moira, tucked under her arm so closely, could hear nothing without her aid. She steered the little girl into her own bedroom, helped her undress, and tucked her into a long flannel nightgown before taking time to root out one of the spare hearing aids.

'I'm all right,' the child said, studying Molly's face in order to read her lips as she adjusted the volume of her replacement aid.

'I'm glad,' her adopted aunt said slowly, repeating in sign language. 'Tell me again about your puppy—your dog?'

'Bertie went missing,' Moira said in a rush. 'I didn't think he could jump out of that box, he must have. I hunted the whole house and couldn't find him. And then you said that about waking Shag, so I did. Your dog went to the front door and scratched, so I grabbed my coat and opened the door—and then he ran like blazes for the observation platform, and he jumped up at the edge of that stone garbage thing, so I looked inside, and there was Bertie, lying in the bottom, just squirming and crying. It was kind of hard to get him out 'cause that garbage thing is so deep, but I got my hands on him, only when I tried to stand up I slipped on the ice, and that's all I remember until you were there.'

'You didn't see anyone else?' Molly signed.

'No. Not nobody.'

'All right, love. Now, I'm going to get a washcloth and clean you up a little bit, and then I want you to take a good long nap.'

'But I'll miss Daddy's birthday party!' The child was so excited that she had to do the signs twice. Her vocabulary was extensive, but her fingers were not yet nimble enough.

'Not to worry,' Molly signed. 'Your daddy is a thousand years old, and I'll save you a piece of cake. Right?'

'Right.' Moira laughed for the first time since coming home, picked up Bertie from Molly's arms, and climbed into bed, where she became instantly solemn. 'I feel safer now with you here,' the child said, and lifted up both her arms in the signal for a hug. Molly leaned over and provided that service. 'I love you, Aunt Molly,' the child whispered in her ear. 'I've never been so happy, not any time or anywhere. Daddy tried to explain to me—about what was going to happen to me. He always said, "Be brave." And I wanted to be because *he* wanted it. But I was always scared. It frightened me. But now I've got you, and I think I can face it.' And then, much more wistfully, 'I wish—I wish I could just wave my magic wand and that *other* person would disappear!' Molly dabbed at her own eye to stop the little tear, and went for the washcloth. By the time she returned from the bathroom both Moira and little Bertie were fast asleep again.

So it was back to the bathroom for a very thoughtful Molly, where she managed to put her own face and person back in order while she gave the whole evening a good think. Sorting for the truth was like trying to follow a straight line through a well-planted maze. There was little Moira and her happiness, Tim and his confusion, Susan and her hatred, and even Gerda with her—scheming?

Only Captain Francis stood unaccused—well, that of which he *might* be accused was a simple problem between two consenting adults, as the new state laws described it. Molly shrugged that off.

But Tim—there was *another* problem entirely. He claimed that he wanted to marry her. But his reasons were so mixed that Molly could hardly decide what to do. Did he want to marry her for Moira's sake? That stood high on the list—very high. Or was his offer merely a ploy to get Susan out of his hair? That too rated highly. Certainly unrated was the crazy idea that he had finally fallen in love with Molly Patterson. Nice going, girl, she told her mirror image. You win first price for wild imagination! And with that she shrugged, tugged her blouse around in front, and marched herself down the corridor. In Susan's room she busied herself for a few minutes, then headed for the stairs. It was not sweet soft-hearted Molly going down those stairs, though. She *had* come to *some* answers; it was Joan of Arc Patterson stepping very determinedly down the old staircase, with more than a little anger in her eyes. And perhaps, she thought, with the strength of a fairy godmother, to do a little wand-waving?

They were all at table, having arrived at the main course, the Cornish rock hen, and conversation was fulsome. Molly peered into the dining-room. Captain Francis was sitting nearest to the door. At her small noise he looked around, and she beckoned. He excused himself from the table and joined her in the hall, where she murmured some very firm directions, at which he smiled, agreed, and escorted her back to the table.

'All's well?' Tim asked anxiously.

'All's well with Moira,' Molly qualified her answer. The table talk was renewed. Tim was at the far side of the big round table, with Gerda on his left and Susan on his right. Captain Francis had the chair beside Gerda, and Molly took the place opposite Tim. It irritated her intolerably. She managed two bites in a matter of twenty minutes. When the others had completely demolished their servings, hers was still big enough to feed a grown man. Shag, who grew fat on the leavings of others, sensed this and moved close to her leg. She patted the old dog's head. Ordinarily he knew better than to beg openly, but for this once, this night, Molly needed all the sympathy and support she could gather. And still her anger grew. Sweet, lovable Molly Patterson was out for blood!

'Well, I'll bring in the cake, shall I?' said Gerda. 'A special—Tim asked for it, I made the cake, and Molly decorated it.' The men made half-hearted moves to get up as she rose and went to the kitchen. In a moment she was back, bearing the massive cake. The strawberry juice was running freely; the whipped cream was a little liquid too. The whole thing looked like a mushy red and white confection.

'Just the way I like it,' said Tim with a big grin. 'But then Molly knows everything about me, so one would expect the perfect cake!'

A lot you know, buster, Molly told herself as she rose in her place. What I know about you—for sure—could be written on the back of one of the new twenty-five-cent postage stamps with a heavy-duty pen! But this is all the time I intend to wait!

'I have a small problem to be solved before you cut the cake,' she announced. The conversation stopped. Tim frowned, Susan glared, and the other couple looked as if they were holding hands under the tablecloth—and holding their breaths as well.

'Go ahead,' Tim invited cautiously.

Molly pushed her chair back and walked around so that she was standing between Tim and Susan. 'A long time ago,' she said quietly, 'a very dishonest woman stole my man.' Susan was laughing up at her; Tim's mouth was half open. 'But I deserved that, so it didn't set me off. And then that same woman was monstrously cruel to a very lovable child who couldn't defend herself.' Susan had lost her smile; Tim shifted anxiously in his seat, as if a flock of soldier ants were invading the chair. Gerda and her Captain leaned back in their chairs, very self-satisfied.

'But I can't act on something like that, because she wasn't my child—at that time.' Molly folded her arms over her breasts and took a deep breath.

'But then this same woman did a very terrible thing to a little dog—and that's where I draw the line!' Her voice had been gradually rising up-scale, until at the end of the sentence she was in full voice. Susan was turning various shades of pink, her mouth working at a rebuttal.

'You can't prove that,' she snarled, half rising. Molly put one hand on top of Susan's head and pushed her back down into the seat.

'I can't?' she retorted. 'And me an old Perry Mason fan? Well, let's see. Whoever was responsible took that puppy by the scruff of his neck, carried him outside in below-freezing weather, and dumped him into the old stone garbage container—and left him there to die!'

Susan made one more effort to get up. 'Prove it,' she snarled again, baring her lovely teeth like a mastiff.

'Yes, prove it,' Molly sighed. 'But first, while Moira was hunting that puppy, with Shag's help, she slipped on the ice and almost did herself a serious damage.'

'Do you think I'd do something like that to hurt my own daughter?' Susan screamed.

'Yes, I do,' Molly returned calmly.

'Then prove it!'

'Yes, prove it,' murmured Molly. 'Did you know that if you wet a dog's fur with some smelly liquid the dog will smell for hours and hours?'

Susan looked down at her hands, squirrelled up out of her chair, and backed away from Molly, holding her hands behind her back.

'Did you know that today, in this house, I rubbed Tim's back with eucalyptus oil?'

'So then you're the one who handled the dog!' Susan screamed. She was shaking, and almost seemed to be frothing at the mouth.

'Not exactly,' Molly continued inexorably. 'When I gave Tim that massage I wore rubber gloves. Tim got all his share on his back, so it couldn't have been him. But you, Susan. Remember? You spilled the bottle of oil, and it ran all over your hands? Remember, Susan?' Molly took a step in her cousin's direction, and Susan raised her hands defensively. 'And when you picked up the puppy, Susan, remember—you spread that eucalyptus oil all over Bertie's fur. Remember?'

'Tim, I don't know what this madwoman is talking about! Tim?'

'I'm very interested to hear,' he said judiciously, not moving a muscle.

'And let me tell you,' Molly continued, spitting the words out one at a time like slugs from a submachine gun, 'there's nothing in this world I hate worse than a person who would abuse a little dog just for the sake of vengeance.'

'You're mad,' Susan stammered. 'Totally mad!'

'Probably,' Molly continued. 'But this is *my* house, and I don't intend that you contaminate it for another second, Susan, cousin or no.' With which she leaned over Susan's place at the table, picked up her glass of red wine, and gently poured it all over the other woman's head.

'Well, you can't put me out on a night like this,' Susan spluttered. 'Tim, you can't let her——'

'It's Molly's house,' Tim said nonchalantly as he tossed her a napkin. 'I can't stop her if she wants to throw you out. In fact, I might even cheer a little.'

'Why, you——' Susan seized one of the silver candlesticks on the table and tried to used it as a club. One step forward, Molly told herself, and then turn, and—once again, just the way it had been explained in her martial arts class, there she was with the candlestick on the floor, and Susan's hand locked up behind her back in a painful hammer-lock. And with that hold in place, Molly urged her cousin towards the door, where Captain Francis was already waiting, the suitcase that Molly had just packed in his hand.

Molly halted the procession at the door, and turned. 'You will all excuse me?' she asked politely.

Ten minutes later she was standing in the cold doorway, rubbing her hands in a washing gesture as her Bronco, with Captain Francis at the wheel and a suddenly subdued Susan at his side, ploughed down the street and turned westward towards the Boston highway. When the red lights on the back of the truck faded out of sight, Molly shut the door gently and went back into the dining-room, shivering from anger more than from the cold. The others had hardly moved in her absence.

When she reappeared, both Gerda and Tim gave her a smile of welcome, although Tim's seemed just the tiniest bit apprehensive. She plumped into her seat at the foot of the table. 'I guess we're ready for the candles and cake now,' she said softly. In that one short period of time she had run out all her anger—well, almost all. And here was

Gerda, with those concerned eyes, and Tim, with those——

'She's gone?' he asked.

'Yes. The Captain is taking her to Logan Airport. And I don't think she'll ever come back. Not after our last few words.'

'I never would have expected it of sweet lovable Molly,' Tim chuckled. 'It did my heart good!' He jumped at that second, as if his aunt might have kicked his ankle under the table.

'It was a surprise,' Gerda said. 'But then I always knew you had it in you, Molly Patterson. Now, if we can put all that nastiness behind us, where the devil is that lawyer fellow?'

'Alfred?' Molly mused. 'Well, I—made him a proposition at the hospital, and he decided—he decided he didn't want to play in my league after all. I can see Alfred now, trying to borrow enough money to get back to the big city.'

'Well, then' said Tim in a burst of false enthusiasm, 'maybe we could drink a toast?'

'To what?' Molly, suspicious even of her lifelong love, felt that something was missing.

'To what?' Tim grinned. 'Why, how about this? You've solved all my problems, Molly Patterson, and now you won't *have* to marry me if you don't want to!'

A deadly silence came over the room. Molly staggered to her feet and stared over the distance between them. Too far. She pushed her chair away and this time walked round to stand between Gerda and Tim. He sat still, almost frozen in position.

'You're telling me, Tim Holland, that you don't want to marry me? That your proposal was all a trick?' Ice words from an ice maiden!

'No,' he responded anxiously. 'I'm not telling you that at all. I'm telling you that if you don't want to marry me, you don't have to.'

'You know something,' she mused, 'I've loved you for a long time, Timmy. But in between spates of loving, I think I've hated you. Did you know that?' Her desperately searching eyes travelled the table, and found what she wanted.

'Now, Molly,' he protested. 'Molly, you don't want to do that!'

'Don't I?' she shouted at him as she picked up the juicy mess that was his birthday cake. 'Don't I really, Tim Holland? Well, you unconscionable—oaf—I think I've wanted to do this since I was eight years old!' And with that she cradled the cake in both hands, and very gently pushed the entire mess into his face.

Tim sat there quietly, with strawberries and whipped cream gradually oozing downward across the bridge of his patrician nose. Gerda was quietly applauding. Molly, shocked back to sensibility, was appalled at what she had done. She backed away from them both a step at a time, until her nerve broke. The tears began, accompanied by the repressed sobs of a dozen years or more. She wheeled and ran for the front door.

Gerda was having trouble suppressing the laughter. When it finally broke loose she rolled in her chair, while her favourite nephew lifted one hand and cleared a strawberry out of his eye. 'There's hope for you yet, lad,' Aunt Gerda managed to choke out.

Tim shrugged his shoulders and his finger went to his mouth. 'Not as perfect as I thought,' he said philosophically. 'She didn't put enough sugar in the whipped cream.'

CHAPTER ELEVEN

MOLLY came back in out of the cold at eleven o'clock, about the time when Captain Francis arrived back from his trip to the airport. They entered hand in hand, the old man and the troubled young woman. Tim and Gerda had just finished the dishes, and were heading into the living-room to relax. Gerda came over and kissed the Captain on his cheek before offering him a brandy.

'Here's to crime,' he toasted. Tim smiled half-heartedly—cleaned-up Tim, with no trace of the shortcake in view. Gerda joined the toast. Molly, who had decided in the last twenty minutes to give up alcohol and men and to enter a nunnery—if any still existed—flopped herself down in a chair.

'So where did you leave the spider lady?' Gerda asked.

'At the airport,' the Captain responded. 'She wasted the entire trip mouthing off about how bad New England was, and how she hated it, and the snow, and the people. But mostly about the snow.'

'You just dropped her off at the terminal?'

'Oh, no,' he laughed. 'Miss Molly here asked me to give her any help that I could, so I did. She wanted a ticket on the first plane out of the city, she told me.' He stopped long enough to take a sip from the brandy glass. There was a laugh hiding under his bushy grey eyebrows.

'So don't sit on it,' Gerda commanded. 'Where was the flight going?'

'Well, there wasn't any choice,' the Captain mused. 'The airport had just reopened. She didn't ask me any questions, just got on the plane at the gate. It was a charter flight, headed for Nome, Alaska.'

'Yes, that will be great,' said Gerda in awe. 'You old reprobate! Luckily they don't have snow in Nome at this time of year.'

'Yeah,' the Captain responded. 'Let's you and me go in the kitchen and talk. This fancy living-room leaves me nervous.'

'Yeah, talk,' said Aunt Gerda, and winked at Tim as she followed Captain Francis out of the room.

'That pair,' Tim said after a moment of silence. 'They've debated it for thirty years or more, but she tells me they've decided to get married.'

'Lucky,' Molly sighed. 'Tim——'

'Molly——' he said at exactly the same time. They both laughed nervously. 'You first,' he said. 'Ladies first.'

'I'm not a lady,' she told him, disgusted with herself. 'And I'm not about to apologise for dumping that cake all over you. I'm not sorry—I enjoyed that very much. It's been something I've wanted to do for years.'

'Yes, I could tell,' he replied solemnly. 'Even an oaf like me gets the message after while.'

'Tim——' she stammered. '*That* part—I do apologise for that. You're not an oaf. Well, not very often, anyway, but——'

'I think you'd better let me have my say first,' he interrupted as he came over and sat down beside her. 'We have to go back ten years, to your eighteenth birthday, Molly. Remember?'

'I could never forget,' she sighed.

'Nor me either, Molly.' She had been staring straight ahead up until that moment. Now she turned and looked squarely at him. 'Do you know why I came over that morning?'

'I—didn't remember your coming in the morning,' she half-whispered. He was leading her back into the dark jungle-land of horrors, of things she didn't want to remember.

'I thought your father was going to tell you,' he sighed. 'I came over to ask you to marry me.'

'But—Tim? I don't understand. You didn't ask—and you married Susan!'

'I know. Look, Moll. Your father invited me into the den. He said he had something important to say. I followed him. Susan was there, waiting for us. And your father told me that Susan was pregnant—and I was the man! I know that Moira's age has puzzled you ever since we came back, my dear. Susan and I were married ten years ago; Moira is nine and a half years old.'

'Oh, God, Tim. Then it was true?' Molly buried her face in her hands and sniffed back the tears.

'It *could* have been true,' he muttered. 'It wasn't, but it *could* have been. That's why I went along with it. Susan and I tried it on one time. It wasn't until a couple of years later that I found out that every dog on the north shore had been sniffing around Susan. She should have sold tickets to keep the men in order. When she discovered she was pregnant she picked me out of the crowd because my family had the money. That's not much of an excuse, Moll, but I was a hot-blooded kid, and she was offering without strings—and I really screwed up our lives, Molly, yours and mine.'

'But, Tim, you never said a word to me. And you were gone—ever so long!'

'I had no right to say anything to you, Molly. I'd done the deed, and I figured it was up to me to make the marriage work. But instead—well, you know what happened now. And what could I do after my divorce? I didn't have the nerve to come back here looking for you—I thought at first that you would have been snapped up by one of half a dozen men. And when Aunt Gerda told me that you were still single—I just couldn't understand.'

'But even then you didn't come back,' she accused as she lifted her head back up. Poor Tim, she thought, all those troubles. And I thought *I* had a hard time!

'No,' he sighed, 'I didn't come back. There was always Moira. Lord, Molly, I can't tell you—I wandered all over Europe, from one hospital to another, from one specialist to another. I didn't dare stop. There was always the thought that the next man was the one who could come up with the miraculous cure! So I stayed away—until the last man, at Heidelberg, told me that the chase was fruitless.'

'And here you are,' she concluded.

'And here we are,' he agreed sombrely.

Molly sat quietly, thinking. Tim moved a little closer. Out of the corner of her eye she could see his hands signalling, but her mind paid no attention. Dear Tim, and Moira too. I *want* that dear little scrap to be my own. I *want* her. But do you marry a man because you want his daughter to be yours? That makes for a strange sort of marriage, doesn't it? Can I marry for Moira's sake? Or would I do better to skip the wedding and just be a maiden aunt? Look at Gerda. All the years she's spent, avoiding the fact that she loved the Captain. Can you see Molly Patterson, forty years from now, doddering up to Tim Holland and saying, 'Tim, we should have gotten married all those years ago!'

Suddenly something pierced her cloud of thought. Her head snapped around and she stared at the tall thin lovable man sitting next to her. His hands were signing something, over and over again. 'I love you.'

'Tim,' she said tentatively. 'We were fooling you, Moira and I. That doesn't mean *good morning*.'

'I know what it means,' he answered gruffly. 'Aunt Gerda gave me a book of American Sign on Thanksgiving morning. I just didn't have the nerve to say it out loud!'

'Oh, Tim!' All her speculations collapsed, all her battle flags surrendered. With a little cry of happiness Molly hurled herself at the man who had once left her behind. Like a puppy she coiled up in his lap and squirmed to get as close to him as possible. His warm kiss was the seal. She gave herself up.

Out in the kitchen the two schemers listened intently. 'Well,' Aunt Gerda whispered, 'either they've made up, or he's killed her.'

'Or she's killed him,' the Captain corrected. 'But I have the feeling that your witchery has succeeded. Not only in there; out here too. This sitting around on hard chairs is not for people our age, love, no matter what those two are up to. What do you say—shall we go upstairs?'

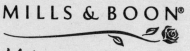

MILLS & BOON®

Makes any time special™

Mills & Boon publish 29 new titles every month. Select from...

Modern Romance™   Tender Romance™

Sensual Romance™

Medical Romance™   Historical Romance™

MAT2

The perfect gift this Christmas from

MILLS & BOON®

**3 new romance novels &
a luxury bath collection**

for just £6.99

Featuring

Modern Romance™

The Mistress Contract
by Helen Brooks

Tender Romance™

The Stand-In Bride
by Lucy Gordon

Historical Romance™

The Unexpected Bride
by Elizabeth Rolls

0011/94/MB7